PRAISE FOR 1998 HOLT MEDALLION WINNER EUGENIA RILEY!

EMBERS OF TIME

"Ms. Riley's plot stimulates the senses and her characters leave a lasting impression."

—*Rendezvous*

"This story had me spellbound. It is a must read!"

—*Kathy's Faves and Raves*

LOVERS AND OTHER LUNATICS

"Versatile author Eugenia Riley delivers a delicious romp. . . . Pure reading fun!"

—*Romantic Times*

"Witty, over-the-top characters, sparkling dialogue, and scintillating sensuality combine to make this novel one of Ms. Riley's very best. An absolute must read!"

—*Rendezvous*

BUSHWHACKED BRIDE

"Ms. Riley's . . . characters are delightful, as are the various subplots that make this a wonderful romance."

—*Romantic Times*

"An uproarious adventure from start to finish. This book has it all: humor, passion, and a cast of endearing characters that the reader won't soon forget. Ms. Riley has crafted an amazing tale that leaps right off the pages."

—*Rendezvous*

TEMPEST IN TIME

"Eugenia Riley spins a brilliantly woven web, ensnaring readers with her ingenious plot twists, endearing characters and an unforgettable love story."

—*Romantic Times*

A TRYST IN TIME

"A unique time-travel novel interlaced with mysterious secrets and intense emotions. Ms. Riley focuses on the magical potency of love, as it transcends the web of time to meld bleeding hearts together."

—*Romantic Times*

W9-BZS-121

SEDUCTIVE INTENTIONS

"Tell me, was getting me pregnant part of your plan, too?"

He flinched as if she'd slapped him. "Courtney, how can you even think that?"

"Well, I didn't see any big interest in family planning on your part that night."

"Darling, we were both pretty tipsy."

"Be honest with me, Mark. Did you want to get me pregnant?"

He smiled. "Courtney, I never intended to get you pregnant. That's the God's truth, I swear. But do I mind that you're carrying my child? No, not in the least, darling."

Cheeks hot from his frank words, she accused, "You intended to seduce me."

He drew a teasing finger down her throat, and he spoke very huskily. "Courtney, how could I ever look at you and not want to seduce you?"

Other *Love Spell* books by Eugenia Riley:

EMBERS OF TIME
STRANGERS IN THE NIGHT
LOVERS AND OTHER LUNATICS
BUSHWHACKED BRIDE
TEMPEST IN TIME
A TRYST IN TIME
NEW YEAR'S BABIES
A TIME-TRAVEL CHRISTMAS

The Great Baby Caper

EUGENIA RILEY

LOVE SPELL ◆ NEW YORK CITY

A LOVE SPELL BOOK®

December 2001

Published by

Dorchester Publishing Co., Inc.
276 Fifth Avenue
New York, NY 10001

If you purchased this book without a cover you should be aware that this book is stolen property. It was reported as "unsold and destroyed" to the publisher and neither the author nor the publisher has received any payment for this "stripped book."

Copyright © 2001 by Eugenia Riley Essenmacher

All rights reserved. No part of this book may be reproduced or transmitted in any form or by any electronic or mechanical means, including photocopying, recording or by any information storage and retrieval system, without the written permission of the publisher, except where permitted by law.

ISBN 0-505-52461-9

The name "Love Spell" and its logo are trademarks of Dorchester Publishing Co., Inc.

Printed in the United States of America.

Visit us on the web at www.dorchesterpub.com.

*To my adorable baby grandson,
Tony Alexander, with much love and thanks
for his "technical support" on this project.*

*Special thanks to Susan Krinard
for her continuing support and excellent feedback,
and to Louisa Brown for so patiently answering
my U.K. questions, on this book and my last.*

The Great Baby Caper

Chapter One

This has got to be the craziest caper I've ever suffered through in my life, Courtney Kelly thought as she clipped across Bourbon Street, avoiding piles of manure and cursing her demented boss, M. Billingham Bootle, with every step she took.

She could not believe the ridiculous mission she was undertaking tonight. Dressed in her best navy blue raw silk suit, her wheat-blond hair neatly bobbed, her green eyes looking straight ahead, she was slogging through the steamy streets of the New Orleans French Quarter, ruining her expensive leather pumps and searching for . . . *a man.* Ten yards behind her, her driver cruised along in a silver limo, tailing her. He must be having a really good laugh about now.

How on earth had she landed in this insane predicament? Courtney was an MBA with five years of experience as a corporate rising star. Indeed, only twenty minutes ago, she'd been at a posh hotel back on Canal Street, sipping daiquiris with several associates at the five o'clock mixer that had opened her company's annual convention.

Then chaos had descended in the person of Mr. M. Billingham Bootle himself, president and CEO of Bootle's Baby Bower, a Denver-based baby products company with retail stores in Colorado and several other western states. Among corporate gurus, Mr. Bootle was politely referred to as "eccentric"; among his staff, he was known to be totally bonkers. He was famous for his practical jokes and the outlandish capers he sometimes staged at the company's annual convention—like last year in Dallas, when he'd hired actors to perform an Old West style shootout right in the middle of the company's awards banquet. Courtney shook her head at the memory. In the midst of fake bullets popping and actors yelling epithets, several frightened women had run from the room; other attendees had sat in stunned silence. Most, however, had only laughed, well-used to the "crazy" old chairman and his outrageous antics.

This year had proven to be no exception, Courtney mused glumly. In fact, M. Billingham's latest stunt might well take the cake. She recalled the moment back at the ballroom when Mr. Bootle had ascended to the podium, his crafty blue eyes gleaming, his shock of white hair catching the light. "Ladies and gentlemen, welcome to New Orleans and the twenty-fifth annual convention of BBB Ltd. As all of you are aware, when you came to work at Bootle's Baby Bower, I made you only one promise: that working here would never be dull."

Waiting for the predictable laughter to die down, he had continued, "Tonight, I fully intend to keep that promise. But first of all, I have a very important announcement to make. I don't suppose it's a secret to any of you that I'm getting along in years. So, I've decided it's time to get off the corporate fast track. Although I will remain active on the board, I'm ready to relinquish the reins as your CEO, and am prepared to begin the process of selecting my successor tonight."

Even as startled murmurs rippled over the room, Courtney's heart raced with excitement and anticipation. This was the announcement she'd been waiting for, praying for, ever since she'd come to work for BBB four years ago. She'd already accomplished much during that time and was currently vice president in charge of product management, supervising the acquisition of merchandise for all their stores. She knew that of the corporate executive staff, only she and a few others were high-powered enough to qualify as potential CEO candidates.

Her hunch was proven correct by M. Billingham's next words: "Ladies and gentlemen, I am pleased at this time to announce the four finalists for the position of your new CEO: Ms. Kelly and Messrs. Gilchrist, Gideon, and Getz."

Courtney grinned at the news, accepting the polite congratulations of those standing nearby. Inwardly she was sailing high and totally unimpressed with her three male competitors. Wally Gilchrist was the corporate manager of operations; Al Gideon, the comptroller; and Gil Getz, the head of planning and development. The three men were so similar in their names, thick-lensed glasses, paunchy stomachs, and balding heads that everyone in the company frequently got them mixed up. More importantly, though, of the four, only Courtney stood out as the hard-charging CEO type. The other three were efficient workhorses, team players who occasionally indulged in fits of whining when things didn't go their way.

The news could not have been more thrilling—yet just as quickly M. Billingham had burst Courtney's bubble. For no sooner had he made his stirring announcement than he'd taken one of his all-too-frequent laps around the bend.

Struggling to hold back a roguish grin, M. Billingham declared: "In keeping with our festive surroundings and our competitive company spirit, I thought we should make the contest for new CEO really interesting and fun. Thus, I've decided to organize a scavenger hunt—a trial by fire if you will—to determine who shall win the promotion. Each of the four executive candidates will receive secret orders to bring back a certain—well, shall we say *item*—and the first one to bag his kill will win the prize. Just to keep the match spirited, each set of marching orders will have a unique New Orleans flavor." M. Billingham clapped his hands as if bursting with pride at his own cleverness. "So there you have it—the competition in a nutshell. And may the best man—or woman—win."

Courtney remembered the hush that had fallen over the ballroom, amid whispers of "Has the old coot *really* lost it this time?" and "Yeah, looks like he's completely flipped his wig!" Meanwhile, four clerks were dispatched bearing official looking envelopes for each of the four contestants. Even as Courtney's missive arrived, she had watched her competitors rip open theirs and, to a man, grow ashen-faced.

Then one look at her own edict had twisted her insides into knots.

Her orders still lay in the pocket of her jacket, and she retrieved them now with a shake of her head. The instructions were engraved in black on a plain parchment card: COURTNEY, DEAR: YOU MUST FIND THE MOST ELIGIBLE BACHELOR IN THE FRENCH QUARTER AND MARRY HIM BY MORNING. BEST OF LUCK, M. BILLINGHAM.

Horror and outrage consumed Courtney on reading those audacious words. She was to . . . *what?* Pick up some drunk in a seedy bar—and *marry* him?

She had rushed up to the chairman just as he'd descended the podium. Waving the card in his face, she declared, "You're joking."

The old guy merely grinned at her. "Courtney, dear, never let it be said that I lack a sense of humor. But in this case, suffice it to say the outcome of this little scavenger hunt will be deadly serious."

"B-but this is preposterous!" she sputtered. "You can't mean you expect me to go find a—"

"Shhhh!" he interrupted, glancing around at several people intently watching them. "I said the instructions were *secret,* my dear. Divulge them, and you haven't a prayer of winning."

"And you haven't a snowball's chance in hell that I'll obey this ridiculous dictate!"

The old man gave a shrug. "Suit yourself, then. I'm sure one of your opponents will prove more amenable."

Temper surging, Courtney snapped, "But this is unfair, sexist, why it's sexual harassment—"

"Sue me, then," he interjected calmly.

"I damn well may."

M. Billingham shook his head. "Courtney, dear, why get into such a dither? It's all in good fun, you know."

"Fun? But from what this says, you expect me to . . ." Leaning toward him, she whispered fiercely, "To get married."

"Indeed, I do," came the unabashed reply.

15

"*What?*"

He stepped closer, his bright blue eyes boring into her own. "Courtney, may I remind you that ours is a *baby* products company? We may be on the brink of major expansion and an initial public offering, we may need a savvy new CEO, but that does not mean we should lose sight of our core values."

"What does *that* mean?"

"Do you actually think I'd give this promotion to someone lacking in—er—family perspective?"

"But—I have a family. A very large one."

"Not one of your own. Now consider your three competitors: All of them are married, with children, even though I must admit they're clones and drones about it. Why, last year at the company picnic, they even got their wives mixed up, as I recall. And didn't one of the babies end up going home with the wrong family?"

Courtney waved the card at him. "Why are you wasting my time with this?"

"Why are you wasting yours?" He nodded toward the ballroom doors. "Your rivals, Gilchrist, Gideon, and Getz, have already departed on their respective missions. Just to reassure you, let me state that their assigned tasks are every bit as daunting as your own. But if I were you, I wouldn't allow any grass to grow under my feet."

"Meaning what?"

He winked. "If you want the promotion, my dear, you'd best hustle your butt."

"Hustle my . . . you are a horse's patooty, sir!"

The old guy had roared with laughter. "So it's taken you this long to figure that one out?"

Courtney had seethed inside, all the while realizing she was cornered and hating M. Billingham to the core.

"Very well," she'd agreed at last. "I'll go on your idiotic mission. Besides, if I stay here, I'm certain to strangle you."

The old man had only chuckled. "I knew I could count on your fiercely competitive nature, my dear."

Courtney had stormed out of the ballroom, and now she gritted her teeth at the memory. She'd been struggling with her dilemma ever since. How dare the old codger dictate that she must take a husband in order to gain a promotion!

At first she'd been tempted to go hire a lawyer, or march straight down to the E.E.O.C. Then, once she'd begun to calm down, she'd looked at the situation more rationally. Yes, the old man was a lunatic, but if she sued, she'd only brand herself a troublemaker, not the best route to go in the stuffy, conservative corporate world.

The bottom line was if she wanted to salvage the situation in any kind of positive way, she had no choice but to cooperate.

But what about taking a husband from the seamy Vieux Carre? As a passing drunkard tossed her a leer, she had her answer: unthinkable.

On the other hand, was it really all that complicated? After all, she was an MBA; she ate daunting dilemmas for breakfast. Besides, surely all she really needed to do was to hire some respectable-looking guy with half a brain to pose as her fiancé for a few hours. That should be enough to appease her delusional employer. Once the promotion was in the bag, she could kiss Romeo good-bye.

But that didn't make her task any less intimidating. The very thought of picking up some stranger in a squalid bar and paying him to . . . When she'd complained about her predicament to her chauffeur, the insufferable man had only laughed, even daring to say, "It's the Big Easy—just enjoy it, *chére*." Then he'd deposited her here on Bourbon Street.

Enjoy it, indeed! Courtney hadn't been club-hopping since her college days. And New Orleans was as bawdy and disreputable as they came. Horns belted out raunchy jazz from the bars on either side of her. The scents of decay and sour beer filled the air. Revelers with flushed faces, sloshing cups of beer, tripped down the uneven sidewalks past gin mills and strip clubs.

She grimaced and tugged at the collar of her silk blouse. Even in mid-April, the air was warm, humid and sticky, and above, the overcast skies threatened rain. Not that she could really become any more uncomfortable than she already was.

Where to begin? she wondered, surveying a sea of gawdy neon signs. Unfortunately she wasn't very familiar with New Orleans, much less the bar-clogged Quarter. Crossing the street, she decided she might as well dive into the first dive she encountered. She swept through the opened double doors of a corner tavern.

She grimaced at the odor of smoke as her eyes adjusted to the dimness. The jukebox belted out "Rambling Rose," while several couples nursed drinks in the shadows. At the bar slouched four men, all with their backs to her. One head was gray, another bald, a third graced by a ponytail. But the fourth—neat, blond, attached to a body ensconced in a presentable polo and khaki slacks—well, he looked decent. He *might* do.

Exuding a confidence she hardly felt, she crossed the room and tapped her candidate on the shoulder. "Excuse me, sir."

Her mistake. All four men turned to ogle her.

"Yeah?" they inquired in unison.

Courtney gulped. She hadn't expected *this*. Not a group reception. And what a group. All four of them were drunk and disreputable. Baldie had an ugly scar running down his cheek, Ponytail sported a crooked nose, and Gray Hair had a stubbly face and a cigar dangling from his mouth. Worst of all was Blondie—the one she had thought was respectable. He was bleary-eyed, with a red nose and florid skin.

Retreat was clearly the best possible option. "Oh, sorry, gentlemen," she muttered, backing away.

"Need some help, lady?" slurred Blondie.

"Certainly not."

"Then why are you hitting on us?" teased Gray Hair.

"I'm not hit—I'm doing nothing of the sort." She wheeled about toward the door.

But Baldie was quicker, sliding off his bar stool and striding into her path. "Hey, wait a minute, honey—we really want to help. We don't bite—honest Injun."

Courtney gave him a dubious look. A winner he clearly wasn't, but perhaps he might point her in the right direction. "Well, actually, I just had in mind . . . the truth is, I'm here on business for Bootle's Baby Bower—"

"Bootle's *what?*" he asked.

"Hey, what's a bootle?" Ponytail asked, laughing.

"Whatever it is, I'd sure like to bootle *her,*" jeered Gray Hair.

The men fell into gales of raucous laughter.

"Oh, of all the nerve." Courtney glared at the men. "That's not what I meant at all. I just meant I need to hire someone—"

"I'm for hire, honey buns," slurred Baldie. "Though I don't come cheap."

19

That comment brought the house down, the men rolling about on their stools. Courtney pulled a twenty from her purse and tossed it at Baldie. "Here."

His eyes lit with lecherous pleasure. "Is this for what I think it's for, baby doll?"

"Oh, yes it is," Courtney said, simpering. "Be my guest and *go screw yourself*."

She dashed out of the exit to the sounds of the men's ribald chuckles. Lord, she was so stupid! What had she expected? Prince Charming sitting in a den of sin? She cursed M. Billingham for putting her in this ludicrous situation and cursed herself for even attempting to comply.

Now what? She gazed about the teeming street, just catching a distant flash of lightning. Great! Rain was clearly on the way, and she hadn't thought to bring along an umbrella or an overcoat.

Perhaps she could find someone on the street. . . . She carefully studied the throng of humanity trooping by. Couples walking arm in arm, derelicts and drunkards, clumps of tourists. At last she spotted a likely-looking lone candidate ahead, a tall, brown-haired man wearing a neat black suit. Quickly approaching, she called, "Sir, may I have a word with you?"

He turned to smile at her. "Yes, miss, may I help you?"

Courtney groaned. Another totally unsuitable candidate, but not for the same reason as the quartet in the bar. "Thanks, but I'm afraid I mistook you for someone else—er, Father."

The priest smiled politely, then turned and continued on his way.

Courtney ground her teeth. Darn! From sinners to a saint! Was there no suitable bachelor anywhere in this town?

She heard the limo roll behind her, and turned to the driver. "Don't you dare say anything."

The grinning, dark-eyed Cajun chuckled. "You try to pick up the good father, no? We have limits, *chére*, even here in the Big Easy."

"Oh, hush."

He gazed at the skies. "Don't you think you should get in, *chére?* It look like rain, eh?"

Courtney glanced at the brooding skies. "No, not yet."

At once, thunder boomed overhead and fat raindrops began to fall.

"Damn it!" Ignoring the driver, Courtney shielded her head with her purse and charged on, tearing into the next bar. Standing in the doorway, panting to catch her breath, she spotted a pair of handsome yuppies playing pool, one guy with short brown hair, the other with blond. Both appeared to be about her age, were tall, slender, and wore impeccable casual clothing.

Thank God. At last, a couple of gentlemen.

She made a beeline to the pool table. "Hello," she began rather breathlessly. "Hey, could I ask you guys a favor?"

The blond guy turned, smiling at her. "Well, that depends on the favor."

"I've a business proposition for you gents—that is, if you can respond without turning into a couple of sex maniacs."

The two laughed, then the second man turned to Courtney. "We'll certainly try our best."

Courtney decided that this time, simply telling the truth might work best. "Well, you see, I'm here in New Orleans at a convention, and my boss is something of a eccentric. To make a long story short, he has sent several of us out on a scavenger hunt as a competition for an important promotion. My assigned task is to find a man to be . . . that is, to pose as, my fiancé."

Both men broke up again. "Sweetie, you can't be serious," the second man said. "Your boss really did that to you?"

"He sure did."

"Looks like you have grounds for a lawsuit, honey," added the blond one.

"I know, but that's really beside the point," Courtney continued. "For the moment, I think it's best just to indulge the old tyrant. So, if one of you would just help me out by posing as my fiancé, I'll pay you. Anything reasonable."

The two men exchanged a look, then both chuckled. "I'm afraid we wouldn't be of much help," the brown-haired one replied.

"Why not?"

He wrapped an arm around his friend's shoulders and winked solemnly at Courtney. "Because Stevie and I are an item."

Courtney gave a groan. "Well, good for the two of you. But frankly, it makes no difference to me at all. I mean, can't one of you pretend or something?"

"You mean like Rupert Everett's character did with Julia Roberts in *My Best Friend's Wedding*?" the blond asked.

Courtney snapped her fingers. "Yes! Precisely like that!"

He rolled his eyes. "Sorry, sweetie, but this is the real world."

"Don't I know it," Courtney said, groaning.

Spirits sagging, she stalked toward the door, only to gasp when a seedy-looking man in shorts, a T-shirt, and a golf hat stepped into her path and grabbed her arm. "Hold it, lady."

She shrugged off his fingers. "Leave me alone. I'm not interested."

"But I am." He reached into his pocket and pulled out a badge, flashing it at her. "New Orleans vice, lady. I been following you—"

"You've *what*?"

He shook a finger at her. "And let me tell you, what I just seen comes dangerously close to solicitation."

Courtney was outraged. "Oh, I never."

He looked her over with distaste. "Now I'd a'thought a well-heeled dame like you would know better than to proposition a priest, much less a couple of fruitcakes like them two over there, out looking for Lord only knows what kind of kinky kicks."

"Kinky *what*?"

"Why, I should haul you in—"

Furious, Courtney cut in, "And I should report you for gross stupidity, as well as for bias toward persons of alternative lifestyle persuasion."

He gave a snarl. "Can the lip, babe, and let this be a warning to you. Flash your cash at any more of our citizens, and I'll pack you up in the paddy wagon along with the rest of the floozies. Now get out of my sight."

"With pleasure!"

She stormed out into the light rain. This was too much! She was going to strangle M. Billingham Bootle. For the sake of her promotion, she had not only been propositioned, but had been accused of solicitation herself.

Just as she thought things couldn't possibly get any worse, she heard an ominous boom, and the skies above her began to pour.

"Great! Just great!"

She heard a horn honk, then her chauffeur called, "*Chére*, won't you please get in the car?"

Courtney glanced back at the limo and reluctantly nodded. As she started for the vehicle, the chauffeur jumped out, fighting a grin as he opened her door.

"You're really enjoying this, aren't you?" she accused, sinking into her seat. "I'm warning you—one more smirk and I'll personally mop up the streets with your ugly face."

He made a clucking sound. "*Chére*, I not ugly."

"Get this vehicle moving."

"Yes, ma'am." Shutting her door, he returned to the driver's seat. Rolling down the connecting window, he said, "They some tissues in the compartment."

"Right—tissues to sop up Noah's flood." Nonetheless, she grabbed a handful and began dabbing her dripping face. "Now what do you suggest?"

"*Chére*, I just the driver."

"Baloney. You're a local, aren't you?"

"Sure am."

"Where would I go around here to hire a husband?"

He roared with laughter. "Oh, no, Miss Kelly. You boss, he already warn me about you. He say carry you around, but no helping you. That be cheating, no?"

Courtney rolled her eyes. "Come on, he'll never know the difference if you help me out just a little. I mean, you're a presentable-looking guy—"

He chuckled. "So you change your mind, now you need my help, eh?"

"Don't you have a friend or relative I could hire?"

He wagged a finger at her. "You boss man, he smart. You try that and you be caught, *chére*."

"Damn it."

With a smile, he relented. "Well, maybe I help you just a wee bit."

She lurched forward. "Oh, please. I'll give you a huge tip."

He eyed her image in the rearview mirror and frowned. "You know, you not exactly dressed to entice a man, *chére*."

"Believe me, I enticed plenty," Courtney rejoined, remembering the drunkards in the bar. "In fact, had I been any more enticing . . . well, I shudder to think what might have happened to me."

"Maybe so, but you still looking for love in Slime Alley, *chére*."

She waved a hand. "My orders said the French Quarter, damn it. And you're the one who let me out on Bourbon Street, remember?"

A wickle chuckle escaped him. "Well, maybe I have a bit of fun with you, eh?"

"*What?*"

"The truth is, you boss man, he say have a bit of fun with you."

"The jerk! Why am I not surprised?"

"Now the Vieux Carre, it mostly clubs where scuzz buckets hang out," he continued rather philosophically.

"Don't I know it. Where would you suggest I look?"

"On the edges, *chére*, at the hotels. That where all the rich tourists are."

"Ah. Like where?"

He pulled up to a posh corner establishment, an old stone building with handsome shutters and an iron-lace balcony on the second floor. "Like there. La Belle Duchesse. The hotel bar, it face the street."

"Ah." She peered past the open double doors at a softly

lit interior with a handsome bar and bistro-style tables. "It doesn't look too bad."

"You try the bar, then." He turned off the ignition, got out of the car and opened her door. "I be waiting, *chére*. Good luck."

"Thanks. I'll need it."

Courtney emerged on the walkway and stood gathering her resolve. She was still wet, but there was no cure for that. She whisked straggles of hair from her eyes, brushed down her damp suit, and bravely marched inside the hotel bar. Her eyes perused the dim expanse. Damn, the place was deserted, except for . . .

Then she saw him, sitting at the bar, like her knight in shining armor. Tall, dark, magnificently handsome. Around thirty, she judged. Thick dark brown hair, perfectly cut, flawless features, dark-rimmed glasses adding a distinguished touch. He was dressed in an understated green tropical shirt, pressed khakis, and Italian loafers, and wore an expensive watch with a leather band. Although he was sipping a mai tai, he appeared anything but drunk. A class act if she'd ever seen one. Perhaps the chauffeur had been right. One didn't reel in a prize marlin while fishing in a sewer.

But would he help her?

Squaring her shoulders, she approached him. Within feet of him, she watched him turn and smile. Heart thumping, Courtney smiled back.

Chapter Two

Close up, he was even more handsome, she noted. His eyes were bright and deep-set, his brows beautifully arched, his nose perfect. His cheekbones were high, and his mouth was fine and straight, with just a hint of seductive fullness. When his smile deepened in apparent approval of her approach, her pulse surged giddily.

Through it all she was nagged by the feeling that there was something vaguely familiar about this stranger. Yes, there was, she quickly decided. He resembled any number of tall, dark, and sexy male movie stars she could think of.

Clearly she had a winner! But in order to enlist him, she would have to be her most clever and charming self. Possibly even flirt with him.

How long had it been since she'd flirted with any man?

Suddenly, however, she found the prospect of flirting with this stranger enormously appealing.

At the bar, he spoke first. "Well, hello there, miss," he murmured in a deep, British-accented voice.

"Hello," she managed, charmed by his accent.

He stood, and at once she admired how lean and tall he was. The scent of an expensive male cologne wafted over her. "A bit beastly, the weather out, isn't it?" Eyeing her damp clothing, he clucked under his tongue. "I can see that you have already reaped the vengeance of the elements. May I offer you a libation to ward off pneumonia?"

At his droll commentary, Courtney had to chuckle. He was certainly all British and very quaint, she had to give him credit for that. She also couldn't believe her good fortune, for here was a true *gentleman* who had greeted her not with the usual crude come-on, but with actual concern for her plight. "Thank you. That's very kind of you."

"Splendid, then. So you'll join me?"

"Don't mind if I do," she replied, taking a seat.

Resuming his own seat, he remarked, "The mai tais are quite palatable here, if you'd like a recommendation."

"By all means," she agreed.

He turned to the bartender and ordered her a drink, then flashed his dazzling smile again. "So what brings a beautiful young lady like you out on this stormy evening?"

Courtney was feeling coy. "What makes you ask?"

He looked her over, though with a respectful eye. "Well, you're not exactly dressed to go clubbing in the Vieux Carre, I must say. Looks to me as if you've just come from some corporate board meeting."

"Actually, I've come from . . . something like that. And from the sound of you, you've just come from merry old England."

He grinned wryly. "How did you guess?"

"It's written all over your—er—accent. Are you here in the States on vacation?"

His response, too, proved teasing. "Something like that."

The bartender deposited Courtney's drink, and she lifted it toward her companion. "To us, then. Two strangers passing in the night in the rainy French Quarter."

"Ah—how romantic that sounds. Hear, hear." He clicked his glass against hers and took a slow sip. "So, was I correct? Are you here in the Big Easy on business?"

She nodded grimly. "My company's annual convention."

"Ah. Stodgy affairs, conventions, aren't they?"

Courtney had to laugh at the irony. "You said it."

"So you're an escapee from the unmitigated boredom."

She sipped her drink. "Hmmmm . . . could be."

"So what company is it? If you don't mind my asking."

"No, I don't mind. It's Bootle's Baby Bower."

He lifted an eyebrow. "You don't say."

"That's right, actually the company has its roots in England."

"Indeed. Why, I pass your London outlet all the time. Just around the corner from where I live—St. Katherine's Dock."

She nodded. "Ah, yes, I'd heard that was the latest haven for London yuppies."

He winked. "They're called highfliers over there. But, yes, it's quite a posh quarter, with plenty of quid lying around to be squandered in pricey boutiques like Bootle's."

She regarded him with keen interest. "Do you have a

family?" Feeling a rush of warmth at his sudden, sharp scrutiny, she quickly amended, "I mean, children for whom you might shop at Bootle's?"

He shook his head. "Not ones of my own, though I've two younger sisters, both married, and a bumper crop of young nieces and nephews coming along."

"You're kidding!" she replied. "I'm pretty much the last holdout, marriagewise, in my family, too. Three married older sisters and one younger brother, complete with fiancée. All of my sisters have children."

"Do your siblings also exert intolerable influence on you to proceed to the altar?"

"Do they ever!" she declared, thoroughly enjoying herself. "And my parents! You'd think they'd be content with their brood of seven grandchildren—"

"Seven!" he repeated.

"But, oh, no—they won't be satisfied until I take the plunge."

He scowled. "Ah, yes, all that pressure to take the plunge, matrimonially speaking."

Courtney struggled not to smile; he appeared so serious and sympathetic that she was hard-pressed to figure out whether he'd meant the double entendre.

"At any rate," he continued, "there's nothing worse than parents determined to marry off their offspring."

Courtney had to laugh as she considered her own plight. "Well, that depends. I can think of something worse."

"What do you mean?"

She eyed him skeptically. "If I tell you something, will you promise to take me seriously, and, well, not to laugh?"

At once his expression grew grave. "Absolutely."

"You asked me what I'm doing here tonight."

"I did."

She leaned closer and spoke in a conspiratorial whisper. "Well, it's all the fault of my boss, M. Billingham Bootle."

"Ah. I take it he must be the head of Bootle's Baby Bower?"

"CEO and chairman."

"I see. What does the *M* stand for, if I may ask?"

She gave a shrug. "I don't know. Money, most likely. Anyway, M. Billingham is about to retire from active leadership in the firm. In fact, I've just learned that he's about to select his successor."

"Really? Might you be in line for the post?"

She laughed. "Yes, if I can 'bag my kill.' "

"I beg your pardon?"

"You see, M. Billingham is . . . well, something of an eccentric. He has ordered a scavenger hunt in order to select his successor."

He gave an incredulous laugh. "A scavenger hunt? Why, how peculiar."

"My thought exactly, but unfortunately, my boss is certifiable, a madman with a long history of bizarre practical jokes. To make a long story short, he simply refuses to listen to reason. He has ordered me and three male colleagues out on the streets here, to hunt up whatever *items* his demented mind has conjured up. The first man—or woman, in this case—to successfully complete his mission wins the promotion."

"I'll be deuced. What exactly did this old crackbrain ask you to do?"

"That's where you have to promise not to laugh."

He solemnly crossed his heart. "On my honor."

She sighed. "I've been ordered to find the most eligible

bachelor in the French Quarter, and to marry him by morning."

His reaction was predictably extreme. First he choked on his drink. Then he burst out laughing.

"And you promised!" Courtney accused.

Still half-choking, half-laughing, he pulled off his glasses and wiped away tears. "Sorry! But, great Scot, you cannot be serious. Your boss is trying to force you to wed a stranger? Why, that's the most outlandish scheme I've ever heard of."

"Tell me about it."

He looked at her then, and Courtney struggled not to gasp as she found herself staring into the stranger's brilliant blue eyes, eyes that were even more vibrant than she'd first thought. Excitement and a second spark of recognition swept over her. It seemed downright criminal that any man could be so handsome. And still he seemed hauntingly familiar. Had she met or seen him somewhere before?

"Miss?" he asked with concern. "Are you all right?"

"Oh, it's nothing," she replied, forcing a casual tone. "It's just that—well, you have such vivid eyes."

He wagged a finger at her. "If I didn't know better, I'd swear you were flirting with me."

Courtney smiled. She found she was having a lot of fun with this stranger. "Could be. But that doesn't solve my dilemma, does it?"

"No, it doesn't. Just how were you planning to solve it?"

She bit her lip. "Well, I guess I need to find someone— a man, that is—to help me."

"Ah, yes," he murmured, "a male of the species. They do sometimes come in handy, I suppose."

Liking him more by the moment, she gathered her courage. "Would you do it?"

"Me?"

She nodded solemnly.

He leaned closer, his seductive scent filling her lungs. "Do you mean, will I marry you?"

His question was so wry and disarming that she choked out a laugh. "No, no, I mean, would you be willing to pose as my fiancé, just for a little while, so I can—"

"Bag your promotion?" he politely supplied.

"Well, yes. You're pretty quick on the uptake, aren't you?"

"I suppose I am. So you're just enlisting me in a sort of—acting assignment?"

"Precisely. Well put."

"But are you sure our pretending will be enough?"

Although his words sparked a stab of doubt, she squared her shoulders with bravado. "Sure, why not? After all, the old man is crazy and has a short attention span. As long as I show up with a warm male body, I'm sure everything will be fine. So . . . will you do it? Will you help me out?"

He scowled over this for a long moment, then broke into a grin. "Sure. Why not? I don't think I've had such fun since my Cambridge days."

Relief swept Courtney. "You mean you'll really help me?"

"Of course."

She clapped her hands. "Oh, this is wonderful. And there's no time to waste. Come on, drink up so we can get back to the hotel."

He flashed her a puzzled frown. "But aren't you forgetting something?"

Eugenia Riley

Disappointment burst Courtney's bubble. "Oh, so you're just like the others—"

"Others?" he asked mildly.

"The others I approached before you."

A look of feigned dismay darkened his features. "You mean there were others before me? Darling, I'm crushed."

"Come on, quit teasing me."

"You think I'm teasing?"

She forged on with the issue at hand. "The others, well, they expected me to . . ."

"To what?"

"You know what!"

"To compromise your virtue?" he asked in a shocked tone.

Courtney burst out laughing again. He was just too much!

"Why, the scoundrels!" he blustered with that same air of mock outrage. "That's utterly despicable. I'd call them all out for insulting my fiancée—pretend fiancée, that is—if only I knew who they were." He paused to pat her hand. "And I assure you, my dear, that I have no such dishonorable intentions."

"I'm relieved to hear it." She sobered somewhat. "But if that's so, then what exactly do you think I've forgotten?"

He could hardly contain his own amusement. "Why, introductions."

As his meaning sunk in, she chortled. "Good grief, how silly of me. You're right, of course. I can't exactly pass you off as my fiancé if I don't even know your name, right?"

"Righto."

Grinning, she extended her hand. "Courtney Kelly."

He shook her hand. "Mark."

"Mark who?"

He gave her a chiding look. "Now *you* have to promise not to laugh."

"Okay."

"Mark Wiggleshaft."

She gasped, then burst out laughing.

He wagged a finger at her. "Naughty girl. You promised."

"Sorry. But that can't actually be your—"

"It is, indeed."

Courtney grimaced. "Oh, brother. You mean I have to go back to the hotel and introduce Mark *Wiggleshaft* as my fiancé?"

He affected a look of chagrin. "Having second thoughts already, darling? And we've only just gotten engaged."

"Well, it *is* pretty funny. And probably just what Mr. M. Billingham Bootle deserves."

"Yes. And if you want to talk about silly names, there's one for you."

"You're right. And I really shouldn't berate your heritage. For all I know, the Wiggleshafts might cringe in horror at what I'm asking you to do."

Merriment twinkled in his eyes. "Truth to tell, I suspect my stuffy ancestors might well roll in their graves at this daring episode—especially Sir Hugo and the Dowager Biddlespoon."

"Ah. So you come from an old English family?"

"We've traced our lineage back to Elizabeth I. A couple of dukes, a bumper crop of marquesses and earls—even a black sheep or two. Present company excepted, of course."

"Goodness, I'm impressed. And, just for the sake of

35

our current situation, what exactly do you do, Mr. Mark Wiggleshaft?"

Modestly he replied, "I'm a management consultant and entrepreneur. I handle my family's holdings in London, as well as a few companies I've managed to acquire or start up on my own."

"My, my. You do sound like quite a catch."

"The most eligible bachelor in the French Quarter," he quipped with a devilish air.

"And you've really managed to stay single?" she continued casually.

He sighed. "My family has a suitable young lady picked out for me, and I suppose in time I'll bow to the pressure—queen and country, and all that."

"Ah."

He grinned. "But for tonight, love, I'm yours."

His words thrilled her so much that suddenly, Courtney wished he were hers for much more than just a night. In the back of her mind, it nagged her a bit that he was being so cooperative and had accepted her outlandish story so readily. But at the moment, she knew she couldn't afford to look a gift horse in the mouth.

Mark took out his wallet and laid several bills down on the bar. "Shall we go, then? I mean, didn't you say you must bag your prize with all haste in order to win?"

"Precisely. My chauffeur is waiting outside."

"Good show."

In true gentlemanly fashion, he offered her his arm and escorted her out of the bar. The sleek silver limo sat at curbside. The chauffeur hopped out and opened the back door for them. Mischief gleaming in his eyes, he glanced from Mark to Courtney. "So you met with success, Ms. Kelly?"

"Yes." She got in and watched Mark slide in beside her. "Back to the hotel, please."

"Yes, ma'am." The chauffeur shut the door.

She turned to Mark. "You'll let me buy you dinner afterward, to thank you for this?"

Now he teased her with a pained look. "*Allow?* Well, if you insist. I'm sure it will be torture, but someone has to do it."

She playfully poked him in the arm. "Oh, hush."

"But I do have a question."

"Yes?"

"Just what are you planning to tell your boss about us?"

She shrugged. "Oh, I don't know. I guess that we met in the French Quarter, and it was love at first sight."

He frowned. "I'm still rather afraid he might call your bluff and insist we marry."

"And you're saving yourself for the girl back in England, right?"

"Something like that."

She responded with bravado. "I wouldn't worry too much about our being forced into matrimony on the spot. Besides, doesn't a marriage take time, a license and blood tests, all that?"

He scratched his jaw. "True. So you just might pull it off. Only there's one aspect it might be hard to fake."

"Oh? What's that?"

He stared straight into her eyes, and all at once the mood changed from one of playfulness to one of breathless anticipation. "Don't you think it will be difficult for us to pretend to be in love unless there's some spark of chemistry between us?"

Courtney gulped. His gaze, his words, seared her with

unexpected sexual heat. "Well . . . I hadn't thought of that."

"Wouldn't your boss expect us to be lovely dovey, to hug and kiss as engaged couples are known to do?"

"I hadn't thought of that, either."

He took her hand, raised it to his mouth and slowly, gallantly kissed it. "Well, you'd best think, Courtney. For me personally, it would be difficult to simply pretend consuming passion for a woman I hardly know."

His words made a certain sense, provocative though they were, and she was already feeling hot from the touch of his lips on the back of her hand. "What are you suggesting?"

A hint of roguishness gleamed in his eyes. "I think we must share a kiss."

"A kiss?"

At once he grew utterly solemn. "You know, strictly in the name of gamesmanship, to make our pretense believable."

He had a point—a truly valid one—Courtney had to admit it. And he made his argument with the charm of a master.

Who was she kidding? This man was sexy as hell, and he wanted to kiss her—not just her hand, but her mouth. A brigade of bulldozers couldn't stop her from accepting his offer.

"Well, okay," she conceded demurely, raising her face toward his. "I guess one kiss wouldn't hurt."

Smiling tenderly, he leaned over and pressed his mouth to hers. It was a sweet, gentle kiss, and never would Courtney have expected her world to be so rocked by it. But jolted she was. As his lips held hers and the heat of his breath seared her mouth, a current of sexual need warmed her midsection then arced treacherously lower. She gasped against his mouth and felt his strong arms move to envelop her. The protectiveness of his gesture further melted her. For a preppie Brit, this man certainly knew how to kiss. When his hot tongue teased the contours of her lips, she went light-headed and could feel her insides melting.

"Well?" he asked a moment later.

"I-I think we'll be believable," she managed huskily.

He nuzzled his mouth against her flushed cheek. "Do you, love? I personally think we could use a bit more practice."

"Sure," Courtney replied recklessly, shocking herself to the core. Then she stunned herself even more when she kissed *him*.

Chapter Three

As Mark opened the hotel door for her, Courtney flashed him a giddy little smile. Goodness, this man was some charmer. Pretending to be attracted to him was no longer—well, a pretense.

Once both were inside the glittery lobby with its posh rugs and gleaming crystal chandeliers, he glanced about. "Which way?"

Courtney pointed ahead. "The Pelican Ballroom."

Nodding, Mark took her arm and ushered her onward. Courtney couldn't believe her good fortune. Although Mark had insisted on some kisses in the limo, he'd been clever and charming about it, unlike the previous boors with their crude come-ons. By contrast with them, he seemed a prince in every way. To be frank, she hadn't minded that intimate interlude at all. In fact, she'd enjoyed it tremendously, doubtless the reason she'd rashly kissed him back, in defiance of her usual reserve.

Inside the vast room with its elegant murals depicting shorebirds, people milled about in small clumps. Courtney scanned the room, relieved to spot neither Gideon,

Gilchrist, nor Getz present. Good—she was the first back with her haul—and what a haul!

Her gaze settled on the chairman, who stood across the room chatting with two elderly male board members. She tugged on Mark's hand. "There he is."

Mark scowled at M. Billingham. "So that's the old tyrant."

"M. Billingham Bootle in the flesh. Come along."

As they stepped up to the group, M. Billingham turned to eye Mark and Courtney with amusement and interest. "Well, what have we here, Courtney?"

Proudly, she proclaimed, "What you have here, sir, is the winner of your scavenger hunt—and the promotion. Mr. M. Billingham Bootle, meet my—er, my fiancé, Mr. Mark Wiggleshaft."

Amid chuckles from the board members, M. Billingham raised an eyebrow in amazement, then offered Mark his hand. "Mr.—er—Wiggleshaft. Such an interesting name."

Mark firmly shook the older man's hand. "Mr. Bootle. I must say I find yours equally quaint."

A twinkle in his eyes, M. Billingham murmured, "So, it appears you've swept fair Courtney off her feet, young man."

"Hardly an easy task, but I managed somehow," Mark modestly replied, wrapping an arm around Courtney's shoulders. "Isn't it true, darling?"

"Of course." Courtney turned to M. Billingham. "Mark literally carried me away. Now all that remains is for you to declare me the victor."

A frown brought M. Billingham's bushy white brows rushing together. "Not so fast, my dear. You were ordered to find an eligible bachelor. I surmise from his accent that this young man is a Brit, which speaks well of him, of course. I'm always proud to meet one of my countrymen." With a bemused glance toward Mark, he finished, "However, is he otherwise worthy of you?"

"Oh, definitely."

"I do feel I'd past muster with Dunn and Bradstreet," Mark remarked wryly.

"Furthermore, you of all people should approve, Mr. Bootle," Courtney went on. "Mark's from an old, mon-eyed British family, and he's also an entrepreneur in his own right."

M. Billingham regarded Mark with interest. "An entrepreneur, are you, Mr. Wiggleshaft? And what might be your field of specialty?"

"I own a number of retail and Internet enterprises based in the U.K."

A look of pleasant surprise flitted over the old man's features. "I am impressed indeed. So, you are well-fixed and of good stock. An eligible candidate, I must say. But tell me, are you willing to commit to our fair Courtney for the rest of your life?"

Even as the chairman's question filled Courtney with unease, Mark gave her a quick squeeze and gallantly replied, "Absolutely, sir. I'm hers."

Courtney flashed both men a frozen smile.

M. Billingham clapped his hands. "Splendid, then. Well, Courtney, I'm prepared to declare you the winner— just as soon as we dispense with one small formality."

Courtney felt a sudden sinking sensation in the pit of her stomach. "Oh. What might that be?"

"Just a quick trip to the airport, so we may all hop the corporate jet to Vegas for the wedding."

"The—er, *what?*" Gasping, Courtney exchanged a mystified glance with Mark, then turned back to the chairman. "W-wedding? Why, I've only just met this man!"

M. Billingham scowled. "Did you not take seriously your assigned task in the scavenger hunt?"

"Well, I . . ." Floundering, Courtney stammered, "Of course I did, but . . . I thought, well, I mean I assumed I'd have some time, time to get to know this man better—"

"Time to wiggle out of your commitment with Mr. Wiggleshaft here?" M. Billingham quipped. "No dice, Courtney. If you want the promotion, you must comply with my terms—fully—which means you must marry this chap tonight."

"Tonight?" Now Courtney was suffering full-fledged panic, and a look at Mark's face revealed that he, too, had gone pale. "But that's preposterous! You can't expect me to actually marry a complete stranger—"

"And I thought you said it was love at first sight," M. Billingham scolded. "Were you trying to trick me, Courtney?"

"No, but you were obviously trying to trick me!"

"Trick? I put all my cards on the table and made my terms crystal clear."

"Well, your terms are a bunch of terrorist tactics."

Now Mark intervened. "Sir, I agree with Courtney. I do think you are rushing matters a trifle."

M. Billingham shot him a glower. "We hardly need input from the groom here. You, sir, are but a technicality—"

"A technicality?" Mark repeated, voice rising.

"And see that you remember your place. As for you, Ms. Kelly . . ." M. Billingham swung on Courtney. "Kindly make up your mind. My patience is not limitless. In fact . . ." With a superior air, he gestured toward the doors of the ballroom, where a crowd was gathering. "It appears your competition is close on your heels. Pardon me, please."

"Pardon *you?*" With mouth hanging open, Courtney watched the chairman calmly stride away. "Can you believe this?" she asked Mark. "He's actually insisting we fly right off to Vegas to be married."

He nodded grimly. "Yes, I was afraid something like this might happen. Didn't I warn you?"

"Yes, you did, but I never dreamed . . ."

"I don't suppose we could just indulge the old psychopath, fly to Vegas and marry, then get a quickie annulment?" Mark suggested.

Courtney was horrified. "Are you joking? The way he's going at it, he'll likely demand a . . . well, a ringside seat at our wedding night."

He actually blushed. "Ah, you have a point, my dear."

Craning her neck to view the activity near the door, she added, "And damn, now it looks as though my illustrious opponents are returning with their haul. Come on."

Before he could protest, she grabbed his hand and pulled him toward the others. Virtually all the convention-goers had now gathered near the door, and the sounds of laughter and snickers filled the air. As Mark and Courtney broke through the wall of people, she discovered the source of everyone's amusement. At the center of the crowd stood the chairman, and next to him a grinning Gilchrist and his companion, a skimpily clad, heavily made-up female dancer with a live boa constrictor dangling around her neck!

Even as Courtney struggled to absorb this astounding scene, Al Gideon marched into the ballroom, escorting a large African-American woman wearing a turban, along with a brilliantly patterned skirt and scarves. In short order he was followed by a limping, grimacing Gil Getz, in tandem with a short, wiry man who mouthed blasphemies in French while tugging along a small alligator on a leash! As the obviously irritable creature snapped at several onlookers, the crowd began to scatter.

"My Lord, can you believe what we're seeing?" Courtney muttered to Mark.

"I think you work with a gaggle of lunatics."

"Agreed. Let's get a closer look."

He touched her arm. "Yes, but mind the gator, love."

She rolled her eyes.

They arrived in the center of the crowd just as Gilchrist was addressing the chairman. "Sir, in compliance with my order to bring back an exotic dancer with a snake, may I present Miss Cuckoo La Clerque and her dance partner, Barry the Boa Constrictor."

While laughter erupted all around them, Cuckoo grinned at the chairman and undulated her bosom, shaking the snake as well as her billowing breasts. "You want I put the moves on you, honey?" she teased M. Billingham.

Amid more merriment, the chairman grinned. "Charmed, I'm sure, Ms. La Clerque, but I'll take a rain check. Well done, Gilchrist, but I'm afraid Ms. Kelly may have already beaten you to the punch by bringing back her assigned eligible bachelor." He jerked a thumb toward Mark.

With a quick glance toward the couple, Gilchrist frowned. "Damn. You mean I had to go to all this trouble, and she just had to pick up some guy?"

"Not just any guy, as you'll soon see," M. Billingham said. "Although you may still win against Ms. Kelly by default as she's not yet fulfilled all the terms of her assignment."

Gilchrist brightened. "Really, sir?"

M. Billingham glanced smugly toward Courtney. "Yes, Ms. Kelly seems to have a small problem with follow-through . . . or perhaps commitment."

Courtney shot him a nasty look.

M. Billingham took no note, turning instead to Gideon. "Well, Alfred, who have you there?"

Gideon gestured toward the large woman with cocoa-colored skin and noble features, who stood with her chin thrust high, scowling magnificently at the others. "Sir, as you know, I was ordered to bring back a voodoo priestess to perform a spell to rid the company of evil spirits. Thus, I present Mamma St. Mambo, the most respected practitioner of black magic in the Big Easy."

M. Billingham nodded to the woman. "Madam St. Mambo."

"M'sieur," she responded archly.

"And is she ready to perform her incantation?" M. Billingham inquired.

"She is indeed." Gideon gestured to her. "Tell him, Mamma."

She drew herself up. "I ready to throw the bones, *cher.*" Retrieving a small bundle from her pocket, she knelt, threw out a handful of sinister-looking bones and feathers, then stood and began to chant, dance and wave her arms. Several onlookers shrank away, while others watched in wide-eyed fascination.

Shaking his head at the demonstration, M. Billingham turned to Getz. "Well, Gilbert, it looks as if you've complied as well, even if you are a day late and a dollar short."

Wearing a frown of supreme frustration, Getz hobbled forward, followed by the still-cursing man tugging along the ill-tempered alligator. "Sir, may I present Hal the Alligator and his handler, Gabe the Cajun. You've no idea the trouble I went to to find these two. Why, I had to visit a carnival out near the airport. Then the damn lizard nipped me on the ankle, and afterward he made a dreadful mess in the taxi—"

"Yes, yes, I'm sure you've been thoroughly abused," M. Billingham interjected patiently.

Struggling with the gator, the wiry little handler spoke up in a thick Cajun twang. "Sir, Hal, he don' like these people."

M. Billingham grimaced as the animal snapped at him. "Never fear, we don't like him, either." Clapping his hands, he turned back to Courtney. "Well, Ms. Kelly? As you can see, your competition has made a formidable showing. Are you prepared to fulfill your end of the bargain, or default to Gideon here—that is, Gilchrist?"

With so many eyes focused on her, Courtney was feeling desperate. She glanced at Mark and caught his look of keen compassion. Swallowing her pride, she decided to try pleading. "Mr. Bootle, please. It's utterly absurd for you to expect me to marry this man in order to get the promotion."

"She has to *marry* him?" Gilchrist gasped to Gideon.

"Wow, didn't we get off easy?" answered Gideon, fanning his flushed face with his hand.

Mark spoke up again. "Yes, sir, I think you're taking this matter a bit beyond the pale."

M. Billingham turned on Mark. "I said, sir, that we don't need any comment from you."

Mark was clearly indignant, too, a vein jumping in his temple as he advanced toward M. Billingham. "Well, sir,

I have every right to comment, and furthermore, you *are* going to listen to reason."

"Why should I listen to you?" M. Billingham sneered.

"Because I say so, Grandfather!"

As gasps sounded out, Courtney turned horrified eyes to Mark. *"Grandfather?"*

He offered her a sheepish grin. "Ooops, it just slipped out."

Courtney could not believe what she was hearing. "Ooops? He's your *grandfather*, and all you can say is 'Ooops, it just slipped out'?"

"Sorry, love, I forgot to mention it."

"My God!" Appalled, Courtney whirled on the chairman. "You two are *related*?"

The chairman burst out laughing. "Indeed we are. You didn't *really* think I'd expect you to marry an utter stranger, did you, Courtney? For a smart girl, you're a bit slow on the uptake, aren't you? And you must admit I've found a most clever way to pair you up with my grandson—and get you to marry him."

Courtney could only stare from the chairman's triumphant face to Mark's suddenly guilt-stricken visage. She'd been so caught off-guard and confused, it took a long, agonizing moment for everything to sink in. When it did, the emotional impact was devastating. "You mean this whole thing was a set-up, a practical joke?"

"It was deliberate, all right, Courtney, but I'm hardly joking," the chairman replied.

"Both of you were in on this?" she demanded.

Mark's miserable expression confirmed his involvement.

"Yes, the two of us and your chauffeur," M. Billingham admitted proudly. "I had to bribe him, of course."

She turned on Mark. "How could you?"

Helplessly, he beseeched her with an outstretched hand. "Courtney, please, you're taking this all wrong. You must allow me to explain—"

"Explain! You deceived me, you son of a bitch!"

Sounds of horror erupted around them as Mark implored, "Please, Courtney, I never intended for matters to run amuck this way."

"Sure, you didn't," she snapped. "Lies and betrayal must be a spectator sport for you, as they are for your grandfather."

Undaunted, M. Billingham chided, "Courtney, really, I think you're being rash, and perhaps a bit arrogant—"

"Arrogant? Rash? I'll tell you what arrogant and rash are: requiring me to marry your grandson as part of my job description."

Mark spoke up sternly. "Yes, Grandfather, Courtney is right. Fun is fun, but you're taking this too far. It is utterly absurd of you to try to blackmail her into marrying me."

She glared at him. "Butt out, I said. I don't need your help." She addressed the chairman. "Well, what do you say? Are you going to back down on this preposterous dictate, or should I hire a lawyer and sue you?"

M. Billingham gave a shrug. "My terms stand. If you want the promotion, you'll marry my grandson. Otherwise, it goes to Gilchrist."

Courtney stared from one man to the other with tears burning her eyes. "Then I quit. And I'll see you both in court."

She wheeled about and exited the room.

Chapter Four

Mark felt stunned, watching Courtney flee the ballroom like Cinderella rushing to get home by midnight. He thought of running after her, but soon realized there was little point in doing so as long as she remained so furious.

Not that he blamed her. He couldn't believe what his grandfather had just done, ruining his chances with a woman who had fascinated him for more than a year now. He'd gone along with his grandfather's crazy scheme only because he'd thought the scavenger hunt might be a fun way for him and Courtney to meet. Never had he dreamed his dotty relative would actually follow through and try to force Courtney to wed him on the spot. Now M. Billingham Bootle had ruined everything, his rash strategy backfiring in both their faces.

He observed the old man, laughing with Gideon and Gilchrist and several other colleagues . . . as if he hadn't just destroyed a woman's life. He heard him remark, "Well, Gilchrist, it seems you may be the winner, after all—"

That did it! Mark could not abide any additional insults from the old geezer. He quickly stepped between the men and tapped his grandfather on the shoulder. "Sir, a word with you, if you please."

Casting his grandson a forbearing look, M. Billingham grinned to the others. "Pardon me, gentlemen. I must speak with my grandson."

Mark curtly nodded toward the ballroom doors. "Outside, sir."

"As you wish."

Mark turned and marched out of the room, with his grandfather close on his heels. Outside in the corridor, he turned on the older man. "Have you lost your mind, sir?"

M. Billingham chuckled. "Not in the least. I think I have performed quite admirably."

"You mean you just single-handedly ruined my chances with the woman I want to marry!"

M. Billingham sighed. "Grandson, you overdramatize so. You're just like your mother, Pamela, in that regard."

A sudden pain clenched Mark's throat. "Do not speak ill of the dead, Grandfather."

A look of regret crossed the old man's eyes, and he waved a hand in irritation. "Dash it, boy. Must you be so touchy about everything? You never did have much of a sense of humor."

"I have a splendid sense of humor—except when my grandfather is acting like a maniac and ruining my life— and that of an innocent bystander."

"Now you're being entirely too judgmental—"

"And you're blaming me and changing the subject, as always," Mark interrupted. "May we cease discussing my character defects and have a go at yours?"

M. Billingham shook his head. "Dash it if you aren't

51

dogged and stubborn just like your father—"

"I said enough insults regarding my parents, may God rest their souls," Mark cut in with more venom than he had intended. "Let us return to the subject at hand."

"Which is?"

"Damn it, Grandfather!" Mark waved a hand in exasperation. "When you enlisted me in your scavenger-hunt scheme, you assured me that the entire escapade would be only a practical joke, a novel way for Courtney and I to meet."

"So I did."

"Then you lied to me. What was this preposterous business just now? The corporate jet? A quickie marriage in Vegas? Did you actually intend to force Ms. Kelly to marry an utter stranger on the spot? Have you gone daft?"

"Now you're ranting and raving like a—"

"Stop it, Grandfather, and answer my questions."

"Very well." The old man's expression grew sheepish. "The truth is, I thought you and Courtney would suit each other admirably, and so, like the seasoned executive I am, I took charge and gave you both . . . well, a bit of a nudge."

"You mean you all but pushed us both over a bloody cliff."

"Would you have cooperated if I'd confessed my true intentions?"

"Of course not."

"Then you have your answer."

"Ah. The end justifies the means, then?"

The old man grinned baldly. "Have you ever known me to operate under any other precept?"

Mark shook his head in disgust. "My God, I can't believe I'm hearing this. You are utterly without scruples."

"So I am. Get to the point, boy."

"The point is, what are we going to do about Courtney?"

M. Billingham gave a shrug. "Why should we do anything about her? The woman is as irritable and highstrung as a marsh wren. Let Courtney deal with Courtney is what I say."

Mark was tempted to throttle his exasperating grandfather. "Now you're trying to shift the blame to her."

"And why shouldn't I? She's the one who just stormed out."

"After *you* tried to blackmail her into marrying me."

"But isn't that what you wanted?" the old man responded innocently.

"To blackmail her? Heavens, no."

"To marry her."

Mark drew a steadying breath. "Grandfather, you know damn well I never expected you'd try to strongarm her this way."

"But that's what it takes to win over a willful creature like Courtney. You'd certainly have never gotten the job done on your own."

Mark felt angry color creeping up his face. "What do you mean by that crack?"

"I mean, for all your intelligence and charm, grandson, you're more an observer of life than a real participant. For more than a year now, you've admired our Ms. Kelly from afar, watching videos of her at board meetings. I knew it would take more than a minor prodding to move you from voyeur to potential husband."

Mark could feel the heat intensifying in his face. "That's not fair, Grandfather. I watched those videos to help you select your successor as CEO."

"You couldn't take your eyes off her."

Mark coughed. "She has an intriguing style, I must allow."

"Especially when she devours her colleagues like a man-eating shark."

"Then that should have alerted us both that she was the last woman on earth either of us should have tried to maneuver this way."

"Oh, balderdash. She'll come around."

Mark's brows shot up. "And you're certifiable. Didn't you listen to her, Grandfather? She's planning to sue you—probably me as well, if I may hazard a guess. And I'd say she has ample grounds—sexual harassment, discrimination, extortion—"

M. Billingham dismissed his grandson with a wave. "Quit pestering me with such trifles—"

"Trifles? Grandfather, she's probably going to end up owning the company and see us both incarcerated as well, before this is over."

"How you exaggerate."

"I'm telling the God's truth."

M. Billingham gestured dismissively. "If you're so worried, go after her. She's staying in room 1424."

"And will no doubt hurl me from her balcony."

"Cease these histrionics and go mend your fences."

"Mend my fences? If my fences are in need of repair, sir, may I point out that you're the one who demolished them in the first place?"

"Ah, quit nitpicking and decide if you want the girl or not."

"Of course I want her."

"Then what are you waiting for?"

Breathing hard, Mark eyed his grandfather suspiciously. "I'm not sure this situation is salvageable, but . . . will you promise me you won't award the promotion to anyone else while I'm gone?"

"I'll hold the promotion—as well as the corporate jet."

"Grandfather! Even if Ms. Kelly should forgive me—and that's an extremely remote possibility—there's no way she's going to jet off with us to Vegas to marry me tonight."

"I'll give her until tomorrow then."

"You are mad."

"Mark, I've exhibited ample patience with you," M. Billingham snapped back. "I've snagged the fish, and it's your job to reel her in." He consulted his watch with an air of boredom. "Now if you'll excuse me, I've a convention to run."

Mark tried to protest, only to watch his grandfather calmly stride away. Now what was he to do? The old man was as stubborn and mule-headed as the lovely woman he'd just met. The two were clearly at loggerheads, poised to blow each other away, and he was positioned squarely in the middle of both their sights. Whichever way he moved, his own annihilation was certain.

How had things ended up in such a damnable muddle?

And he'd so looked forward to this day. Meeting Courtney Kelly had exceeded his expectations in every way. She was even more beautiful, intelligent, and spirited than he had hoped she would be. Kissing her had all but blown him through the roof of the limo. There had truly been an instant attraction and rapport between them. Now all of that was in peril thanks to his grandfather's interference. Dash the old coot!

But perhaps he was partly responsible, too. He *had* gone along with his grandfather's practical joke, when he should have known better. He should have remembered the old guy's penchant for surprise maneuvers and outlandish capers—and thought twice.

He'd also braved uncharted waters with undue confidence. He'd fallen for Courtney Kelly from afar when her image on a screen touched something in him and drew him out of his shell. He'd seen how much like himself she was; he'd fantasized that she would make the perfect executive wife.

But meeting Courtney had moved the process from fantasy to reality. Now he had a tiger by the tail, a real woman who was stubborn and mad as hell. Given all that had transpired, winning her over would not be easy. It would require putting his heart and his emotions on the line, risking hurt again.

He frowned, remembering more of his grandfather's criticisms. Was the old man right? Was he more of an observer of life than an active participant? Was he capable of admiring Courtney from a distance, but not executing the deal up close and personal?

One thing was certain: He was in the thick of it now.

Chapter Five

Still trembling, Courtney stood on the balcony of her room, sipping a scotch and soda and staring out at the gray waters of the Mississippi River. It seemed incredible that her career with Bootle's Baby Bower had just ended. She'd struggled so hard to get to her current rung on the corporate ladder. At twenty-nine, she was not only the youngest female vice president the company had ever known, she was the *only* female vice president.

Not that it had been easy . . . Men! They had certainly done their best to undermine Courtney every step of the way; so many of them were threatened by a young, powerful woman. In her first job, three male colleagues had kept her out of the information loop in order to make her look bad; in her second, her male boss had tried to make her take the fall for a bad deal he'd made with a supplier. Courtney had fought back both times and had come out on top.

But M. Billingham Bootle's latest move had topped them all—and had toppled Courtney, as well. She didn't know how to fight insanity, and this was clearly insanity.

All her dreams had been dashed at the whims of the crazy old chairman. She still couldn't believe he had tried to blackmail her into marrying his grandson. She'd been such an idiot—the chauffeur had even been in on it, and like a nincompoop, she'd suspected nothing and had allowed herself to be maneuvered.

As for Mark, that rat was clearly in it up to his pretty blue eyeballs. What a fool she had been to be seduced by his charm. Calling himself Mark Wiggleshaft indeed! He was clearly as big a snake as was his grandfather.

Now what was she to do? She could sue the company and would likely win. But just as she'd reasoned before, that would only brand her as a pariah, a troublemaker. Besides, Bootle's Baby Bower's reputation might be ruined in the deluge of negative publicity that would surely follow. Much as she yearned to crucify M. Billingham, she had a lot of friends left at the company and enough of a sense of loyalty that she would hate to see the enterprise scuttled in the wake of all the litigation and bad press.

No, the best thing to do would be to start over, get a job with a competitor and defeat M. Billingham that way—fairly and squarely, the good old American way, unlike his own devious and underhanded tactics.

She gave a groan of sheer exhaustion and frustration. Wouldn't her family laugh if they could see her now? Though a dedicated career woman herself, Courtney came from a large, traditional Irish Catholic family. All her parents and siblings had ever wanted was to see her married with a family of her own. They'd never taken her career seriously and might even secretly applaud M. Billingham's sneaky methods.

Well, *she* would take herself seriously even if no one else did. She would . . .

The Great Baby Caper

Her thoughts scattered at the sound of a rap at her door. Who could that be? Room service had already brought her drink.

She tiptoed over to look through the peephole, then caught a sharp breath. Mark whoever-he-was stood outside, looking quite tense.

As well he should be. How dare he show up here, after what he'd just done! Every angry cell in her body yearned to throttle him.

Far better to ignore him. Not that she would feel any real compunction about murdering him, but she didn't relish the prospect of spending the rest of her life in a squalid Louisiana prison.

Perhaps if she waited, he'd go away.

No such luck. "Courtney?" he called. "May I please have a word with you?"

She cursed under her breath.

"Courtney, I heard that. May I come in for just a moment?"

"Go away."

"Courtney, no. We must talk."

"There's absolutely nothing in the world I want to hear from you, Mr. Wiggle—whoever you are."

"Not even an apology?"

"Especially not that."

"Courtney, please."

"I said get lost."

"Not until you speak with me."

"Damn it!" At her wit's end, Courtney swung open the door and glared at him—although, handsome and contrite as he appeared, it was much harder than she would have thought.

Mark gave her a look of compassion mingled with anxiety. "You're furious at me, aren't you?"

"Brilliant deduction, Holmes." She jerked her head toward the other side of the room. "The balcony's over there. Want to jump—or should I push you?"

He laughed nervously. "That's just what I told my grandfather you'd say. I was jesting, of course."

"Oh, really?" She took a reckless gulp of scotch. "Well, you got it all wrong."

"And why is that?"

"Because I'm *serious*."

Solemnly he stepped inside her room. "I know you are, love." He sighed. "Courtney, can we please discuss this rationally?"

She seethed silently. He stood with hands extended in supplication. Much as she wanted to kill him, she couldn't help feeling somewhat moved by the look of pleading and vulnerability in his bright blue eyes. Memories of the exciting kisses they'd shared in the limo pushed to the surface, further weakening her resolve. And observing him now, she suddenly realized why he'd seemed so familiar before. He resembled M. Billingham—a very young, very handsome M. Billingham.

Damn it, she was being a pushover, going all mushy at the sight of a handsome man. She had to remind herself that his looks and sex appeal concealed a blackhearted scoundrel.

She squared her shoulders. "Rationally? Are you taking a lesson from your grandfather, who has been the soul of sanity in all of this?"

"Courtney, I know the old guy can be exasperating—"

"Exasperating? Try criminal."

"Believe me, I sympathize. Indeed, I was just warning him that he's put himself and the company in legal peril through this absurd stunt—"

"Oh, so that's why you're here," she cut in. "To protect your grandfather's legal interests?"

"No, not at all. I'm here to apologize on behalf of us both."

She made a sound of contempt. "Save your breath, Romeo. Besides, I'd never believe an apology coming from the likes of Mr. Billingham Bootle."

He took a step closer. "Would you believe one coming from me?"

"After the way you just duped me?"

"Courtney, will you please allow me to explain?"

"There's no possible explanation for what you did." She moved to the door and held it open. "Right now I just want you to leave."

He stubbornly held his ground. "Courtney, you must know it was never my intention to try to force you into marriage—"

Intrigued despite herself, she cut in, "Then what *was* your intention, Mr. Mark Wiggleshaft? If that's even your name."

He smiled sheepishly. "When my grandfather recruited me for this mission, he assured me it would all be in jest, for good fun. I went along because I thought it would be an interesting way for the two of us to meet. I never intended that it should result in—well, virtually a shotgun wedding as you Yanks would put it."

"So you were just a dupe, like me?" she inquired sarcastically.

"Precisely."

"Likely story. A dupe would never meet me under false pretenses like you did."

"Courtney, it's the truth. I never suspected my grandfather was—well, so serious about all this."

She frowned, tempted to believe him. "If that's your

61

story, tell me, why *did* you want to meet me? Were you just trying to score points with Gramps?"

"No, not at all. In fact, I must say I was a rather eager recruit."

She closed the door and stepped toward him. "What the hell does that mean?"

He smiled sheepishly. "You see, Courtney, for some time now I've admired you from afar."

"You've *what*? How?"

"My grandfather has spoken about you for years—your intelligence, your spunk. I've always assumed you were his heir apparent, the one he would want to succeed him as CEO of Bootle's Baby Bower."

"You'd never know it by the way he treats me."

"If it makes you feel any better, he's equally irascible toward me. But to get back to my story, in the last year or so, Grandfather has requested that I watch you in action, through videos of your board meetings."

"Good grief," Courtney muttered. She knew the meetings were videotaped for legal purposes, but had no idea M. Billingham was sharing the videos with his grandson. "You mean you spied on me?"

"Courtney, aren't those videos pretty much public record?"

With a dry laugh, she conceded, "Point taken. In fact, they must have been boring to watch."

A look of admiration came over him. "On the contrary, Courtney, watching you in action, seeing you take charge and brook no nonsense from the others, left me extremely impressed—and concluding that my grandfather was absolutely correct in his choice of you as successor."

Feeling complimented more than she wanted to admit, Courtney sputtered, "B-but all of that is moot now.

I haven't been chosen as your grandfather's successor, not at all. I just resigned."

He stepped closer. "I'm hoping I may dissuade you there. The woman I watched in those board meetings was hardly a quitter."

"I'm *not* a quitter! I simply refuse to be coerced, or to compromise my principles."

"And well you shouldn't," he stoutly agreed. "I'm sure we can find a way to bring Grandfather around in this. We just need to team up, put our heads together."

She gave a disbelieving laugh. "Teaming up with *you* is what got me in this mess. I'm not interested in you, sir—or your head."

He grinned then, and, realizing what she'd said, she blushed deeply.

"Reconsider, Courtney, please?"

She shook her head. "Sorry, Mr. Wiggleshaft, but you've flunked Credibility 101."

He appeared crushed. "Don't you believe me at all?"

She hesitated. "Number one, however innocent you claim to be, you were involved in this, something I can't easily ignore. Number two, you tell a pretty nutty story, and a lot of it doesn't make sense."

"Such as?"

"Well, for one thing, why haven't I ever met you?"

"I beg your pardon?"

"I've worked for your grandfather's company for four years. Don't you and he share holidays, vacations, that sort of thing?"

"We do."

"Then why have I never seen M. Billingham showing you around the company? Why has he never even mentioned you?"

He glanced away. "Grandfather and I live on separate

63

continents, and we've always chosen to keep our business and personal affairs separate. I don't visit his enterprises, nor he mine."

"But you just said you helped him select me as his successor."

"That was the exception to the rule, a one-time favor. And I only watched the board meeting videos."

She frowned in puzzlement. "And that's really what attracted you to me?"

His eyes glinted with amusement. "Actually, it was the video of your May 4 meeting."

"Why that one?"

"You were delivering quite a spirited speech, pacing about and lecturing the others on the finer nuances of product liability, when you caught your heel on a carpet tack or something—"

Courtney was mortified. "Oh, my God! That was recorded?"

He nodded. "And you accidentally tumbled into Wally Gilchrist's lap." He laughed. "I still can't decide who wore the more comical expression—you or Wally."

She chortled. "So you wanted to meet me because I'm clumsy?"

"No, because when you tumbled into Gilchrist's lap, you blushed that becoming little blush, just as you did now, and that made me see the vulnerable, sensitive woman buried beneath the hard-charging executive veneer."

At his unexpectedly disarming words and the look of sincerity in his eyes, Courtney could feel her face growing warm yet another time, even as her pulse pounded. He had an uncanny way of probing beneath the surface with her. "I-I see. I think. Look, you've made your appearance now and have acted appropriately contrite. But I *really* think you should leave."

"I'm making you uncomfortable, aren't I?" He moved a step closer and lowered his voice a notch. "Or am I getting to you, Courtney?"

Was he ever! "I'll take the fifth. I'll also try to give you the benefit of the doubt as far as your explanation goes. But I really think there's no point in our discussing the matter further."

He feigned a woebegone look. "And after you promised to buy me dinner?"

Her mouth dropped open. "You would bring *that* up now?"

He pressed a hand to his heart. "Courtney, you're dealing with a desperate man, one who, under the circumstances, would be more than happy to buy you dinner, even crawl out to the kitchen and prepare his own plateful of crow—or humble pie, if you prefer."

Tempted to give in, she glanced away. "I really think I should be alone right now."

"To do what? Watch the telly, brood, drink warm milk, and go to bed early? Woman, this is New Orleans."

She grudgingly smiled. "I know it is."

"In fact, I think it's a criminal offense here to go to bed before midnight."

"You're making that up," she accused.

"Relent, please?"

She laughed but shook her head. "Sorry. I can't."

"Meaning you won't."

"Very well, I won't." Then, seeing his disappointment, she softened further. The truth was, she had just lost her job, and everyone she knew was at the convention. She *didn't* exactly relish the prospect of spending the entire evening alone. "Just dinner?"

His face lit with pleasure. "Just dinner. No strings attached. What do you say?"

She gave a shrug. "Well, okay. If we make it quick—that is, early."

Mark grinned. "Sure, love. Whatever you say."

Minutes later, down on Royal Street, Mark proudly escorted Courtney past trendy antiques shops and posh hotels. He could not believe his own good fortune, that this beautiful woman now walked beside him, that he would have an evening alone with her. Somehow he'd managed to snatch victory from the jaws of defeat.

Before they'd left her room, she'd slipped into the bathroom, changing into jeans, loafers, a knit top and a light blazer. He highly approved of her choice of attire, which made her appear much warmer and more feminine than she had in her stuffy suit. Admiring her lovely, wheat-blond hair, he caught her glancing at him covertly. "Something on your mind, my dear?"

"Yes," she admitted. "What happened to your glasses?"

He tapped his breast pocket. "They're in my jacket."

"But you were wearing them earlier."

"I sometimes do for reading."

"Ah—so you were reading the menu at the bar?"

"Very well," he admitted. "I wore them deliberately then, hoping the specs might make me appear more genteel."

"I see. So you were out to con me, to appear perfect?"

"You think I'm *not* perfect?" he countered innocently.

Ignoring that loaded question, she asked, "And what is your real name? It can't be Wiggleshaft."

Mark laughed. "You're right, that was but another ploy. Actually, my first name is Mark, but my surname is Billingham, not Wiggleshaft—though there is a Wiggleshaft or two on our family tree."

"Admit it—you used Wiggleshaft just to rattle me."

He pretended a look of horror. "Me? Desire to rattle a lovely lady such as yourself? Never!"

"Come on, 'fess up."

"Very well. It was rather fun watching you squirm."

"Thanks loads."

"You're welcome."

"So you're Mark Billingham, then."

"In the flesh."

She frowned. "Wait a minute. I can see how you got the Billingham from your grandfather, but what happened to the Bootle?"

He chuckled. "As a young man, my dad had a falling out with my grandfather, so he had his last name legally changed to Billingham as a sort of rebellion."

"Wow, what a fierce revolt."

"Truth to tell, I think Dad changed it more because of all the ribbing he took at Cambridge for the Bootle."

"No doubt. Where are your parents now?"

His features tightened. "Passed away, I'm afraid. They perished ten years ago, in a ferry accident near Thailand."

"Oh, how awful."

Appearing even more uncomfortable, he cleared his throat. "Those are the sorts of risks taken by world travelers, I'm afraid."

"So your grandfather must be—"

"Like a second father to me?" he supplied.

She nodded.

"He is, indeed."

She touched his arm. "Mark, I'm really sorry."

Pleasantly surprised, he asked, "Why?"

"Well, that you lost your parents. And also for the way I've . . ."

Intrigued, he pressed. "You've what?"

She gave a sigh. "It's true that I'm furious at your grandfather and not particularly thrilled that you were in on his little charade. But I've said such terrible things about him, thinking only of my own situation, not realizing how important he must be in your life."

Touched by her words, Mark replied, "Thank you, Courtney. And never fear. Grandfather may be dear to me, but let me assure you that I'm hardly blind to his faults."

"Tell me about it. Like trying to order our marriage by corporate decree." She snapped her fingers. "Hey, when you said your family had picked out a young lady for you, were you referring to—"

"Grandfather and his matchmaking?" he supplied. "Yes. He picked you, all right, though I never dreamed he'd try to serve you up on the spot like fast food."

Courtney had to chuckle.

He winked. "Of course, we could always defy the old chap and have a torrid affair."

"Mark!" She punched him in the arm.

"Courtney, I'm ribbing you."

"Right," she agreed with a nervous little laugh.

But as he took her arm and guided her around a corner, Mark wondered if he really was. He couldn't remember when he'd had more fun with a woman. Courtney was clever, brash, and outspoken, very American, but also feminine, vulnerable and appealing. Irate though she was, she had agreed to see him for the evening, demonstrating a grace that he admired. And it must have taken a great deal of humility for her to admit that, while she remained furious at his grandfather, she recognized how important the old boy must be in his life.

If only M. Billingham Bootle possessed one iota of the sensitivity and thoughtfulness of this woman he had trampled on without conscience. Well, Mark intended to remedy that, to make things up to Courtney in every way.

In the meantime lovely Courtney Kelly was his for one glorious evening, and he intended to relish every second.

Chapter Six

Courtney eyed Mark covertly over the edge of her menu. He'd put on his glasses again, and, perusing the menu, he appeared even more intelligent and refined.

An hour ago, she'd been furious with him. Now she was feeling all too charmed by him. He was handsome, sympathetic, with a wonderful sense of humor. Logic argued that she should have nothing to do with him, that he might well be cut from the same black cloth as was his crafty grandfather, but her heart suspected otherwise. Besides, she had just endured a major upset in her life, one that really wasn't Mark's fault but that of his grandfather. She could use some cheering up.

And she did feel buoyed at the moment. Mark had ordered frozen daiquiris, and several sips had already lightened her mood. Their surroundings couldn't have been more elegant or romantic. The cozy Creole restaurant was softly lit and tastefully decorated with brass ceiling fans and green plants. The mouthwatering aromas of succulent foods filled the air. Their linen-draped table was positioned next to a sheer glass wall looking out on a charming courtyard with sparkling fountain, ferns, and blooming flowers.

"It's so lovely here," she murmured.

"Indeed it is."

Courtney glanced at Mark to see he was staring straight at her. Gracious. This man was too irresistible for her own good. She countered with small talk. "Have you decided what you want for dinner?"

He closed his menu and removed his glasses. "Actually, I'm not that familiar with New Orleans cuisine."

"Me either. It's been years since I've visited here." She perused the menu. "But actually the Creole Sampler sounds pretty good. A bit of everything—*bouillabaisse*, oysters Bienville, shrimp creole, crawfish étouffée . . ."

"Sure, why not?" he agreed, gesturing at a passing waiter. "Let's blow the limits."

Blow the limits. With him, that was an appealing prospect!

Moments later, as they nibbled on the excellent oysters, Courtney said, "So, Mark. Tell me more about your background."

He made a face. "Not the usual tedious drivel."

She wrinkled her nose at him. "You are from another continent, you know. I doubt I'll find the details of your life boring."

"Very well, don't say I didn't warn you." Taking a sip of his drink, he murmured, "I grew up in London, in one of those moldly old mansions in Mayfair."

"Born with a silver spoon in your mouth, eh?" she teased.

He nodded wryly. "The Bootles hail from a long line of titled aristocracy. My dad acquired quite an impressive trust once he came of age and married well shortly thereafter. Unfortunately, soon after my birth, he and my grandfather had their falling out."

"Oh, yes, you mentioned that. What was the rift about, if I may ask?"

He sighed. "Actually, it was over my grandfather's desire to have my dad join the family business, Bootle's Baby Bower."

"You're kidding me."

"No."

"Let me guess: M. Billingham saw your father as his heir apparent, and your father had other ideas?"

"Precisely, though their relationship was a bit more complicated than that. Grandfather always was something of a maverick, you see. As I've mentioned, we hail from noble stock, but there were a few heretics among our forebears. One was my great-grandfather, who married a commoner—a firebrand of an Irishwoman, no less—a circumstance that the rest of my family was only too eager to sweep under the proverbial rug."

"Do you have something against the Irish?" she challenged.

"Of course not," he hastily reassured her. "Don't think I've not noticed the Kelly, as well as those green Irish eyes of yours."

Courtney smiled. "My Irish blood comes from my father's side. My mother is actually of German lineage."

"Ah—and quite a nice combination that makes for you, if I do say so, Ms. Kelly."

"Thank you."

"At any rate, it is his great-grandmother's Galway blood that ofttimes seems to run in my grandfather."

"I have always wondered where M. Billingham got his audacious streak."

Mark nodded. "However, disposition-wise, my dad

took after my grandmother Enid, may God rest her soul. He was the typical, stiff-lipped Englishman. So, after Grandfather and he parted ways, he had our name legally changed and ventured forth on his own, establishing Billingham's, a London-based clothier with the finest upscale casual wear for the highflier."

Courtney snapped her fingers. "Billingham's—don't they have an outlet here in the States?"

"Yes, but only one, in New York on Madison Avenue."

"You know, I think I visited it once when I was in Manhattan. Quite a handsome store."

"Thank you. We have a dozen outlets in the U.K., and two more in the works."

"Impressive. Your father must have become quite a success, though he didn't venture far, going from clothing for yuppie babies to attire for their parents."

Mark grinned. "Precisely. As I said, the traditional, no-nonsense Englishman."

She sipped her drink. "So tell me, Mark Billingham, do you take after your staid, conservative father, or your devil-may-care grandfather?"

Mischief gleamed in his eyes. "Perhaps I'm a mixture of both?"

"Nothing like a direct answer," she grumbled. "And your mother?"

His features darkened with regret and pain. "Quite the society queen, leaving me and my two younger sisters to the tender mercies of our nannies. The three of us endured the typical, uppercrust English childhood."

"I'm sorry. But what of your grandparents? Did you see M. Billingham at all?"

"Oh, certainly we saw Grandmother and Grandfather on birthdays, Christmas, that sort of thing. My parents and Grandmother were too socially conscious not to keep up appearances. Things were strained between Dad and Grandfather, but really not much more awkward than the typical reserve practiced by so many British families. However, years later when Grandmother died, Grandfather decided to start afresh overseas by expanding his baby products company to America—that good old Irish pioneering spirit, I suppose. As you're aware, he established himself here with great success, and now there are only two Bootle's Baby Bower stores left in the U.K." He paused. "As for me, it was prep school at Cheam, followed by Eton, then in due course I finished up my MBA at Cambridge."

"That's some achievement." She hesitated. "When did you lose your parents?"

He hesitated, lowering his gaze. "Er—my junior year at Cambridge. My sisters were at boarding school in Switzerland, and my parents had gone on a world tour with friends. That's when I learned of the ferry accident off the coast of Thailand." He cleared his throat awkwardly.

She touched his hand. "I'm so sorry."

"Thank you." A muscle jerking in his cheek was his only betrayal of emotion. "Grandfather was wonderful then, taking charge of everything. After that, we spent holidays and summers with him in Denver. Indeed, he wanted the three of us to settle with him there and seek American citizenship."

"With you joining Bootle's Baby Bower?" she suggested ironically. "Perhaps an attempt to rewrite history?"

"Indeed, but I felt obligated to take on my father's ventures instead."

"Of course you would have," she agreed sympathetically. "And I imagine you also adopted your dad's policy of keeping his and your grandfather's business enterprises separate?"

Mark nodded. "You're a smart girl."

"Well, I did wonder earlier why M. Billingham never brought you around BBB. Now I know."

"Yes, I suppose I did honor family tradition there. And besides, by the time I finished my education, both my younger sisters were engaged to chaps in London. So I took the helm at Billingham's. I signed on at a propitious time, too, around the time the Internet took off. I established our online store early and did it right, as well as starting up one of the largest online pharmacies in the U.K. I also bought up a few failed e-companies—music, electronics, fine jewelry—and reorganized them into successes."

"So you've become quite an achiever in your own right."

He gave a shrug. "I make out nicely."

Courtney was about to comment, only to pause when the waiter came by, depositing their main courses. Seeing that Mark was watching her expectantly, she picked up her fork.

"Now that you've endured my background," he remarked, "tell me more about yourself."

She laughed. "I'm afraid my upbringing's not nearly so interesting. I come from the typical, middle-class American family. I grew up in west Denver, where my dad owns a residential air-conditioning company. My mom was a bit unusual in that she stayed at home—but who can blame her with five children? As I've already mentioned, I have three older sisters and one younger brother. I pretty much followed the path of my sisters—dancing lessons, Girl Scouts, cheerleader—that is, until I graduated from high school. At that point, my older sisters had gotten jobs, followed soon after by marriage. By contrast, I broke the high school quarterback's heart and went on to college."

He winked at her solemnly. "You do strike me as a heartbreaker, Courtney."

She coughed and forged on. "I got my BBA from the University of Colorado and won a scholarship to Harvard Business School for my master's."

"My kingdom, woman," he muttered. "Now you're making me feel like an utter pedestrian."

"Sure I am," she mocked. "To continue, my first couple of jobs were stepping-stones, until I landed the position as junior executive in charge of products at Bootle's Baby Bower. From there . . ." Voice fading, she narrowed her gaze. "Well, you know the rest."

"You're on the verge of becoming the new CEO."

She shot him an admonishing look. "Mark, I just quit."

He held up a hand. "Peace, Courtney. We'll get to that later."

"Mark, there's nothing to get to—"

"Peace," he reiterated firmly. "All right?"

"Okay," she conceded grudgingly. As a tense silence descended, she added, "You know, much as I do resent them at times, I must say I don't know what I would have done without my parents. What I mean is—I'm really sorry you lost yours."

"I know you are," he replied quietly. "Although our family was not as closely knit as yours seems, I do miss my folks, as I know my sisters do. They compensated by quickly forming families of their own. In my case, I went from being a dedicated student to becoming a die-hard workaholic."

"Ah, so you have a fault after all," she teased.

"And it seems we have something in common."

She lifted her drink. "Touché. I'll admit that I'm quite dedicated to my career—or I was."

Ignoring her dig, he responded smoothly, "Yes, I've sensed that about you. In fact, that's one aspect that attracted me to you."

Pleasantly surprised, Courtney asked, "Really? In what sense?"

"Well, with all my various enterprises and responsibilities, I may never have a great deal of time for a family. Most women I've dated have not been particularly understanding there."

"Ah. So you're seeking that perfect corporate wife?"

His mouth curved devilishly. "What makes you think I want to marry?"

She rolled her eyes. "Really, Mark. Remember that little scavenger hunt earlier this evening?"

He chuckled. "Again, Courtney, the marriage part was strictly my grandfather's idea."

"Right. Strictly. Then you're just the debonair Englishman playing the field. You've no plans to marry, ever?"

From the way he suddenly shifted in his chair, he was definitely squirming. "I didn't say that. I hope that even with us, perhaps eventually there might be . . . well, possibilities."

She couldn't resist a smile; he could be the artful dodger when he wanted. "Yes, the prospect does come up eventually in most people's lives."

He met her eye. "Actually, whomever I marry, she will have to be—well, very understanding of my unconventional lifestyle."

"Unconventional?" She leaned closer. "Do you have girlfriends in every port, Mark, or are there aspects of your lifestyle—you know, weird, kinky stuff—that you're keeping in the closet?"

He leveled a mock-scolding look on her. "I don't have girlfriends in every port, nor any skeletons in my closet. But I am apt to dash off on long business trips at a moment's notice, a reality that most wives doubtless will not well tolerate."

"Unless you had someone who was as busy as you are," she muttered, thinking aloud.

"Precisely."

"Like a female clone of yourself?"

He shuddered. "How unromantically you put that, my dear."

"I'm just being logical, like you. We do seem to think alike in some ways."

"We do." He cleared his throat. "So tell me, does marriage fit into your life plan?"

She slowly shook her head. "Not really. I've pretty much decided the domestic scene isn't for me."

She was perversely thrilled to see a look of disappointment wash over his handsome features. "It isn't? May I ask why you've concluded that?"

"Oh, mostly from observing my three older sisters. They all have young children, and almost all of the housekeeping and child-care responsibilities fall on them. Don't get me wrong—I adore my nieces and nephews. But I don't want my life to be a series of trips to the grocery and dry cleaners, not to mention the soccer field and the pediatrician. Two of my three sisters are doing all that plus holding down part-time jobs."

He whistled. "Haven't your siblings ever heard of nannies or housemaids?"

"Mark, I don't hail from a wealthy family. Although

The Great Baby Caper

I'm doing well, my sisters and their husbands have had to struggle financially."

"Ah. Sorry if I sounded glib there."

"Apology accepted. What my sisters are doing is fine for them. But my point is, if you can't devote yourself to your partner and your children, then you have no business getting married in the first place."

"An interesting perspective."

"You disagree?"

"I tend to think one can have it all."

She stared him straight in the eye. "That's because you're a man, Mark."

He laughed. "Oh, Courtney. You are delightful."

Courtney lowered her gaze. The truth was, he was delightful, too. And though she hated to admit it, Mark Billingham was already getting under her skin. . . .

Chapter Seven

After dinner, Courtney walked with Mark along the levee, watching passengers disembark from a dinner cruise on an old-fashioned riverboat. The air was balmy and sweet, still scented with rain.

"Oh, the Mississippi is glorious tonight!" Courtney exclaimed.

He followed her gaze across the wide gleaming waterway to the beautifully lit bridge to Algiers in the distance. "It is indeed lovely. You know the Thames can sometimes nave that kind of glow on a really clear spring night." He reached out and took her hand. "Have you ever seen London, Courtney?"

It seemed so natural, his taking her hand that way, and she hadn't the heart to pull away, especially not with the new surge of excitement sweeping through her at his warm touch. She struggled to keep her voice casual. "Yes, my high school class went to Paris and London for our senior trip."

"That must have been some trip."

"Three years of car washes and bake sales, and a lot

of help from our parents. But it was worth it. London is a beautiful city, with so much history. You must adore living there."

"Having grown up there, I tend to take a lot for granted. The States I find interesting, though. Very brash and contemporary."

"Especially compared with stodgy old England?"

"Indeed. New Orleans provides a nice contrast—it's free-flowing, unrushed, unbridled . . . rather sensual, don't you think?"

The word *sensual* slammed Courtney straight in the gut. She managed to remain outwardly cool. "You're right, it's different here. More erot—I mean, exotic."

He smiled at her little slip of the tongue, pausing by a daiquiri stand along the levee, where several couples were lined up to get drinks. "Thirsty?"

Even though she was still feeling a slight buzz from the liquor consumed at dinner, Courtney decided, why not? This was New Orleans, after all. "Sure, I could use another of those daiquiris."

After Mark bought their drinks, they sipped them as they descended the levee, crossed the street and entered Jackson Square, where a stand of ancient, moonlit oaks guarded the historic cathedral. Along the old stone buildings flanking each side of the square were gathered clumps of people listening to street musicians, drinking at patio tables, or waiting for tarot-card readings. A few feet away from Mark and Courtney, a trumpeter was belting out a jazz version of "Rock of Ages."

"That music is divine," she murmured.

As they passed the man, Mark stepped away to drop several dollars into his musician's case. Moving back to her side, he slipped an arm around her and nodded toward the square. "Look there, love."

She gazed at the oaks just as the wind did a silvery dance through the leaves. Then, directly ahead of them along the iron fenceline, she spotted a young couple locked in an embrace, oblivious to the world as they passionately kissed.

Was *that* where Mark had been directing her attention? Glancing back at him and catching the tender though conspiratorial look in his eyes, she had her answer. Things were becoming far too romantic!

Still appearing to savor a wicked secret, Mark remarked, "Wonderful the light over there on the cathedral, isn't it, love?"

On a whim, she reached out and mussed his hair.

"What's that for?"

She wrinkled her nose at him. "Oh, you seem a little too perfect, when you can be a real rascal at times."

He chuckled. "Once when I was at Cambridge, I substituted a naughty video for one of my professors' lectures on the pitfalls of investing in third world economies."

"You didn't!"

"That turned out to be quite a lively session. The professor blamed one of my pals, his teaching assistant who had unwittingly given me access to the lecture hall, so I felt duty bound to confess. Luckily the old boy had a sense of humor and didn't turn me in to the dean."

Courtney was laughing over this when a carriage rattled past in the street behind them, and the driver called out, "You folks want a ride?"

Simultaneously, they both turned to see the driver sitting in the canvas-topped open carriage, holding the reins of a large gray horse. "Sounds like a splendid idea," Mark agreed.

He took Courtney's hand to help her on board, and as

she placed her foot on the step, he caught her about the waist and gave her a boost. Heat surged through her where his strong, warm hands had touched her. Then he joined her, his hard body pressed next to hers, his exciting male scent firing her blood. When he slipped his arm around her, she couldn't resist and nestled even closer to his heat.

The contraption rattled off, and Courtney sighed dreamily as they turned onto a quiet street with beautiful old town houses draped with iron lace balconies. It felt so wonderful to be with Mark, to leave her troubles behind.

"How are you doing, love?" he asked quietly.

The word *love* rolled tenderly off his tongue and excited her deeply. "Oh, I'm fine, perhaps a bit tipsy."

He leaned over and whispered at her ear. "Are you trying to tempt me by telling me that?"

"Tempt you?" she asked in mock outrage. "In front of a horse?"

He chuckled, then grew more serious. "Courtney, this has been such fun."

"Yes, it has," she murmured.

He drew a deep, steadying breath. "I know we agreed not to talk about it, but . . . Will you let me speak with Grandfather tomorrow, see if I can set matters straight? I'm sure I can talk him into reinstating you in your post, minus all this malarkey."

Though touched by his offer, she shook her head. "Mark, that's kind of you, but I think you were right in the first place. We really shouldn't talk about this now. Besides, I think the best thing for me to do is just to move forward. But tonight . . ." She glanced ahead at the stately facade of Antoine's Restaurant, watching a laughing young couple enter. "I feel as if I've stepped into a different world, and I'd just like to enjoy it a little while longer. Do you understand that?"

"Of course. Too much nose to the grindstone can be quite dispiriting. I think tonight I feel much the same way." He took her chin in his hand and spoke soulfully. "As if I have discovered quite a different world."

"Mark—"

His voice grew rough. "My Lord, you're so very lovely."

Her next protest was token at best, and she actually welcomed the warmth of his lips descending on hers. Sweetly and deeply he kissed her, and with the clip-clop of the horse's hooves, the scent of night and mist, the brush of the wind against her face, the moment oozed romance. She sighed ecstatically and moved her lips against his, heard a groan rise in him. Although he ended the kiss too soon, she was left reeling.

She breathlessly eyed him. "Mark, do you think we should . . . I mean—"

"Courtney, I think you've given us both the best advice of all," he said huskily. "Let's just enjoy this night."

His sexy words left her shivering, and she almost moaned aloud. How could she argue with *that*? As if he sensed her agreement, he snuggled her closer.

The conveyance turned down quiet Royal Street with its shops and hotels. Rain began to fall again, pelting the canvas cover on the carriage. The sound was treacherously sensual and romantic.

"That rain smells so good," Courtney said, breathing. "What's New Orleans without a shower?"

The driver pulled up to the awning of an art shop. "I'd best let you folks off here, where there's cover."

Mark handed the man some cash. "Thanks." He slid to the ground, then helped Courtney down. Her body brushed the hardness of his as she alighted. All at once she felt dizzy, and she was glad his strong arms supported her.

She glanced up to see his eyes glowing with passion. "Mark."

The word was half a protest, half a plea. With a groan he caught her close and lowered his face to kiss her, this time greedily. His lips tasted of rain, and thunder boomed in the background, a sensuous accompaniment as his tongue slid deeper, possessing her mouth. Courtney felt she might explode right then and there, so intense was the hunger she felt. With the torrid New Orleans night surrounding them, all her senses were on fire.

A moment later he pulled back and smiled at her, a smile of pure joy. "Come on, love," he said.

Courtney needed no further prompting. She linked her hand with his. Like happy children, they ran down the rain-splashed street together.

Chapter Eight

The night was magical. Courtney left all logic behind. Her entire being was centered on the fascinating, sexy man walking beside her.

They strolled all over the Quarter, buying frozen daiquiris from street vendors, ducking under awnings to kiss during the off-and-on thunderstorms. They returned to Jackson Square to listen to the jazz musicians and walk beneath the massive, dripping oaks. They had their fortunes told off Pirate's Alley, and both laughed when the tarot lady told them their destinies were linked. They ate hot, sugar-coated beignets as they wandered through the colorful street market.

They talked—about friends, relatives, hobbies, the differences in their countries and upbringing. They shared jokes and memories from their college days.

Midnight found them heading back toward their respective hotels. Strolling along with Mark's arm around her waist, Courtney knew she had a healthy buzz on from all the daiquiris. But she didn't care. She couldn't remember when she'd had more fun. For years she had

86

been far too serious, chained to her work. Tonight she had been set free, and although the future could prove daunting, for now she allowed herself to glory in her emancipation. And Mark. Just hours ago, he'd been a stranger whom she'd despised. Now she felt as if he was a good friend.

As they turned a corner, she spotted the regal pillared facade and soft light of a stately hotel. "What a beautiful old hotel."

"It's where I'm staying," he replied.

"How lovely. Our convention hotel is nice, too, but it's all modern. This one has some real Creole charm."

Near the front doors, he paused. "Care to come in and have a look?"

Courtney was taken aback. "Well, the hotel does look interesting . . ."

"Wait till you see the view from my room," he said enthusiastically. "There's an inner courtyard, and it's just spectacular."

Courtney gave a dry laugh. "I-I'm not sure visiting your room right now would be wise."

"Then we'll have the bar serve us a nightcap out in the courtyard. How 'bout that?"

"Now that sounds too picturesque to resist."

He escorted her inside the gorgeous, marble-floored lobby, with its gleaming gold chandeliers. As they started toward the bar, a bellman stepped toward them. "Sir, the bar is closed for the night."

"Ah, what a shame. I'd hoped to show the lady the courtyard."

"I'm afraid the patio is closed for the night as well, sir—except to our guests with a view from their rooms."

Mark pulled out his wallet and handed the man a ten.

"Tell you what—why don't you ask room service to send two cognacs up to Suite 415?"

The man grinned. "I'd be delighted to, sir."

Before Courtney could protest, Mark firmly led her away. "The lift's over here, love."

Courtney shot him a scolding look. "Mark, this isn't what I had in mind. I just wanted to see the courtyard—"

"But you can't, love, unless you come upstairs with me." The elevator doors opened, and he steered her inside the car. "I assure you it will be worth the trip." He winked. "Besides, we're two mature adults. We can handle this, don't you think?"

She fought a smirk. "That's just what I'm afraid of."

His low, half-wicked chuckle only confirmed her fears.

They alighted on the fourth floor and proceeded down the softly lit corridor. Mark unlocked door 415, pushed it open and motioned for her to proceed him inside.

Courtney stepped into the suite and glanced around. "Nice."

"You like it?" he asked, shutting the door.

Courtney studied the softly lit room, with its cathedral ceiling, walls papered in gold silk, plush carpets, expensive traditional furnishings and tasteful art picturing New Orleans street scenes. The suite's best feature was a free-standing spiral staircase that curved upward to a loft; a large bed was just visible beyond the railing.

"You must like to travel in style," she remarked.

"I enjoy tasteful surroundings," he replied, setting down his key. "You must, too. That is, I assume my grandfather pays you a livable wage."

"He *did*," she replied pointedly. "I'll have to watch my pennies for the time being." She gestured at their surroundings. "Still, I think I would always find this kind

88

of setting extravagant. My middle-class upbringing, I suppose. Why get a suite when a simple room will do?"

He stepped closer and murmured huskily, "Perhaps to charm the socks off a beautiful lady?"

"Watch your step, Mark," she managed.

He succumbed to a self-deprecating smile. "At any rate, I find your practicality endearing." Playfully he touched her chin with his index finger. "Especially as it allows me room to spoil you."

She was staring back at him rather breathlessly when a discreet rap came at the door. Mark answered it, murmured a few words to the room-service attendant, then returned with a small tray. Setting it down on an end table, he approached her holding two small glasses. "Cognac?"

She took hers. "Thanks."

With his free hand, he took her arm. "Now I'll show you the suite's best feature."

He led her to the French doors, and opened them.

"Oh, Mark." Courtney stepped out onto the balcony, eyes filled with wonder as she stared at the courtyard below. The lush tropical expanse dripped with palms, ferns, philodendrons, and dozens of varieties of flowers. A three-tiered stone fountain provided a lovely focal point. Soft recessed lighting enhanced the exotic, seductive atmosphere.

Courtney took a breath scented of nectar, mist, and greenery. "You're right, the courtyard is wonderful."

"Worth making the trip up here?"

All at once she felt a bit choked up and was confused by her own feelings. "Oh, yes."

He eyed her curiously. "Is that a tear I see?"

She nodded, feeling a bit embarrassed as she wiped it away. "Yes. You know, this evening has been so special."

"I agree completely."

She gazed out at the courtyard. "I've been so busy, so devoted to my career, that I hadn't realized there was a big, beautiful world out there that I had totally ignored."

"I know. My life has been much the same."

She turned to gaze at him. "Until tonight. I feel as if I've stepped into a different world, a world of fun and romance, where anything is possible."

He leaned over and gently nuzzled her cheek with his lips, until she gasped. "And what would you like to see made possible, Courtney? What would make your world perfect tonight?"

His question was a loaded one, and they both knew it. Catching her breath with an effort, she backed away and lifted her glass. "Perhaps a toast?"

He smiled. "Good save, love. To us, then."

They clicked their glasses together and solemnly sipped. The cognac was sweet and strong, burning Courtney's throat, an erotic reminder of the heat still building elsewhere in her body.

"Sit with me a moment, Courtney?" he asked.

"Sure."

They sat side by side on the patio chairs, quietly sipping, drinking in the beauty of the courtyard, listening to the tinkling of the fountain.

After a moment, he took her hand and squeezed it. "You know, I hate to see this end."

"Me, too."

For a long moment he sat quietly, his thumb sensuously caressing the inside of her palm, until she thought she would scream if he did not kiss her again. Then softly, poignantly, he asked, "Stay with me tonight, Courtney?"

The question, though expected, set Courtney reeling.

The Great Baby Caper

There was nothing she wanted more than to make love with Mark. Over the last hours he'd evolved from being her enemy to becoming a kindred spirit. But she realized succumbing to him now would be foolish. She still didn't know him *that* well, and he was the grandson of the man who'd betrayed her. Though instinct argued that he probably wasn't part of that betrayal, how could she be sure? Besides, after tonight, their paths would diverge, perhaps forever.

She spoke unsteadily. "Mark, I don't think that would be wise. Tomorrow I'll be heading who knows where, and surely soon you'll be going back to England—"

"All the more reason for us not to miss this magical opportunity."

Growing more and more afraid she might succumb, she stood unsteadily, setting her empty glass down on the patio table. As she straightened, a new wave of dizziness staggered her. Lord, she hadn't realized she was quite this tipsy. "Mark, I really should go."

He stood, too, grasping her arm to steady her. "I'll escort you back to your hotel."

"Don't be silly. I can get a cab."

"Nonsense. Better yet, stay here. You're not too steady on your feet, love. You can have the bed upstairs and I'll take the couch."

"No, I don't think so."

"Why, Courtney?" He pulled her into his arms and spoke huskily. "Because you're afraid you won't be able to resist temptation?"

She gasped. "Mark, please don't."

He brushed her lips with a teasing kiss, his breath hot and sweet. "Then answer me, Courtney. Are you afraid you'll succumb to what we're both feeling?"

"Oh, yes. And I must go."

He gave a long sigh. "Very well, darling, but I insist on taking you back."

"Well . . . okay."

They started off with his arm around her waist; however, just inside the door, she stumbled badly.

Mark tightened his grip on her. "Are you okay?"

Dazedly Courtney shook her head. "Just a little bit woozy."

"That does it." He swept her up into his arms and headed purposefully for the stairs.

She was shocked and amused by his caveman tactics. "Mark, you can't carry me up a spiral staircase! You'll trip and break both our necks."

At the foot of the staircase, he gently set her on her feet. "Very well, but I'm helping you upstairs. And you're staying here tonight."

"Mark, please—"

"Courtney, do you really think you won't be safe with me?"

Tempted to blurt out, *Will you be safe with me?*, Courtney instead managed to reply, "Yes, I know I will be. But—"

"No buts. Up the stairs to bed, woman."

To bed. Now that was a decadent prospect, especially coming from him. Courtney didn't resist further as he nudged her up the staircase, keeping a steadying hand at her waist. In the loft, she stared at the king-size bed with its plush quilted bedspread. The loft was cozy, with only the bed, nightstands, and a dresser filling the space.

Mark crossed over to open a drawer, returning momentarily with a large beige T-shirt emblazoned with "Billingham's, the Strand, London." Handing it to Courtney he said awkwardly, "I hope this will suffice for you to sleep in. There's a fresh toothbrush and a bathrobe in the bathroom."

"Thanks," she murmured. Starting away, she wobbled again.

He grabbed her arm. "Need some help?"

She raised an eyebrow at him. "Not in the bathroom, thank you."

He retreated, and, tossing him a crooked smile, she was off. Inside the large marble bathroom, she brushed her teeth and prepared for bed. Moments later as she emerged, Mark popped up from the bed. He'd removed his jacket and unbuttoned several buttons on his shirt, and looked very sexy.

Though his eyes burned with secret desires, his manner was in all respects polite. "Feeling better?"

She nodded. "The water on my face helped. Though I hesitate to think of how I'll feel in the morning."

He chuckled. "If you're done, I was hoping to grab— er, a quick, cold shower, before I venture downstairs."

Courtney had to laugh. "Cold, Mark?"

He shook a finger at her. "Stop it, woman, before I lose what remains of my gentlemanly restraint."

Though Courtney's expression was devilish, she didn't reply.

With a groan, he pulled her close and gave her a quick, hard kiss. Then he made a dash for the bathroom. But at the door he turned to give her a last wink. "If you change your mind, you can still save me from death by cold water."

Then he was gone.

Courtney drew a shuddering breath. *If you change your mind . . .* The words tortured her, along with the promise of passion they represented. Mark's scent still lingered in the air, enticing her. Touching her mouth, she could still feel the heat of that searing kiss; licking her lips, she could still taste him.

Making a sound of frustration, she removed her robe and got into the soft bed. At once she was tossing and turning, especially when she heard the shower rush on in the next room. She imagined him undressing, imagined him . . . And what would he do when he finished, try to climb into bed with her? Oh, she hoped so. Then she quickly realized he wouldn't, that he was too much of a British gentleman not to honor his word.

That realization made her burn for him even more. Funny how his masculine reserve sparked her own feminine aggression. She flipped over and punched down the pillow with her fist. What was wrong with her that she was considering abandoning all her fine resolve and attacking him in the shower?

The truth was, she was dying for him. She hadn't had sex in a long time, and this man was both charming and irresistibly sexy. She was like a starving woman, lying just feet away from a sumptuous feast. And as he'd pointed out only moments earlier, tonight was probably their one chance to be together—their one chance to love.

That realization pushed her over the edge. Would it be so bad to just go take a little peak at him?

Long afterward, she would wonder what demon drove her to her feet, propelled her across the room, forced her itchy fingers to gently turn the doorknob, until temptation appeared before her.

Mark stood with his back to her at the open shower door. He'd removed his shirt and the muscles of his tanned back rippled like smooth steel. He was leaning inward, adjusting the shower knobs, the fabric of his pants pulling against his beautiful buttocks.

She winced. There was only so much a woman could take. She crossed the room, wrapped her arms around his waist and whispered, "Make that hot."

Obviously taken unawares, Mark jumped, then turned in her arms and gazed down at her with mingled delight and surprise. "Courtney, my Lord, you shouldn't be—"

"Saving you from death by cold water?" She cut off further protests by throwing her arms around his neck and kissing him hungrily.

He responded with a moan, then seized her in his embrace and plunged his tongue inside her mouth. His hands roved her body, boldly stroking, kneading. Then he grasped her hand, almost roughly guiding it to the front of his trousers.

Courtney almost collapsed then, tearing her mouth from his so she could catch her breath. He was very aroused, and so hard; her fingers felt riveted to the enticing spot. At once her passion-starved brain conjured a thousand erotic images of him inside her.

She smiled in joy when he pulled the T-shirt over her head so she was standing before him in only her panties. Reverently he raked his gaze over her, then touched one of her breasts. At once both her nipples tightened. When he looked up at her, his gaze was very intense. She stared at him in the explosive silence, only the sounds of their ragged breathing filling the void. Then he leaned over and took a taut nipple in his mouth. She all but screamed with the passion she felt.

"I believe you said hot, my love." He turned away to flip on the warm water. Turning back, he hesitated slightly. "You're sure, love?"

"Oh, yes."

Eagerly she went into his arms, hugging him tightly. She couldn't comprehend her own tears, the rush of emotion burning at her eyes, at the back of her throat. She wanted to belong to him, to be possessed by him. Their mouths collided, ravenously kissing. Her hand fumbled for his belt, and she heard his groan of delight. His hands grasped and kneaded her breasts. Then she was pulling off his trousers, and he buried his face between her breasts. Sexual heat radiated from his mouth, sending powerful currents streaking through her body. When he pulled off her panties and began boldly stroking her, she thought she would lose her mind.

A moment later Mark pulled her into the shower with him and closed the door. Warm water pounded her body as his fervent gaze raked over her. "Courtney. You're so beautiful."

"So are you." Indeed she couldn't take her eyes off his glorious naked body, noticing how his tanned flesh gleamed with moisture, how the short black hairs plastered against his skin lent him an incredible aura of masculinity. Moisture glistened on his long black eyelashes, and his eyes were an incredibly vivid blue.

He kissed her face, her mouth, her throat, then slid to his knees, his mouth touching her in a most intimate spot, his tongue parting her flesh. She sobbed, coming apart inside, quivering with the desire she felt. When he slipped a finger inside her, she dug her fingernails into his shoulders and moaned wantonly.

He rose, sitting down on the shower seat, then pulled her onto his lap. Smiling, he penetrated her fully. Courtney cried out in delirious pleasure. He was slick and so hard, warm, and big. Her insides pulsed and throbbed around him, and she felt a sense of joining with him that brought new tears to her eyes.

His mouth locked on hers, and he began to move, thrusting upward powerfully while rocking her into his potent strokes. All the while the warm water beat upon them. Soon she tore her mouth away, breathing in sharp gulps, then kissing his face, nipping his ears.

He caught her closer and quickened his pace to the tumultuous strokes preceding climax. As her cries intensified, he held her fast and found his heaven inside her. With a wrenching shudder, Courtney found a pleasure to equal his own.

Holding her there in the shower, feeling her sweet flesh quivering about him, Mark couldn't believe Courtney was his. For over a year now he had yearned to meet this incredible woman. Tonight that wish had been granted. But never had he dreamed that within a single night they would be one. That she'd be here, her body joined with his.

For a long moment they sat with bodies melded, breaths mingling. With the shower still beating its hot, sensual tattoo, he listened to her little sobs and whimpers, comforting her with his mouth. Their bodies were so tightly locked that he wondered if they could ever be parted.

At last he rose, gently uncoupling them. Courtney appeared slightly dazed, her cheeks beautifully flushed as he pulled her out of the shower. He kissed her wet, delicious mouth, her cheeks, and briskly rubbed her down with a towel. He gathered her into his arms and lifted her, realizing he was trembling all over. She gazed up at him with languid green eyes, large and trusting. She was gorgeous, her body smooth, supple, and so very curvaceous. She had delicious breasts just perfect in size, and a rounded bottom he had adored kneading with his hands as he'd plunged into her. The torrid memory made him pause to kiss her again, thoroughly, before carrying her to the bed.

He laid her down and joined her, covering her soft body with his own. Quickly he spread her thighs and eased inside her again. Her reaction enthralled him. She tossed her head and made a hoarse sound, her fists grabbing the sheets. God in heaven, how he wanted her! He seized her lips with his own and slipped his hands beneath her, lifting her hips into his thrusts. He felt her flesh hotly squeezing him, heard her soft moans. She was so wet and snug, he had to struggle not to succumb before he brought her to ecstasy.

He leaned over and gently caught her taut nipple between his teeth. She cried out, and that erotic sound sent him plunging deeper. Her hips arched upward again to take all he offered, her arms locked around his neck, and her lips eagerly sought his. . . .

Tears welled in his throat at the sweetness of her surrender. Somewhere in the back of his mind, he knew she must be still tender from their first coupling, but he lost all reason in the haze of the desire consuming him. His, she was his. Their cries mingled, then collided in a shared sob of joy.

Chapter Nine

Courtney jumped awake to feel her brain pounding against her skull with the force of a shotgun recoil. She winced at the pain, then gasped as she spied Mark lying beside her. Torrid memories of their unabashed love-making hammered her senses, and looking at him now was even worse torture. Still sound asleep, he appeared far too sexy with his tousled hair, long dark lashes resting against his cheeks, and heavy whiskers. His chest was bare, the sheet tangled about his middle.

She sat up in bed and grimaced a new wave of dizziness hit her. She was sore all over from using muscles she hadn't given a good workout in ages. How many times had she and Mark made love, anyway? Four? Five? Had they ever really stopped?

And she'd gone to him! He'd been all set to tuck her into bed and sleep on the couch downstairs, when she'd all but jumped his bones.

Heavens, had she lost her mind? With a moan, she buried her face in her hands. She didn't understand what had happened to her. One-night stands were not

Eugenia Riley

her cup of tea at all. Had the shock of the chairman's actions and the loss of her job pushed her over the edge? Had it been one too many frozen daiquiris, or the sensual atmosphere of the French Quarter? Not to mention meeting the world's most sinfully handsome and charming man?

Yes, she found Mark Billingham very appealing, but the truth was he was still in many ways a stranger to her. Now that the cold light of day had dawned, she could see that clearly. Usually, her will and logic managed to overrule her weaker emotions. But not last night.

Why had she succumbed to *this* man, when becoming intimate with Mark could only exacerbate her own difficulties? He was the grandson of her sworn enemy, and for all she knew, he might even be in on his grandfather's scheme to ruin her life.

How could she have lost her control so quickly, so completely, and what must he think of her now?

As if he sensed her silent turmoil, Mark opened his eyes and grinned up at her sleepily, his hand boldly inspecting the contour of her thigh. "Good morning, love."

She recoiled, drawing the sheet up to her neck. "Don't you 'love' me."

Frowning slightly, he sat up, offering her a closer view of his tanned, muscled shoulders and chest. "That's not exactly the tune you were singing last night, love."

"No, last night it was more like 'Fools Rush In,' " she confessed ruefully.

Ignoring her sarcasm, he leaned over and quickly claimed her lips. "How 'bout the old standard 'Bewitched, Bothered, and Bewildered'?"

Fighting the potent pleasure of his kiss, she replied, "I'm plenty bewildered, I'll admit."

He frowned. "Darling, what's wrong?"

"You don't know?"

He pulled her resisting body close. "Come on, tell me."

Waving a hand, she confessed, "I'm upset, confused, hungover."

He chuckled. "But with very pleasant memories, I hope?"

"More like nightmarish ones at the moment."

"What?" he replied. "I thought we got on spectacularly well last night."

"You would." She nervously brushed a strand of hair from her eyes. "Look, would you mind if we don't discuss this in your bed?"

He leaned over to nuzzle her neck. "I think this a jolly good place to discuss it, love."

"*Please*, Mark."

He groaned. "Very well. Hold on a moment."

He hopped out of bed, and Courtney's face reddened. With a wince she took him in—the gorgeous shoulders and chest, the flat belly, the strong male thighs that had abraded hers as she'd absorbed his deep, hard thrusts. He was partially aroused even now, and the sight of it tormented her passion-tender body. Then as he moved past she caught sight of the splendid lines of his back, his taut male butt, and she wondered which was worse torture, the front view or the back.

He strode inside the bathroom, emerging a moment later wearing a white terry robe. Taking hers from the floor, he handed it to her. "Here, love."

"Thanks." Struggling with the sheet, Courtney managed to get the robe around her shoulders, then turned her back to him and shoved her arms into the sleeves. She stood and quickly tied the belt around her middle.

She turned to see Mark regarding her tenderly, and almost melted on the spot.

He crossed to her side and pulled her into his arms. "Come on, darling, it can't be that bad."

Oh, she was so confused, and she needed comfort so badly. For a moment she just let him hold her and inhaled his delicious scent. "But it is," she finally admitted in a small voice.

"What are you so upset about?"

"What do you think? Last night."

Gently he stroked her hair. "But why? Do you think it wasn't real, that it was just some rash, spur-of-the-moment affair?"

She eyed him narrowly. "What do *you* think?"

He hugged her closer and spoke hoarsely. "I think last night was the most wonderful night of my entire life. I don't regret a single moment—and I sincerely hope you don't, either. I don't want this ever to end."

His words were so sweet. Conflicting emotions churned inside Courtney. In truth, her sentiments were similar to his own, but that didn't change anything. They were two strangers who'd met in the night and now must go about their business. Gently, she pushed him away and slipped out of his arms. "But it *has* ended, Mark."

He paled. "How can you say that, Courtney? You came to me, remember?"

She began pacing about. "Yes, and I'm not claiming I don't deserve to be shot over that—er, lapse. However, in my defense, you're the one who maneuvered me here . . . and upstairs to your bed."

"Courtney, let's try not to assign blame. And we can keep this going if we want to."

"Right," she muttered ironically. "We'd have such a

great future together. Two continents, your grandfather . . ."

"But I think we can have a good future, love." He paused to take a deep breath, then announced, "I want you to marry me now."

"What?" Stunned, she turned to him. "Marry you? Why?"

He gave an incredulous laugh. "You can ask that after last night? Because we get along so famously, of course."

Her own laughter was derisive. "You mean in bed we do."

"Courtney, don't say that," he chided. "You know as well as I do that we really got to know each other last night, and something very special happened between us. Something that was much more than just chemistry. A lot led up to those moments in bed."

"Yeah, a lot of rum and seduction."

He appeared crestfallen. "Courtney, how can you reduce what happened between us to just sex?"

"And how can you extrapolate it into—"

"Extrapolate it?" he interrupted. "Now you sound like some legalese-spouting corporate guru."

She began to pace again. "Well, maybe last night was a lot more corporate than you're willing to admit. That is, if—"

"If what?"

She turned, trying to discern his motives in his face, but spotting only tension and suspicion. Well she felt damn suspicious too! His proposal of marriage had set her reeling and had made her question her own hasty acceptance of him and his motives last night. Now with just a few rash words, everything had changed.

How could Mark Billingham be so certain he wanted to marry her so soon? Hadn't he made it clear last night that he, too, felt wary about marriage? Why the sudden shift? Did he have a loony streak like his grandfather? Or was he allowing his grandfather's scheme to dictate his own choices? Had that been the real game plan all along?

This last question was sobering to Courtney in the extreme. She found herself wondering if perhaps Mark wasn't so innocent in all this, after all. Was the one-hundred-proof night on the town all part of his and his grandfather's game, a more subtle way to bring her around after direct methods had failed? Had she been a complete dupe?

She certainly felt like one now! She stared him in the eye and spoke with all the courage she could summon. "Mark, I can't possibly marry you because you're clearly proposing for all the wrong reasons."

"Such as?"

She raised her chin. "Isn't it obvious?"

Anger hardened his jaw. "No, I must be dense. Explain it, please."

"Well, you can't seriously want to marry a woman you've known for less than one day. Which means you must be doing your grandfather's bidding, so he'll win in his power play to control me."

A shocked sound escaped him. "You actually believe that? That I'd act strictly on his behalf, and not out of genuine attraction toward you?"

Feeling torn, she replied, "Mark, look at this from my perspective. First, M. Billingham tries to strong-arm me into marrying you, resulting in both my refusal and my resignation from the company. Then you come around, all smiles and charm, and claim to be on the side of the angels in all this. In the guise of smoothing things over, you romance and seduce me, stating all the while that like me, you're reluctant to marry. Then this morning we're strangely back to the same proposition your grandfather tried to force on me yesterday—that I should marry you, at once. I feel like some kind of naive little rabbit being maneuvered into the pot. But whereas my former boss did his dirty work with a shotgun, you offer a carrot instead."

"A carrot." He appeared even more irate, a vein popping out in his temple. "Am I supposed to find the phallic symbolism amusing, love?"

"Find it what you will. But it's the truth, isn't it? You're just as much your grandfather's pawn in this as I am. I mean, you lost your parents, didn't you? You told me he's all you have left, so you must want to please him."

He made a sound of disbelief. "Enough to try to ruin a woman's life strictly on his whim? How can you even think such a thing after last night? Wasn't what we shared much more than just a one-night stand? Wasn't it magical? Didn't I convince you my feelings were genuine?"

Feeling swayed by his words, Courtney stepped over to the window and gazed out at the courtyard, now sunsplashed, with hotel guests already gathered for breakfast. The last time she had looked at that courtyard, she'd felt so happy. Now, it took every iota of her will not to burst into tears and go rushing back into Mark's arms. That might feel good for the moment, but could prove disastrous for her future.

Turning back, she flashed him a sad smile. "Of course it was magical. We were in sensual New Orleans, with stars in our eyes and too many daiquiris in our blood. But everything has just happened too fast. I can't trust your motives in this, or my own feelings. Besides, any future between us will be doomed by your grandfather's interference."

His voice went very quiet. "So you feel nothing for me, Courtney?"

She almost lost her resolve then. "That's not what I said. Mark, even if your motives are more noble than I think they are, this is just . . . too complicated."

"So you'll give up on us simply because we have a few hurdles to overcome?"

"A few hurdles? Even I can't leap over Mount Everest in a single bound."

"No one's asking you to, love." He stepped closer. "I'll admit you have a point about my grandfather. I can't completely blame you for not trusting me under the circumstances. But here's a thought: Why don't we take marriage off the table for now and just date? You can even go back to work for the company again if you want to. I'm certain I can bring Grandfather around to such an arrangement."

For a moment Courtney vacillated, then she sadly shook her head. "No, I can never work for your grandfather again, not after the way he betrayed me and demeaned me as a woman. It's out of the question."

Courtney regretted her words the instant she saw the hurt and outrage spring into Mark's eyes. In a heated voice, he demanded, "And what happened between us last night . . . Tell me, did that demean you, as well? Because that's precisely how you're acting at the moment."

Courtney bit her lip. "I'm sorry, Mark. I-I just can't deal with your grandfather again, which means I can't deal with you, either. We're going to have to make a clean break of this. Anything else, I . . . I just can't take."

Perilously close to tears, she acted before he could protest. She dashed into the bathroom and slammed the door.

Chapter Ten

"Courtney, please, won't you lis—"

Mark Billingham winced at the clicking sound of the phone as Courtney hung up on him for the third time that morning. Setting down the receiver, he turned to his grandfather, who lounged nearby in a leather wingback chair, nonchalantly sipping his tea. How dare the old codger appear so blasé in the face of the worst disaster in Mark's life!

After Mark and Courtney had parted company back at his hotel, Mark had hastened to his grandfather's suite at the hotel on Canal. He'd come partly to seek his grandfather's help and partly to upbraid him. Of course he'd been discreet as far as Courtney's reputation was concerned, for he was too much the honorable Englishman to do any less. Although he'd admitted to his grandfather that he and Courtney had had dinner together the night before, he'd concluded his account simply by stating that they'd parted company with nothing resolved. He hadn't told the old guy about their spending the night together.

Eugenia Riley

Even as he prepared to give his grandfather his third dressing down of the morning, the old man held up a hand. "Don't start up again with me, Mark. I've a convention to run, and I don't have time for this."

"You haven't the time? Well, you've had ample time to turn my life into a living hell with your machinations."

"You mean Courtney Kelly has."

"After you provoked her beyond all reason."

"Well, if she can't take the heat, then she'd best get out of the executive suite kitchen."

Mark flung a hand outward in exasperation. "There you go with more of your sexist remarks. You know she's going to take us both to the cleaners once she files her lawsuits, which I'm sure will be too numerous and devastating even to contemplate."

"Spare me your melodramatics regarding Courtney's alleged legal tactics," M. Billingham scoffed. "She hasn't the balls to try it."

"Aptly put," mocked Mark. "But, strictly in a metaphoric sense, not true at all. Courtney has ample courage, and you deserve to bear the brunt of it."

M. Billingham waved him off. "She's all smoke and no fire, that one. She'll be back with her tail between her legs before we know it."

Mark was incredulous, his eyes imploring the heavens. "Grandfather, if that's what you really think, all I can say is that you've been running a baby company for too long. You're living in a fairy tale."

M. Billingham only chuckled. "On the contrary, grandson, I know human nature, and I know Courtney. She'll be back."

"When pigs fly, she will."

"You see, Courtney's quite ruthless, and she wants

that promotion in the worst way. I'm betting her ambitions will win out in the end and she'll be back to assume her place as CEO—and as my grandson's wife."

Mark's jaw dropped open. "You *actually* think I'd want her on that basis?"

M. Billingham gave a shrug. "It's a beginning. Some of the best marriages start out as hostile takeovers."

"I can't believe I'm hearing this! Hostile takeovers, indeed. Well, my marriage won't start out that way. You don't understand anything, Grandfather. I really *care* for Courtney. Now you've killed my chances with her."

"There you go being melodramatic again, just like your moth—"

"Don't you dare speak ill of my mother again," Mark cut in heatedly. "As if you're some paragon of familial virtue."

At last he got a rise out of the old man, who surged to his feet with fire in his eyes. "Mark, I always wanted what was best for you—"

"Now that's a laugh. You wanted what was best for *you*. You're a puppeteer who expects the entire world to dance to his demands. Well this puppet has broken its strings—and so has Courtney."

Mark strode out of the room, leaving his grandfather to scowl after him.

Hands shoved in his pockets, Mark marched along the levee, the churning waters below matching his turbulent state of mind. What was he to do? He'd spent last night with the most incredible, beautiful woman. He was all but convinced he loved Courtney Kelly. Now he'd lost any chance with her due to his grandfather's intrigues.

Well, to be honest, he hadn't helped his own cause by so rashly proposing marriage that morning. Courtney's shock had been visible. Why hadn't he practiced a modicum of caution and kept his damn mouth shut?

Now Courtney distrusted his motives, and he couldn't blame her. Now she believed his seducing her had been only part of his grandfather's scheme, when nothing could be further from the truth.

But could he tell Courtney the truth—that until twelve months ago, he'd been a wretchedly lonely man, immersed in his own private world? That he'd seen that first video of her at the board meeting and had become fascinated?

Of course she knew he'd become acquainted with her that way. But could he tell her how obsessed he'd *truly* become? How he'd endlessly replayed the videos, studying her every unique facial expression, her every body move, the mystery of her smile, the confident yet provocative way she walked? The cool authority of her voice?

Could he admit she was everything he had ever dreamed of in a woman—and a wife? Could he tell her he'd fallen in love with an image flickering on a screen? And that when his grandfather had proposed his insane scheme, he'd rashly gone along, just to have a chance with her?

Could he tell her that the *real* Courtney was so much beyond his wildest dreams that he was still reeling from his moments alone with her? Could he tell her that making love with her was the grandest bliss he had ever known, that he had lost himself in the depths of her warm, tight body, the hot eroticism of her mouth, the tender warmth of her breasts, the gorgeous depths of her eyes, the soft comfort of her arms? That he could make love with her until time itself ceased and still never get enough of her?

Could he *ever* tell her, much less hope to win her over? How could he convince her his motives were sincere? How could he win her back? Somehow he must. He simply must, or he'd lose his mind.

Chapter Eleven

"What do you mean, *none* of the Christmas merchandise has been ordered?" Mark bellowed.

In late June, he stood in his posh office at the headquarters of Billingham's in London, shouting at his young male assistant, Riggs, a fair-haired man with glasses who stood trembling across from him, holding a sheaf of papers.

"Sir," Riggs replied in quivering tones, "these special purchase orders have been sitting in your in box for months now, awaiting your signature."

"Then why did you never direct my attention to them?"

"Sir, I tried to, but you either ignored me or cut me off."

"It was your job to make sure I took notice."

The other man gulped. "Yes, sir."

Mark began to pace. "I can't believe this. We can't have Christmas at Billingham's without having our special Christmas robes and sweats for the entire family, as well as the exclusive table linens we feature for the holidays. My father must be rolling in his grave."

"Yes, sir."

"Is there no way we can get the stock in time?"

"The Birmingham factory said it can still produce the order, at a twenty percent surcharge."

"Twenty percent!"

Riggs all but cringed. "That's their standard rate on a holiday rush order."

"It's highway robbery, and by all rights should come out of your salary."

Riggs went pale. "But, sir, you know I tried to warn you—"

Mark shook a finger at him. "I don't want to hear any more of your lame excuses. You are undoubtedly the worst executive assistant I've ever had. One more incident like this, and you're discharged."

Mark realized he'd gone too far when he saw Riggs begin blinking rapidly. His voice shook badly as he replied, "I'll save you the trouble, sir. I've tried to be patient with you, but even I have my limits. I-I resign . . . and consider that effective immediately."

To emphasize his point, he tossed the papers at Mark's feet. Then he spun about and strode out of the office.

Mark started to go after him, then collapsed into his desk chair with a groan. Perhaps it would be best to wait until tomorrow, give Riggs a chance to cool down, then perhaps try to bribe him back with a hefty bonus.

Damn, he'd acted like such a jackass—really, much like his own grandfather, whose abrasive manner he least wanted to emulate. He hadn't meant to be so sharp with Riggs, over something that was technically his own fault.

But he'd been hell to live with ever since his last trip to America in April. His staff avoided him like the plague, and he was seriously off his game. He kept forgetting things—like approving the Christmas purchase orders for Billingham's—and his latest planned acquisition of a telecom company was going down the tube as well due to several tactless remarks he'd made during the negotiations.

All because of her. Courtney Kelly. His life had been utter chaos since the day he'd met her. Worse yet, only weeks after their encounter in New Orleans, she had disappeared, fallen off the face of the earth. On top of missing her, he was worried sick about her.

One day he'd feel desperate to find her and win her back, so his life could return to normal. The next, he would think, damn her anyway for doing this to him. Endlessly he wondered: Was he more miserable with or without her?

He had his answer as his desk phone rang and he tensed. "Riggs!" he called. "Answer the damn—" Then, remembering his assistant had just quit, he snatched up the receiver. "Hello?"

The connection sounded rather fuzzy. A female voice inquired, "Mr. Billingham?"

"Yes."

"Moody and Moody calling from Denver. Can you hold?"

At last! The call he'd been waiting for from the States. "Yes," he tersely replied. "And tell your boss he can't possibly be any more *moody* than I am at the moment. This had better be good."

The woman laughed nervously. "Yes, sir. I'll get Mr. Moody right on the line."

Mark waited in an agony of expectation as the seconds ticked past. . . .

* * *

"What do you mean, the shopping court won't be ready in time?" Courtney demanded.

In downtown Detroit, Courtney, in business suit and hard hat, was standing inside the unfinished retail corridor of a massive new downtown casino complex. She was talking with the construction project manager and his foreman.

Two months ago she'd accepted a job in Detroit as retail liaison for a new casino. Unfortunately things weren't going very well at the moment. It looked as if the shopping corridor would never be finished in time for the gala opening, which was scheduled shortly. Indeed, the covered strip still appeared to be no better than an unfinished glass-and-concrete shell. All around them in the long wing stretched construction debris—sawhorses, tarps, cans of paint, scaffolding. Dust and noise filled the air as workers hammered, sawed, and painted. Courtney scooted out of the way as two men passed carrying a huge lighting fixture.

The project manager gestured at the bare concrete floor. "As you can see, we'll be ready to start laying the terrazzo on the center walkway next week. But it'll still be a good six more weeks before all the plumbing, wiring, and central-air systems will be completed and the tenants can start moving in."

"Six weeks!" Courtney gasped. "My vendors are ready to go now. Many of them are hoping to open by July 4 when the casino itself launches, and your deadline on this project was June 10. You're way behind schedule and over budget."

The foreman gave a shrug. "Sorry, ma'am, but there's just no way we'll make it by the fourth. The concrete in some of the units isn't even dry yet."

Courtney cursed under her breath. "Well, the two of

you had best find a way, because I intend to keep the promises I made to our retail vendors. We've got all sorts of lucrative deals hanging in the balance here. Furthermore, you're in breach of contract on this."

The manager pulled off his hard hat and glowered at Courtney. "Ma'am, there's no need to get nasty about this. We do our best, but sometimes our subcontractors don't show up for work. There's been a Sheetrock shortage, in case you haven't heard. Plus, we can't help the damn weather, and we've had lots of rain this spring. Our contract states we're not responsible for acts of God."

"I don't give a damn what your contract says," Courtney retorted. "And I don't want to hear any more of your lame excuses. I expect you to finish by the fourth."

"Oh, yeah?" he scoffed. "What am I supposed to do, install portable toilets and use sparklers for electricity? Bribe some building inspectors?"

"No. Get the job done, and do it right."

The man's face reddened. "Look, lady, you've said your piece but you're not my boss. Why don't you just get the hell out of here, before a can of paint falls off a scaffolding or something and knocks some sense into you?"

Courtney was furious. "That remark was uncalled for. You'll be hearing from me."

"Yeah. Sure I will."

She spun about to leave, then heard the manager mutter to the foreman, "A bitch in a hard hat."

She whirled to face him, pulling off her hard hat and tossing it at him. He caught it with a grunt.

"I heard that. And if you think for one moment that this *bitch* can't get you fired, think again."

This time as Courtney turned and walked away, there was dead silence.

Leaving the building, she fumed. Great, they wouldn't make the opening. Now her boss would haul her onto the carpet because those construction morons couldn't get their act together.

Men. They were the bane of her existence. If a man had taken those two clowns to task just now, he would have been only doing his job. Have a woman do it, and she was a bitch.

Well, maybe she was acting just a little bit testy these days. Men again. It was all *his* fault, anyway. Mark Billingham. Her having to leave Denver and take a job here. Her having to *think* about him all the time, too. Of course her grouchiness had nothing to do with missing him. Of course.

She sighed. Thank heaven her friend Vanessa Fox would arrive for a visit later today. Vanessa was her sanity, and she needed a little peace in her life right now.

Chapter Twelve

"Courtney, please reconsider and come back with me to Denver."

Two days later, Courtney sat across from her friend Vanessa, who had just spent the weekend visiting her in Detroit. In her mid-sixties, silver-haired, slender, and quite beautiful, Vanessa was dressed in an impeccable green linen suit. The two women were having a quick dinner at an Italian restaurant before Courtney took Vanessa to the airport for her flight home to Denver.

"Vanessa, it's been great having you here, but I can't live in Denver anymore, not with M. Billingham there, not to mention, his grandson. Following the disaster in New Orleans, Mark drove me crazy with the phone calls, flowers, you name it. He might still be in the States for all I know."

"And right now you just want to be left alone." Vanessa was frowning as she took a sip of hot tea.

"Exactly."

Vanessa smiled cynically. "Sorry to be blunt, dear, but

do you think that's why you spent the night with Mark in the first place?"

Courtney sighed. She kept no secrets from Vanessa. She'd first met her friend four years ago when she'd been hired on at Bootle's Baby Bower. Vanessa's husband had been senior vice president in charge of profit and loss, and both had been members of the board. From the day the two women had met at a corporate dinner party, Courtney had found Vanessa spunky, outspoken, charming, kindhearted—and brilliant. Vanessa possessed both a highly creative and practical brain, a rare combination. She was as adept at computers and complex mathematics as she was at fashion design.

Most importantly, Vanessa had always approved of Courtney's career aspirations, becoming in many ways the mentor Courtney had never quite found in her own parents. She was something of a second mother to Courtney. Even after her husband, Floyd, had died of a heart attack two years ago, and Vanessa had left the board, the two women had remained fast friends.

Now Vanessa knew that Courtney had spent the night with Mark—indeed, she was the only one among Courtney's circle of friends and family who *did* know. But why was Vanessa trying to second-guess her motives?

"Why do you keep bringing up the fact that I spent the night with Mark?" she challenged. "I thought you were convinced I'd made the right decision in sending him packing. And haven't you always argued that a woman my age must put her career first?"

Vanessa's expression grew pensive. "Yes, but perhaps I'm judging you on my own terms, and that may not be fair to you. Not all women are cut from the same cloth, you know."

"But you and I are a lot alike. That's why we became friends."

"We're also from different generations."

"Baloney. You're more twenty-first century than I am. How many times have you helped me out when my computer crashed?"

Vanessa chuckled. "When I graduated from college magna cum laude back in the late fifties, with a double major in fashion design and accounting, I was considered to be one of the most promising potential female executives in this country. I had three job offers from major manufacturers in Chicago and New York, something unheard of for a woman of that era. Then I met Floyd, foolishly got swept off my feet and became pregnant in short order." She paused to clear her throat.

Feeling a stab of uneasiness, Courtney lowered her eyes and took a bite of her salad.

"I was, of course, expected to give up my career aspirations in favor of being Floyd's wife and raising his children. In our early years, I took in other people's taxes and bookkeeping just to help out. But I never really knew what it might have been like to fly my own kite—especially in fashion design."

Courtney frowned. "But you loved Floyd, didn't you?"

A wistful look came over Vanessa's pretty face. "I was extremely fond of him, and I wouldn't trade our four children and eight grandchildren for all the tea in China."

"But it's like the poem about the road less traveled," Courtney mused. "Do you regret having taken the path you did?"

Vanessa fell pensively silent. "That's a difficult question to answer. My identity became that of wife and mother. I felt I never fully evolved into a person in my own right."

"Vanessa Fox, Fashion Designer."

"Something like that. I did get a taste of the business world when Floyd joined Bootle's Baby Bower ten years ago and suggested I fill a vacancy on the board."

"That was very sensitive of him. He knew there was something missing in your life."

Vanessa nodded. "Indeed, I do feel I made a contribution there. That old rat Ham Bootle even used my drawings to launch the 'Bootle Baby Layette Collection.'"

"Designs on which you still collect royalties to this day," Courtney pointed out proudly. "I'm also aware that you were the true genius behind Floyd's suggestions about revamping our accounting procedures—ideas that saved the corporation so much money."

"Our work together allowed Floyd and me to share something as a couple." Vanessa blinked at a tear. "You know, I still miss him. Of course, after he was gone, there was no point in staying on the board and battling it out with old Ham Bootle. He and I always had such a personality clash."

"I do wish you had stuck it out a little longer," Courtney remarked with regret. "You know I was on your side and tried to intervene with Mr. Bootle."

"Yes, my girl, and had we both persisted, it would have cost you your job."

Courtney sighed. "Perhaps so. But I would have tried."

"I know. At any rate, I do despise the old coot, so it's probably just as well that I left. He certainly put Floyd through the wringer with his demands and tirades. In fact, I hold him partially responsible for the stress that contributed to Floyd's massive coronary. Even after

Floyd's first attack, Ham never let up on him." She brightened. "But enough about me. Getting back to you and Mark Billingham—"

"There is no me and Mark Billingham," Courtney interjected.

"I'm not so sure. You're not the type to indulge in one-night stands, Courtney."

"Tell me about it."

"In fact, since I've known you, this is the first time you've been seriously involved with any man."

"I'm not sure how serious an overnight fling is."

"You might not want to think about this, but I have a feeling that young man means a great deal more to you than you're willing to admit—even to yourself."

Courtney bit her lip. As usual, Vanessa's insights were right on target. "So you're saying I should give up all my aspirations in favor of becoming Mark's wife?"

"I'm saying, first of all, that we live in a different age, my dear. Today women *can* have it all."

"You can say that after the way M. Billingham treated me?"

"But he offered to make you his successor as CEO."

"*If* I'd marry his grandson."

"So?" Vanessa's expression was unrepentant. "The boy is handsome and charming, is he not? From what you've told me, he can't be nearly as obnoxious as the old man."

"Vanessa! Are you actually suggesting I should cave in? For the world's first liberated woman, that is heresy."

Chuckling, Vanessa held up a slender hand. "I'm saying that, unlike me, Courtney, you've been offered the brass ring. Why not grab it? Is it pride?"

"Of course not!" Courtney fell thoughtfully silent. "It's just that it's hard for me to trust Mark after New Orleans. And I'm not ready for a husband, either."

"Ah," Vanessa murmured. "Still remembering your bad experience in high school?"

Courtney gave a groan. "Well, it *is* pretty bad when your whole family gangs up on you, wanting you to marry the high school quarterback. I'm not sure my parents will ever forgive me for breaking up with Tyler." She laughed. "I do know marrying him would have been a huge mistake. All he wanted was a little groupie to follow him around from game to game. I hear he's done pretty well in the minor leagues—and is on his third wife."

Vanessa nodded wisely. "So you don't trust men. Is it fair to take that out on Mark?"

"It's not just trust," Courtney replied soberly. "Men are threatened by powerful women, as you well know. When I was in college, I fell hard for one of my classmates, and he for me. Love at first sight and all that. Until I won the scholarship to Harvard for my master's, and Brent was turned down. Immediately he dumped me in favor of an elementary-ed major whose career path didn't compete with his."

"So he was a rat. The world has its share of them."

"But my experience demonstrates some important points," Courtney continued passionately. "Men don't want to marry women who are smarter and more successful than they are. And love at first sight is a myth. My God, Vanessa, Mark proposed to me in New Orleans only hours after he met me. It was all just too fast, too intense. Real love doesn't just pop up like a dandelion. He had to have been influenced by his grandfather's desire to force my hand."

Vanessa gave her a chiding look. "Courtney, that's not

fair. Didn't he deny this numerous times—and also rise to your defense?"

Courtney glanced away. "What else could he have done under the circumstances?"

"Okay, let's assume for the sake of argument that he's guilty as sin. Hasn't mankind been conspiring against womankind ever since time in memorial?" Vanessa winked. "You know, my dear, sometimes it can be fun to lose."

"Vanessa, you are unbelievable," Courtney scolded.

Vanessa only grinned. "You always knew I was deeply practical, didn't you, my girl?"

"Well, yes, but—"

Vanessa patted Courtney's hand. "I want to see you on top of the world. I want you to be CEO and president of Bootle's Baby Bower. I want to watch you toss M. Billingham Bootle on the garbage heap like the relic he is. So I say, take what they offer you—marry the boy. You can whip his cute little British behind into line, and beat Ham Bootle at his own game."

Courtney was incredulous. "Vanessa, I've known you for years but never realized . . . You are a monster!"

"You've only now figured that out?"

"This isn't war, you know."

"Isn't it? I know you decided not to sue Ham, but wouldn't the best revenge of all be to go back to Bootle's Baby Bower and demand your rightful place? Take that old codger for everything you can get?"

Shaking her head, Courtney consulted her watch. "Look, we need to get you to the airport."

"Hogwash. We've plenty of time. You're just avoiding the issue."

"You bet I am." Courtney motioned for the waiter. "And we don't have nearly as much time as you think.

It's a real hike to the airport, especially at this time of day—"

Vanessa touched Courtney's arm. "For the last time, please come back with me to Denver."

"I can't," Courtney replied heavily.

"What are you accomplishing here, working for that casino? All those vultures do is fleece the public."

Courtney bit her lower lip; she was beginning to have doubts about work herself. "Well, I'm helping to bring new prosperity to the Detroit area. Besides, my work is in retail liaison, not the casino itself."

Vanessa harrumphed. "Same difference. Besides, I'm convinced you're working for the mob."

Glancing about, Courtney whispered, "I am not! And I'm tired of hearing that all casinos are run by the mafia. I'm working for legitimate businessmen—"

"That's what they *all* say," Vanessa cut in with an air of superiority. " 'I'm just a poor little businessman.' Right before they're sentenced to twenty years at Leavenworth."

"Vanessa, really."

"Furthermore, Detroit is an eyesore. I don't believe anyone here has even heard of the term 'urban renewal.' "

"That's not fair. This weekend, we haven't had nearly enough time to visit the finer areas such as Grosse Pointe—"

"I don't need to visit them to know that you belong back in Denver, my girl."

The waiter walked up then, and Courtney tossed him a credit card before Vanessa could protest. "Look, no more arguing. You're going to miss your plane."

* * *

Later, driving home after dropping Vanessa off at the airport, Courtney couldn't get their conversation out of her mind. She realized Vanessa was right. She didn't belong here in Detroit. Her heart remained back in Denver.

In fact, she was still paying out the lease on her apartment back home, and had only rented furniture for her apartment here. Somehow she'd known from the outset that she was only passing through Detroit.

Of course, two months ago, with Mark still hot on her trail, she had jumped at the chance to almost double her salary by accepting an offer from the casino. It had been a quick way to get out of Denver and back on her feet elsewhere. And there were advantages. So far, her role had been behind the scenes. Mark hadn't been able to find her, though she was certain he must have tried. She kept in touch with her parents and siblings through her cell phone, and only Vanessa knew of her exact address here. So far, the two women had been quite circumspect.

But Vanessa had made some valid points at dinner. The more Courtney learned about her new job, the more uneasy she felt. Now she realized that Vanessa was probably right. Casinos might be glitzy and alluring, but their bright lights tended to seduce precisely the wrong people—hardworking types who couldn't afford to be gambling.

And she missed her job at Bootle's Baby Bower. Much as she hated to admit it, she also missed Mark. Was Vanessa right that she was letting pride get in the way? Should she simply take all that Mark and his grandfather offered? Was living well the best revenge, as Vanessa had seemed to argue?

Courtney was worried about something else, too, a

matter that had nagged her endlessly over the past months. It wasn't just the expected feelings of uneasiness over all the changes in her life. No, it was *real* physical nausea, appearing at most suspicious times. An obsessive need for sleep, and a body that tingled in odd places.

She remembered Vanessa's pointed look at dinner. Did her friend already suspect the truth that Courtney had been avoiding?

She gritted her teeth as the lights of a drugstore beckoned. She had to smile, for the sight was almost like a portent. Bracing herself, she pulled into the parking lot.

"Oh, my God," Courtney murmured.

She stood in the bathroom of her apartment in Southgate, staring at the pregnancy test strip. Both windows had turned a pinkish color in record time. Tears filled her eyes and emotion clutched her belly. At least she knew the truth now.

But hadn't she really known she carried Mark's baby for weeks now?

Before she could even consider the implications, much less try to figure out what she felt, her phone rang. She gasped, and a chill streaked down her spine. Could it be Mark? Could some weird kind of parental telepathy have told him that his seed was growing inside her?

With a trembling hand, she grabbed the receiver. "Hello?"

"Well, what's the verdict?"

"Vanessa!" she cried. "How can you be calling me?"

"From the plane, silly. Now 'fess up. Are you expecting or not?"

"Am I . . . ? My God, how could you know?"

She heard Vanessa's low chuckle. "My dear, I'm old,

but I haven't forgotten what a good attack of nausea feels like. Nor am I deaf. I heard you heaving in the bathroom at six this morning. Then you seemed just fine at breakfast, and I, of course, was too polite to comment. But ever since then I've been on pins and needles, waiting for you to bring it up, and I can't bear the suspense any longer. So tell me, are you or aren't you?"

"Vanessa!"

"Come on. This cell phone is costing me something like five dollars a minute."

"You're exaggerating, as usual."

"Tell me!"

Courtney sighed. "Vanessa, you're a mind reader. The truth is, I picked up a test on the way home—"

"Aha! I knew it!"

"—and the verdict is . . ." Taking a deep, bracing breath, she said it for the first time.

"I am."

"My gracious. Congratulations. How do you feel about it?"

"I don't know! I no sooner saw the result than the phone rang."

"Are you going to marry him now?"

Courtney groaned. "And follow the same path you did with Floyd? I'm just not sure."

Vanessa's tone grew solemn. "Think about it seriously, dear. You *can* have it all. And congratulations again."

"Thanks."

"Must run now. They'll be bringing round champagne. I'll have one for you and will give you a ring as soon as we land."

"Sure, Vanessa. Take care."

Courtney hung up, not sure what to feel. But once

again before she could really even consider it, she was interrupted—this time by the doorbell.

"Damn it, what now?"

She rushed over and peered through the peephole. Her heart skipped a beat. Talk about weird parental telepathy!

Mark Billingham stood outside her door.

Chapter Thirteen

"Courtney, darling," he said.

Courtney felt as if she'd just seen a ghost. But there he was standing across from her, Mark Billingham in the flesh. Having him so close to her, with her emotions still in chaos from the new found knowledge that she carried his child, knocked her totally off balance. He looked so handsome in his sport shirt and khakis, and the expression on his face was so forlorn. His face seemed more striking than she'd remembered, his eyes more vibrant, but deep lines etched beneath his eyes attested that he hadn't slept well in weeks. Her throat tightened painfully as she realized she had missed him terribly and longed to comfort him now.

Comfort *him*, when he was the source of her problems? She marshalled her courage. "Mark, what are you doing here?"

"Isn't it obvious? Won't you let me come in for a moment?"

"How did you find me?"

"It wasn't easy. You covered your tracks well."

"Yes, I did. And I repeat: How did you find me?"

He glanced away uneasily. "Vanessa," he finally admitted.

"Vanessa? You *followed* my friend?"

"I hired private detectives."

"My God." Courtney was stunned and outraged. "I can't believe your gall, Mark. I want you to leave, now."

Even as she tried to shut the door, he placed his foot between the panel and the jamb. "Courtney, please. Just give me a few minutes of your time. I've come a very long way to see you."

"Kindly remove your foot from my door."

He smiled, but didn't budge. "Courtney, I feel as if I've had my foot in my *mouth* almost from the moment we met. Please, give me a chance to make amends."

"Damn it, Mark, we've already been all over this—"

"Ten minutes of your time," he argued doggedly. "You may as well say yes, Courtney, because I'm not leaving until you agree."

She hesitated, wavering.

"Please."

"Damn you!"

"Ten minutes."

"Five."

"Very well. Five." As she backed away and held open the door, he moved inside, his eyes never leaving her as she shut it. Then he quickly leaned over and kissed her cheek. "I've missed you, darling."

Courtney almost died inside then. She hadn't expected that kiss, so chaste yet somehow so sexy, nor the caress of his voice, the way *darling* rolling off his tongue so sensuously, heating her flesh like his erotic touch. And the well-remembered scent of him further fired her blood, bringing to mind a dozen sensual memories. She backed away. "Mark, you said you wanted to talk."

"I did." His gaze burned into her. "But I just had to kiss you once, Courtney. It's been so long, and you look so damned beautiful. When I remember touching you, holding you . . . well, I've scarcely thought of anything else."

Courtney was drowning in those same memories herself, but she managed to lift her chin and face him. "Please, Mark, state your case. You don't have much time."

"Courtney, that is my case." He drew a deep breath. "I'm here as a desperate man. You've turned my life upside down. Until two months ago, I was just a typical chap, buried in my work, with no thought of a personal life. Then I met you and something unexpected and magical happened. I fell for you Courtney. Hard."

His words tortured her already raw emotions, for weren't her feelings similar to his own? Hadn't meeting Mark and spending the night with him rocked her world, as well?

"It was like the proverbial bolt from the blue," he went on.

"That's very romantic," she quipped, though in trembling tones.

"Now everything's changed. My life is a disaster without you. I can't concentrate on my work—my executive assistant resigned thanks to my volatile temper, and I just botched up a deal that was potentially worth millions—"

"Poor baby."

"Courtney, give me another chance."

Though it was very difficult, she swung away from him. "I can't, and you know the reasons why."

"Are you really happy here, working for that casino?"

She gasped, turning toward him again. "My Lord, your detectives are thorough, aren't they?"

"Are you happy?" he pressed.

Courtney blinked at sudden tears. "That's none of your business."

His eyes teemed with emotion as well, and he moved a step closer. "Because you're miserable, aren't you, just like me? You can't be content here all by yourself. I just can't believe you'd want to spend your life, your career, in Detroit."

"Well, it sure beats Denver at the moment."

He edged even closer, until she could feel his warmth. "Here's a thought: Come with me to London, Courtney. Married or not, it's your choice. We'll build a life together there, away from all the pressures and issues that have pulled us apart here."

Though his pain seemed genuine and his proposal was tempting, she shook her head sadly. "Mark, it's not that simple. My life is here, and after what happened in New Orleans, I'm not sure I can ever trust you again."

"I don't blame you, but—"

"And if I'm with you, I'll never be able to get far enough away from M. Billingham Bootle."

He was silent, scowling.

"Well, can you deny it?"

He gave a sigh. "What can I say, Courtney? He's an old rascal, yes, but he's still my grandfather, and I love him."

"That's just my point." Her voice softened. "You've lost your parents, Mark. I don't want to rob you of the only real family you have left. And M. Billingham and I will never did see eye to eye—"

"That's true, Courtney, but just as they say in the marriage ceremony, a man reaches a point where he must 'forsake all others' and cling only to the woman he loves."

Again Courtney found herself fighting tears. Was Mark saying he actually loved her? Was he truly as sincere as he sounded? Could she risk believing him when her own prior experiences dictated otherwise?

Did it make a difference? She just wasn't ready for him, for anything that was happening in her life right now. And his admission seemed additional proof that he had "fallen" for her all too suddenly and impetuously.

She regarded him with keen regret. "Mark, you may think you have feelings for me, but the truth is, we're two strangers who rushed headlong into a situation, and must now get over it. As for M. Billingham, even if we moved to London as you suggest, we'd still have to see him. I mean, wouldn't we? Wouldn't you end up hating me if I tried to cut you off from him?"

"Courtney, I could never hate you."

"Yes, you would, if I took you from the only parent you have left."

"We could see Grandfather strictly on a limited basis," he suggested. "Holidays, that sort of thing. And later on, if there were children . . ."

Children. Courtney hadn't expected that last remark. Warmth suffused her belly and shot up her face, and she quickly turned away—but not before Mark had spotted her reaction and responded with a look of shock and wonderment. She stood reeling, praying she hadn't given herself away, knowing all the while that she had.

She heard his voice, cracking with emotion. "Courtney, my God . . ."

Courtney's voice trembled badly. "Mark, I think your five minutes are up."

"To hell with my five minutes!" She felt his hands

134

on her shoulders, firmly turning her. "Courtney, are you . . . ?"

She gazed into his starkly emotional face. "Am I what, Mark?"

He gave a groan. "One reason I had to find you is that we didn't . . . I mean on that night, we . . ."

"Didn't use any precautions?" she provided.

He swallowed hard. "Are you pregnant, love?"

Heart hammering, she glanced away.

He caught her chin in his hand, turning her to face him. "Tell me, please."

Though it was tempting, she couldn't lie to him; she owed him that much. There had been too many lies between them already. "Yes."

His face lighting with joy, he clutched her close. "Oh, darling, that's wonderful news."

"Is it?" His arms were so warm and comforting, Courtney was tempted just to let him hold her, let him carry her burdens. Yet her conflicting emotions prompted her to challenge him. "Tell me, was getting me pregnant part of your plan, too?"

He flinched as if she'd slapped him. "Courtney, how can you even think that?"

"Well, I didn't see any big interest in family planning on your part that night."

"Darling, we were both pretty tipsy."

"Be honest with me, Mark. Did you want to get me pregnant?"

He smiled. "Courtney, I never intended to get you pregnant. That's the God's truth, I swear. But do I mind that you're carrying my child? No, not in the least, darling."

Cheeks hot from his frank words, she accused, "You intended to seduce me."

He drew a teasing finger down her throat, and he spoke very huskily. "Courtney, how could I ever look at you and not want to seduce you?"

Feeling dangerously aroused by his provocative touch, she backed away, catching a sharp little breath.

He sighed. "But I didn't sleep with you for any nefarious purpose, as you seem to think. Anyway, we're forgetting what's important here."

She laughed ironically. "And what is that?"

"The child, darling." He pulled her into his arms again, then drew back and eyed her with touching wistfulness. "How do you feel about being pregnant?"

"I-I really don't know," she admitted honestly. "I just now found out. I only took the test a few minutes ago. And before I could even think about what I felt, the phone rang. It was Vanessa, calling from the plane. Then as soon as we hung up, you arrived. So I still don't know how to react, what to feel."

"You aren't thinking of—of doing something?" His voice was very tight.

She immediately shook her head. "No, Mark. If I were considering 'doing' something, I'm sure I would have taken the test right away, instead of waiting two months."

Pleasure and pride lit his eyes. In a tender, awed voice he asked, "Then you want my baby?"

That question hit Courtney like a fist to the gut, driving home emotionally, for the first time, that it truly was *Mark's* baby growing inside her. They were inexorably linked now for the rest of their lives. "Yes, I want this baby."

"Thank God." He breathed a relieved sigh and tucked her head under his chin. "I'm so glad I'm here, because it would kill me to think that you would consider going through this without me."

She pulled free. "What does that mean?"

He appeared confused. "Well, the baby is half mine. We'll marry at once, of course."

"Mark, what century were you born in?"

He scowled. "I may be from another country, Courtney, but I can't believe values here are that different. A baby needs two parents."

"You can be a parent without marrying me."

"Not a very effective one. And what about the child?"

"What do you mean?"

"What about when he or she is older? Won't our child be angry at you, knowing you had a chance to marry its father and refused to out of pride alone?"

"Pride alone? Mark, that's terribly unfair."

"Is it?" He drew closer. "Then why won't you give us a chance?"

"Mark, I think I've explained all that. I can't really trust you after New Orleans, nor be with you because of your grandfather."

"And you don't think your pregnancy changes things?"

"Of course it changes things."

"Then you'll marry me?"

She waved a hand in exasperation. "Mark, we're going around in circles. You say marry you, but our situation is much more complicated than that."

He sighed. "At least consider it seriously. Look, I've an idea."

She rolled her eyes. "Mark, I think I've suffered enough from your ideas."

"Hear me out. I've been thinking about it ever since I arrived in Michigan. Courtney, one of my favorite childhood memories is of when my family came to the States

137

on holiday, and my parents took me and my sisters to spend a week at Mackinac Island. We boated, fished, hiked, and generally had a wonderful time."

"Why are you bringing that up now?"

"Because I'm asking you to go there with me."

"What?"

His voice was intense with pleading. "We need some time alone, just you and me, to work this out. Mackinac Island is one of the most romantic and isolated spots on the planet. Let's get in the car and drive there tonight, just the two of us. I think we can take care of your doubts in short order."

Courtney shook her head. "Mark, our going off alone is not going to solve anything—even in bed."

He winced. "Courtney, there's much more than sex between us, and you know it. I want to give us time, and the right setting to recapture the magic, the genuine affection between us." His eyes gleamed passionately. "You know it's there, Courtney, and if you are honest you'll admit it. We found it together in New Orleans, and it's still sizzling in the air between us tonight."

She held up a hand, more in an attempt to keep her own emotions at bay than to restrain him. "Mark, please. That kind of spontaneity and passion is what got us into this dilemma, and is what I trust the least. It clouds the other issues too much."

"And I say all these other 'issues' are just a bunch of nonsense. I want them out of the way. I want it to be just you and me—and our baby."

"But it can't be that simple, Mark," she replied miserably. "I feel like ever since we met, you've been trying to pull me into the deep end with you. You can't just merge two lives with a snap of your fingers. Why can't you understand that?" She glanced at her watch. "Look, it's way past time for you to go."

"Forget it, Courtney," he retorted. "Things have changed in the last few minutes. Now we have a child to think about."

"You're right," she acknowledged. "We do have a child to think about. But all of this is too much for me right now. You're overwhelming me, Mark."

Surprisingly, he smiled. "I tend to do that, don't I?"

"Do you ever!" she retorted, and for a moment they both smiled. "I-I need some time to think about this, absorb it, see how I feel."

He nodded. "You want to sleep on it? Well, at least that's a beginning." He reached out and slowly, sensuously caressed her lower lip. "You know, I'd love to sleep on it with you."

She pulled away. "That would be a mistake and you know it. Give me the night—then we'll meet in the morning to negotiate this further."

He playfully touched the tip of her nose. "Negotiate. I love it when you talk dirty, darling."

"Mark, get out of here."

Unabashed, he quickly kissed her. "We'll have breakfast, then. I'll pick you up at eight A.M. Pleasant dreams, darling."

Certain now that he would haunt those dreams, she watched him leave.

Afterward Courtney couldn't keep her mind from spinning. So much had happened in such a short amount of time. In the space of a few minutes, she had learned she was pregnant, then Mark had appeared at her door. Both were major events in her life, but she still wasn't sure what either meant.

Would the baby be part of her future, but not Mark? Was that what she wanted? Did she even know?

How did she feel about being pregnant? There she had to smile. Much as she oftentimes resented the interference of her large family, she was fiercely loyal to them. She might be a hard-charging businesswoman, but she knew that at her core, her values were their values. Being pregnant with a child meant taking responsibility.

In truth, she loved children; she often baby-sat for her nieces and nephews. Indeed, being far away from "the Rugrats" and the rest of her family was one big minus about living here in Detroit. She missed them all dearly. She'd always wanted children of her own . . . someday.

But not *this* day, not this soon. Not before she'd accomplished some of her career goals—and definitely not before she'd gotten married!

Still, there was no doubt in her mind that she wanted this child and would keep it. The very thought of her baby brought a tear to her eye as she touched her lower belly. It seemed incredible that the miracle of life grew within her—

Mark's life. His seed. His baby. His love living inside her. As he'd aptly pointed out, the child was half his, and therein lay her dilemma.

She knew how she felt about her child. She just wasn't sure how she felt about its father. Her anger toward M. Billingham had clouded her judgment, her ability to read her own emotional pulse, for too long. She did remember how attracted she'd been to Mark during that magical night back in New Orleans. The chemistry between them had been explosive. She'd even questioned whether she might be in love with him. He was handsome, charming, sexy. He'd definitely swept her off her feet. Seeing him tonight had sent her emotions into a tailspin all over again.

But was that enough to build a lifetime commitment? All Courtney's instincts urged her to proceed with more caution. Back in college, she'd allowed herself to be "swept up," had succumbed to an intense love affair—a relationship that had turned out to be a serious error in judgment. It had taken her years to recover from the heartache, the blow to her self-esteem. All of which demonstrated that critical life choices, such as she and Mark must make, required a clear head.

But it was all so complicated. She remembered his arguments about the child. Would her child one day resent the fact that she hadn't married its father? Would he or she be better off with two strangers plunged into a marriage of convenience—or with her as a single mother?

She did know how her large, conservative family would feel about her having a child out of wedlock. To be honest, the prospect made her just as uneasy as she knew it would make them.

And what about Vanessa's argument, that she could have it all? Marry Mark, and insist M. Billingham hold up his end of the bargain by making her the new CEO? Was that being mercenary in the extreme—or simply accepting her due?

Oh, she was so confused! She only had till morning to get her thinking straight, and she suspected she needed a lifetime.

Courtney was carrying his child.

This amazing revelation kept replaying itself through Mark's mind as he drove back to his hotel. His emotions were in chaos, and his frustration level was excruciating.

These last months with Courtney hidden away from him had been hell. At times he'd suspected he was losing his mind. When the private detectives he'd hired had been unable to uncover any promising leads on her whereabouts, he'd bellowed at them without conscience. Then at last he'd gotten his break when Vanessa Fox had flown off to Detroit to see Courtney. He'd received the fateful call in London, the day poor Riggs had quit.

He couldn't believe he'd finally managed to locate Courtney. She was as beautiful and spirited as ever, and the sight of her, after the weeks of torturous waiting, had been overwhelmingly emotional. Then he'd briefly held her, kissed her, touched her. Even now his arms ached to embrace her softness again.

She'd appeared tired and as shaken to see him as he'd felt on seeing her. Nonetheless she'd sent him away. Now, when she needed him so much. Now, when she carried his baby.

He needed her, too. His life was meaningless without her. With her by his side, he could get his life back on track again, though he knew it would never quite be the same.

Funny. Until he'd seen Courtney in the videos, he had not even considered marrying or having children. A breathtaking night in New Orleans had changed that. He had come to Detroit seeking a person he desperately loved. Now he could hope to leave with two.

He had to convince Courtney that he wasn't his grandfather's pawn, that he wanted her in his own right, that she could trust him—and he would do whatever it took to win her over.

He had to convince her that the baby changed things. Indeed, it changed everything.

Chapter Fourteen

At 7:35 A.M., Courtney was putting the finishing touches on her makeup when she heard her cell phone ring. Buttoning her silk blouse, she dashed into the living room to grab it. She suspected the caller was Mark and wondered how he'd gotten her cell-phone number. But then, nothing should surprise her after he'd tracked her down through Vanessa.

She punched the receive button. "Hello?" she asked tensely.

"Courtney, dear, are you all right?" inquired a concerned feminine voice.

"Vanessa!" Keenly relieved, Courtney asked, "Did you make it home okay?"

"Fine, although we encountered some turbulence north of Denver. I tried to call you late last night, but there was no answer."

"Sorry. I was in the bathtub when I heard the phone ring and I thought it might be . . . well, I've been through so much."

"That's why I didn't try to call you again. I figured you

were there, but asleep—or just feeling overwhelmed. After all, you've been through the wringer."

Courtney laughed ruefully. "Vanessa, you don't know the half of it."

"What do you mean?"

"After you called me from the plane, Mark showed up."

Courtney heard a gasp. "You're kidding. He showed up *there*?"

"Yep."

"However did he find you?"

"Evidently he tracked me through you."

"He, what? Of all the . . . But how through me?"

"He hired private detectives, and I guess they must have been watching you for clues and followed you here from Denver."

"Oh! I've never heard of anything so outrageous." Abruptly, Vanessa chuckled. "You know, that's one very determined young man."

"Tell me about it."

There was a brief silence, then Vanessa exclaimed, "Oh, my God! I just thought about . . ."

"Uh-huh."

"Does he know?"

"He guessed."

"My heavens!"

"It's my fault, though. He casually mentioned children, and I went red as a beet."

Her usually sedate friend giggled. "What happened then?"

"What do you think? He proposed marriage again, this time using the baby as additional leverage."

"Well, to be fair, dear, it is his child, too."

"You think I don't *know* that?"

"So what did you say?"

"I said I would think about it."

"And?"

"I tossed and turned almost all night long and still haven't decided what to do."

There was a long pause.

"All right, Vanessa, what are you thinking?"

Solemnly, Vanessa said, "You can't run from your life, Courtney."

A chill washed over Courtney. "What do you mean by that?"

"You're a smart girl. You know precisely what I mean. You don't belong in Motor City, my girl. Your home is here. And you've allowed Ham Bootle and his grandson to run you out of town."

"Vanessa, that's not fair."

"It's true. It took private detectives for Mark to find you."

"Should I have wanted to be found?"

"Were you planning on keeping this man in the dark regarding his own child?"

"Vanessa, I only found out I was pregnant five minutes before Mark appeared. I hadn't even had time to think about it."

"You mean you *confirmed* your pregnancy only five minutes before Mark appeared. Your encounter with him was, what, almost two and a half months ago? If I remember correctly how these things work, that makes you almost three months along. Surely you had suspicions, from the way I heard you heav—"

"Very well," Courtney admitted. "I had suspicions."

"If you are indeed the honorable young woman that I know you to be, you were going to have to face Mark about this sooner or later. It's just as well that it happened now."

"You're probably right. But is a baby enough reason to bring two people together?" Courtney sighed. "I don't mean to be blunt, but you're the one who should know."

"Indeed, and I can think of worse reasons for two people to marry," Vanessa replied frankly. "Moreover, it seems to me that the baby wasn't more than a wish hanging on a star that night you and Mark got together in the French Quarter."

"You're right," Courtney rejoined. "Something else brought us together then. Rum and a steamy New Orleans night."

"How cynical you are, my girl. But let's get back to the issue at hand: What are you going to do?"

"I don't know." Sighing, Courtney glanced at her watch. "And I need to decide quickly. Mark is picking me up for breakfast in twenty minutes."

"You know what I think—"

"Yes, I know. That I should go for it, grab the brass ring, take the promotion . . . and Mark. Now who's being cynical?"

"If I didn't think you had feelings for this young man, I'd never suggest it. If I thought Mark was cut from the same cloth as Ham, I'd personally ship you off to Timbuktu before I allowed you to marry him. But I sense that young Mr. Billingham is a gem of a different water, that he has far more integrity than Ham."

"Probably so. But that doesn't mean this will last."

"If you want a guarantee, dear girl, buy a car. At any rate, this situation with Mark must be resolved."

"Agreed. But, unless my answer is yes, Mark won't give up."

"My point precisely. And doesn't that give you a hint as to what you should do?"

Courtney mulled this over. "You know what really bothers me?" she asked wistfully.

"Tell Vanessa."

"Mark lost his parents. His *parents*, for heaven's sake, while he was still in college."

"Yes, I heard about the tragedy years ago. I understand there were some sisters—"

"Yes, two, back in London, now with families of their own."

"But your point is, I'm sure, that now obnoxious Ham is really all Mark has left as a sort of elder statesman in his life."

"Exactly. And although he doesn't talk a lot about losing his folks, I know it must have devastated him, and . . ."

"And?"

Voice growing hoarse, Courtney asked, "How can I keep this man from his own baby?"

Vanessa paused for a long moment, then said, "My girl, I think you have your answer."

Before Courtney could comment, Vanessa quietly hung up.

Courtney stood frowning at the sound of the dial tone; then the doorbell rang. She laughed, setting down her cell phone. This was becoming comical. First Vanessa called, then Mark rang her doorbell.

He was fifteen minutes early, too. Was she surprised?

Feeling like one of Pavlov's dogs, she ran over and opened the door. Mark, freshly pressed and cleanly shaven, stood in her doorway. Surprisingly, he broke into a grin at the sight of her. She should have taken that as her cue that he was about to catch her off guard.

Not missing a beat, he quickly caught her in his arms, swept her inside the door, shut it, and gave her a hearty kiss. Even as she reeled in the aftermath, he drew back and began unbuttoning her blouse.

"Mark!" Outraged, she slapped his hands away.

He burst out laughing. "Courtney, have a look at yourself."

She looked downward. "What?"

"Your blouse is buttoned perfectly crookedly, my dear."

She scowled at her blouse, and at last spotted the extra flap of fabric, with buttonhole, at the bottom. "Oh. Excuse me."

She started toward the bedroom, but he caught her arm. "No way. You've been out of my sight too long. Allow me." He began freeing the buttons, his amused gaze fastened on her, and this time Courtney was too flustered to resist. Once her blouse was completely undone, he backed off, stared at her breasts in the lacy wisp of her bra, and a low wolf whistle escaped him.

"Mark!"

"Can I help admiring a masterpiece?"

To hide her discomfiture, Courtney busied herself buttoning her blouse. His provocative behavior left her deeply rattled. She had seen Mark passionate, persuasive, angry, distraught. Now he was back to being his most tender and teasing self, and somehow that was most unsettling of all.

This was going to be difficult. Damn difficult.

"Well?" Mark asked tensely, moments later at the coffee shop. "Have you come to a decision, Courtney?"

Taking a bite of fluffy scrambled eggs, Courtney set down her fork and faced Mark over the tabletop. With his expression so tense and filled with expectation, he seemed a different man from the rascal who had appeared at her door earlier. But this was their moment of decision.

As to what she would say to him, she had gone around in circles endlessly, only to come back to the same sobering facts. Perhaps Vanessa had said it best: *You can't run from your life.*

"Courtney?" Mark nudged.

"Yes, I've come to a decision." Steeling herself, she said quietly, "I'll marry you, Mark."

His face lit with joy. "You will?"

She held up a hand. "Not so fast. There are conditions."

"I'll agree to anything reasonable."

She lifted her chin. "If we marry, I want to go back to Bootle's Baby Bower as CEO."

He flinched slightly. "Go back? But why? You mean you see this as agreeing to my *grandfather's* terms?"

"Mark, I'm marrying you to give my child a name."

"What about a father?"

"That, too." She smiled. "In fact, I think you'll be a good father."

"Go on."

"I think we should marry for the child's sake. But there are no guarantees that we'll make it—"

"Speak for yourself there, Courtney. I'm playing for keeps."

She felt her face go hot at that and quickly glanced away. "Mark, I am willing to try. I think it's better that a child grow up with two parents rather than one. And we do seem to be—er—compatible in some ways—"

He grasped her hand. "In all the ways that count, darling."

Even though his words set her pulse hammering, she retrieved her fingers and cleared her throat. "I don't think we should draw any hasty conclusions from the short amount of time we've spent together. What happened in New Orleans was probably just a fluke—and definitely not enough to build a lasting marriage on."

"I found it a damn fine place to begin."

"That's another thing," she went on in a shaky voice. "Just because we're getting married doesn't mean that we—"

"Oh, doesn't it?" he cut in, guessing her meaning at once.

Bravely, she stated, "I don't want to repeat the mistakes of New Orleans."

"Love, if you do any research on the institution of marriage, you'll find it's all about repeating the mistakes of New Orleans—and as often as possible, if I have my way."

He was agitating her even more, as if he had power over her and were savoring it; she twisted her fingers in her lap. "You're missing my point. I don't want us rushing things—"

"Courtney, you've agreed to *marry* me," he reminded.

Marshalling her courage, she stared him in the eye. "That doesn't mean that my emotions will immediately follow suit—or that your feelings will last."

"So what are you saying?"

"I'm saying we need time, Mark. I don't want to sleep with you, not until I'm ready. If I ever am."

"You mean one of those classic marriages in name only?"

"Yes." She lifted her chin. "If we're meant to be, our relationship will stand the test of time."

"And you want to go back to work, even with the child

150

coming? Won't that mean my grandfather will win?"

"Mark, I've already lost." Watching him blanch, she quickly added, "I mean, I've agreed to marry you."

"And you see that as losing?"

Contrite, she said, "I'm sorry if I said that wrong. But when I spoke with my friend Vanessa about this, she urged me to take it all, everything I've been offered. In thinking it over, I see that her point of view makes a lot of sense."

His gaze grew hard. "So I'll never know whether you're agreeing to marry me because of our child, or because you want the promotion."

She leaned toward him and spoke earnestly. "Mark, I'm marrying you because of the child. I'm taking the promotion because I *earned* it. If I thought I hadn't, I'd never accept it. So . . . will you arrange things with your grandfather?"

"Yes, but . . ." He fell silent, frowning.

"What?"

His brow knitted in a tense frown. "Courtney, it's going to be damn difficult for me to run my business ventures from the States."

"I'm sorry, Mark, but—"

"And I think you're being shortsighted, wanting to return to work with a baby on the way. Why not go with me to England and take it easy until our children are older—"

"*Children?*" she cut in, eyebrows shooting up.

"I'm well off, and there's really no need for you to work."

Courtney gave an incredulous laugh. "I can't believe I'm hearing this! But I should have known. It's like I'm back in high school and you're my boyfriend, Tyler, expecting me to drop everything and help him live his life."

"I beg your pardon?"

"You're threatened by my career, aren't you?" she demanded.

"Of course not."

She rolled her eyes. "That's just so typical, just what the others said."

"Others?"

"Has it ever occurred to you that having a career satisfies a need in *me?* Oh, no. Now that I'm with child, guess I'm just the 'little woman,' who's better off staying at home, while you're the big shot with the well-stroked ego."

"Courtney, you don't have to stroke my ego." Abruptly he grinned. "In fact, where stroking is concerned, I'd prefer—"

"Let's not take a detour here," she interrupted sharply. "Let's return to the issue at hand, which is, you don't want me to go back to work, right?"

"I'm sure your career is fulfilling," he answered patiently. "But why can't it wait a while? Why can't you put the child first? It's unrealistic to think otherwise. Why, both of my sisters had to give up their jobs once their children were born. Even though they both had help, they didn't want their children to be given short shrift—as the three of us were growing up."

"Ah—so now I'm responsible for making up for your bad childhood?"

He blinked rapidly. "I'm talking about our baby's childhood."

"Fine. Then why don't you quit your job and raise our child?"

"Courtney, that's not fair."

"Of course it's fair. What's sauce for the goose is sauce for the gander, as they say. Furthermore, my terms are not negotiable. If you don't like them, there's a simple solution: We won't get married."

For a moment he ground his jaw, appearing supremely frustrated. Then he waved a hand. "Very well, I accept your conditions. But I have a few of my own."

"I'm listening."

"We'll marry here in Detroit as soon as the arrangements can be made."

She caught a sharp little breath; heavens, he wasn't allowing any grass to grow under their feet. "Well, I hadn't expected it to be that sudden, but I suppose it makes sense."

"My grandfather will attend the service."

"Mark!"

His expression was obdurate. "It's a deal breaker, Courtney. He and your friend Vanessa may act as our witnesses."

She hesitated a long moment, then conceded, "Okay. But you know they hate each other—"

"They can bury the hatchet for one day, then. And there's more: Before we return to Denver, we're going on a honeymoon together."

"But, Mark, I told you I wouldn't—"

"Separate bedrooms if necessary, Courtney. Which brings me to my next term. Look at me, Courtney."

She did, and found his gaze burning into hers. "Yes?"

He took her hand. "I'll agree not to claim my husbandly due for a time. But I have still the right to woo you, Courtney."

"I . . ." Absorbing the impassioned look in his eyes, she had difficulty breathing. "I still have the right to say no."

"That you do, darling." But all at once Mark appeared very relieved, and his wide grin attested that he didn't believe she would.

*   *   *

The rest of the meal passed with Courtney feeling uneasy and Mark looking proud enough to burst his buttons. They discussed their wedding plans in greater detail. Later, outside the restaurant, he stopped on the deserted walkway, pulled her into his arms and tenderly kissed her. Courtney clung to him but found the moment bittersweet. They were going to marry, but they faced so many challenges, and she remained so confused. Would they make it?

"My future bride," Mark breathed afterward. "Do you know how proud it makes me to say that?"

"Mark, let's not expect too much."

"Darling, I expect it all."

He pulled a small velvet box from his pocket and extracted a ring. Before she could even gasp he slipped the stunning, round-cut diamond on the third finger of her left hand.

Courtney felt awed and touched. "Mark, you shouldn't have. It's beautiful."

"You're beautiful."

"When . . . where did you get it?"

"In London, a few weeks ago."

"Confident, weren't you?"

"Hopeful, darling. Always hopeful."

After another long, lingering kiss, he led her to the car. By now, Courtney felt as if her heart were permanently lodged in her throat. She had agreed to marry Mark as a practical solution; she hadn't expected him to be so romantic about it. She'd insisted on a marriage of convenience; he'd made it clear he intended otherwise.

How would she survive a honeymoon alone with him? She really needed to be cautious, especially now that he'd laid his cards on the table and admitted he wanted her to give up her career and move to London with him. She had really hoped Mark might be different, but he was in fact just another man who didn't accept her as an equal or take her seriously as a woman. And that definitely spelled trouble for their future.

Driving Courtney home, Mark felt proud enough to burst. She'd agreed to marry him. She still had her doubts, and to be honest, so had he. Was she marrying him only to secure her promotion, or to have a father for their child? Could she come to care for him and the baby? Or would he never be more than a stepping-stone in her career path? It bothered him a lot that Courtney was so adamant about returning to work and remaining in the States, that she seemed so unwilling to sacrifice for him or the child. She'd accused him of being threatened by her career, and perhaps he was.

Obviously Courtney had been burned before, for she doubted his motivations and that his feelings would last. He had to convince her he was different from the men she'd known before.

And he'd feel so much better if they could be intimate together from the outset of their marriage. But she'd been unyielding there, too, and he had to take her any way he could get her. Already she tended not to trust him, and he couldn't risk destroying their fragile rapport. At least she had agreed to the honeymoon plans; once they were alone, surely she would succumb to the same magic that had swept them up in New Orleans.

The worst part was over now. They would be together, the two of them and their child. He had his work cut out for him with Courtney, but he intended to see that this became a marriage in every way. Both their futures depended on it.

155

Chapter Fifteen

Late on an afternoon a week later, four tense people sat in the waiting room of a Detroit area justice of the peace. Courtney and Mark shared an uncomfortable wooden bench, with Vanessa and M. Billingham sitting on equally stiff chairs across from them.

Despite the lovely beige suit she wore and the bridal bouquet of roses she held, Courtney was a nervous wreck. She glanced at Mark seated beside her, appearing so handsome and sober in his expensive gray pinstripe suit. Attractive though she found him, she couldn't believe she was marrying this stranger whom she barely knew. She couldn't believe she was having his baby.

Their two agreed witnesses, M. Billingham and Vanessa, weren't helping matters at all as they shot each other hostile looks; Courtney fully expected warfare to erupt between them at any moment. In the two hours since she and Mark had picked the pair up at the airport, they'd been sniping at each other constantly.

The atmosphere had been far more restrained between Courtney and M. Billingham; so far, she'd exchanged only a few stiff words with her former boss. Of course, the arrogant M. Billingham had been unable to resist making a snide comment or two about how Courtney had "come around" to his way of thinking. But Courtney also had her own small victory to relish; she'd managed to convince Mark not to tell his grandfather about the baby—at least, not yet. After all, it was humiliating enough to know that she had, in effect, bowed to the old man's dictates; if he knew she'd slept with his grandson practically on first sight, his gloating would never end.

As if she needed all these tensions to top off a most stressful period in her life. The last week had been a blur—resigning her job at the casino, seeing a doctor to confirm her pregnancy, rushing about with Mark to get their marriage license and blood tests, arranging for her own move back to Denver. Not to mention fighting over their "honeymoon." Mark had insisted they spend at least a week alone; Courtney, preferring no honeymoon at all, had finally whittled that down to five days.

She was marrying a most stubborn and determined man—a reality that hardly comforted her, considering that they would soon be alone together.

She'd also had to call her parents and break the news about her sudden marriage to Mark. They'd been shocked, then hurt and confused when she'd insisted she didn't want them to arrange a big church wedding back in Denver, or hop a plane and come here. They were happy to hear Courtney was moving home. But when Courtney's mother had insisted she would throw a reception for the newlyweds back in Denver, Courtney had refused even to discuss the matter. Then, feeling guilty, she had promised she and Mark would attend the already scheduled birthday party for her sister Caryn's twins the following week.

She hadn't told her folks about the baby, but she was sure they suspected something was amiss, due to the rushed and almost secretive wedding plans. She'd felt bad about shutting them out, but she was having a very difficult time maintaining her own emotional equilibrium. It was hard enough having to deal with a sudden marriage, not to mention M. Billingham's presence as witness. If she'd said yes to her parents, her entire family would have come storming up to Detroit, complete with rabid curiosity and endless questions regarding the hurried nuptials. That kind of stress she could not have tolerated.

M. Billingham's voice cut into her thoughts. "Well, this is a swanky little place," he drawled, glancing about the small, utilitarian office. "About as comfortable as the coach compartment on our flight up from Denver."

Mark addressed his grandfather with a pained look. "Grandfather, please don't start up again regarding your plane ride."

M. Billingham emitted what sounded like a growl. "I wouldn't have to start up at all, except for *that woman*." He jerked a thumb in the direction of Vanessa.

"Oh, don't you flip your finger at me, Ham Bootle!" responded Vanessa tartly.

"It was a *thumb*, woman."

"I don't care if it was a pickled herring. Are you blaming me again because your corporate jet blew a gasket?"

"It didn't blow a gasket," M. Billingham grumbled. "An engine overheated, so I had to book a commercial flight at the last moment, never knowing *you* would be on board."

"Excuse me for attending my dear friend's wedding," Vanessa retorted.

"That *is* excusable. What was unconscionable was your refusing to board the same airplane with me unless I would sit in coach, so you could have first class all to yourself. Of all the gall! Why, I haven't ridden in coach since—well, since I was a very young chap and took a junket through the Middle East as a tourist."

Vanessa smiled nastily. "I think a person of your insufferable arrogance deserves to take *every* flight in coach. Besides, you're lucky I didn't demand the entire airplane to myself."

"I should have allowed the airline people to put you off as they were threatening to do," he continued crossly. "But I figured Courtney would likely refuse to marry my grandson without you here—though God knows why she's so partial to you." He flashed Courtney a forbearing smile.

"You're absolutely right there," Courtney agreed sweetly.

"Thus I was forced to bow to your terrorist tactics and retreat to coach. Are you satisfied now that you've humiliated me with your little power play?"

"Power play?" Vanessa scoffed. "You're one to talk. Seems to me you rather enjoy blackmailing others into untenable positions."

"How dare you!"

"Grandfather, please," interjected Mark. "It's our wedding day. Can't you two display a modicum of courtesy?"

Vanessa was the first to appear contrite. "I'm sorry, Mark, Courtney."

"I apologize as well, grandson. But this woman is unbearable. It's no wonder we had to expel her from the board of directors—"

"You mean *you* did!" Vanessa cut in.

Mark surged to his feet. "Enough, I said."

The two culprits were staring at him guiltily when a middle-aged woman emerged from the adjacent office. "The judge will see you now."

With a relieved smile, Mark turned to extend his hand to Courtney. "Ready, dear?"

Thinking she might *never* be ready, Courtney took his hand and smiled back with a courage she hardly felt.

The four trooped rather glumly into the wood-paneled office. The judge, an elderly man with a shock of white hair, greeted them all with friendly handshakes, then got straight down to business. As he began a short, stock sermon on love, commitment, teamwork, and family values, Courtney glanced about to see that M. Billingham and Vanessa both appeared cool and immovable as statutes. Then she covertly looked at Mark. His expression was solemn, and slightly vulnerable.

What was he thinking, feeling? Was he as confused as she was? Was he glad that they were marrying, or did he feel troubled, and rushed, as she did? Did he really care about her and the baby, as he had claimed? Or was he deceiving her and possibly himself as well? Was he really doing his grandfather's bidding, after all? If only she could know for certain what was in his heart, and her own. . . .

Doing his grandfather's bidding was actually the farthest thing from Mark's mind as he listened to the judge and stared at the woman he loved. Though she was trying to put on a brave front, Courtney's eyes gave her away. In those lovely green depths, he could spot her uncertainty and vulnerability. In the slight trembling of her lips, he could sense her hesitation, her turbulent

emotions, her doubts about the course they had selected.

He had none of those reservations. He was convinced
they were making the right choice. Thank heaven they'd
soon be alone on Mackinac Island, where he'd have her
all to himself. Surely before their honeymoon ended,
he'd be able to woo her over to his side, and she would
see that they were meant to be together, always. . . .

Courtney felt almost unreal as she repeated her vows
to love, honor, and cherish the stranger who would soon
become her husband. Before she knew it, the two had
exchanged their wedding rings, and the judge was giving
Mark permission to kiss her. She watched him turn, saw
him smile a smile of pure joy. Then he pulled her into
his arms and pressed his lips so lovingly to hers. She
didn't expect the rush of emotion that brought tears to
her eyes.

After a moment they moved apart. Mark winked at
her, then turned, shaking hands with the judge and
thanking him.

"Bravo!" cried M. Billingham, striding forward to clap
Mark across the shoulders. Then he stepped toward
Courtney and kissed her cheek. "Welcome to the family,
my dear."

"Thank you, sir."

"What's this 'sir'?" he asked in outrage. "We're all kin
now. You must call me 'Grandfather,' just as Mark
does."

Courtney bit her lip to keep from issuing a less-than-
polite retort.

"I don't think we should push things there straightaway," Mark admonished his grandfather.

M. Billingham gave a shrug but did not directly comment. "At any rate, Courtney, we're delighted to have

you among the Bootle clan, and we'll also look forward to seeing you back at work next week."

Courtney nodded stiffly.

As he retreated, Vanessa rushed forward, warmly embracing Courtney. "Congratulations, dear."

"Thanks, Vanessa."

Vanessa smiled back and whispered, "I know this must be hard for you right now, but I'm sure in time you'll see it's for the best."

"I hope you're right."

After attending to some legalities and exchanging some final pleasantries with the judge, the four exited the office. In the waiting room, Courtney extended her bouquet toward Vanessa. "Here, I want you to have this."

Surprisingly, the older woman shook her head. "Thanks, but don't you think that would be a bad omen?" She shot a blistering look at M. Billingham. "I mean, the woman who takes the bride's bouquet *is* supposed to get married next, and with *him* here . . ."

"Ah, yes, better to have Jack the Ripper along, eh?" M. Billingham mocked.

"Quite so," came the chilly response.

"Vanessa, please, don't be silly," Courtney scolded, pressing the flowers into the other woman's hands. "I want you to have the bouquet. And you don't have to marry anyone if you don't want to."

"Oh, very well." Giving Courtney another hug, Vanessa accepted the roses.

M. Billingham clapped his hands. "Well, what say I take us all out for a grand dinner?"

"Thanks, Grandfather," answered Mark, "but I must ask you and Vanessa to celebrate in our stead." He wrapped an arm about Courtney's waist and grinned. "I'm absconding with my bride on our honeymoon."

Courtney felt her stomach jump, but didn't comment.

M. Billingham appeared eminently pleased. "Good show, boy. I can't blame you at all for carrying off this beauty." He glanced expectantly at Vanessa. "Hungry?"

"Not on your life," she retorted. "I'd rather eat prison food than break bread with you, Ham Bootle." She turned to squeeze Courtney's hand. "Best of luck, dear. I must run along. I'll see you back in Denver."

"Thanks, Vanessa."

Vanessa slipped out of the office, leaving Courtney and Mark alone with M. Billingham. The old guy winked conspiratorially. "Well, grandson, tell me where the two of you are going."

"Grandfather, you know better than to ask that," Mark chided. "Honeymoon plans are invariably state secrets."

"I suppose," M. Billingham replied with obvious disappointment. "Well, good luck, you two. I'm going to go back to my hotel and order room service, then await the corporate jet in the morning. God knows I can't risk running into *that woman* on another commercial flight."

Mark smiled. "Good luck, grandfather. May we drop you off?"

"No, no, I'll catch a cab. Have a pleasant honeymoon, you two."

After giving Courtney another quick hug and shaking Mark's hand, the old man slipped out, leaving the two of them in the deserted outer office. Mark surprised Courtney with a delighted laugh.

"What?" she asked.

With a look of joyous anticipation, he caught her close

for a brief though ardent kiss. "Congratulations, Mrs. Billingham. At last I have you alone."

The knot in Courtney's stomach tightened. *Mrs. Billingham. At last I have you alone.* This was what she'd been afraid of all along!

Chapter Sixteen

"You okay?" Mark asked.

Three hours later, Courtney sat next to Mark in the posh black sedan he had rented for their honeymoon. Around them night had fallen as they drove through the heartland of Michigan, with the wispy silvery shapes of trees stretching along the rolling landscape on either side of them. They were headed due north, for the promised honeymoon on Mackinac Island.

"Guess I feel kind of numb," she admitted quietly.

He flashed her a sympathetic smile. "I know what you mean, darling. Everything has happened so suddenly. That's why I'm so glad we'll have this time away."

Courtney was unable to voice her true feelings—that the most tense period between them might well be just beginning, now that they were truly alone. Now that she felt so vulnerable to him and his charms.

"Plus, our moments with my grandfather and your friend Vanessa today—well, the antagonism between them hardly made our wedding ceremony pleasant," Mark went on.

"I know," Courtney agreed. "At least Vanessa's hostility toward M. Billingham made it unnecessary for me to rake him over the coals again."

Mark chuckled. "There truly is bad blood between those two."

"Indeed. As you may know, Vanessa was married to Floyd Fox, senior vice president in charge of profit and loss, until he died of a heart attack two years ago. Vanessa always resented M. Billingham's demands on Floyd's time, and in many ways felt your grandfather deprived her of a husband."

"I'm familiar with the story, and how she was also on the board."

"Yes, *was*. Within six months of her husband's death, Vanessa was forced out by M. Billingham."

"She couldn't get along with my grandfather."

"Can anyone?"

"Well, I'm trying."

Feeling a stab of guilt, she murmured, "I'm sorry. Of course, you have to defend him."

His jaw tightened. "Don't get me wrong. I've been tempted to disown the coot many times. Much he's done has been indefensible—including the way he treats his employees and their families. Vanessa is hardly the first wife or widow who has wanted to hack him into chopped liver." He quickly glanced at her. "Actually, darling, much as I am concerned about your taking on too much while you're pregnant, I'm happy the company will have new leadership."

Although pleased by this seeming vote of confidence, Courtney remained doubtful. "Mark, do you actually mean you're endorsing my career choice, even though it may be at odds with what you want? I thought you wanted to whisk me off to London with you, and my career be damned. You surprise me."

He reached over to pat her knee. "My dear, you may be in for a lot of surprises on this honeymoon."

That last statement reduced Courtney to silence.

"Will this do?" Mark asked.

It was almost midnight. He and Courtney had just arrived in Mackinaw City. Since they wouldn't be able to take the ferry to Mackinac Island until the next morning, he had booked them a two-bedroom suite at a resort along Lake Huron.

They now stood on the balcony just outside the living room, staring out at the lakeshore as small, silvery waves slapped the beach. Beyond stretched the spectacular lights of the Mackinac Bridge, and the winking lighthouses along the shoreline.

Courtney was spectacularly lovely in the moonlight, the breeze off the lake rippling her heavy hair and whipping her casual dress around her shapely body. The moonlight softened the lines of fatigue and worry on her beautiful face.

"It's fine, quite lovely," she replied.

He stepped closer and touched her shoulder. "I meant what I said, Courtney. I won't try to sleep with you. Not until you're ready."

She nodded and stared back at the water.

"Are you tired?" he asked.

"Yes. The doctor said to expect that early in pregnancy."

"We've been so rushed, I didn't get a chance to question you about your doctor's visit, other than to learn everything is fine."

"He said my due date is January 9."

Mark grinned. "Ah. A winter baby."

"But I warned him that we tend to deliver early in my family."

Mark was seized with worry. "You mean, like preemies?"

"Technically, yes, but it's nothing that scary. My older sister delivered her girl two weeks early, and my oldest sister's boy was almost three weeks premature. But both babies were almost six pounds, and healthy."

"Ah, I feel reassured. Only, considering the risk, perhaps you should cut back on work?"

She tensed. "No, Mark. The doctor didn't think that was necessary at all."

He decided it would be best not to press the issue again for now. Instead he reached out to touch her soft cheek. "So, we might have a Christmas baby."

"Perhaps."

He frowned pensively. "And you could have a tax deduction this year."

"Mark!"

"Just kidding, darling." He quickly kissed her cheek. "I'll let you go to bed, then. We've a big day ahead of us tomorrow."

"Thanks. I do feel ready to turn in."

He kissed her again, this time touching his lips to her sweet, soft mouth. "Good night, Mrs. Billingham."

Her voice shook slightly. "Good night, Mark."

Mark died a little as he watched her step back inside and turn toward her room. This was wrong. It was their wedding night. She was his bride. They should be together. Every iota of his being cried out that he should rush after her, grab her, hold her, woo her with his passionate kisses.

But he knew he had to let her go. He couldn't afford

to rush things. Right now, Courtney's trust in him was but a fragile thread that could snap at any moment, with the least hint that he would not honor his word. All thanks to the fiasco back in New Orleans, and his grandfather's interference. And the fact that she knew now that he really would prefer she quit her job and move with him to London.

Had he been wrong to state his case so frankly there? But it did seem the best way to put their baby first, even though Courtney still didn't see the matter in that logical light.

The bond between them would have to be strengthened slowly and patiently—that, or not at all. For now, he must be content with the knowledge that she was his wife, even if it was, so far, in name only . . .

As Courtney headed toward her room she could feel Mark watching her. She turned to see his gaze riveted on her with desire, tenderness, and torment. Suddenly she felt so lonely. This was her wedding night. Why was she running away from this handsome and sexy man who wanted her?

Because she couldn't trust him. They'd rushed into this marriage too quickly, and he wanted more from her than she was prepared to give—that she sacrifice her career, her own life and sense of identity, for him.

The barriers between them would have to be overcome slowly, if ever. Mark would have to prove to her that he was a much better man than his grandfather was. He would have to show her his love was genuine, and not some sudden and impetuous emotion he'd fallen into much as one might plunge into an ocean. He'd have to demonstrate that he saw her as an equal partner in this marriage, that he respected her career choice, her individuality.

Still, she longed to go to him, to kiss away the pain on his handsome face, to find comfort for her own misery in his embrace. Yet until she was convinced they would make it, physical intimacy might only make matters worse.

Quashing the urge to go running back into his arms, she hurried into her room and shut the door.

Chapter Seventeen

Courtney stood with her husband on the deck of the jet ferry while its noisy engines propelled them across Lake Huron toward misty Mackinac Island in the distance. Since no civilian automobiles were allowed on the island, their car had been left in a lot back in Mackinaw City. A brisk breeze was blowing and the temperature was in the low seventies, the air scented of the lake, with seagulls swarming overhead. Both she and Mark wore slacks and windbreakers.

"Have you ever seen the island before?" he asked.

Staring ahead at the long, forested island with its high limestone ridge, she shook her head. "No, though I saw the movie *Somewhere in Time*. I've wanted to go there ever since."

"Ah, so I've managed to fulfill a secret fantasy."

She wrinkled her nose at him.

He pointed to the west. "That's the Grand Hotel."

She spotted the long, white, magnificent edifice sitting majestically on a high shelf of the bluff. "Oh, wow, you're right. Are we staying there?"

Mark shook his head. "I've heard it's out of this world, but I had something a bit more intimate in mind."

She raised an eyebrow at him, but his only response was a wicked grin. She wondered what he was plotting. She recalled him saying, "I have the right to woo you."

And from what she remembered of the movie, there could not possibly be a setting more perfect for romance than Mackinac Island. She watched in fascination as the land mass grew clearer. A striking harbor zigzagged along the edge of the lake, lined with everything from yachts to fishing boats. A whimsical old lighthouse stood in the distance. Behind the harbor stretched a line of charming Victorian houses and hotels. To the west a grassy park lined with blooming lilacs gave way to a forested bluff. On the ridge above loomed a large fort with an American flag. Beneath it farther to the west, she glimpsed a quaint business district.

"Excited?" Mark asked.

"It looks wonderful."

The boat pulled into its space at the pier, and Mark escorted Courtney down the gangplank with the other tourists. At dockside stood a bearded man in a red English tailcoat, buff-colored breeches, and a black top hat. He held a card on which was written BILLINGHAM.

"Mark—is he here for us?"

"Yes. Only a few public vehicles are allowed on Mackinac Island, so I've rented us a carriage and coachman for the week."

"I'm amazed."

Mark spoke to the man. "I'm Mark Billingham, and this is my bride, Mrs. Billingham."

The middle-aged man removed his hat and grinned at her, his gold tooth twinkling in the morning light. He spoke in a feigned Cockney accent. "Aye, sir, ma'am. I'm

Terrence Mastingham, your coachman. If you would be kind enough to point out your valises, we'll be on our way."

Courtney had to smile at the man's deliberately quaint speech. After Mark indicated their suitcases, the coachman grabbed them and led the couple away to a gleaming black, folding-top carriage harnessed to two matched grays. As the man loaded their bags in the boot, Courtney could not take her eyes off the lovely conveyance, which even boasted a gold coat of arms on its door. She felt touched in spite of herself. "Oh, Mark, it's gorgeous. Are we really going to drive around in this all week?"

"We certainly are."

"I feel rather like Princess Diana at her wedding."

He winked. "Indeed. But we'll hope for a much better outcome than the Prince and Princess suffered."

Approaching the door, the coachman spoke. "Would you folks like to get settled in first, and then we'll have a roundabout?"

"Sounds great," Mark agreed.

The man opened the door, and Mark helped Courtney step inside, then settled in next to her on the plush burgundy velvet seat. The coachman secured the door, and Courtney heard the springs squeak as he climbed into the driver's seat above them. The coach rattled off, down a lane bounded by the harbor on one side and Victorian houses on the other. The scents of greenery and blossoms filled the air. Soon they ascended a steep incline toward another road lined with massive Greek revival style mansions and cozy Victorian cottages.

Before long the coachman pulled into the driveway of a yellow-and-white Queen Anne–style cottage with a slate roof and a screened side porch. "Mark, are we staying here?"

"Yes. It's the summer home of some Detroit potentate. It wasn't easy finding a rental for July 4 week, but luckily, the man and his family are in Europe for a month."

"The house is precious. And . . ." She hesitated. "Well, as you said, intimate."

He patted her hand. "Don't worry, love, there are two bedrooms. I checked."

She cast him a forbearing look.

The coachman opened their door and bowed. Mark hopped out, then helped Courtney alight. Meanwhile the coachman had retrieved their luggage. "Sir, I have your key, so I'll just go open up and deposit your luggage upstairs."

"Thanks."

He hurried ahead, and Mark and Courtney strolled through the yard, past a lovely oak tree and flower beds filled with blooming petunias and geraniums. By the time they climbed the steps to the porch, the coachman was reemerging.

He handed Mark the key and made another bow. "There you are, sir. Shall I call back for you in an hour?"

"Please do."

The man left, and for a moment the two stared at each other. "Well, Mrs. Billingham, shall we explore our honeymoon haunt?"

"Sure."

But as she started ahead, he touched her arm. "You're forgetting something." With fluid grace, he lifted her into his arms and carried her over the threshold.

Courtney laughed. He was certainly acting gallant. For a moment he stood gazing at her so tenderly that her heart did somersaults.

She cleared her throat. "Ready to put me down?"

"Perhaps never." He leaned over and kissed her. "Happy honeymoon, Mrs. Billingham."

An eternity seemed to pass before he finally let her down. Her heart fluttering, Courtney glanced about at the long central hallway. On their left stood a beautifully carved mahogany table, a bowl filled with roses sitting on its marble top, the reflections of the crystal and blooms glittering in the goldleaf mirror above. Beyond was the graceful archway to a parlor. On their right, another opening led to a dining room. Straight ahead, at the end of an Oriental runner, curved an oak staircase leading to the upper floor. She took a deep breath and smelled roses, timeless antiques, and furniture polish.

"This is so lovely," Courtney remarked. "Just look at those wooden floors."

"Ready to go exploring?" he asked.

"Sure."

Courtney stepped with him into the cozy room. Her eyes scanned a delicious mix of plush imported carpets, period chairs and a Victorian sofa, all done in shades of mauve with gold accents. The ceiling featured painted murals of cherubs and a glittering brass chandelier. Stepping over to a gold inlaid table, she fingered a cobalt blue Sèvres vase with painted classical courting scenes. On either side of the vase sat fabulous Faberge eggs.

"The owners must be connoisseurs of antiques," she murmured.

"Perhaps that explains their insistence on a hefty deposit, plus enough references to give me the same security clearance as Agent 007."

She chuckled. "You went to a great deal of trouble to put this together, Mark."

"Anything to please my bride." He kissed her cheek. "Let's look at the dining room."

They stepped into the large room with its Duncan Phyfe table and chairs and handsome matching sideboard. Courtney was charmed by the antique blue-and-white dishes on the table. She picked up a plate and studied its classical design. "Wedgwood," she murmured, setting it back down.

Mark strode toward a door at the end of the room and opened it. "Looks like there's a nice modern kitchen, as well. There will be a housekeeper coming along tomorrow to make our breakfast and tidy up. But today I wanted you all to myself."

"Hmmmm," Courtney murmured. "When did that coachman say he was coming back?"

"Let's check out the upstairs."

Like two excited children they climbed the stairs, emerging in a dark hallway. Spotting a flood of light, Courtney proceeded through the first open door. "Oh, Mark, it's exquisite."

They looked around at the large, airy bedroom. A mammoth cherry four-poster bed dominated the space with its full canopy, lacy white bed drapes and bedspread. A matching dresser and highboy completed the ensemble. Belgian lace curtains hung at the windows, and white wallpaper with an oak leaf pattern graced the walls. Beyond, an opened door revealed a white tiled bathroom with an old-fashioned, claw-foot tub.

Then Courtney's gaze fixed on Mark's suitcase, placed next to hers near the foot of the bed. "Um, I think the coachman had the wrong impression."

His expression was devilish. "Yes, that we're newly-weds."

"Mark!"

"Never fear. According to the real estate agent, there are two full bedrooms and baths up here. I'll retire to the other room and let you freshen up."

"Thanks, Mark."

Grabbing his suitcase, he dipped into a bow like the coachman's, and left her laughing. Hearing his door click shut down the hallway, Courtney was surprised to find herself swept by a wave of wistfulness, and missing him already. He'd been such fun this morning; she longed for him to come back and tease her some more.

Tease her and what else? What was wrong with her? Mark was less than fifteen feet away. This wasn't the way things were supposed to proceed. This was a marriage of convenience, for the sake of their child. She wasn't supposed to be feeling so drawn toward her new husband, so emotionally involved.

But involved she *was*, despite herself. Mark had put so much thought, so much sensitivity, into planning their honeymoon. He was proving himself to be a man of caring and depth. Much as she hated to admit it, this was what they both needed after all the stress of the previous months—to get away to a quiet, genteel, beautiful place like Mackinac Island.

A place where their thoughts were bound to turn to romance. . . .

Down the hallway in the smaller, more masculine bedroom with its tall bookshelves and cozy wing chairs flanking the fireplace, Mark was carefully unpacking, placing his shirts and underwear in the chest of drawers. He smiled to himself. He was certainly making excellent progress with Courtney. He could feel her warming up to him since they'd arrived here. He'd been obliged to pull quite a few strings and call on the help of an old friend from Detroit, now a real estate broker, in order to make the arrangements for this fabulous cottage. But if Courtney could relax here, all his efforts would be worthwhile.

He hadn't been on Mackinac Island for many years, not since he was twelve and had come with his parents and sisters. That year, the entire family had come to America to celebrate his grandfather's fiftieth birthday, and they'd done extensive sightseeing afterward. He remembered how his mother and dad had seemed estranged that September. At the time, he had blamed the tensions on their oft-overheard disagreements regarding his grandfather; his father hadn't wanted to come to America at all, but his mother had insisted.

Mark hadn't understood the true reason for the rift between his parents until years after their deaths, when he had discovered among his mother's effects a letter from his dad begging her forgiveness for his infidelities, a letter dated only weeks before they'd made that trip to America.

He did know that his parents had renewed their love for each other here on Mackinac Island. He remembered them spending countless hours together holding hands on the veranda of their hotel, or taking long walks along the lakeshore drive.

He desperately hoped that same magic would work between himself and Courtney now. Certainly, he would never be unfaithful to her, but so much else stood in their way: The fact that they were from separate cultures and lived on two different continents; the question of how they would adjust their lives to suit the baby; the horrible tensions between Courtney and his grandfather.

Perhaps with time and love, they could overcome all that.

Chapter Eighteen

Courtney sat next to her bridegroom in the open-top carriage as the coachman drove them away from their cottage. To their left down the slope of the bluff stretched a fabulous view of the town and harbor; to their right rose more quaint, late nineteenth-century houses. In the distance ahead of them she could see the bastions and flag of the fort.

The coachman began what seemed a stock lecture about the island. "To tell you a little about Mackinac, it was first settled by French fur trappers and missionaries. The French government established a fort here in the late 1740s to protect the fur trade. In 1861, the British took charge after defeating Canada in the Seven Years War. The fort as we know it was begun by the British in early 1780 and completed when the Americans took charge after the revolution. The Yanks battled the Redcoats again during the War of 1812, after which the Americans permanently took charge. During the nineteenth century, the economy was built on fur-trading, including the American Fur Company owned by Mr. John Jacob Astor himself. Later in the century the fur trade faded and fishing and tourism became more important."

As they began to descend into a wooded area, they passed a long tour carriage coming up the hill, crammed with tourists wearing shorts and hats and wielding cameras and binoculars. They wound through a lovely forested ravine and emerged on Fort Street. To their left stretched the grounds of the fort, with barrackslike structures peeking out at them from the bluff.

The driver gestured toward the green area with its lovely blooming lilacs. "That's Marquette Park, the entrance to Fort Mackinac State Park. You should see the fort while you're here. Lots of history."

They turned onto Market Street, its long expanse of historical facades heralding stores and hotels, its sidewalks crowded with sightseers. The driver gestured toward an old story-and-a-half house on their right. "That's the Beaumont Memorial, named in honor of William Beaumont, an Army doctor at the fort in the 1820s. There's a famous story regarding him. In 1822, he cared for a young man who was accidentally shot in the stomach. The doctor never could get the hole in the man's belly to heal, and therefore he did experiments on him to study the human digestive system. As a result, Dr. Beaumont is considered a pioneer in the field." As they passed another tour carriage, he pointed ahead. "There are all kinds of historic sites to see on Market Street, including the Astor warehouse, the Stuart House, and an old blacksmith's shop."

They turned around the block and emerged on Main Street with its shops, restaurants, and hotels. Courtney sniffed at a tantalizing aroma on the air. "What's that I smell?"

The coachman chuckled. "Mackinac Island's famous fudge. You must sample some while you're here."

As they passed one of the shops, she spotted employees working the fudge on marble-topped tables. Already her mouth was watering. "I can't wait."

"Nor can I," added Mark. He addressed the coachman. "Hey, hold up, will you?"

The man pulled the horses to a halt. "Aye, sir."

Courtney raised an eyebrow. "You're buying fudge already?"

"Your wish is my command," came Mark's gallant response. "Chocolate or vanilla?"

"Well . . . how 'bout pecan?"

Mark grinned at the coachman. "A feisty one, isn't she?"

"Well, sir, she knows her own mind and, frankly, I think our pecan fudge is the best."

"Then nothing but the best for my bride. Wait right here, love."

He hopped out of the carriage and dashed into the shop, emerging in a couple of minutes with a white box. He climbed in beside Courtney, opened the box, and handed it to her.

Courtney took an ecstatic breath. The aroma drifting out of the interior was irresistible. "My heavens, it's still warm. But you can't expect me to eat the whole thing."

"Indeed not," he retorted indignantly, then called to the driver, "Fudge, my good man?"

"Thank you, sir, but not while I'm driving," Terrence drolly replied. "I might lose my head and plunge us straightaway into a ravine."

"Then carry on."

"Aye, sir."

As they clopped off, Mark took a small chunk of fudge

from the box and raised it to Courtney's lips. "You first."

Courtney took a bite of the warm fudge, felt it melting in her mouth, tasted pecans and an incredible sweetness, and thought she had died and gone to heaven. "That's the most delicious candy I've ever tasted in my life! It should be outlawed."

Mark chuckled, leaning over and whispering at her ear, "Perhaps we can invent a few more guilty pleasures that should be outlawed before we leave this island."

Courtney didn't dare comment, for her face was already burning. She didn't doubt for a moment that Mark would do his best to invent those "guilty pleasures," and to seduce her into succumbing!

They headed away from the town, into another wooded area. "Mackinac is ringed with parks," the driver explained. "While you're here, be sure to take a few hikes and smell the balsam."

Courtney inhaled deeply. "I do already, but I still like the fudge better."

"Amen," added Mark, and they both laughed.

They wound down a shady trail with a large golf course on their right, eventually climbing up a ridge where Courtney spotted a magnificent pillared white hotel that stretched seemingly forever on a high ridge to their left. The building's huge colonnade was lined with American flags, and a jaunty cupola provided the crowning touch for the fabulous edifice.

"Yonder is the Grand Hotel, where the movie *Somewhere in Time* was filmed," the driver announced. "The daily buffet luncheon is fabulous."

"The hotel itself looks good enough to eat," Courtney declared. "Like a grand steamboat, or a huge, tiered wedding cake."

The driver laughed, and Mark patted her hand. "Ah,

so you're craving wedding cake now? Stick with the fudge, darling. There are limits."

She stuck out her tongue at him, suddenly enjoying herself more than she would have ever dreamed, and didn't object at all when he wrapped an arm around her waist. They wound through the interior of the island, past stately cottages and shady old cemeteries. Eventually they emerged near a high arched rock formation on the eastern side of the island fronting the lakeshore.

Courtney gazed at the large ring-shaped limestone formation, an opening at its center giving a view of the lake. "Is that a breccia formation over there?"

Terrence called back, "Yes, ma'am, you're exactly right. That's Arch Rock, the island's most famous natural wonder. It rises up more than a hundred and forty feet. Scientists say the hole in the rock was formed by water and wind erosion over time, but the Indians have handed down a more interesting tale. Evidently long, long ago an Indian maiden fell in love with a spirit brave, and her heartless father tied her to the bluff to keep her from her true love. It's said her tears, washing down the limestone, created the circle in the rock. Later her lover came back to claim her and took her with him to heaven."

"What a sweet story," Courtney remarked.

"If you folks want to see the stone closer up, there are steps yonder."

"Believe we will," Mark answered.

They left the carriage and ascended Arch Rock, standing together at the railing near the top of the formation. Courtney gazed down at the woods behind them, the beautiful blue lake stretching for miles ahead of them, where tankers and a cruise ship glided past in the distance. The sea breeze felt wonderful on her face.

183

"This is quite a natural wonder," Courtney remarked. "I know a little about rocks."

"So I've surmised. How did you learn about them?"

She gave him a self-deprecating smile. "Oh, it's a long story, one better reserved for another occasion."

Mark wrapped an arm about Courtney's shoulders. "If your father tied you to that rock and kept you from me, would you cry until your tears created a beautiful breccia sculpture?"

She laughed. "I wouldn't like being tied to a rock."

He frowned, watching a seagull sail past over their heads. "No, you're one of those birds who likes to be free, eh?"

She met his sober gaze. "In charge of my own life, yes."

"And where does that leave me?" he asked quietly.

"I'm not sure." She sighed. "Mark, give me some time."

"I'm pressuring you again?"

She nodded. "You know, this island has to be one of the most beautiful spots I've ever been. I think you're so thoughtful to do all of this. But—"

"But?"

"Guess I am feeling a bit overwhelmed by it all."

"I don't mean to overpower you, love," he replied sincerely. "Spoiling you rotten is more like it."

"You're definitely doing that, as well."

"Good." She was pleased to see a smile spring to his lips. "You'll get used to it in time."

"I hope so, Mark. Forgive me if I'm still a little numb. I mean, we're still strangers, and I've spent almost no time with you. Now all of a sudden we're plunged into this provocative situation as husband and wife."

"Provocative, hmm?" he teased.

"Guess I'm just confused about a lot of things."

Mark took her hands and addressed her earnestly. "Courtney, we're here to clear up your confusion. We're here to get to know each other better, apart from the world and our responsibilities."

"I hope you're right and I hope it will work out that way."

He sighed. "Looks like I've got a lot of persuading to do."

"Not too quickly, please," she cautioned. "Let's just become better acquainted as you suggested. That should be our first goal."

"I'm with you there, love." But as he leaned over and tenderly touched his lips to her own, she realized that he had far from given up on doing "a lot of persuading."

Chapter Nineteen

Courtney had never known she could have so much fun.

For the remainder of the day, she and Mark strolled through the business section of the island, stopping at charming little shops and sampling additional fudge. They toured the historic fort, watched a re-enactment of a skirmish between the Americans and the British in the War of 1812, and took a quiet walk through a nearby forest. Later in the day, Mark rented them a small sailboat and took them out on the lake.

Sitting next to him on the port side of the boat, she marveled at his skill in working the tiller and the sail as he maneuvered the craft through the choppy waters of Lake Huron. The afternoon was mild, the breeze crisp and sweet. In the distance she watched a barge glide past. Ahead she could see the wooded outline of the mainland and a lighthouse near the point.

"Where did you learn to sail a boat?" she asked Mark.

"I've enjoyed sailing all my life. My dad taught me the rudiments when I was a lad. How I looked forward to those times with him when I was home from boarding school."

"That must have been a pretty lonely childhood."

He glanced away. "I suppose it could have been worse. I had plenty of chums at school. And I still spent some time with my parents. Ofttimes in the summers we'd go on holiday up to Windermere where my folks had an estate, and my dad and I would go out on the lake. I still keep an eighteen footer at the yacht club back home, and take it out on the Serpentine when weather permits."

Watching him maneuver the bow of the boat into the wind, she slowly shook her head. "Strange to think of you as a sailor. Guess I'm more familiar with your 'high-flier' image."

"Sailing is my sanity, the way I keep my peace of mind." He sighed. "And going out always brings up lots of fond memories."

"You must miss your parents terribly."

"Yes," he admitted, then flashed her a smile. "Which makes it all the more important to me to have a family of my own now."

Noting the emotion tensing his mouth, she wondered about his last statement. She had grown up in a warm though bustling family atmosphere, but this man had not. She knew people tended to pattern their own homes according to their history. Mark's background was of nannies and boarding schools, of formal distance between himself and his parents. Would he be able to build an intimate family unit with her and their child?

Plus, at a very critical age he had lost his folks and was left with only M. Billingham Bootle—who, if Courtney was any judge of character, was an even poorer example of a parent.

She bit her lip. "After you lost your parents—was it difficult for you to reestablish a relationship with your grandfather?"

"You mean because of the rift between him and my father?"

She nodded.

"No, not really. I never felt a part of that, and as I mentioned before, our family did keep up appearances. Of course I didn't see him nearly as much after he moved to America, until after my parents died, that is. When we met at the airport, I recall that I sobbed rather shamelessly, and the old boy did his best to comfort me."

She touched his hand. "He was all you had left."

Mark's hand grasped hers with surprising strength. "Courtney, he was always important to me. I won't try to lie to you there."

She glanced away and they fell silent.

"What about you, Courtney?" he asked after a moment. "Did you have a passion as a child?"

Thinking back, she smiled whimsically. "If I tell you, you'll laugh."

"No, I won't."

"Actually, as a little kid, I was something of a tomboy. Climbing trees, riding skateboards with the boys."

He grinned. "You, a tomboy? I suppose it does make a certain sense. Even then, you were trying to succeed in a male-driven world."

She rolled her eyes. "I was also an amateur rock-hound."

"Ah, yes. The reason for your commentary at Arch Rock."

"Do you find my interest strange?"

"Not especially. After all, you lived in the Rockies."

She laughed. "That's right. A rockhound in the Rockies. I used to have this wooden box, and everywhere we went I'd fill it with rocks. I know I drove my mom crazy on some of our family vacations. I had a hammer that I used to bang the rocks open, and goggles to protect my eyes."

"You hammered the rocks open?"

She nodded. "Imagine the wonder I felt the first time I shattered a plain-looking rock, and found inside a beautiful piece of flint, or even a geode or quartz."

"Ah—rather like finding a woman with a hard exterior who's a warm and loving person inside."

Ignoring that, she went on, "Then when company came, I'd display my collection and give everyone the appropriate lecture."

"Tell me, did this scientific bent of yours continue?"

She shook her head. "Not in high school. Guess that's when I began to discover my own femininity—and boys. Lectures on mineral formation during the Mesozoic Era don't exactly mix with football and the Homecoming Dance."

"For my own sake, I'm eternally grateful," he replied with feigned gravity. "Otherwise I'm sure we'd be spending this entire week hammering limestone about the island, or attempting to scale the Sugar Loaf formation that we passed today."

She playfully punched his arm. "You're exaggerating."

"My grandfather has accused me of that."

"Anyway, in high school I started getting interested in makeup and clothes, became a cheerleader—"

"And broke the quarterback's heart when you went on to college."

She glanced at him sharply. "Right. I told you about

that, didn't I? He . . . wanted too much of me." She was tempted to add, *like you*.

Though his frown bespoke his concern, Mark didn't comment directly. "Then it was on to earn your MBA, the scholarship to Harvard and all that. I'm impressed."

"You have your MBA as well," she put in.

"But I didn't have to work at it as I know you must have. There was never any doubt that I would continue on at Cambridge, no financial necessity for a scholarship."

"Yes, I encountered a lot of well-fixed types like you at Harvard. Rich, spoiled, and arrogant."

"Is that how you think of me?" he asked in mock horror. He pulled her closer. "Come hither, woman. It seems I've a major job of proving myself to do."

She laughed softly. "This sailboat is a good beginning. A part of your personality I find unexpected—and charming."

"Charming enough to win a kiss?"

"Don't push your luck." She nodded toward the west, where the skies had grown gloriously red as the sun began to sink toward the horizon. "The sunset promises to be spectacular."

"Indeed."

He eased closer to her, and they sailed along quietly for a few more moments, until a gust of wind hit the sail, and the boat hiked over. As Courtney held on, Mark valiantly worked the sail and the tiller, and after a few dizzying seconds, he managed to right the craft. It wasn't until after it was stable that Courtney was swept by a wave of nausea.

Mark glanced sharply at her pale face. "Are you all right?"

"Sure. Just a bit startled."

"You look ill, love."

"Well, I am a bit nauseous, but I'm sure I'll be all right in a moment."

"Damn. I'm sorry, Courtney. I should have known better than to take you out on the lake in your—er—delicate condition."

"Mark, quit being so stuffy and British," she protested. "I'm a modern, healthy woman—"

"Who is pregnant with my child and shouldn't be jostled. Time to get you back home for some pampering."

"Mark."

But he proved adamant, turning the sailboat toward the harbor where the coachman was waiting for them. Within twenty minutes they had arrived back at the cottage.

Inside the front door, Courtney laughed when he swept her up into his arms. "Mark! What are you doing?"

He headed for the stairs. "I promised you some pampering."

"You're being ridiculous! I'm not Scarlett O'Hara, and you're not Rhett Butler."

He wiggled his eyebrows. "Frankly, my dear, you're giving me ideas."

"Mark, you're being a rascal."

"I'm taking care of the mother of my child."

The mother of his child. Somehow those brief, electric words startled Courtney into silence even as a treacherous heat swept through her belly.

He easily carried her up the stairs. On the second floor, he strode into her room and whipped back the quilt on her bed while still holding her, then laid her down, removed her tennis shoes and draped the quilt over her. Courtney had to admit the bed felt wonderful, but when Mark grinned down at her, she stuck out her tongue.

He crossed the room and lit a fire. She breathed in the seductive warmth of the blazing cedar logs; the crackling sound they made was so soothing.

He stood and brushed off his hands. "Don't you dare move, or there will be dire consequences."

Though she grinned at his melodramatics, she actually felt too cozy to move. She did wonder what he was up to.

Her question was answered minutes later as she heard the soft rattle of dishes out in the corridor, followed by the smells of warm tea and cinnamon buns. A moment later Mark reentered the room bearing a silver tray with a doily and an exquisite china tea set.

"Oh, Mark." She sat up.

He strode to the bed and set down the tray. "Tea, madam?"

"Yes, thanks. You *are* pampering me."

He began pouring her a cup. "And what do you take in yours?"

"Just a bit of lemon."

He squeezed some lemon into her cup, then placed it on a saucer and handed it to her. "Roll?"

She wrinkled her nose at him. "You're going to make me fat."

"Aren't you supposed to grow fat, my dear?" he teased back.

Courtney blushed and accepted the bread dish he handed her. "These smell delicious."

"The housekeeper brought them this morning. Just heated up a couple in the microwave."

"Ah—so you do have a domestic streak."

"A slight one. I do live alone, and so far have managed not to starve."

"You mean you've had no English beauties at home, waiting on you hand and foot?"

He made a clucking sound. "Courtney, you know I haven't had time for a serious relationship—up until now."

"Most men hardly have to be serious in order to take advantage of a woman."

He leaned close, until she could feel his breath on her cheek. "I do. Besides, now I'm taken. I have a wife." He skillfully kissed her.

"So you do," she murmured back, enjoying the kiss more than she should have.

For a moment they fell silent, both nibbling and sipping as the treacherous warmth of the fire heated the room. Then Mark set down his dishes and turned to Courtney, his dark eyes very serious. "How do you feel about it, Courtney?"

Flustered, she asked, "About what?"

His hand stole under the covers until he touched her lower belly. Heat seared her to the core as his gaze continued to hold hers.

"About carrying my child inside you."

Courtney would long wonder why such a simple statement could be so sexy. Mark looked so solemn and so sweet. His hand was so warm, touching her intimately, yet there was an innocence about it, too. How could she tell him not to touch her there, when he was connecting with his own life inside her?

She smiled at him shyly. "I'm really not sure just how to feel as yet. I never expected this would happen at this stage in my life."

"But you didn't want to have done with it."

193

Those words brought unexpected tears to her eyes and tight emotion to her throat. "Oh, no. I never could."

He nuzzled her cheek. "Me neither."

Shivering from his kiss, she pulled away slightly. "It's just that I had so many goals I wanted to accomplish before . . . this."

He appeared sad. "Are your goals that important?"

"Are *your* goals important, Mark?"

He clutched her hand. "You know, we don't have to go back to Denver at all. As I've already suggested, we could go live in England, even buy a cottage like this one and spend summers here in America."

"That sounds so simple, Mark, and would make things so convenient for you."

"Yes, it would."

"But what about me, my future, what I want?"

"Are either of us lacking for money? Why not make our marriage, our child, the most important thing?" Earnestly, he continued. "Courtney, I grew up with nannies and maids, and emotional distance from my parents. I want my child to have more than that."

She nodded, carefully considering his words. "Actually, I can relate to your feelings of being neglected as a child. As the fourth of five children, I too often felt my needs were put on the back burner. In my case, there were no nannies or maids to pick up the slack while my parents socialized. Instead, my mom was an overburdened housewife with five kids to raise, my dad an overworked businessman struggling to support a large family." She drew a heavy breath. "That's one reason I'm not sure I'll have enough to give to a child, plus a career and a husband. I'm afraid I'll be spreading myself too thin."

He squeezed her hand. "Not if we simplify things and make some sacrifices."

"But I'm the one being asked to make them all."

His tense expression revealed his disappointment. "I hadn't realized you saw things in that light."

Gently she replied, "Mark, we still have a long way to go on this. But that doesn't mean we won't be able to work things out somehow."

He was silent.

"The one thing I know is that I must go back to Denver. Like Vanessa said, I can't just run from my life and my responsibilities there. I must try to make sense of all of this—you, me, the baby, my career."

"That disappoints me, Courtney."

"Why?"

He leaned close and spoke very huskily. "Because I was hoping you *would* run away—with me."

As he ardently kissed her again, Courtney was sorely tempted.

That evening Mark suggested they eat in. Like teenagers, they ordered pizza and soft drinks. Mark brought the food up to Courtney's bedroom, poured her a soft drink and set the pizza box on the bed.

He crossed over to the small entertainment center next to the dresser. Squatting, he spoke over his shoulder. "Good, they have a VCR, and several movies. *Somewhere in Time,* of course."

"Oh, I love that one!" Courtney declared.

"And the lady of the house must be a Cary Grant fan. Let's see, we have *That Touch of Mink, Charade, People Will Talk . . .*"

"*People Will Talk!*" Courtney exclaimed. "I *adore* that movie, and I haven't seen it since I was a child. My grandmother was a big Cary Grant fan, too."

"*People Will Talk* it is, then," Mark said, taking out the tape and placing it in the VCR.

They snuggled under the quilt, nibbling pizza, and watching the old black-and-white movie. Several times Mark cast meaningful glances Courtney's way, and she was intrigued to note the similarities between the movie plot and her and Mark's situation: a pregnant woman, a marriage of convenience, a potent sense of attraction between the main characters. Before long Mark's hand reached out to grip hers, and when he raised it to his lips for a lingering kiss, the gesture seemed sexier than the most passionate caress.

When the film ended, she caught Mark staring at her, his expression both amused and smug. "What?"

"Now *that's* what I call a marriage of convenience. I hadn't remembered how romantic that movie was, with the strong chemistry between Cary Grant and Jeanne Crain."

She shrugged with bravado. "I'd say it's more like a fairy tale."

"Come on, Courtney. That movie was very realistic for its time."

"True."

He raised an eyebrow meaningfully. "And Cary Grant certainly fell in love suddenly enough."

"You mean fifty years ago, he did."

Mark gave an incredulous laugh. "I can't fall in love quickly because I'm a millennium man?" When she didn't respond, he added sternly, "*Courtney?*"

"Hmmm . . . I'll consider the possibility." Though her lips were twitching, she forged on. "May we watch *Charade* next? And after that, *Somewhere in Time*?"

Her attempt to sidestep the issue won her a quick,

possessive kiss. "Courtney, I'm going to get you yet," he warned fiercely.

No doubt, she thought, as, wagging a finger at her, he went off to change the tape.

Chapter Twenty

The next few days passed idylically. Courtney enjoyed Mark's company as they went biking, hiking, and riding about the island. They played tennis at the public courts and skated along the lakeshore road near town. They explored all three of the old cemeteries, as well as natural formations such as Devil's Kitchen and Skull Cave. They spent long interludes sitting on the side porch of their cottage, sipping tea and staring out at the lush balsam forests.

All the while, the romantic tension kept building between them. Although Mark made no overt attempts to seduce Courtney, his desire for her was ever apparent in the way he touched her hand, or looked at her, in the protective way he wrapped an arm about her waist as they walked along, or paused beneath a tree or awning to grace her lips with a quick, provocative kiss. He bought her little things at antique and curio stores: a cameo ring, a crystal perfume bottle, a hand-painted cachepot, an afghan picturing island scenes.

One of their most touching moments occurred in an

antique furniture store. Mark was examining some old picture frames when Courtney spied a beautiful old oak spindle cradle. No sooner had she touched the satiny wood than she heard Mark say, "It's yours."

She turned to see him gazing at her with tenderness. "Mark, that's sweet, but . . ." She glanced at the price tag. "Gracious, it's five hundred dollars."

"A bargain to get a smile out of you."

"Mark."

The male clerk stepped up. "Does the cradle interest you, sir? It's really an excellent example of early Americana. And such a reasonable price—"

"Can you ship it to Denver?" Mark smoothly interrupted. "My bride fancies it."

Courtney had no hope of hiding the warm blush that heated her cheeks then. She was sorely tempted to tell Mark what *else* his bride fancied at that moment—her husband!

"Of course, sir," said the beaming clerk. "If you'll just follow me."

As Mark was starting off, Courtney caught his arm. "Mark, this is too much."

He leaned over and kissed her cheek. "You're a bride. You're entitled."

She would have argued with him further, but knew it was hopeless. Besides, she did love the cradle.

Their last day on the island turned out to be July 4, and a festive atmosphere prevailed all day. With other tourists and islanders, they picnicked at the park, and afterward watched a stone-skimming contest at the lake. That evening they had dinner in the dining room of one of the island's posh hotels. Seated with Mark in a charming bay window at the front of the room, Courtney could see the winking lights of the harbor as she and Mark sipped champagne and ate excellent swordfish; along the shoreline, a small crowd had already gathered to await the fireworks later. Both had dressed up for this special occasion—Mark in a stylish dark blue suit, Courtney in a jade-green silk dress. Several other couples dined nearby, but the room was quiet except for the sounds of a small band setting up in the background.

"You look so lovely," he murmured. "That dress is the perfect complement for your rosy skin and bright eyes."

"Are you trying to disarm me with flattery?"

"Definitely," he replied with a chuckle.

"Well, as far as that goes, you look pretty dapper yourself."

He grew pensive a moment. "Are you sorry it's our last night here?"

She sighed. "It has to end sometime, Mark."

"That sounds grim."

"You know what I mean. We have to return home . . . and to reality."

"Reality. I think we could both do with a bit less of it."

Quietly she asked, "Do you think the best way to solve our problems is to avoid the truth?"

"And what's the truth? That we're married, having a child together?"

"That we still have many obstacles to overcome."

"Then let's be about it," he replied with returning good humor. He gestured toward a passing waiter. "Ready for dessert, darling?"

Courtney set down her fork. "Well, I'm pretty full."

"You'll just have to make some room, then." As the waiter grew closer and gave Mark a questioning look, Mark nodded back, and the man hurried off. Noting Mark's smug expression, Courtney wondered about the private signal between him and the waiter.

Her curiosity was assuaged shortly afterward when two waiters stepped up, one bearing an exquisite two-tiered cake with cream-colored icing, the other an ice bucket with champagne. As the first man proudly set the cake before Courtney, she gasped in surprise and joy. Before her stood a swirling confection crowned by a small plastic lighthouse, with an even smaller bride and groom standing next to it.

"Oh, Mark!" she cried. "A wedding cake?"

"I hadn't forgotten that you've been craving it," he teased. "And we didn't get to have one in Detroit."

Courtney smiled from Mark to the waiter. "It's lovely."

"We ordered it specially from town, ma'am," the man explained. "Your husband said you had to have pecan fudge icing."

"He did, eh?" Courtney glanced at Mark and melted at the look of tenderness and pride on his handsome face.

"May I cut you a slice, ma'am?"

"Oh, it looks too pretty to eat," Courtney protested.

Mark winked solemnly. "Shall we have it bronzed instead?"

"No, silly." To the waiter, she added, "By all means, please cut the cake."

He did so, handing her a plate with a large slice. "Congratulations, ma'am."

"Thank you."

The waiter cut Mark a slice as the other man poured them both flutes of champagne. After the men withdrew, taking the cake to be boxed up, Mark lifted his glass. "To us, Courtney."

She lifted her glass and clinked it against his. "To us." She took a sip of the excellent champagne, then tried a bite of the cake and sighed ecstatically. "Mark, this is scrumptious beyond belief."

"Like my bride," he teased.

She laughed in delight and continued eating the delicious cake.

After a moment, Mark set down his glass and listened thoughtfully as the small band began playing "Can You Feel the Love Tonight?" "Care to dance, darling?"

Courtney nodded. "Sure."

Hand in hand, they went out to the small dance floor. Then Mark drew Courtney close and led her in a slow fox trot to the seductive music. As the refrain swelled to a romantic crescendo, he drew her closer and kissed her hair.

Courtney realized she was on very dangerous ground. Mark had been so incredibly sweet to her tonight, really over the entire honeymoon. She gloried in the strength of his arms surrounding her, in his warmth, his spicy scent. She knew just what he wanted—what she wanted, too. She *felt* the love, just as the melody of the song poured it out, and she wanted nothing more than to make love with Mark tonight.

Then her more cautious nature urged her to slow down. She'd gotten in trouble before by rashly pursuing her attraction to Mark. Of course he couldn't get her pregnant again—but he could break her heart. She still doubted his "instant" love for her, was convinced that he'd wake up one day soon, realizing how impetuous he'd been, that he'd made a mistake. It had certainly happened to her before—an intense relationship quickly fizzling. Besides, she and Mark had so many practical problems still to work out—his opposition to her job, not to mention the logistics of a bi-continental marriage!

She felt so wary of risking her heart, yet she wanted him so much . . .

Mark was also lost in thought, glorying in the woman he held in his arms. She was so soft, so warm, so incredibly beautiful. Never had he felt so close to Courtney as he did tonight. The look on her face when the waiter brought the cake had thrilled him deeply. She'd appeared delighted, yet so vulnerable, so genuinely touched. How he prayed that before this night was over, they would draw closer still. . . .

After a moment he murmured, "I feel so happy, Courtney. Are you happy, too?"

Her smile was slightly troubled. "I—suppose I'm as happy as I can be under the circumstances."

"Said with a strong note of caution."

"Guess I'm thinking about our going back tomorrow, the challenges I'll face. My life is really going to change."

"And mine hasn't? I have a wife, and I'll shortly have a child."

"Men seem to accept all that with equanimity. For a woman there's a lot more to consider—setting priorities, juggling home, family, and career, deciding what's most important."

"You mean you don't already know?" he asked sadly. "I think I do."

"And I think you're oversimplifying."

Mark glided her into a turn. "Forgive me, darling, but I'd like to keep things *very* simple tonight."

Courtney would have replied, but Mark captured her open lips in a long, soulful kiss. He tasted of cake and champagne, passion and need. The low moan escaping her had him pulling her closer still. But after a moment both drew apart at sudden, popping sounds.

Courtney shook her head as if coming out of a daze. "Goodness, Mark, am I seeing stars?"

He nodded toward the bay window. "Fireworks."

She caught his hand. "Oh, Mark, let's go see."

Along with several other couples, they emerged on the front porch of the hotel, just as a roman candle exploded in a fountain of brilliance in the night sky over the lake. Then half a dozen more rockets burst forth, sending a dizzying, multicolored shower of light raining down from the heavens. Along the shoreline, cheers could be heard from the small crowd as the dazzling show continued.

"Happy Fourth of July," Mark murmured, rubbing Courtney's back to warm her.

"Happy Fourth of July to you, as well," she replied happily. "You know, I've never seen anything so beautiful."

Mark wrapped his arms around his bride and kissed her cheek. "I know, darling. I know."

By the time they arrived back home, Courtney was reeling from Mark's sexy kisses. In the upstairs hallway, he caught her close again and slowly, sensuously claimed her lips, stroking her with his tongue in a way that made her toes curl. He pulled back to study her face with fire in his eyes.

His voice was rough. "Courtney . . . it's our last night."

Sadly she shook her head. "Mark, I'm just not ready yet."

Though his eyes revealed his disappointment, he braved a smile. "Would you like a cup of warm tea before retiring?"

"Thanks, but I think I'll just have a long soak in the tub."

"Want your back scrubbed?" he asked wickedly.

"Mark, you know better."

"Do I?"

Making a scolding sound, she turned and walked off.

Moments later, as she reclined in the old claw-foot bathtub, having a good soak in the lavender-scented water, Courtney found she did miss Mark, although she recognized the folly of calling him in now. Still, she coveted his warmth. The large room was chilly, with only a small electric heater placed on a chair near the door providing some heat.

But the warmth she yearned for was much more than just physical. . . .

She considered her husband's earlier words. So they were here to simplify everything. That would be fine until they returned to Denver, and then, just as she'd argued, the situation would be a great deal more complicated for her than it was for him.

Each day now, Courtney could feel more strongly the pull of new life growing inside her. The physical changes of pregnancy had overtaken her—the fullness of her breasts and the sensitivity of her nipples, the dull aching she swore she sometimes felt as her womb expanded to accept the small life pulsing and growing within it. Part of her wanted to give up all her dreams for the sake of that precious life. Part of her still resented how Mark, and his grandfather before him, had taken charge of her, taking her destiny out of her own hands.

Part of her very much feared being hurt, when the marriage they'd both rushed into foundered on the rocks of reality. . . .

Getting out of the tub, she was so preoccupied with her thoughts that she didn't notice when she snagged her foot on the heater cord. The next thing she knew, the heater and the chair holding it toppled to the tile floor with a loud crash. Startled, Courtney cried out and jumped out of the way just in time. Fortunately the heater had an automatic shut-off that instantly kicked in.

A split-second later, the bathroom door burst open and Mark, shirtless but still wearing his dress trousers, came barreling into the room, eyes filled with frantic worry. "Courtney, are you . . ." Then he gulped, his eyes riveted to her naked body.

Courtney blushed to the roots of her hair. "Mark, get out of here!" she cried, frantically grabbing a towel and wrapping it around her middle.

He ignored her, staring flabbergasted at the overturned heater and chair. "What the hell . . . ?" Quickly he leaned over, unplugged the heater and righted it, as well as the chair. "What are you doing with an electric space heater in this bathroom?"

"Trying to stay warm!" she snapped back.

"By jerry-rigging it on top of a chair? Don't you realize you could have been instantly electrocuted if the device had tumbled into the tub?"

"Mark, it was at least five feet away from the tub."

"That doesn't matter. Just the thought of you having it running so close to water makes me cringe."

"Mark, can we please have the lecture on home safety later? As you can see, I'm hardly clothed."

He stared at her again, hard. "You're wet. And shivering. I'll help."

And before Courtney could even protest, Mark snatched the towel from her fingers and began rubbing her down. "Mark!" she shrieked.

As he worked, his burning gaze was riveted to her naked flesh. Then his hand stopped and he swallowed hard. Abruptly he dropped the towel and pulled her close. "Hell, I'll warm you."

In the next instant his mouth was plundering hers, his tongue plunging deep. An inarticulate moan escaped Courtney. Suddenly all the tension building between them over the past week exploded in a moment of searing hunger. Time slipped away, and it was like that steamy night in New Orleans again. Ravenously she kissed him and clung to him.

His lips moved hungrily down her throat. "Darling, when I heard that crash, I was so scared. I thought you had taken a bad fall, hurt yourself and the baby. You need someone to take care of you, woman."

Though sinking fast, she managed to protest, "The heck I do."

"The heck you don't."

Mark hauled her up into his arms and carried her into the bedroom. As he laid her down on the bed, his lips slid from her throat to her breast, his tongue lapping greedily. She writhed, her hips coming up off the bed. He slipped his hands beneath her, kneading her bare bottom, and she shuddered in ecstasy.

"Delicious," he murmured at her breast. "I'll lick all the moisture off you."

"Mark," she managed weakly. "Don't you think—"

"Don't think at all. Not tonight."

In the next moment his mouth latched on to her tender nipple, and she gasped helplessly, knowing she was lost to him. She tangled her fingers in his hair. "Mark, I'm very sensitive there."

"Because you're having my child," he murmured huskily, gently running his lips over the swollen peak. "Is that better?"

"Oh, yes."

His fingers slid down her belly, dipping low, then one of them pushed inside her. "Are you tender here, too? Can you feel my baby growing?"

"I can feel you," she managed, kissing him recklessly. "I want you. All of you."

She got her wish as he rolled on top of her. She grabbed for his zipper, slid it open, slipped her fingers inside his briefs and touched him. He was so hard, ripe to fill her.

He paused to look down at her a moment, his eyes brimming with passion. Then she got her wish as he pushed fully inside her. She whimpered in pleasure and clutched his body tightly to her own. Oh, how had she ever fought this? He was sheer heaven, and the feeling of joining herself with him was beyond rapture.

"Warm now?" he murmured.

"Oh, yes." And then, to each powerful stroke, she repeated, "Yes, yes, yes . . ."

Plunging into his wife's delicious body, Mark couldn't believe that Courtney was his again. She lay completely open to his thrusts, taking them, meeting them, and her soft arms and legs were tangled about his body. Her mouth was heaven on his, and the soft, inarticulate sounds of her surrender propelled him onward as he lost himself in her.

"You're mine, now," he uttered hoarsely. "My wife. Say it, Courtney."

There were tears in her beautiful eyes as she whispered back, "Your wife."

Mark knew she would have said it again, and again, but his mouth was claiming hers once more.

Chapter Twenty-one

At Bootle's Baby Bower's corporate headquarters in west Denver, Courtney sat at her desk staring at a sea of paperwork. She couldn't believe how backed up things had gotten during her absence from the company. Although Courtney had assumed that Wally Gilchrist had been appointed CEO after she'd quit, in reality, M. Billingham Bootle had reneged on the promises made in New Orleans, semi-retiring without ever naming a successor.

Until her return. It amazed Courtney to realize that the old guy had held the position open during her absence. The reins of power had been officially transferred in the boardroom early that morning. Courtney half shuddered as she recalled her chilly reception, particularly from former competitors, Gilchrist, Gideon, and Getz. None had come forward to shake her hand. She could fault Al Gideon and Gil Getz as sore losers, but Wally Gilchrist was entitled to be miffed, since he really should have won by default back in New Orleans.

Nonetheless, she'd felt a surge of pride at the moment

of her triumph. She'd prevailed over M. Billingham Bootle, perhaps the worst male chauvinist she'd ever had the misfortune to work for. And here she was, only twenty-nine years old and already CEO of her first company.

Of course, her victory had been dampened somewhat by the knowledge that she couldn't really share it with Mark. He didn't want her back here, or working for his grandfather.

She also had a lot of fence-mending to do here at corporate as a direct result of M. Billingham's machinations. With the company rudderless for more than two months, Gideon, Gilchrist, and Getz had fallen into infighting that had further snarled operations. The company would be going public within the year, yet the legal framework and paperwork were way behind schedule, with deadlines swiftly approaching on some critical SEC filings. Inventory for the upcoming Christmas season was sadly lacking. Planned store openings in Colorado Springs and Pueblo might have to be postponed. It would take her months just to get the operations back up to speed.

All at the worst possible time in her personal life. She was a partner in a marriage supposedly "in name only" that her husband already found more than convenient. In about six months she would deliver Mark's child.

She remembered her moments of weakness on Mackinac, how she had succumbed to Mark and his love-making. The atmosphere between them had been tense since then, although on the airplane ride home, she'd made a point of insisting he not tell anyone—especially his grandfather—about the baby without first consulting her.

Then when they'd arrived at her apartment the previous night, he'd followed her into her bedroom and boldly set his suitcase down next to hers at the foot of her bed.

That was when Courtney had put *her* foot down. "Mark, please, put your bag in the guest bedroom."

He looked incredulous. "You're banning me from your bedroom after what happened between us last night?"

Courtney sighed. "This is just what I was afraid would happen. Just because I succumbed to you—"

"Succumbed? I thought you made love with your husband." Drawing closer, he asked poignantly, "Don't you want to make love with me, Courtney?"

That question made her feel altogether too vulnerable.

"Tell me the truth now. You owe me that much."

Bravely she faced him. "Yes, I want to make love with you. I think what happened last night is certainly evidence of that." Seeing him advance toward her, she held up a hand. "But I just don't think it's fair to lead you on when I'm not sure we'll make it."

"Lead me on?" He gave an incredulous laugh. "We're married and expecting a child, Courtney. Don't you think that puts us way beyond the 'leading on' stage?"

"I'm sure you want to believe that," Courtney gently replied. "But the truth is, I married you for our child's sake, to give him or her a name. I made it clear from the beginning that I had doubts about our relationship, and I never made any promises that we'd stay together always."

He was silent, clearly brooding.

"Mark, if we keep making love and eventually we do split up, both of us are going to be even more deeply hurt. I have to be more certain than that. On Mackinac we got the cart before the horse again. We gave in to our emotions before our minds were ready to follow, just like we did in New Orleans."

"Courtney, I don't care what you say. You may think you're not ready, but I am. I'm with you one hundred percent, and have been from the day we met."

His expression was so sincere that guilt lacerated Courtney. "I'm sorry, but I don't feel the same way. And I'm still afraid you may be deluding yourself, trying to please your grandfather, or blinded by what could be just an infatuation."

"Courtney, my eyes are wide open."

She sadly shook her head. "Mine aren't. Not yet."

"And what about our child? What is he or she supposed to do while you decide if you want me in your life?"

"Mark, our child isn't due for six months. For now . . . please, just remove your suitcase."

He picked it up, his eyes gleaming bitterly. "I'm surprised you aren't suggesting separate quarters."

"Actually, I'd prefer it."

"Then you have your wish."

With a slam of the door, he'd been gone, and she hadn't heard from him since. The memory made her wince. She hadn't intended to be so harsh with him, and in fact would have gladly shared her apartment with him. But she'd known if she did not vigorously assert her own rights, she'd end up in his arms again. When he touched her, her logic turned into mush. She had to keep a clear head in order to gauge her own heart, her own mind, in order to decide what was best. Coming back and facing the mess at work had more than demonstrated to her that it would be difficult for her to give her husband everything he needed and wanted and still pursue her own career goals. The child would need much of her attention, too, would have to come first in many respects. Already she felt pulled in so many directions at once.

A rap at her door interrupted her thoughts. Praying it wasn't Mark, she called, "Come in!"

M. Billingham Bootle himself stepped through the door. Dressed in a gray pinstripe suit and red bow tie, he grinned at her broadly. "Well, hello, dear Courtney. I'd have thought you'd still be on a high from netting your promotion this morning. Instead you're sounding a bit peevish . . . especially for a blushing bride."

Courtney stood. "What do you want, Mr. Bootle?"

He whistled. "Such formality. I'd have expected a bit more warmth and gratitude. You may be the new CEO, but this is still my company."

She waved a hand at the accumulated paperwork on her desk. "One would never know it from the way you've allowed things to slide around here."

"Only because you ran off and neglected your duties."

"I ran off? You mean I refused to be blackmailed?"

"Call it what you will, though it seems you grew amenable in the end."

"Unlike you, I didn't have much of a choice."

He made a clucking sound. "On the contrary, Courtney, you had all kinds of choices. You chose to run initially. And I saw no reason to postpone my scheduled tour of the Orient just because of your little hissy fit in New Orleans."

"My hissy fit? What about your ultimatum?"

The old rascal grinned. "You accepted my terms readily enough in the end. Are you sorry you're now at the helm?"

"No, but that's hardly the point."

"It's precisely the point, my dear. The company

needed you, and you bailed out. Now you have a mess to clean up. For as you can see, none of your competitors, neither Gilchrist, Gideon, nor Getz, was equal to the task before you."

Realizing that arguing with him was futile, Courtney sat back down. "Fine. Will you kindly leave so I may work?"

He laughed. "Temper, temper. We'll hope you show more patience with my grandson."

Courtney was silent.

"Actually, I'm pleased to see signs of hope there," M. Billingham went on. "My grandson informed me only this morning that the honeymoon was entirely satisfactory."

"He—said what?" Courtney stammered.

"I think you heard me the first time."

"Those were his exact words?"

"Indeed."

"Where is he?"

He raised an eyebrow in amazement. "Courtney, my dear, you mean to tell me you don't even know where your own husband is?"

She fiddled with papers on her desk to hide her discomfiture. "Not at this precise moment."

"I assumed he would be at your apartment, though when he's in the States, he does sometimes conduct his own business at the BBB corporate penthouse in the Richardson Building. Your assistant would have the keys."

Courtney marched to the door and opened it. "Thanks. Now if you'll excuse me . . ."

Grinning, M. Billingham stepped out. A moment later, Courtney grabbed her purse and followed.

* * *

" 'Entirely satisfactory'?" Courtney demanded, striding inside the corporate penthouse.

Sitting behind his desk with its dramatic backdrop of the Denver skyline and the Rocky Mountains, Mark removed his reading glasses and watched his irate wife storm into the room, looking every bit the hard-charging executive in her navy linen suit. When the doorman had rung him to let him know Courtney was in the lift, Mark had realized something was amiss, for his wife was too busy to desert her post this early in the day. Now the heat of anger on her lovely face confirmed his worst suspicions.

Nonetheless, he got to his feet with a grin and hastened to her side. "Good morning, darling," he murmured, reaching for her.

She flinched. "Don't you dare touch me after what you did."

"And what was that?"

"Telling your grandfather that our honeymoon was entirely satisfactory."

"What should I have said? That it was entirely disappointing?"

"It was none of his damn business!"

"Courtney, he's my grandfather."

"And I'm your wife."

That statement, unintentional though it clearly was, brought a proud grin to Mark's face and a telling blush to Courtney's.

He drew closer, until he could smell the sweetness of her perfume and hear her rather rushed breathing. "I'm pleased to hear you acknowledge that."

She crossed her arms over her bosom. "What I mean is, what happened on our honeymoon should be between you and me. It's personal."

Unable to resist, he pulled her into his arms. "Yes, I agree. It's *very* personal—and my fondest hope is to keep it that way."

She squirmed. "Mark, don't twist things around. You shouldn't have been talking to your grandfather about our—our love life."

"Love life," he repeated, savoring the words. "You know, I'd like a bit more of that."

"Quit dodging the subject." The quiver in her voice revealed how affected she was. "You know what I mean."

"Ah, yes," he mused cynically. "That my grandfather doesn't have a right to know his grandson is happy?"

That question pulled a response from her, and he was touched to see a certain vulnerability, mingled with uncertainty, spring into her eyes. "Are you happy, Mark? I mean, I know I haven't made things very easy for you."

That bit of humility delighted him. "Yes, darling, you've been quite a handful. Were you not carrying my child, I should likely have you over my knee."

"Mark!" Casting him a scolding glance, she pressed, "Just answer me, please."

He leaned over and pressed his mouth to her cheek, gratified when he heard her breathing quicken. "I'll amend what I said. I was ecstatic with you on Mackinac Island—but miserable without you last night."

She glanced away, biting her lip. Could he hope she'd been lonely, too? At least for now she wasn't fighting to get away from him, and that was definitely progress.

"Courtney, let me come home," he pleaded. "Or, you move in here. Grandfather says there are no guests scheduled to stay in the penthouse over the next few weeks. We'll have daily maid service, plus a world-class view of the face of the Rockies. What could be easier, or more fun?"

Though a grudging smile pulled at her mouth, she sadly replied, "Mark, it's still too soon."

Mark decided to opt for whatever he could get. "See me after work tonight? Take in dinner, perhaps a movie?"

"I don't know. Things really got stacked up during my absence."

He pointed at the desk, where his laptop and briefcase were open, papers scattered about. "Things have gotten pretty snarled up for me, as well. I really ought to fly back to London straightaway to attend to some important matters—and I wish you'd come with me."

She bit her lip then. Was she upset at the possibility that he might leave?

"Mark, I can't just drop my life like that," she said at last. "Look, I really need to get back to work, but I'll call you later."

"Promise?"

"Promise."

He leaned over and just managed to brush her warm lips with his own before she slipped away. He watched her leave with a sigh, almost wincing at the sight of her shapely backside retreating. That last night on Mackinac, things had been so beautiful between him and Courtney. Now she'd moved away from him again, both physically and emotionally. His grandfather doubtlessly hadn't helped matters by taunting her.

Her professional duties were also taking her away from him. He felt threatened and knocked off balance there. Perhaps it was selfish of him to expect to be put before her career, but he was more afraid he would lose her with each day that passed.

Why couldn't she trust him and believe he really cared? Why did she continue to suspect ulterior motives on his part? Why was she so determined to withhold her own heart? Somehow he had to convince her that they belonged together.

Chapter Twenty-two

As Courtney drove back to work, her cell phone rang. She punched on the receive button. "Hello?"

"Well, hello, dear," came a familiar female voice. "How is married life agreeing with you?"

"Vanessa!" Courtney cried. "I've been meaning to give you a ring and . . . Gosh, it's good to hear from you."

"Well, you should be glad I'm not calling you from prison."

"Prison?" Courtney laughed.

"Yes, I somehow managed not to murder Ham Bootle on our flight back to Denver."

"Wait a minute, you're joking!" Courtney exclaimed. "I thought he took the corporate jet back."

"Unfortunately it remained gasketless, or whatever, and was grounded in Denver. You can't even imagine the temper tantrum that man pitched when he discovered he had to ride commercial like the rest of us peons, and found himself once again joining me on my flight."

Courtney had to grin at that delicious image. "Did you force him to sit in coach again?"

"What do you think his tantrum was *about?*"

Courtney was delighted. "Good for you. I'm all for teaching that old tyrant some humility, though it seems an impossible task. I've only just returned to the office, and I'm ready to throttle him myself." She paused. "Anyway, Vanessa, I really did appreciate your moral support at our wedding."

"My pleasure. How was the honeymoon?"

"Oh, fine," Courtney answered a bit too casually. "Mark took me to Mackinac Island."

"How romantic." Vanessa paused, then added wickedly, "From your coy tone, my dear girl, you must have had a major lapse there."

"Vanessa! I'm not being coy."

"Oh, yes you are. Now you're sounding tense, another dead giveaway. Come on, you know you can't hide anything from Vanessa."

Courtney groaned. She did know she had no secrets from her very smart and perceptive friend. Nonetheless, she tried her best to dodge the subject. "If I sound tense, it's probably because I came back to a real mess at work. On top of that, Gilchrist, Gideon, and Getz are all furious that I've been appointed CEO. Then, after the transfer of power in the conference room, Mr. Bootle stopped in at my office to personally torment me." She hesitated.

"Concerning what?"

At last, Courtney confessed, "He informed me that Mark told him our honeymoon was 'entirely satisfactory.'"

Vanessa chortled. "Now I *know* you had a major lapse. Did your husband really say that to Ham?"

"I just confronted Mark, and he admitted it."

"Goodness, what a charmer that man is."

"Vanessa! That 'charming' man has thrown my life totally off balance. In fact, he just mentioned that he wants me to drop everything and fly off to London with him. And several times now, he's suggested I quit my job and go live with him there."

"I'm not surprised. Your job does take up a lot of your life."

"But it's *my* life. I can't just live his, as my sisters seem to do with their husbands. Things are . . . well, getting out of control."

"For a woman in love, that's the best way for things to be, darling girl."

"In love?" Courtney repeated, a bit too sharply. "What makes you think I'm in love?"

Vanessa's soft, knowing laughter was her only response. Courtney brooded about her friend's insights all the way back to the office.

Courtney ran across Wally Gilchrist in the hallway near her office. The paunchy little man adjusted his glasses and faced Courtney with a sneer.

"Ah—so the queen bee returneth," he mocked.

Courtney faced him down with a cold look. "Wally, please. Wasn't the chilly reception you gave me in the board room bad enough?"

"What do you think a thief deserves?" he snapped back.

"Wally, that's not fair, or true."

"Really? What do you call stealing the promotion that I earned fairly and squarely?"

"I didn't steal anything from you. That decision was made by the chairman."

"Who promised it to me, then reneged, then gave it to you when you decided to be a good little girl, come crawling back and marry his grandson."

"If you feel that way, why not sue Mr. Bootle?"

He laughed nastily. "And get myself labeled a turn-coat, a troublemaker? You'd love to see that, wouldn't you?"

Courtney hung on to her patience with an effort. "I know you feel cheated, Wally, but the fact is that we need to work together as a team. That was more than demonstrated by all the bickering that went on here during my absence—"

"If Mr. Bootle had simply honored his word and appointed me CEO, none of that would have happened."

"Perhaps not, but we must face reality. If you don't feel you can continue to work under my leadership, I'll understand if you choose to leave."

Wally whipped off his thick-lensed glasses. "Are you threatening to fire me?"

"No, I'm not. But I am pointing out that, given your strong feelings, you might be happier elsewhere."

Wally's face turned red. "Well, you just try it, lady, and I *will* sue you—and Mr. M. Billingham Bootle, to boot. In the meantime, I'd advise you to watch your back!"

Watching him wheel about and stalk away, Courtney shook her head. This was turning out to be a just peachy morning.

She continued on to her office, and had scarcely gotten back to her desk when the phone rang. Frowning, she picked up the receiver. "Hello?"

"Hi, dear, welcome back."

Courtney sighed. "Hi, Mom."

"I figured you two lovebirds would be back in town by now, but you didn't call."

"Sorry, but we only got home last night."

"How was your honeymoon?"

Courtney bit her lip. "Fine."

"You know your sisters and brother are dying to meet Mark."

"They will in time."

She heard her mother gasp. "You mean you've forgotten about tonight?"

"What about tonight?"

"The twins' birthday party. You promised that you and Mark would attend."

Courtney broke the pencil in her hand. She'd completely forgotten about today's birthday party for her sister Caryn's twin boys—and she had promised her mom, when they'd spoken by phone the week before, that she and Mark would attend. Now she shuddered at the thought of being bombarded by her large—and curious—family tonight.

"Mom, I really think it's too soon."

"But you promised. First you tell us you're marrying a man you hardly know, and you won't let your father and me attend or give the two of you a proper church wedding. Now you don't want to introduce your new husband to your family. What's going on, Courtney?"

"Nothing's going on. Of course I want to introduce Mark. Just not tonight."

"Too tired from your honeymoon?" her mom teased.

"Sure, that's it," she replied flippantly.

"You know it will be an early evening. Barbecue at six-thirty, then you and Mark can be out of here by eight or so—if married life has you so tuckered out."

Courtney was tempted to say a few choice words to her mom about minding her own business. Instead she muttered, "My heavens, you're persistent."

"And while you're here, your dad and I would like to talk to you about the reception we still intend to throw for you and Mark."

"Mother!"

"So we'll expect you both around six o'clock?"

Courtney was silent.

"I mean it, Courtney. We won't take no for an answer."

Realizing further argument was futile, Courtney gave in. "Okay. See you then."

Hanging up the phone, Courtney felt supremely frustrated. She wasn't ready to introduce Mark to her family. Of course she knew that they would all be charmed by him, likely love him at first sight. That was what she was afraid of—that all of them would gang up on her, embracing the idea of her marriage and giving it legitimacy, when she still wasn't at all sure about what she felt, and whether or not she and Mark would make it.

Even as she wrestled with her dilemma, her phone rang again. She yanked up the receiver and snapped, *"What?"*

She heard Mark whistle on the other end. "Darling, are you okay?"

"Hardly," she replied. "What's up?"

"Well, you promised to call me and you didn't."

Courtney had to smile at his impatience. "Mark, I've only been back at the office for ten minutes."

"It seemed an eternity to me," he replied with an air of drama. "Not to mention, your line has been busy for the last five."

"So it has."

"Are you going to tell me to whom you were talking?"

Hackles rising, she replied, "I think that's none of your business."

"As your husband, it's none of my business?"

"You take every opportunity you can to remind me of that, don't you?"

He lowered his voice a notch. "Two nights ago, you

seemed happy enough with that state of affairs your-self."

Not liking this turn of conversation at all, she said, "If you must know, that was my mother. We're expected at my folks' place tonight for my twin nephews' birthday party."

"Sounds splendid. How old are these twins?"

"Two. And I just don't see how we can get out of the party."

"Did I say I wanted to?"

"No, but I'm really not ready to face all of them as yet."

An edge of tension entered his voice. "Ah—so you're not ready to introduce your husband to your family?"

With great restraint, Courtney reined in her temper. "Look, Mark, I'm having a very rough day, and I refuse to start arguing with you—"

"Very well," he interrupted. "At any rate, *I* can't wait to meet your family. What time are we due there?"

"Six."

"I'll pick you up at your apartment at five-thirty."

"Fine."

"Fine. See you then."

At five-forty, Courtney walked with Mark toward his car in the parking lot of her apartment complex. She wore navy slacks, sandals, and a white knit top; he had donned khaki pants, Italian loafers, and a navy plaid shirt.

As they neared the car, she was bemused to see the shadowy outline of what appeared to be two passengers in the backseat. She turned to him with a frown. "Did you bring along guests?"

"Indeed, I did." He opened the back door to the sedan

and made an expansive gesture. "Meet Teddy and Freddy."

"My God." She stared at two plush five-foot-tall white teddy bears that grinned at her from the backseat. "What inspired this?"

"It's a birthday party, isn't it? Doesn't tradition dictate that one bring a gift?" He winked. "Besides, under the rushed circumstances, I thought you might have forgotten."

She was forced to smile. "Actually, I called our south Denver store and had them wrap and send out all the appropriate two-year-old books and puzzles, and asked them to sign both of our names."

"How thoughtful of you."

She gestured toward the teddies. "But I can hardly top these."

"Yes, they'll be an added bonus for the twins." He opened her door. "Shall we go?"

"Sure. Thanks."

He ushered her in, went around to his side and swung in beside her. As they made their way out of the complex, she gave him directions on getting to her folks' house.

Maneuvering the car onto the freeway, he cast her a bemused look. "Are you really so uptight about seeing your family, darling? Surely they aren't monsters."

"No, they're not monsters," she admitted grudgingly.

"Didn't you say your mom's a homemaker, your father an air-conditioning contractor?"

"You have a good memory."

"Tell me more about them, and your siblings."

"Well, there's not a whole lot to tell. My family is pretty ordinary. My parents have lived in the same house in suburban Denver for more than thirty years. My mom,

Brenda Kelly, raised five children there, and my father, Lyle Kelly, Sr., has his residential air-conditioning company nearby."

"That's quite a large family."

"A good Irish Catholic family," she explained. "I have three older sisters—collectively we're known as 'the four C's.' Carla is the oldest. She's married to Jason, and they have three kids—twelve-year-old Sam, four-year-old Brittany, and one-year-old Joshua. Next comes Caryn, who's married to Mike. They were married for almost ten years before she finally conceived, and now they're the proud parents of the twins, Jake and Jeff."

"The two-year-olds whose birthday we're celebrating today?"

"Correct. Then there's Christy and her husband, Steve. They have two daughters, a nine-year-old named Mary Ellen, and a six-month-old baby girl, Hannah. Finally there's my younger brother, Lyle Jr. He's in his senior year at the University of Colorado, getting his degree in mechanical engineering. After graduation, he's planning to join my father's business and one day take it over."

"And he's not married yet?" Mark teased.

"No, but he has a fiancée, Becky. They've been dating since high school."

"Your family seems—well, rather big on family, if you'll pardon the redundancy."

"They are. As I've mentioned before, my parents would have preferred that I marry right after high school as my sisters did, to start providing them with more grandchildren."

"They don't approve of their children having careers."

"Not their daughters, I don't think. You see, Lyle Jr. and I were the only ones who attended college. My parents take a great deal of pride in his accomplishments, but as for mine, they seemed more annoyed than impressed when I went off to college and felt my MBA was a complete waste of time."

He appeared shocked. "They said that?"

"No, but it was obvious from their attitude." She laughed. "Wouldn't they be tickled pink to know I'm pregnant."

He frowned. "You mean you aren't planning to tell them?"

She shot him a heated look. "Not tonight, Mark. Don't you dare."

He expelled a long sigh. "Courtney, I'm sorry if your folks don't take the proper pride in your accomplishments. But you shouldn't withhold the news of their coming grandchild out of spite."

"You think I'm being spiteful?"

He nodded. "Partly spiteful, partly prideful. Not just in withholding this information from your parents, but in your insisting on keeping my grandfather in the dark, as well."

"Well, you're wrong about why I don't want to tell my parents," she asserted. "As for M. Billingham—if you think I'm eager to hear him gloating over my pregnancy, then I'll admit I'm guilty as charged."

She heard him curse, low, under his breath. "Courtney, don't you even want my child?"

Lashed by the unexpectedly bitter question, she replied, "Of course I want the baby. Haven't I told you that several times now?"

"You've told me it's against your scruples to have done with it, but whether you really want it . . ." He shot her a heated look. "Frankly, I'm beginning to wonder."

She closed her eyes. "Mark, please. I'll admit I'm under a lot of stress right now, and maybe I'm not saying everything perfectly. If so, I apologize. But the truth is, I just can't deal with this today."

His reply was gentle but firm. "Well, I'm afraid you haven't a choice, my dear. You're not going to be able to put this off much longer. The reality is right there, growing in your belly. And it needs and wants your total commitment."

"Don't you think I know that?" Courtney felt the unbidden sting of tears in her eyes. "Why are you suddenly accusing me of not wanting our child?"

"Why aren't you planning to tell either of our families?" he countered.

"Mark, I'll tell them when I'm ready. Just not now. And I want your word that you won't spill the beans to my folks before I am ready."

"Do you actually think I would jump the gun, knowing your strong feelings?"

"Mark, I think you've jumped the gun on just about everything."

"Fine, then, Courtney," he snapped. "You get your way. Are you pleased?"

Staring moodily out the window, Courtney felt anything but pleased. Of course she wanted this child. Of course. He was just pressuring her to reveal her pregnancy before she was ready.

On the other hand, she could see his reasoning, and she had to admit he'd been largely right in his criticisms. She was withholding the information about her pregnancy from her parents partly out of pride. Already she could hear them gloating—just as M. Billingham would surely gloat. No doubt they would pressure her to give up her career aspirations and become a nice little housewife for Mark, and a doting mother to their child. That was why she felt especially tense over having to introduce her new husband to her family. It would no longer just be Mark promoting the marriage; all of them would now band together against her.

Then she saw her parents' street looming ahead and felt a pang of uneasiness. "Turn right there."

Mark guided the car around the corner. "Which house?"

"The ranch-style one at the center of the cul-de-sac. The one with all the cars lined up in the driveway."

Mark steered straight for the cul-de-sac, toward a large, beige brick ranch-style home with a massive pecan tree shading the yard and brightly colored flowers spilling from several beds. An air-conditioning van and two passenger cars were parked in the driveway, three SUV's out in the street.

As Mark pulled the car into the driveway behind the other vehicles, Courtney watched the front door of the house open. Her family all but burst out—first her grinning parents, followed by her sisters and their families, her brother and his fiancée. Within seconds the group had surrounded the car like an adoring gaggle of groupies greeting a rock star.

Courtney glanced at Mark to see him grinning broadly. She wished she could have sunk through the upholstery.

Chapter Twenty-three

"Courtney, your husband is just a doll!" Carla declared.

"Yes, and we want to hear the whole, uncensored story of how you two got together," added Caryn.

Standing at the kitchen sink, Courtney flashed her sisters a stiff smile. Caryn, Carla, Courtney, and their mother were all present making last-minute preparations for dinner. Courtney's oldest sister Carla greatly resembled her, except that her hair was red; Caryn was a slightly younger, more petite blonde. Their mom, Brenda, was an attractive brunette in her early fifties.

While the women worked, the rest of the crew was outside. Through the window over the sink, Courtney could see a large contingent of children romping through the grass while her dad manned the barbecue, his Denver Broncos cap obscuring most of his reddish gray hair. Mark stood nearby laughing, drinking beer with her younger brother, Lyle Jr., and her brother-in-law Mike.

"Yes, dear, I think you've kept us all in suspense long enough," put in Brenda from the chopping block island, where she was slicing tomatoes. "First, you come home from your convention in New Orleans with some wild story about Mr. Bootle trying to force you to marry his grandson. You quit your job and run off to hide in Detroit. Then you call up out of the blue and say you're marrying Mark, after all—"

"And none of us are invited to the wedding," scolded Caryn from the sink. "So what gives? Why did you decide to reject Mark in the first place, and then why did you change your mind?"

"Have you guys ever heard of minding your own business?" Courtney countered crossly.

"Mind our own business?" repeated Brenda indignantly. "Why, we're your family."

"Which gives us a right to meddle," added Carla, smirking.

"Well? Are you going to 'fess up?" pressed Caryn.

Courtney sighed. "The truth is, I was drawn to Mark from the outset, but resented his grandfather's interference, that stupid trick he played on me, trying to force us together in New Orleans. So I told Mark then and there that it was no dice on our having a relationship. We said good-bye, then eventually he tracked me down in Detroit and, well . . . he changed my mind." As she finished, she marveled at the truth of her last statement.

Carla ecstatically clapped her hands. "Oh, I just knew it! He swept you off your feet, didn't he?"

"You might say that," Courtney replied dryly.

"And here we thought you'd never marry," remarked Caryn. "But Mark's quite a sexy charmer, isn't he? And that accent . . . no wonder you fell like a ton of bricks."

"Well, I wouldn't put it quite like *that*."

"And taking you to Mackinac Island for your honeymoon," declared Brenda. "Lyle and I have wanted to go for years. Was it spectacularly romantic?"

Courtney was shocked to feel a bittersweet pain clutching at her heart as she found herself wishing she and Mark were still sharing that idyllic interlude, instead of the stress-filled days confronting them now. She busied herself rinsing glasses. "Yes. Spectacularly."

"And what are the two of you planning now?" Carla asked. "Being Mr. Bootle's grandson, Mark must be loaded to the gills. Are you going to return with him to London and become a lady of leisure, have half a dozen children?"

Courtney gritted her teeth; already it was starting with her family. She should quit her job and become a housewife and baby-maker. Her own dreams be damned.

She avoided the question. "Being a lady of leisure and having half a dozen children seems a contradiction in terms."

"But think of all the nannies you could hire," Carla teased.

"And we could all go visit!" added a glowing Caryn. "Oh, I'd love to see London."

"I can hardly wait," Courtney quipped. "But before all of you update your passports and plan out the rest of my life, bear in mind that I'm perfectly capable of taking charge of it myself. And that will include following the career path I carved out for myself years ago—foreign as that concept may seem to you."

Carla's mouth dropped open. "But why would you work at all if you don't have to? I'm so glad Jason's making enough now that I can stay home with Josh and Brittany."

"That decision isn't for every woman," Courtney replied firmly.

"Well, thank you, Gloria Steinem," put in her mother.

A tense silence had fallen when suddenly, four-year-old Brittany came bursting in through the back door. The child was adorable with her wide face, green eyes, and blond bobbing ponytails. Dressed in a pink T-shirt, cutoffs, and sandals, she clutched a rag doll in one small arm.

Brittany was quickly followed by Lyle Jr. and his fiancée, Becky. Lyle was a younger, more slender version of Courtney's dad, complete with red hair and freckles; Becky was a lovely young woman with brown hair and eyes and a willowy frame.

"Hi, Aunt Cor'ney!" Brittany chirped. "I like your daddy."

As everyone laughed, Carla gently corrected, "Honey, he's her husband, not her daddy. And it's Aunt *Courtney*."

"That's just what I said," the four-year-old protested. "Aunt *Cor'ney*. And I like her daddy—I mean her Mark. He's nice. He swung me and Sissy high in the air." She lifted her doll to demonstrate.

"That was good of him, sweetie," Carla replied.

Brittany darted over to Courtney and grinned up at her. "Are you going to have a baby now, Aunt Cor'ney?"

Courtney felt uncomfortable as all eyes seemed to focus on her. "I . . . what makes you ask that, honey?"

" 'Cause my daddy told your Mark you'll pro'bly have a baby now. Then your Mark said something I couldn't hear, and my daddy giggled and slapped him on the back."

"I see," Courtney murmured, frowning.

"Brittany, your daddy doesn't giggle, he laughs," admonished Carla.

"Why can't a daddy giggle?" Brittany demanded.

"Yeah, Carla, I think it *was* a giggle," teased Lyle Jr., who had been listening to the exchange with a fascinated smile. "Hasn't Jason been sneaking off to ballet lessons lately?"

"Oh, hush!" Carla scolded her brother.

Amid more laughter, Brittany tugged on Courtney's hand. "So *are* you going to have a baby now?"

Feeling at a loss, Courtney glanced about at the sea of curious, expectant faces. Then her brother rescued her, swinging Brittany up into his arms. Winking at Courtney, he said, "Honey, give Aunt Courtney a break. She only just got married."

"That's why I'm asking her!" Brittany protested.

Lyle grinned at his fiancée. "Pretty soon you'll be bugging me and Becky about having a baby."

"But you *can't* have a baby," the child retorted. "You aren't married yet."

"You tell him, honey," Becky encouraged the child.

Everyone laughed, and Courtney felt very relieved as everyone's attention was diverted from her.

"Mark, welcome to the family," Courtney's dad said.

"Thank you, sir," Mark replied.

The whole crew was gathered in the dining room. Lyle Kelly, Sr. sat at the head of the large pine table, with Courtney and Mark on either side of him. Most of the adults and older children were seated with them, while the younger set was gathered about an adjacent, smaller table, along with Becky and Lyle Jr., who had offered to serve as chaperons.

Lyle lifted his glass. "A toast—to Mark and Courtney. May they find happiness together for the rest of their lives."

Amid cheers and exclamations, the others clicked

their glasses together and drank up. Although touched by her father's toast, Courtney also felt put on the spot. It seemed so hypocritical to allow everyone to assume she and Mark were seeking eternal happiness, when she wasn't even sure they would stay together after their child was born. Glancing at Mark, however, she saw that he had never appeared prouder.

"Thank you, everyone," he replied, smiling around the table. "I must say I'm deeply honored to be welcomed into such a wonderful, warm clan. Having lost my own parents at a fairly young age, I feel as if I've been granted a new beginning . . . with all of you as my adoptive family."

Mark's announcement was met by sighs from Courtney's sisters and sympathetic nods from their husbands and Lyle Jr. Brenda smiled at him warmly. "Oh, Mark, I think that's the sweetest thing I've ever heard. No wonder my daughter loves you."

Mark stared straight at Courtney then, and she felt about two inches tall. "Thank you, Mrs. Kelly. I'm proud to have Courtney as my bride."

"Please, you must call me Mom."

"Mom," Mark murmured. "I'm very fortunate to have you all."

Beaming, Brenda continued, "As I've already mentioned to Courtney, Lyle and I want to throw you two a reception—just family and a few close friends."

"Mom, please—" Courtney protested.

Mark leveled a stern glance on his wife, then grinned at Brenda. "Sounds lovely, Mom."

"Oh, good. Our favorite restaurant has a private room available. How does brunch sound, a week from Saturday?"

"So soon?" gasped Courtney. "Impossible."

"Perfect," declared Mark.

Courtney shot her husband a warning look, only to get a glower in return. "Mom, may Mark and I think about this and get back to you?"

"No need to, Mom," Mark quickly countered. "We'll be there with bells on."

"Then it's a date," said Brenda brightly.

Courtney was about to protest again when her father spoke up. "So, Mark, are you a Broncos fan?"

"Lyle, please," Brenda said, groaning. "Don't start up with football again."

"I have a right to ask the man," Lyle shot back. "After all, he's a member of the family now. So, are you, son?"

Mark shook his head. "No, sir, we don't watch many of your American football games on the telly in the U.K."

"Call me Dad," Lyle replied. "And don't worry, we'll make you a convert."

"Yeah, watch out for Dad," joked Carla. "He's always looking for fresh recruits to drag along to the home games."

"Actually, I'd be honored to attend," Mark put in gallantly.

"As if your husband minds that I hold four season tickets," Lyle Sr. groused to Carla, tossing a frown toward Jason.

Jason, a handsome, fair-haired man in his mid-thirties, came to life with an indignant laugh. "Do you hear me complaining, Dad?" To Carla, he blustered, "Hey, honey, you're getting me in trouble here. Your dad's about to eighty-six me from the games, and you know I can't wait to see the Broncs stomp Oakland again."

"Yes, I love being a sports widow," Carla replied sweetly.

"Stomp Oakland?" protested Lyle Sr. "Heck, we'll win the Super Bowl this season for sure."

"Hear, hear," said Jason, and the other men cheered.

Brenda waved her hands. "All right, you guys, enough! One more mention of football and you get to wash the dishes!"

Everyone laughed, and Courtney observed Mark's expression of utter contentment. She knew he already loved her family, just as they were all feeling charmed by him. Everyone was having a grand time—except for her, of course.

While part of her wanted to be happy for Mark, she couldn't help feeling miffed because he'd accepted the invitation to the reception without first consulting her. And she was still upset over what Brittany had revealed—that Mark had spilled the beans to Jason regarding her pregnancy.

Clearly he had broken his word to her. She was sure everyone in her family now knew she was expecting, or suspected the truth. Their looks of frank curiosity seemed to confirm it.

Nevertheless, Courtney really enjoyed the moments after dinner when everyone celebrated the twins' birthday. All the adults gathered about the smaller table where one-year-old Joshua and the twin boys, Jake and Jeff, were seated. The birthday boys were darling in their matching navy overalls with white shirts and jaunty paper hats. They sat in awed fascination as Grandma Brenda brought in the cake with its burning candles and everyone sang for them. When Brenda set the cake down, Carla had to grab Josh, who seemed determined to touch a lit candle.

"All right, boys," said Caryn, the boys' mother. "Make

a wish, then blow the candles out, just like we practiced."

Both boys began blowing fiercely, puffing out their little cheeks, to everyone's delight. Afterward they smeared cake on each other's faces and ripped open their many presents.

But the highlight came when Mark went out to his car and returned with the huge teddies. "Here you are, my good lads." He set the bears down near the twins' table. "One for each."

"Teddies!" exclaimed Jake, and he and Jeff were off.

Everyone laughed as the two toddlers grabbed and hugged their prizes, rolling about on the floor with the plush toys, cuddling them and kissing them. The boys' dad, Mike, grinned proudly at Mark. "Looks like you have a real hit there. Thanks so much."

"My pleasure," replied Mark.

Caryn stepped toward her sons, who were still frolicking on the floor with the teddies. "Boys, you know better. Go tell Mark thank you."

At once both grinning birthday boys clambered up, rushing over to Mark and grabbing his legs, amid cries of "Tank 'ou, Mark." Mark hefted both boys into his arms, laughing when Jake smacked him on the face and got blue icing all over his cheek.

"You're welcome, gents," he declared.

Watching Mark so contentedly holding the youngsters, Courtney was touched as she thought about their own child. For just a moment, her resentment faded, and she smiled.

It was past nine P.M. before they finally got out the door and Mark drove them toward her apartment. "What a great evening," he told Courtney. "I love your family. I found every last one of them to be delightful."

"Obviously, they were all quite impressed with you, too," she replied tensely.

He glanced at her in bemusement. "Is something wrong?"

"You have to ask that?"

He sighed. "You mean my agreeing to the reception."

"Ah, so you remember," she mocked. "Your agreeing *for* me."

"For us both. Courtney, it would have been rude of us to refuse your mother's invitation."

"Right. Which means you had no obligation to discuss it with me beforehand."

"Courtney, what would you have done, said no?"

"No, but that's not the point."

"What is the point?"

"We're supposed to be equals in this marriage and decide things together."

"I don't think that's the problem at all. I think you're angry that we're going to have a reception in the first place."

"Mark, I'm angry because you took charge of me, as you've done several times now. And I won't have it."

He shook his head in disbelief. "As if I really could take charge of you . . ."

"Mark, it's true! You try it all the time. You speak for me. You did so at dinner tonight, and earlier with Jason."

"What do you mean, with Jason?"

"Don't be coy, Mark. You know you told my brother-in-law that I'm pregnant. And after you promised me you wouldn't."

"I did nothing of the kind."

She shook a finger at him. "Yes, you did, and don't

you dare lie about it. Brittany spilled the beans."

"But she couldn't have! Courtney, what did she say?"

"Something about Jason saying the two of us would likely have a baby now, and you laughing and whispering something back."

"And *that's* why you're so furious? Courtney! All I said to him was 'One never knows.' "

She gave a rueful laugh. "You think that wouldn't tip off a pack of amateur sleuths like my family?"

"What would you have had me say? 'Perish the thought'?"

"That would have been a lot better under the circumstances."

"Because you don't want this baby?" he countered angrily. "If that's really the reason—"

"No, Mark, we've already been over that. Just because you and I are having problems doesn't mean this baby isn't wanted."

He flung a hand outward. "Great, then. It's me you don't want."

"Now you're twisting things around."

"Am I? Then why all the damn secrecy about our child?"

Helplessly she clenched her fists in her lap. "Because if we don't make it—"

"*If we don't make it.* That ought to be our song." He shot her a dark look. "Courtney, all I've asked was to be given a fair chance, and you're not even doing that."

"I'm not? I married you, didn't I?"

"And you've been fighting me every step of the way since then. I think we need to talk. A long, long talk."

Frustrated though she was, Courtney had to agree that Mark had made some valid points. "Perhaps so, but not tonight."

"Courtney, I must insist—"

"I said not tonight. I just can't . . ." Taking a deep, bracing breath, she repeated, "Not tonight."

He didn't press the issue further, stopping to let her out at the door to her apartment. As she left his car, she could feel his stormy gaze following her.

Driving home, Mark cursed under his breath. He was trying so hard to win Courtney over, but she greeted his every move with suspicion. Why did she always assume the worst of him? Was it because she thought he was cut from the same cloth as his grandfather, or the other men who had previously hurt her?

He was also dismayed that she'd seemed so tense tonight. She had a wonderful family, but she'd hardly been caught up in the celebratory mood. Holding the two birthday boys had been the highlight of the evening for him, making him dream of holding his own child one day soon. Yet Courtney had seemed distant from the rest of her siblings, and even their young children.

Despite her protestations to the contrary, more and more he suspected she didn't want him or their baby in her life, had never really wanted either of them. She might speak differently, but her actions were those of a woman fighting to keep her distance.

She'd also accused him of trying to take charge of her. Well, perhaps he had, but only because he felt so threatened by all the barriers she'd thrown up to keep them apart.

Chapter Twenty-four

Several weeks later, Courtney sat at her desk, numbly staring at the August edition of their corporate newsletter, inanely called *Bootle Babble*. The headline read: "BBB's New CEO Weds Chairman's Grandson." In the lead article, her promotion was mentioned in passing, made insignificant by news of the nuptials, including numerous quotes from M. Billingham Bootle voicing his approval of his grandson's choice of bride.

To make matters worse, the centerfold was plastered with at least a dozen photos of the wedding reception Courtney's parents had hosted ten days earlier. M. Billingham had dispatched the corporate newsletter editor, along with a specially hired photographer, to cover the event.

Courtney eyed the snapshots: her and Mark kissing, cutting the cake, and opening the presents; M. Billingham grinning from ear to ear, with his arms around both Mark and Courtney; Courtney's dad leading all assembled in a toast; Mark being mobbed by Courtney's cheerleader girlfriends from high school; Courtney's mom and Vanessa passing out bags of confetti.

Damn M. Billingham for having the audacity to gloat so! The article and photo spread screamed "happily ever after," making Courtney feel like the worst kind of hypocrite.

With a sigh, she studied a snapshot of her and Mark feeding each other wedding cake. He appeared delighted; she looked tense, her smile frozen on her face. Another indication that the atmosphere between them remained strained. So far, they hadn't had an opportunity for their serious talk, partly because Courtney had been so busy, but also because Mark had been out of the country for a good ten days, attending to business in London. She'd been miserable while he was gone—but she was miserable with him here, too. Three weeks after their honeymoon, they were still living apart.

"Mrs. Billingham?"

Courtney glanced up, startled. She still hadn't quite gotten used to being referred to by her married name. Her young assistant, Deb, a slender brunette in her early twenties, stood in the open doorway. Courtney quickly folded the newsletter, shoving it beneath one of the everincreasing piles of paperwork on her desk. "Yes, Deb?"

"I think we have a problem."

"Tell me about it," Courtney said dryly. "I just completed a conference call with our attorneys and investment bankers, and learned how very far behind we are on the initial public offering. Barring a miracle, I'm not sure we'll ever get all the SEC filings done in time. Our chief legal officer promised to fax over a revised timetable and summary of remaining problems to be addressed. Is that what you're referring to?"

"No, I've received no faxes for you this afternoon. The

problem is with the opening of the north Colorado Springs store."

"You're kidding," Courtney said, waving a hand. "I've got two other openings behind schedule, but I thought that one would go off without a hitch."

"Well, they've got some very unhappy campers there."

"Unhappy? Why?"

Deb gave a shrug. "I don't know. The manager insisted you come see the situation for yourself. She sounded very rushed and couldn't explain further."

"Damn," Courtney muttered. "I don't have time to rush off to Colorado Springs. Get the manager on the phone for me."

"Sure." Deb ducked out.

Two minutes later, Courtney's phone rang. "Yes?"

"I'm sorry, Mrs. Billingham," said Deb. "All lines, including the manager's cell phone, are tied up."

"Darn. Guess I *will* have to drive down there."

Feeling extremely harried, Courtney dashed out the door. She retrieved her car from the parking garage and left the building. Zipping over to the freeway, she began the sixty-mile drive to Colorado Springs. Although it was a bright summer day, she was much too preoccupied even to take note of the dramatic face of the Rockies rising to the west of her.

What on earth could have gone wrong with the store opening? Courtney knew the manager, Erica Lindsey, very well; she was a seasoned veteran with more than fifteen years at the company and ten years managerial experience. Courtney hadn't worried about the opening, because she'd known the store was in such capable hands.

Whatever had gone wrong there, at least the formal celebration wasn't scheduled until that weekend. That was when all the ads would run, and door prizes would be offered. With luck this little disaster would be cleared up by then and they wouldn't have to cancel the press party, or the actors they'd hired to wear animal costumes and entertain the children.

At the mall north of Colorado Springs, Courtney parked her car, rushed in a west side entrance, and sprinted over to the boutique's prime location next to a large anchored tenant department store. From an initial glance at the store's facade, all seemed normal. The grand opening banner was prominently displayed over the entrance, and the front windows were charmingly dressed: in one, the Bootle Baby Pram, a classic English-style black baby carriage that was their premiere product, was stuffed with a collection of plush toys—bunnies, bears, lambs, puppies, and kittens. The opposite window boasted a tempting display of the Bootle Baby Layette Collection, the ever popular basics in white with pink or blue trim, including the elaborate and much-celebrated Bootle Baby Christening Gown designed years ago by Vanessa Fox, and still handmade and imported from Ireland.

A step through the open front doors revealed an upscale baby boutique with racks of expensive clothing and baby shoes, as well as a small section of baby furnishings, including cribs, dressers, high chairs, strollers, and playpens. The decor itself was understated elegance—pale blue walls with murals of storks, teddy bears, and baby carriages.

At the cash register, Courtney spotted three mothers with small children huddled around the middle-aged manager, and a rather bewildered-looking young clerk. Courtney was bemused to spot a handprinted sign taped to the back of the register: "Sorry—Store Closed Until Further Notice."

Noting her approach, Erica Lindsey flashed Courtney a relieved smile. "Oh, Ms. Kelly—that is, Mrs. Billingham—I'm so glad you're here."

Before Courtney could respond, one of the mothers, a slender blond with a toddler in her arms, stepped forward. The little girl appeared anything but happy.

"Are you the woman they called in from corporate headquarters?" the child's mother demanded.

"Yes, I am. How may I help you, ma'am?"

"You can explain why your company is terrorizing my child."

"Terrorizing?" Courtney repeated blankly. "With baby clothes?"

A second mother came forward, tugging along a little boy who appeared about three. "Yes, and you've upset little Tommy, too."

"We did?" Courtney glanced down at the somber little boy with dark blue eyes and black hair. Finding that he reminded her of Mark, she smiled gently. "Did we upset you, sweetie?"

He nodded vigorously. "Yes, I'm 'set."

The third mother, carrying a baby girl about nine months old, joined the others. "My little Jennie isn't happy, either."

Courtney glanced about the group in mystification. "But what could we have done?"

The young female clerk stepped forward and handed Courtney a pair of boy's overalls in a size four toddler. "I think she's referring to this, ma'am."

Courtney examined the overalls and could find nothing wrong. "What's the problem?"

The mother with the infant grabbed the overalls from

Courtney and held up the tag. "This. If it's a joke, let me assure you these children *don't* find it funny!"

Courtney stared flabbergasted at the tag. At first glance it *looked* like a BBB stock sticker, round and made of tan, recycled card stock. But she soon realized the color was slightly off, the tag a fake. And that was hardly the most glaring anomaly—a large orange "Grumpy Face" sticker had been superimposed on the tag. She grimaced at the sight of glaring eyes criss-crossed by angry red lines, wild hair, and a fiercely frowning mouth opened to reveal fierce, jagged yellow teeth.

"Yuck!" Courtney exclaimed without thinking.

"That's just what my little Tommy said," put in his mother.

"Yuck!" repeated Tommy, making a face at Courtney.

The child's expression was so comical that Courtney had to struggle not to laugh. But before she could respond, the baby pointed at the face, curled her lower lip, and began to cry. Then the two-year-old girl joined in, and even little Tommy appeared on the verge of tears.

"See what I mean?" asked Erica. "These stickers are so nasty that they've upset every child who has come in here today." She nodded toward the clerk. "One of the mothers even screamed at Janet here."

"I'm sorry, Janet," Courtney told the clerk.

"What about us?" demanded the woman with the baby, bouncing the child to quiet her.

"Of course I apologize to you, as well. But I'm wondering . . ." Still feeling mystified, Courtney examined the tag from several angles. "How on earth did this happen?"

"Apparently someone substituted these tags on at least half of our merchandise," Erica explained. "All the bar codes are wrong, too. Most of them won't even ring up. One did, charging a grandmother nine hundred and eighty-nine dollars for a tooth-fairy pillow for her grandchild."

Courtney could feel the color draining from her face. "You're joking."

"No. She was going to report us to the Better Business Bureau until I gave her the pillow."

"This is a nightmare," muttered Courtney.

"So what are you going to do about our children being traumatized?" asked Jenny's mother.

By now the three children had quieted down, though all still appeared pouty and were staring at Courtney suspiciously. "Ladies, again, I'm really sorry." She turned to Erica. "You have a pair of scissors?"

"Sure." Erica handed Courtney some scissors.

Courtney held up the overalls. "Which one of you was going to buy these overalls?"

"I was," said Tommy's mother.

Courtney clipped off the tag and handed the woman the overalls. "With our compliments and our apologies." Briskly she turned to the clerk. "Janet, would you find this lady a shirt to go with these—and throw in a stuffed frog for Tommy here?"

"Yes, ma'am."

"A free shirt and toy, too? Oh, thank you," declared the mother.

Courtney turned to the other ladies. "What were you ladies shopping for?"

"A new crib?" asked the baby's mother hopefully.

"Please, anything within reason," Courtney replied diplomatically.

The woman laughed. "Actually, I was kidding. We were shopping for new baby shoes."

"Then be our guest. With a stuffed lamb for the baby, too." She turned to Jenny's mother. "And you?"

"We needed a new Sunday dress."

"A frilly dress it is." She patted the little girl's cheek. "And a stuffed kitten for Little Miss Beautiful here."

By the time the children and mothers were ushered out of the store with their prizes, all their faces were wreathed with smiles. Erica, Courtney, and the clerk locked the store's doors and posted a "Temporarily Closed" notice. Then Erica released Janet to go have lunch.

"Courtney, thanks so much for your help," Erica said.

Courtney pulled one of the tags from her jacket pocket and shook her head. "You're welcome. Do you have any idea how this happened?"

"I haven't a clue. You know how rushed we've been with the opening. I understand the Aurora distribution center hired a special crew to package everything up in time; then we hired temps to stock the shelves here. Unfortunately no one noticed the grumpy faces until after we opened. We might have kept the store open anyway, but nothing was ringing up right."

"Darn. Just hang tight, and I'll look into this. And I'll send some people down from corporate to help you re-tag the merchandise."

"Thanks, Courtney. I hope we'll get everything cleared up before the official opening this weekend."

"I'm sure we will."

The two women said their good-byes, and Courtney left. Driving back toward Denver, she got busy on her cell phone. First, she called up their distribution manager in Aurora and explained the situation.

When she was finished, there was a long silence, then

Hal Pearson said, "*Grumpy* face stickers? You've got to be kidding."

"I'm afraid I'm not. I know the merchandise is tagged at the factory, then shipped to you. Can you explain how the renegade tags got on the product?"

"I have no idea. I know we were rushed and we hired a crew from Woodrow Temps to help pick and pack everything. As to the tags, we spot-check all the factory shipments, and I was never informed about anything out of the ordinary."

"Then someone must have re-tagged the merchandise there at the distribution center, later on. Do you have this temp agency's number?"

"Sure. Hold on a minute."

Courtney called the temp agency, where an assistant manager informed her that, yes, they had received the work order from the Aurora distribution center for a dozen temporary warehousemen. But the contract had been canceled at the last minute.

"Canceled. Are you certain?"

"Yes, ma'am. It's right here in the log book."

"Who made the cancellation?"

"I don't know, ma'am. Someone from your corporate headquarters."

"Thanks." By now utterly perplexed, Courtney called Hal back. "Just spoke with the temp agency, and they said the order for extra workers was canceled."

"Canceled? But that's impossible. The temps reported for work here as scheduled."

"You're certain of that?"

"Yeah, I remember that day very well. One of my supervisors went home sick, so I had to stay until everything was loaded. I signed the temps' time sheets myself."

"Damn. The agency was sure someone at corporate canceled the work order."

"Wally Gilchrist does have the authority to do that. You might try him."

All of a sudden a lightbulb went off in Courtney's head. "Aha! You bet I will."

She started to punch Wally's direct line, then hesitated a moment to steady her spinning head and gather her thoughts. Clearly Wally must be the culprit in this. He had both motive and opportunity. Motive because he had lost the promotion to Courtney. Opportunity, because he was in charge of operations. Now he was out for revenge. Furious at Courtney, he had obviously engineered a little incident of industrial espionage to try to undermine her.

And she mustn't allow him to squirm out of responsibility for this. Her resolve firm, she dialed his number.

"Hello," answered a surly voice.

"Well, Wally, I just saw your grumpy face stickers, and I must say I find them inspired."

"Grumpy face stickers?" replied an astonished voice. "Is that you, Courtney? What are you babbling about?"

"Don't you dare play dumb with me." Quickly Courtney recounted the catastrophe at the Colorado Springs store, and explained how she had tracked him down through the distribution manager.

"Well, Courtney, you've hit a dead end," Wally sneered. "I know nothing about the canceled work order with the temp agency. Furthermore, I know of no one here who was involved."

"A likely story. Wally, I know how much you wanted that promotion. You've done nothing but attack me since I was appointed CEO. Your indulging in petty revenge doesn't surprise me in the least."

Wally gave a bitter laugh. "Well, then, let me deliver a shocker: You can have your promotion, Courtney. I wouldn't touch it now with a forty-foot pole. As it happens I'm drafting my resignation letter even as we speak."

"You're what?"

"I've just received a great offer from a Boston firm. I'll be gone as of the first of the month."

"Ah—so this was your parting shot?"

Wally's voice went low with anger. "Courtney, let me reiterate that I had nothing to do with the situation at the Colorado Springs store. Hell, if you're looking for a culprit, why don't you try M. Billingham himself."

"You think Mr. Bootle did this?"

"He's certainly enough of a loco bird. Look at the crazy stunt he pulled in New Orleans."

Courtney was silent, thinking furiously.

"For that matter, maybe you did this yourself to get back at the old coot."

"That's ridiculous."

"So is your accusing me. Did I mention that my new position is at twice my current salary? And you actually think I would jeopardize that to pull some dirty trick against a company that doesn't even value me?"

Courtney definitely had some ideas there, but before she could respond, Wally clicked off.

Courtney laid down her cell phone and cursed under her breath. Now what? A rat loose somewhere in the company, and she had no clue how to find it. Except that the culprit must be a man. Men always targeted her.

Was Wally right? Might the culprit be M. Billingham Bootle himself? But what would be his motive? Why would he give her the promotion, then undercut her efforts?

Unless that had been his game plan all along . . . The very thought made her boiling mad.

On the other hand, the perpetrator could be Gideon or Getz, both of whom also harbored grudges against her. Or even possibly one of the company's competitors.

And what about Mark? She considered the notion, then shook her head. He might want her to give up her job, but surely this kind of conduct was too extreme for him.

Courtney had no sooner gotten back inside the door to her reception area when Deb popped up, ashen-faced; she could hear weird, snarling sounds coming from the direction of Deb's computer. "Mrs. Billingham, you're not going to believe this."

Courtney laughed dryly. "After what I've just been through, I think I may be shockproof."

Deb motioned her toward her desk. "I doubt it."

"My God, what now?"

Deb pointed at her computer screen. "Our company website."

With a groan, Courtney glanced at the screen. Her mouth dropped open, and she collapsed into Deb's chair. Unable to believe what she was seeing, she gasped, "This is a joke, right?"

"I'm afraid not."

Courtney stared mystified at the screen. Their sedate little website with its stuffed bears and baby gowns had been invaded by pulsating, growling grumpy faces that spit and spewed and snarled at the user. The graphics were vividly distasteful, the sound effects harrowing enough to put a haunted house to shame.

"Unbelievable!" Courtney declared. "Those same

grumpy faces were plastered all over our product line at the new store—"

"I know. I spoke with Miss Lindsey a few moments ago."

"—but now they're alive! And even more revolting."

"You ain't seen nothin' yet."

"What do you mean?"

Deb pushed the mouse toward her. "Click here for animated graphics of babies screaming, having temper tantrums, and—er—fits of projectile vomiting."

Courtney gave a nervous little laugh. "Now you *are* pulling my leg."

Soberly shaking her head, Deb clicked for her. "Welcome to the wonderful world of Internet hackers."

As the next page came up, the one that normally featured carriages and strollers, Courtney was confronted by four animated baby graphics: one was screaming and beating its fists, the second squalling in its cradle, a third sticking out its tongue menacingly and wiggling fingers at its ears, the fourth upchucking up all over the Bootle Baby Black Pram. Off to the side, she spotted a cartoon of a young mother, grimacing and holding her nose as she went back and forth to the diaper pail with a dirty diaper.

The graphics were quite clever, Courtney had to admit.

"Well, anyone looking at this site will learn right off that contented babies are what BBB is all about," she muttered sarcastically.

"Our head of IT called up to say they've been jammed with e-mails from angry customers who've seen the graphics."

"No doubt."

"Plus they're going to have to shut down the entire

website because our secure ordering encryption system may have been compromised, as well."

"Oh, brother. Are we sure one of the eggheads in our web design group didn't do this as a prank?"

Deb shook her head. "They all claimed innocence and swore we've been hacked. They promised they'll have the damage contained, and a new firewall established, by tomorrow. That is, if you can authorize the overtime."

"God, yes." Courtney got to her feet and realized she was shaking. "Look, Deb, take care of it, okay? I need a few minutes alone."

"Sure." Deb touched her arm and flashed her a look of concern. "Are you okay, boss?"

"I'll make it."

Courtney entered her office and collapsed against the closed door. What a disaster! BBB had been targeted in a bizarre and almost comical way by unknown industrial moles—but the impact on their profits would be anything but funny.

Needing a shoulder to cry on, she went to her desk and dialed up Vanessa.

"Hello?" came her friend's voice.

"Vanessa, this is Courtney."

"Oh, hi, darling."

"Are you at your computer?"

She heard a dry laugh. "What makes you think I live at my computer?"

"Come on, Vanessa. I know about all the solitaire you play, though your secret's safe with me."

"Naughty girl. As a matter of fact my laptop is on. Do you need some help with a program again?"

"No, but can you get on the Net and access our website?"

"Sure. Just give me a moment." A few minutes passed,

and then Vanessa gasped, "Good grief! You've been hacked, my girl."

"No kidding."

A low chuckle followed. "Clever graphics."

"That's what I thought."

"What on earth happened?"

"I don't know. Like you said, someone hacked us. And it looks like the same person compromised the merchandise at our new Colorado Springs store." Briefly she explained about the counterfeit tags.

"My heavens!" exclaimed Vanessa. "Who do you think is behind this? Perhaps one of the three men you bested for the promotion?"

"Perhaps. I was hoping you might have some idea regarding who might have penetrated our site."

"Well, off-hand I know of no one at corporate who would have those sorts of skills, unless it's in your IT department."

"I know, but they all swear they weren't involved. Any idea how the hackers did this?"

"My dear, that's way over my head. Firewalls, passwords, HTML, Java . . . You'd need a senior level programmer for this kind of skullduggery."

"That's kind of what I suspected. You know, before I knew about the website, I accused Wally Gilchrist of engineering the sabotage at the Colorado Springs store—"

"Perhaps he did, but as far as your website goes, I can tell you Wally wouldn't know a megabyte from his own behind. Why, one time at a company function, I tried to discuss the latest spreadsheet software with him, and the man was totally at sea."

"You're probably right. Anyway, he denied involve-

Eugenia Riley

ment and told me he's leaving for a position paying twice as much."

"Good for Wally."

"But he mentioned something curious—that maybe M. Billingham is behind this—"

Vanessa chortled. "You know, I wouldn't put it past the old scoundrel at all. Ham's crazy enough and would have the wherewithal to get it done."

"But to sabotage his own company . . ."

Vanessa was silent a moment. "Perhaps he just wants to sabotage *you*, Courtney."

"I've thought of that possibility."

"I can tell you from bitter experience that while Ham may espouse 'equal opportunities' as far as female employees are concerned, at heart, he's a dyed-in-the-wool sexist. Now that he's gotten what he wanted from you—"

"You mean, now that I've married Mark."

"Precisely. Maybe now he wants to give you the proverbial boot, if you'll pardon a pun."

"Maybe so, but how can I catch him—or whoever did this?"

"Don't worry, dear, I'll help you."

But as Courtney thanked her friend and hung up the phone, she was *very* worried.

Chapter Twenty-five

Courtney was exhausted by the time she arrived back at her west Denver apartment. Outside her door, she was startled by the sounds of a clamor coming from within. She heard the laughter of a child, accompanied by a baby's happy squeal.

Unlocking her door, she flung it open to an astonishing scene. Her living room, usually an impeccable blend of contemporary furnishings and tasteful accessories, was littered with colorful plastic blocks and doll clothing. Even more amazing, across from her stood Mark, holding her one-year-old nephew Joshua upside down and gently swinging him to and fro as he gurgled happily, his blond curls sticking out at adorable angles. Nearby, Joshua's sister Brittany was clapping her hands. Both children wore short denim overalls and T-shirts.

Courtney regarded her husband in consternation. "Mark, what on earth are you doing here, and *what* are you doing to my nephew?"

Mark froze in mid-swing. "Oh, hello, Courtney."

Brittany came rushing over, hugging Courtney about

the knees and grinning up at her. "Hi, Aunt Cor'ney. Mark is swinging Joshie bumpside down."

"So I see." Quickly Courtney crossed the room, dubiously eyeing the baby, who was red-faced though still chirping happily. "Hand me that baby at once. What are you trying to do, make him upchuck?"

"Sorry, love," Mark replied sheepishly, righting the boy and settling him in Courtney's arms. "Just having a spot of fun. That is, Brittany suggested . . . Ooops."

Even as he spoke, Joshua spit up all over the front of Courtney's fine suit, then grinned at her crookedly. Courtney grimaced. "Now look what you've done!" She handed the baby back to Mark. "Hold him, please—and this time rightside up."

"Aye, aye, captain."

Courtney rushed into the kitchen and began wetting a clean dish towel. Brittany trailed along and tugged at her skirt. "But Aunt Cor'ney, Joshie *likes* being held bumpside down."

"Does he like getting sick?" Courtney inquired sweetly.

Brittany's cherubic face screwed up in a pout. "I didn't make him chuck up."

"Yes, dear. Sorry." Patting Brittany's head, Courtney glanced up to see that Mark had also followed her with the baby, and now three sets of eyes were focused on her soberly. She cleaned up the baby, rinsed out the towel, and began dabbing at the stains on her suit. In a tone of strained patience, she addressed Mark. "Now will you please tell me what's going on here, and what you're doing in my apartment with the children?"

"Well," Mark began, shifting the baby in his arms, "it all started when I couldn't reach you this afternoon. Your assistant told me you'd gone to the new store in

Colorado Springs, but when I tried the cell-phone number she gave me, I kept getting a busy signal or an out-of-range message."

Courtney tossed the towel into the sink. "Yes, well, we had a bit of a crisis this afternoon."

"Really?"

"Prior to the grand opening, someone managed to put grumpy-face stickers all over the merchandise."

"Bumpy face stickers?" asked Brittany.

"No, darling. *Grumpy* face."

"You must be kidding," Mark said. "How bizarre. Why would anyone do that?"

"Why? I assume to scare off our young customers. And it worked."

"I'm not scared of bumpy face stickers, Aunt Cor'ney!" put in Brittany.

"Good for you, darling." To Mark, Courtney added, "This same terrorist also hacked into our website."

"How strange. Are you certain it was the same person?"

"Oh, yes, complete with the same nauseating orange faces."

"Orange faces," repeated an awed Brittany. "Are they from Florida, Aunt Cor'ney?"

Courtney laughed. "No, darling."

"But how would anyone get access to both your merchandise and your website?" Mark asked.

"Ah, the marvels of technology," Courtney muttered.

"Such as?"

"It's a complicated story. Ask me later." Courtney nodded toward the children. "Now to get back to the issue at hand: What are all of you doing here?"

"Well, that's really fairly simple," explained Mark. "After I couldn't contact you, I decided to come to your apartment and wait for you. Then outside your door I ran across Carla, who was here with the children."

"Go on."

"Well, it seems she and Jason were about to leave on their planned Caribbean cruise. Their older son is staying with a friend, and they were going to leave the younger two with your mom, but she twisted her ankle this morning. Carla stopped by to see if you'd be willing to fill in, so of course I said yes."

"You *what?*"

"The apartment manager, taking pity on us all, let us in," he rushed on. "Evidently she remembered meeting Carla from her previous visits here. At any rate, I've already arranged all the children's things, including the baby's portable crib, in your guest room." He gestured toward the floor and grinned wryly. "And as you can see, Carla brought along ample toys for them, as well. Really, everything's all set."

Courtney had been listening in openmouthed horror. "Mark, have you lost your mind?"

"Well, it's only for five days—"

"*Five* days?"

"And I assumed you wouldn't want your sister and brother-in-law to miss their cruise."

"Perhaps not—but you might have *asked* me, Mark. This is so typical of you, taking charge and making decisions for me."

"Courtney, really—"

"And at the worst possible time for me at the office."

Brittany tugged at Courtney's skirts, and appeared ready to cry again. "Don't you want us, Aunt Cor'ney?"

At once contrite, Courtney swept the child up into her arms, kissing her. "Of course, darling. Certainly Aunt

Courtney wants you. There are just some logistical problems here—"

"Don't like 'gistical po'blums," Brittany said, pouting.

"I know, angel." Cuddling the child close, she glared at Mark over her head and whispered fiercely, "How on earth am I going to *do* this?"

"I'll help," he offered magnanimously.

"Sure you will." Gently she set Brittany down. "Honey, stay with Mark a moment, okay? I just want to call your mommy."

"Okay," said Brittany.

"You can't," stated Mark.

"What?" Courtney asked.

"Their plane left half an hour ago."

"Damn it, Mark!"

Brittany tugged at her skirt again. "Aunt Cor'ney, are you mad at Mark now? Not his fault you can't call my mommy."

"Of course not, darling. Now if you'll excuse me, I'm going to call *my* mommy instead."

Courtney heard Mark's low chuckle as she quickly crossed back into the living room and picked up the phone. Her mother answered on the third ring, sounding pained and tired. "Hello?"

"Mom, this is Courtney."

"Oh, hello, darling."

"Are you okay?"

"Well, I've had better days. I tripped down the back steps this morning and badly twisted my ankle. The doctor says I must stay off it for at least three days."

"Yes, I heard about that, and I'm sorry. Mom, about Carla's kids . . ."

"Oh, yes, I must thank you, Courtney. After I was injured this morning, I tried to see if Caryn or Christy could keep the kids, but as you know they both have work."

Tell me about it, Courtney was tempted to add, though she kept her peace.

"Then Carla called me from the airport to let me know you had agreed to keep them."

"Well, actually, I didn't agree. Mark did."

"Oh." A brief, awkward silence fell. "Is there a problem?"

Courtney bit her lip, then immediately realized she couldn't ask her injured mother to chase after two small, rambunctious children. "No, Mom. No problem at all."

"Because I'd hate for Carla and Jason to have to return from their cruise. It's their first real vacation alone since the baby was born, and I know they've saved for years. It's nonrefundable, too, I understand."

Courtney could only groan. "Yes, we certainly wouldn't want them to miss that."

"Look on the bright side, dear. This should put you more in the family mood."

Courtney was suspicious. "What do you mean by that?"

"Nothing, dear. Only that you'll be prepared when . . . I mean, don't you and Mark want children of your own someday?"

Courtney didn't answer directly. "Well, for the moment it seems we have a houseful. Take care, Mom."

"You, too."

Courtney laid down the receiver and turned to see Mark, Brittany, and the baby once again watching her expectantly. She clapped her hands and forced a cheerful tone. "Well, it seems I've got some very special houseguests for the next five days."

"Don't you mean *we* have some special houseguests?" asked Mark.

"You don't live here," she blurted without thought.

Brittany appeared amazed, her green eyes going wide. "Aunt Cor'ney, why doesn't Mark live here? Isn't he your daddy?"

"Darling, I'm her husband," Mark corrected patiently.

Brittany whirled on Courtney. "Well? Isn't he?"

She met Mark's amused gaze. "Yes, he is."

"Then he can stay!" She beamed at Mark. "You can stay, okay?"

Mark patted Brittany's head. "Well, Courtney? It would be a great deal easier for me to help out that way."

Courtney waved a hand. "Sure, let's make this a complete menagerie."

"Don't like this ma'gery," scolded Brittany.

"Fine. What do you like, sweetie?"

The child broke out in a grin. "Pizza! I'm hungry!"

"Well, that sounds like a splendid idea," agreed Mark. "Come to think of it, I'm pretty well famished myself. What say we all go out?"

"I'll go get Joshie's diaper bag!" volunteered Brittany.

The child danced away. A silence fell between Courtney and Mark; then he smirked. Courtney could have throttled him, except that he looked so darn cute, standing there holding the baby.

"Don't you dare gloat!" she chided. "You're pretty darn proud of yourself, aren't you?"

"Actually, at the moment, I'm pretty darn proud of *you*." He crossed to her side, quickly kissed her lips, then deposited the baby in her arms. "Here. Get used to it, my little mama."

Courtney was about to issue an indignant retort, but

then little Joshua gurgled up at her, brightly repeating, "Mama, mama, mama!" She buried her face in the baby's soft hair, her irate words forgotten in the rush of happiness she felt.

Chapter Twenty-six

"I want strawberry pizza, Aunt Cor'ney!" piped up Brittany.

Half an hour later Courtney, Mark, Brittany, and the baby had arrived at a local pizza parlor. In a booth near the back, Brittany sat on a booster seat next to Mark, with Courtney across from them; the baby, ensconced in a high chair flanking her, was happily chewing on a set of plastic keys. In the background a musician in a bear suit was loudly playing "I'm Looking Over a Four Leaf Clover" on a calliope, while another employee in a clown suit was circulating about, blowing up balloons and twisting them into shapes for the children.

Courtney looked askance at her niece. "You want *strawberry* pizza?"

"Yes, and Joshie wants cheese."

Mark addressed the baby. "Is that right, Joshua? Do you want cheese pizza?"

Joshua gurgled and stuttered back, "Chuh-chuh-chuh!"

"The man wants cheese," Mark pronounced. "Either that, or a toy train."

"But strawberry," pressed Courtney. "I don't think they even make strawberry pizza, honey."

"Sure they do—with bananas and pineapple!"

"Oh, brother," Courtney replied. "I think I feel a headache coming on."

"No, a tummy ache," corrected Brittany. "Joshie gets one when he eats strawberry pizza."

"No doubt," agreed Courtney. "But you don't?"

Brittany solemnly shook her head.

Mark chuckled, and Courtney gratefully watched the waiter step up. She forced a smile and addressed the skinny, blond teenager. "My niece here says you have strawberry pizza."

The boy laughed. "Yes, ma'am, but actually it's a dessert. A round pastry topped with pudding, strawberries, and other fruit."

"Yes, that's just what I want!" declared Brittany.

"But darling, you can't have dessert for your main course," Mark reasoned.

"What's a main cor's?" Brittany asked suspiciously.

"What comes *before* dessert."

"Oh."

"Tell you what," Mark cajoled. "I doubt Josh here can eat an entire cheese pizza by himself, and he also needs someone older to set a good example by showing him how to do it. What say you split a cheese pizza with him?"

"Well, okay," conceded Brittany. "But I still want strawberry pizza for 'sert."

"Absolutely." Mark glanced at Courtney. "What would you like, sweetheart?"

Courtney fought a smile. "I don't care."

The Great Baby Caper

Mark ordered a small cheese pizza for the children, a large pizza with everything on it for himself and Courtney, milk for Brittany and soft drinks for the adults.

After the waiter strode off, the clown stepped up with his balloons and air canister. "Would the children like a balloon, sir?"

Before Mark could answer, Brittany declared, "Yes, I want a poodle and Joshie wants a bear!"

The clown bowed to her. "Your wish is my command, young lady." He winked at Courtney. "Nice couple of kids you two have."

Courtney felt herself blushing. "They're not . . . that is, we're baby-sitting for my sister."

"Ah, practicing up for your own brood?" he asked.

Courtney was about to issue a "none of your business" style retort when Mark grinned at the man and said, "You bet."

She glanced at him sharply, spotted the tender look in his eyes and found herself melting.

Back at Courtney's apartment, she and Mark marched the children through their bedtime rituals. After both had been bathed and dressed in their pajamas, Mark read Brittany a bedtime story in the guest room, while Courtney settled in a wing chair and fed the baby his bottle. Joshua lay contentedly in her arms, his blond curls framing his sweet little face. He stared up at her with his solemn blue eyes, occasionally reaching up to touch her cheek with his small, soft hand.

Listening to the contented sounds he made, Courtney thought of the tiny life growing inside her and was touched. Looking at the beautiful baby, she couldn't help imagining what her and Mark's child might look like. Would he have Joshua's round little face and blond hair? Mark's blue eyes and dark hair? Or would they have a little girl who looked more like herself? Was she capable of becoming the kind of good mother their child deserved?

"You look very natural there," she heard Mark whisper.

She glanced up to see that he had emerged from the guest room. "Brittany's asleep?"

"Yes. We must have worn her out at the pizza parlor because she nodded right off."

Courtney nodded toward Josh. "Well, this one is almost through with his bottle, but he's still wide awake."

Stepping closer, Mark winked. "Who can blame him? He's gazing at a beautiful lady."

"Get out of here," she scolded.

He held out his arms. "Want me to walk him about? That's usually what it takes to get my small niece and nephew to sleep."

"Sure. Be my guest."

He took the baby and walked the floor with him while Courtney looked on from the couch. At first Joshua squirmed and babbled; but before long he laid his head on Mark's shoulder and began to sing softly, sweet, baby babbling sounds. Soon his little eyelids grew heavy, then he fell sound asleep.

Courtney left the couch, came over and kissed the baby's cheek. "You're very good at that."

"So are you," he whispered back.

"What ages are your nieces and nephews?"

He smiled wistfully. "Well, my sister Beth and her husband have two boys, Peter, five, and William, three. My younger sister, Merry, has a girl and a boy. Madison is three and Dillon two."

"Ah—so you've had experience all across the spectrum, like me."

"Indeed. You know, I'd really like you to meet the rest of my family soon."

"I . . ." Feeling a bit put on the spot, she finished, "I'd like that."

He glanced down lovingly at the sleeping baby, then kissed his brow. "I'll just go put him down."

Courtney followed him into the children's room, where Brittany was already sound asleep, her angelic features outlined by a night-light, a rag doll in her arms. She watched Mark gently lay the baby in his portable crib, then cover him with a quilt. She turned and tiptoed out in front of him, then heard him close the door.

She turned to him. "They're so sweet, so special."

"So are you." Catching her off-guard, Mark pulled Courtney into his arms and tenderly claimed her lips.

She backed away. "My, what inspired that?"

His countenance darkened. "Heavens, who knows? Perhaps I quite lost myself in the cozy domestic scene and wanted to kiss my wife."

Though a smile pulled at her mouth, she glanced away uneasily.

"That clown back at the pizza parlor—you didn't want him to know we're married, did you? Or that you're expecting."

She gave him an apologetic look. "Mark, he was a stranger."

"And I'm your husband, but you often treat me like one."

She felt at a loss. "Mark, what do you expect? My entire life has changed in just a few short weeks. Now you won't give me any time or space to adjust."

His gaze narrowed. "You're still angry that I agreed to keep the children, aren't you?"

"Mark, you didn't ask."

"I thought I explained that I did try."

"Still, I wonder . . ."

"Yes?"

She fixed him with her troubled gaze. "If you aren't more like your grandfather than you want to admit. Making decisions for me, trying to take charge. It's happened several times now."

"And just what is it you expected?"

"I needed to be part of those decisions—and you took them out of my hands."

He nodded. "Very well. Point made. But Courtney, I didn't feel I had a choice today."

"Okay, I'll give you the benefit of the doubt there," she replied. "But collectively, these incidents do add up to more than just coincidence."

He was silent, frowning.

She drew her fingers through her hair. "On top of that . . . well, I've just had a very rough day."

At once his expression grew compassionate. He caught her hand and led her toward the couch. "That's right. You were going to tell me more about what happened." At the couch, he gently seated her, then leaned over to remove her pumps. "Come on, put your feet up, love."

She did as bid, stretching out her legs on the long couch. Mark sat down at the end, lifted her feet into his lap, and began massaging her toes through her hose. Though tempted to protest, she found his touch far too soothing. "Ummm, that feels good," she murmured.

"I aim to please," came his husky reply. "My, you must

have been on your feet a lot today. Your muscles seem tense."

"Well, yes, I suppose I was."

"So tell me about this rotten day."

Courtney explained in greater detail about how the Colorado Springs store merchandise had been sabotaged, the website hacked.

When she finished, Mark whistled. "Goodness, sounds like someone with a really weird sense of humor was at work."

"And how."

"But why would anyone do such bizarre things?"

She gave a shrug. "To disrupt our business. Or perhaps for revenge."

"Ah, so you're referring to Gilchirst, Gilhooley, and Getz?"

She laughed. "Gilchrist, *Gideon*, and Getz."

"They're your prime suspects?"

"I've certainly thought of them, and even confronted Wally Gilchrist today. He claimed innocence and informed me he's leaving the company." She shot him a troubled look. "I've also considered your grandfather."

Mark's hands paused on her feet. "You actually think Grandfather would undermine his own company?"

She waved a hand. "After the stunt he pulled in New Orleans, who knows? Besides, I think he'd go to great lengths to make his point, or to ensure that I looked bad."

"Why would he want you to look bad? You've always been his heir apparent. I mean, he gave you the promotion, didn't he?"

"Yes, but look how he reneged on the deal with Wally Gilchrist. He seems to break his word without the slightest twinge of conscience. Besides, he always seemed much more focused on my being your wife than on my becoming CEO." She paused. "As did you."

His eyebrows shot up. "Now *I'm* a suspect?"

"I didn't say that," she quickly denied, "though it seems very obvious that you don't want me working."

"So we're back to that again? My taking charge? Who gets to wear the pants in the family? And you think I'd resort to industrial espionage—a criminal offense, may I remind you—just to keep the little woman in her place?"

He appeared so ferociously irate, he was comical. "No, Mark, I don't. But you must understand. Until a few months ago, I was completely independent. Now everything has changed. I don't like having my life out of control this way."

He leaned close to her, his gaze burning into hers. "You liked losing control with me. You'd love it again if you'd just let yourself. Only you won't admit it."

Courtney was silent, though her steadily reddening face gave her away.

While his gaze continued to hold hers, his hand boldly stroked her calf, and moved higher. "I think you're still angry because my grandfather forced your hand, and now you're taking it out on me. And I think you'll have to forget about your pride before you'll see the truth."

Though his nearness was making her crazy, she pressed her hands to his shoulders. "Mark, that's not true—or fair."

"Isn't it? Then tell me, Courtney—why can't you accept me as your husband, or the life growing within you as our child?"

"I do accept the child—"

"But not me? What's really keeping you from loving me, and him?"

For a moment she could only stare at him helplessly; his expression of hurt and confusion battered her conscience. "I don't know."

"Yes, you *do* know. You're holding me apart with your anger. And considering that there's the life of an innocent child involved here, I find your attitude both selfish and immature."

She bolted upright. "Selfish? Immature? Mark, that's a low blow."

"Then tell me why you're shutting me out."

All at once Courtney's emotions poured forth. "Okay, I'll tell you. Because I don't think you accept me as I am. I think you want to change me into your ideal of a little wife and mother, just as my family does. And as for your falling for me so suddenly—well, I've been there, done that. That kind of shooting star relationship just doesn't last."

There was a moment of terrible silence; then Mark slowly nodded. "Well, at least that's honest."

Courtney was staring back at him when abruptly a sleepy-eyed Brittany stumbled into the room, hair tumbled and rag doll cuddled in one arm. "Aunt Cor'ney, why are you and Mark yelling?"

Courtney rushed up to the child and hugged her. "I'm sorry, darling. We didn't mean to wake you up. And Mark and I weren't yelling, we were just having a—er—spirited discussion."

"Don't like this 'cussion," she muttered sleepily. "I'm for a drink of water, and Joshie has a poo poo."

Courtney had to smile. "Is Josh awake?"

"No, but I can smell it." Brittany held her nose and grimaced for emphasis.

Courtney turned to Mark and gestured toward the guest room. "Be my guest."

Eugenia Riley

He went pale. "You mean, me, er, change the, er—"

"Poo poo diaper," Brittany finished for him.

Mark gave Courtney a woebegone look. "You must understand that I know absolutely nothing about—"

"What? With all those nieces and nephews you claim to tend all the time?" she cut in briskly. "Come on now, Mark. Besides, aren't you dying to become a family man? So, go learn, Papa. Brittany, let's go get that water."

Courtney caught the child's hand and led her toward the kitchen. Glancing back at Mark, she was amused to see him watching them with a look of helpless bewilderment.

Chapter Twenty-seven

Driving to work the next morning, Courtney struggled to keep her eyes open. Mark would baby-sit while she spent a few hours at the office working on the current crisis.

She and Mark had had quite a time getting the two children settled for the night. After she'd gotten up, Brittany had been fretful and calling out for her mommy; the baby had popped wide-awake when Mark changed his diaper, and both he and Courtney had been impelled to walk the floor with him again until he finally fell asleep. It had been almost one A.M. by the time Courtney had tumbled into bed and Mark had dragged himself to the couch.

Thank heaven, duties with the children had postponed any further discussion of their troubled marriage. But now in the sober light of day, Courtney was forced to reconsider her husband's charges of last night. Did she owe it to their unborn child to give her marriage to Mark a better chance?

It would be so easy to give in to Mark, especially as

much as she missed him. But her resistance was motivated not out of pride or anger, as he seemed to think, but fear. Fear that Mark's sudden love for her just wasn't real. Fear that she and Mark couldn't make it in the long run. They were from different continents, with different goals. Both of them were so strong-willed, so determined to have things their way. Plus, she still questioned whether she was capable of becoming a good wife or mother. Last night's experience trying to care for Brittany and Joshua had been draining and an eye-opener.

Of course she loved her young niece and nephew, and she was already deeply connected to the baby growing inside her. But the truth was, she *was* scared. Could she have it all—the baby, her job—plus become the kind of wife Mark wanted?

She remembered the night they'd met in New Orleans, when he'd indicated that his future wife would have to be very understanding of the demands his career placed on him. She remembered how, several times now, he'd urged her to quit her job and move with him to London. It seemed obvious that Mark wanted to shape her into the kind of traditional wife who would sacrifice her own aspirations for the sake of home and family, the kind of wife she wasn't sure she could ever become. She didn't want to fall into the same trap that had claimed Vanessa.

Her cell phone rang, and fearing Mark had already encountered a crisis, Courtney hurriedly punched it on. "Hello?"

"Hello, dear," said Vanessa. "How's it going this morning?"

"Oh, Vanessa, I was just thinking of you. Believe it or not, things are worse."

"My heaven, how ever could they be worse?"

"Well, aside from the cute little episodes of industrial

espionage at work, Carla and Jason decided to go off on a cruise, and dumped their two youngest on me."

"My heavens. And you agreed to baby-sit under the present, chaotic circumstances?"

Courtney gave a short laugh. "Actually, darling Mark agreed for me. I came home yesterday to find him, Brittany, and Joshua happily ensconced in my apartment."

Vanessa laughed. "Mercy me, that must have been quite a shock. Although having the children sounds like fun."

"Normally it would be. You know I've never hesitated to baby-sit for my sisters."

"I know, dear."

"But it's just a lot of responsibility right now, along with everything else."

"I see. By the way, where are the children now?"

"Mark has them for the morning while I go into the office for a while."

"That was nice of him. Any progress on tracking down your industrial terrorist?"

"Not yet, though I'll be giving everyone the third degree today, you can bet."

"Well, let me know if I can help with the children, dear. I do love baby-sitting."

"Thanks, Vanessa. Believe me, I may be calling on you."

At the office, Courtney attended to several urgent matters, then had meetings with staff members pertaining to the mischief at the Colorado Springs store. In particular she grilled Gideon and Getz regarding any possible involvement, but both men vehemently denied any knowledge of, or participation in, the chicanery. Although Courtney still had her suspicions, she tended to believe both men were simply too dull and unimaginative to come up with such an off-the-wall scheme.

She did ask her head of security, Lon Wilson, to drive out to the Aurora warehouse, meet with their distribution manager and other employees, and try to figure out how the wrong crew could have ended up picking and packing the merchandise for the Colorado Springs store.

By late morning, Courtney was feeling quite frustrated and harried when her phone rang. The caller was Roger Cambridge, manager of the south Denver store. He got straight to the point: "Courtney, we need you at the store immediately."

"Is there a problem, because frankly I'm—"

"You might say there's a crisis."

"Let me guess. Grumpy face stickers."

"I beg your pardon?"

"I take it then that you're *not* referring to grumpy face stickers mysteriously appearing on your merchandise?"

"No—but I think you'll have to see this to believe it."

Courtney didn't like his tone—not at all. "Very well. I'm on my way."

She was in her car when the cell phone rang yet again. "Hello?"

"Aunt Cor'ney, where are you?" came a plaintive young voice.

"Brittany? Is that you?"

A teary voice replied, "Joshie misses you, and Mark."

Panic seized Courtney. "You mean Mark isn't there with you?"

"No,'course he's here. He just misses you, too." Lowering her voice, Brittany added, "Joshie did another poo poo."

"Oh." Courtney smiled. "Would you put Mark on?"

"Okay, Aunt Cor'ney."

A moment later, she heard Mark murmur, "Sorry, darling."

"What's going on there?"

"Nothing. Brittany just misses you."

Before Courtney could reply, she heard Brittany whine in the background, "No, *Joshie* misses her!"

"Sorry, love," she heard Mark say to the child. "Courtney, dear, where are you, anyway?"

"On my way to the south Denver store. It seems there's a fresh crisis there."

"Sorry to hear that. But don't worry about us. We're fine."

Courtney was amused by the air of martyrdom she heard in his voice. "Look, I'm sorry I'm taking so long. I'll just check out the problem at the store, then come right home, okay?"

"Hurry back to us."

"I will."

The south Denver store was in an upscale strip center with a large bookstore, a clothing store, and a linens discounter. Courtney parked her car and hurried to the entrance. This time she stepped inside to quite a curious scene. Plump white take-out bags and boxes were piled near the service counter, and the smell of Chinese food was ripe in the air. At least six Chinese men were lined up at the counter, waving bills and clamoring for the attention of the manager, Roger Cambridge. Roger, an attractive, fair-haired man in his early thirties, appeared harried. He was talking rapidly and waving both hands as if to keep the men at bay.

Even more astonishing, several small children sat on the floor munching on egg rolls while their mothers shopped. A baby girl in a pink dress was gleefully pulling apart the rolls and globbing shredded cabbage in her hair, while two toddlers tossed eggrolls back and forth—and squealed with laughter.

Courtney grimaced. Already the store's carpeting was a horrible mess. What was going on here?

She rushed up to the counter. "Roger, what on earth—"

Before he could reply, an irate deliveryman turned to her, shoving a bill in her face. "Lady, you the manager? Who pay for this?"

"For what?"

"Delivery. Ten dozen egg roll."

"Ten *dozen?*" Courtney gasped.

Another man stepped up. "Yeah, lady, you order twelve dozen from me, too. Now you pay."

"*I* ordered?" asked a flabbergasted Courtney. She whirled on Roger. "What *is* this?"

"A major crisis, I'd say," he drolly replied. "Massive, unsolicited egg-roll deliveries."

Courtney stared aghast at the sea of boxes and bags. "You mean you didn't order any of these?"

He waved a hand. "Of course not. I'm allergic to cabbage, anyway." He sneezed to demonstrate.

A third Chinese man stepped up to Courtney. "The order come from Bootle Baby Bower. That you, ma'am. Now you got to pay."

"But we didn't order—"

"That fraud!" claimed a fourth man, waving his fist.

"Yeah, that stealing!" added a fifth. "I call the cops."

"Now wait just a minute—all of you!" Helplessly Courtney turned back to Roger. "Do you have any suggestions?"

"I'm at a loss."

Even as Courtney spoke, she felt a tap on her arm. She turned to see a young mother glowering at her. The woman held a small boy who was chewing on an egg roll.

"Lady, my son is allergic to MSG," the woman informed her nastily. "If he has a reaction, I'm suing you!"

"No MSG, lady!" scolded one of the deliverymen.

"Yeah, no MSG!" seconded another.

"That's what all you guys say," the mother retorted. "You don't have to stay up all night with a kid with a runny nose and a splitting headache—"

"Madam, please," pleaded Courtney. "I have no idea how these egg rolls even got here."

The woman sneered at Courtney. "Like heck you don't. You're trying to entice customers by bribing their children with egg rolls. Have you no shame?"

Courtney was at her wit's end. "Madam, please—"

"Save it for court, lady."

Whirling about with her child, the customer marched out, almost colliding with a smiling young woman with a camera.

Watching the newcomer start snapping pictures, Courtney rushed over to her. "Excuse me, what are you doing here?"

The woman, who appeared about twenty-two, with curly brown hair and an overeager smile, asked brightly, "Are you the manager here?"

"I'm from corporate," Courtney snapped back. "And I repeat, what are you doing here?"

"I'm a reporter from the *Southside Gazette*," the woman explained. "I was in the mall when a mother told me you had ordered thousands of egg rolls and refused to pay for them. Thought it might make a good human interest story." She glanced around. "Are the cops here yet?"

Courtney saw red. "Get out of here, before I *call* the cops!"

"Well, you don't have to be rude about it." Glaring at Courtney, the young woman quickly made her exit.

Courtney started back for the counter, where half a dozen scowling deliverymen still awaited her. "Gentlemen, I'm sorry, but we didn't order the egg rolls."

"Then who pay?" one demanded.

Courtney glanced at Roger. "Do you have cards with the number of corporate headquarters?"

"Sure do."

"Give each man a card, then." She turned to the delivery men. "Gentlemen, please leave your bills with Mr. Cambridge, then call our company headquarters tomorrow and ask for our public relations manager. We'll try to work something out." She gestured at the bags and boxes stacked everywhere. "In the meantime, I'd suggest you gentlemen take the egg rolls with you."

"No!" shouted one. "You order, you eat."

"Whatever," Courtney said, groaning.

As the men lined up before Roger to turn over their bills and receive cards, Courtney wondered what on earth was going on. Yesterday grumpy face stickers at the new store and projectile vomiting at their website. Now this. Someone with a decidedly whacky sense of humor was targeting the company.

"Aunt Cor'ney!"

The sound of Brittany's bright voice wrenched Courtney from her thoughts. She turned to watch her beaming niece come dancing through the door, followed by a grinning Mark, who was carrying Joshua. Unexpectedly, her heart leaped at the sight of them. She could use some smiling faces at the moment.

She quickly crossed over, hugged Brittany, kissed the

baby, then glanced, puzzled, at Mark. "Well, hello. What are you three doing here?"

"Joshie missed you," announced Brittany, hugging Courtney.

Courtney mussed her niece's hair. "I missed him, too."

"We thought you might need some moral support in your current crisis," added Mark.

"That was thoughtful of you."

Brittany was glancing about. "Aunt Cor'ney, where did all those egg rolls come from?"

"You tell me."

"May I have one?"

Courtney waved a hand. "Sure. Why not?"

"Joshie wants one, too!"

"Okay."

As Brittany danced away toward the take-out boxes, Mark inquired, "So this is the fresh crisis?"

" 'Massive, unsolicited egg-roll deliveries'," she quoted.

"You're kidding."

"Wish I were. Some unknown person bombed us with the stuff, and I just had to deal with six irate delivery-men."

He shook his head. "Looks like someone is out to make your life very interesting."

Gently she took the baby from him. "You're wrong. Someone is out to wreck it."

Chapter Twenty-eight

After alerting several key staff members at corporate regarding the new calamity, Courtney had a quick lunch with Mark and the children, and persuaded him to watch them for the afternoon. She rushed back to the office and called a meeting. Gathered around her in the conference room where Gilchrist, Gideon, and Getz, along with the corporate legal counsel, Milton Davies, PR manager Janis Jacobs, and head of security, Lon Wilson.

"As everyone knows," she began, "in the last two days we've been hit by some rather bizarre industrial espionage. Yesterday, it was grumpy face stickers appearing on the product line at our Colorado Springs store, as well as an assault on our website. Today, it's an eggroll avalanche at our South Denver Store."

Amid chuckles, Al Gideon held up a hand, then grimly spoke. "Don't laugh, folks. We'll likely be out a couple of thou on those egg rolls."

Janis Jacobs followed with an affirming nod. "Yes, indeed. Al, Milt, and I spent our entire lunchtime chewing the fat on this egg roll situation. Plus I had to go to great lengths to smooth things over with one of the mothers. Seems her son had an MSG attack."

Courtney frowned, turning to Lon. "Were you able to track down the person or persons who called in the orders?"

The middle-aged, balding man shook his head. "Not yet, though I've already questioned a few of the vendors. Whoever made the orders claimed to be from BBB, and gave them our south Denver store number. A couple of the restaurants had caller I.D., but the actual numbers came up anonymous."

"Great," said Courtney.

"I'll check out all the restaurants, of course—but we might have better luck if we brought in the police."

Courtney considered this, then shook her head. "No, if we call in the police, we won't be able to keep the press out of it. Let's try to keep a lid on this for now."

"I agree," put in Janis. "Publicizing this might only invite copycats."

Courtney groaned at that prospect.

"Dare we hope for chicken wings next time?" quipped Wally Gilchrist, and again everyone laughed.

Janis tossed Wally a stern look. "At our conference, Al, Milt, and I also decided it might be best to just go ahead and pay for the egg rolls. It would be good P.R. with the restaurants and should also insulate us from lawsuits."

"I suppose you're right." Courtney turned back to Lon. "Were you able to find out anything about the tampering with our product line out at the warehouse?"

"Negative, Courtney. I went out there yesterday afternoon, but I'm afraid I reached another dead end. The distribution manager hired a temporary crew to package merchandise for the new store. Then, according to the temp agency, some unknown person from corporate canceled the work order. No one at the warehouse or at corporate knew that the order had been rescinded. A crew did show up claiming to be from the temp agency, but it seems they were impostors who must have planted the renegade stock stickers, and no one was the wiser."

"My heavens, how bizarre," declared Courtney. "But how could this counterfeit crew have even gotten into the warehouse in the first place?"

"We're very tight on security, but when people show up from the temp agency, we generally take them at face value."

"Well, no longer," Courtney said.

"Yes, ma'am."

"More importantly, why would anyone do this?" Courtney asked. "And how would they get enough access to our business procedures and online services to pull it all off?"

"Obviously, the culprit must be someone who knows a great deal about our company," ventured Milton Davies, a handsome, white-haired man in his late fifties. "Perhaps a former employee with a grudge."

"Or a current one," put in Courtney.

"Yeah," agreed Gil Getz rather nastily. "Plenty of us here have grudges."

As a tense silence fell, Wally Gilchrist asked, "What about one of our competitors?" He rattled off half a dozen names. "They might target us, especially now that we're going public and threatening their market share."

"Good point." She shifted her gaze to Lon. "Any suggestions as to how we find out?"

He mopped his brow with a handkerchief. "I'm trying, Courtney, but this is a tall order. On top of all these headaches, I've got security for twelve stores to worry about—and three of them brand new."

"Yeah—and from what's been happening for the past two days, you haven't done a very good job," groused Al Gideon.

When Lon would have protested, Courtney raised a hand. "Enough. We're not going to solve this through infighting."

Milton spoke up again. "Courtney, Lon's right that we can't expect him to take on all this. I'd suggest we hire a private detective firm to do a thorough internal and external investigation."

"Great idea." She swung about to Lon. "Are you willing to spearhead that with Milton?"

After glancing at the other man, Lon nodded. "Absolutely."

"Count me in, Courtney," added Milton.

"All right, then, everyone. I'm counting on all of you to do your part and cooperate with Lon, Milton, and Janis. I think we all have our work cut out for us. We'll meet again in a couple of days for progress reports."

As the meeting broke up, Courtney felt no closer to a solution than she had before. Nor had she picked up any substantive hints regarding who on her staff might be involved.

To make matters worse, she stepped back inside her office to see M. Billingham himself sitting behind her desk, smirking at her. "Well, young lady, how's my grandson's bride doing today?"

Courtney glowered at him. "Don't start up with me today, Mr. Bootle."

"So married life *isn't* agreeing with you?"

"I don't think that's any of your business. Now if you'll excuse me—"

He stood, raising an eyebrow at her. "Frankly, Courtney, I'm wondering if I should excuse you. Only a few weeks on the job, and you already seem to be losing control of our operations—that is, if the reports I'm hearing are true."

Courtney was tempted to groan aloud. Great, now M. Billingham knew about the tampering. She wondered who had spilled the beans to him—most likely his assistant, Mildred.

She realized there was no point in denying the facts. "Very well, the reports are correct. We're having a small problem with industrial espionage."

"Small?"

"I've got it covered," Courtney went on coolly. "In fact, I've just come from a meeting where we've been working on solutions."

M. Billingham gravely shook his head. "You know, I thought I could entrust you with the welfare of this company, Courtney, but now I'm not so sure."

She strode toward him. "Ah, so you're already prepared to renege on our deal?"

He thoughtfully scratched his jaw. "You might say I'm having second thoughts. Besides, why deny yourself the pleasure of being a full-time wife for my grandson?"

"Spoken like a true chauvinist," Courtney shot back. "And just what I've been expecting from you. I'm sure you've wanted this all along—for me to resign, rush home to Mark and bake crumpets or something. And perhaps you've conjured up a clever little intrigue to encourage my departure."

"Courtney, my dear, whatever are you insinuating?"

"You know exactly what I mean! You and your penchant for practical jokes. Is this little debacle with grumpy face stickers and egg rolls simply your latest attempt to undermine me, to make me throw up my hands and quit?"

He gave an incredulous laugh. "You think I would sabotage my own company?"

"In a New York minute, you would, if it suited your purpose."

"What purpose?"

"To boot me out the door."

He laughed ruefully. "Boot you out? I do love your fondness for double entendre. Besides, Courtney, you give me too much credit."

"I think not."

He shook a finger at her. "Such spirit, Courtney. I'll let your accusations pass for the moment. As to your duties here, I think I'll just give you enough rope to hang yourself."

"Aha!" she cried. "So you admit you engineered this latest disaster."

"I admit nothing—except that you're skating on thin ice, my dear. Get a handle on this crisis, or you may well reap the whirlwind."

Courtney marched to her door. "Kindly take yourself—and your mixed metaphors—and get out of my office."

She could hear M. Billingham's insufferable chuckle as he strode away. She slammed the door, returned to her desk, sat down and hurled a pencil across the room.

When Courtney returned to the apartment, the first thing she noticed was a handsome black leather suitcase sitting next to the front door. Then she spotted Mark, on the floor playing with both children, amid a pile of blocks.

"Hello," she called. "You going somewhere?"

"Hi, Aunt Cor'ney!" called Brittany.

"Hi, sweetie."

"Hi!" yelled Josh, waving a block.

Courtney smiled at the baby. "Hi, darling."

Mark stood and came to her side, leaning over to kiss her cheek. "Hello, sweetheart. How was the meeting? Any clues as to the culprit?"

"No, none, but we're starting up a thorough investigation." She nodded toward the suitcase. "You didn't answer my question."

"Oh, that." He smiled sheepishly. "I'm afraid I must make a quick hop to London."

"A quick what? But you were just there."

He scowled. "You're not the only one with business problems, and I've neglected mine too long. This morning, I received several urgent calls. It seems there's been an unexpected hostile takeover bid for Billingham's."

"Your clothing chain?"

"Yes. And my solicitors have informed me I must be present for the stockholders' meeting tomorrow in order to convince some of our biggest investors to tough it out with us over the long haul, rather than go for the quick profit of selling out to the sharks. Also, my online bookstore is facing an audit from the Inland Revenue. I'm afraid my staff is rather sadly in disarray, and my newest executive assistant just threw in the towel. I wish I could resolve it all from here, but I'm afraid it's too much of a muddle."

"So you're leaving?"

He touched her arm and gazed at her earnestly. "Only for a few days. Look, I'm really sorry to leave you in the lurch with the children. Normally I'd offer to take you with me, but that's clearly impossible under the circumstances. All I can do is to get back here as soon as possible."

Lowering her voice, she asked, "And what am *I* supposed to do with these kids while you're gone?"

"I noticed several good nanny services in the yellow pages."

She waved a hand. "Great. That's tremendous help."

"I'm sorry, love." His expression grew forlorn. "I'll miss you terribly, you know."

"Sure you will."

"Look, I'll hurry back." He turned to the children. "Children, come say good-bye."

Brittany popped to her feet, followed by Josh. "Are you leaving, Mark?"

"Just for a little while, darling."

Brittany rushed over to Mark, with Josh crawling along behind her. Tugging on his shirtsleeve, she pouted, "But I don't want you to leave, and neither does Joshie."

Mark hugged the little girl, then scooped up the baby, who cooed and hugged Mark's neck. "Don't worry, loves, you'll have Aunt Courtney."

Brittany glanced suspiciously at Courtney, then crossed her arms over her chest. "Don't like Aunt Cor'ney. I want my mommy back."

"Brittany," admonished Mark. "I know you miss your mommy, but Aunt Courtney is nice, too."

She pouted a moment, then muttered, "Okay, I like her. But I like you best."

Mark glanced at Courtney almost helplessly, and she relented. Smiling at Brittany, she said, "Don't worry, darling, we'll have lots of fun, and you'll see Mark again soon."

"Promise?" Brittany asked.

"Promise. Now tell Mark good-bye."

"Okay. 'Bye, Mark," Brittany said dully.

He touched her cheek. "Good-bye, dear. Be good." He kissed the baby, then handed him over to Courtney. "Guess I'd best go."

Realizing he really was leaving, Courtney found herself unexpectedly fighting tears, and struggled to keep her emotions in check. She deliberately stared toward the window. "Right. You don't want to miss your plane."

His expression miserably torn, he kissed her cheek, grabbed his suitcase and left.

Courtney fumed afterward. How dare Mark leave her, especially when she was in the middle of such a mess? Yes, he clearly had a crisis brewing with his business ventures at home, but couldn't he have anticipated this before he'd agreed to take on the children? Now, thanks to him, the entire responsibility had fallen on her shoulders, and at a time when she was ill-prepared to deal with it.

But she tried not to show her hurt feelings to the children—cheerfully playing with them, feeding them, bathing them, and getting them to bed. But in the lonely evening hours, tears once again threatened to come. She realized that Mark's leaving was causing her more distress than all her other problems.

Mark was her husband and had become an important part of her life, whether she liked it or not. Much as she fought it, he endeared himself to her more each day. Now, suddenly, he was gone—his smile, his laughter, his kisses, his teasing. There was a big void in her life, in her heart, a void that she hadn't expected to feel.

She missed Mark. Damn him to hell, she really missed him.

* * *

Sitting in the plane over the mid-Atlantic, Mark found he was missing Courtney. He would have given his eye-teeth not to have to return to London right now. But his companies had been too long neglected, and financial disaster clearly loomed if he failed to take charge again. In particular, he couldn't lose Billingham's to a hostile takeover bid. He owed that much to his father's memory.

He knew he had disappointed Courtney. He didn't want her to think he'd be one of those cavalier husbands who disappeared whenever a crisis arose or responsibilities became too heavy. But she must think that now.

On the other hand, this emergency had also brought their dilemma into sharper focus. How *would* they juggle all the responsibilities of their careers, and a family, too? These last couple of days with the children had demonstrated to him how important and time-consuming such responsibilities would be. Right now, he didn't know how things could work between him and Courtney unless one of them made some sacrifices. Should Courtney give up her career? Should he give up his? Should they live in the States, or in England?

Were they both too strong-willed to make any compromises on this at all? Again he recalled Courtney's accusing him of taking charge of her, of insisting on having things his way, of not accepting her the way she was. He wanted to see her as an equal, to be fair and share decisions with her, but perhaps he was spoiled in that regard. Like her, he was used to living independently and making all his own choices. And he was so accustomed to his career, to carrying the weight of responsibilities left him by his father, that he wasn't sure he could live without that, either.

Yet he expected her to do just that.

That put the two of them at loggerheads, and he was so afraid of losing her. But most of all he missed her more than he could bear.

Chapter Twenty-nine

For Courtney the balance of the week passed in a flurry of busy days, and the torture of lonely nights. Thank heaven, Vanessa was able to step in to baby-sit with Brittany and Joshua during the day so Courtney could attend to things at the office. However, she, her staff and the private detectives BBB hired made no progress in investigating the instances of industrial espionage. Thank heavens they had stopped, at least for the moment.

The day after Mark left, Wally Gilchrist departed the company, with no more fanfare than a last-minute luncheon Courtney had catered in the conference room. Bidding Wally farewell and noting the smirk on his face, Courtney hoped that he'd been behind the tampering, after all, and that the incidents would end with his departure.

She also couldn't help noting that the lull had occurred while Mark was out of the country, and in a moment of doubt she again wondered if he might be involved. But would he really stoop to criminal conduct in order to force her out of her job? She tended to believe he possessed a lot more integrity than that.

Courtney was able to make progress in other areas, meeting with the lawyers and mortgage bankers regarding their plans to go public. Her evenings were spent with the children, and she enjoyed them tremendously. Fortunately, by the second night, she and the kids had their routine established, and now Joshua and Brittany were asleep by eight or so each evening. But that left Courtney with the rest of the night to spend thinking about Mark. She just hadn't counted on missing him so much. She hadn't *wanted* to miss him—or to need him so much. It had just happened, and now she was left feeling vulnerable.

Late on Thursday night she was dozing off when her phone rang. She grabbed the receiver and mumbled sleepily, "Hello?"

"Hello, darling. Did I wake you?"

Instantly she was wide awake. "Mark. Is that you?"

"Yes, of course it is. Sorry if I woke you. I'm at my flat watching the sunrise over the Thames, and I was just wishing you could be here to share it with me."

Feeling a lump in her throat, she murmured, "How sweet."

"How are things there? I've been very worried about you."

"Well, Vanessa was available to pinch-hit with the kids, so I've been able to go to the office."

"Thank heaven. How are Brit and Joshie?"

Courtney felt touched that Mark already had his pet names for them. "Just fine."

"And you? Feeling okay?"

"Never better."

"Any progress on your investigation?"

"No, but at least there have been no more incidents. How about you? How are things there?"

"Well, I've managed to ward off the takeover and patch up several other matters, but I'm not sure I can continue to be away so long in the future."

Courtney gritted her teeth. "I see."

"Guess we'll have to talk about that when I get back."

"Yes. Guess we will." She hesitated, then asked, "When will that be?"

His voice lowered an octave. "Do you miss me, Courtney?"

"Well . . ."

"Because I miss you terribly, darling."

His words all but melted her, made her yearn to throw caution to the winds and admit how lonely she was, too. Then she remembered the predicament he had left her in. "You still haven't answered my question."

He sighed. "I'm taking an overnight flight on Friday, which means I should be back by mid-Saturday."

"Oh. Guess I'll see you then."

"Will the children be back with their parents by then?"

"Yes. Carla and Jason should pick them up Friday evening."

"I'll miss seeing them. I've presents for them both."

"They miss you. All Brittany talks about is her Mark."

"How sweet." He paused. "Courtney, when I get back . . . could we go off somewhere together Saturday night, just the two of us? Talk things over?"

"You mean spend the night away?"

"Yes."

"And you *seriously* think we'd talk?"

He chuckled. "I'm trying to be high-minded about this."

"Why do I doubt that?"

"Will you go away with me, Courtney?"

She sighed. "Let me think about it."

"Okay, but while you're thinking, pack a bag."

"Overconfident, aren't you?"

"Perhaps. See you on Saturday, then." He hesitated, then added. "Love you."

Taken aback, Courtney replied, "I-I'll see you then."

Hanging up, she felt shaken. If sleep had proven elusive before, it would be impossible now! Mark had said he loved her. Well, not exactly. He'd said "Love you," not quite "I love you." Still, it had been thrilling, frightening, touching—and the most sexy thing he'd ever said to her.

He'd said he missed her. He wanted to go away with her. Just the two of them alone. . . . Whatever was she going to do? She missed him desperately, too. How could she hide that from him? How would she resist him when he returned? They might still know eventual heartache, for his absence more than demonstrated the long-term challenges they would face.

At his loft in St. Katherine's Dock, Mark hung up the phone and gazed out at the sunrise painting the Thames a tawny gold. He was filled with tenderness. These last days had been frantically busy but also wretchedly lonely without Courtney, and his heart was filled with warmth now that he'd spoken to her.

She had sounded sleepy—and lonely. Or so he hoped. Did she miss him as much as he missed her?

And he'd finally admitted the feelings in his heart. He loved her. Yet when he'd made his declaration, she'd seemed not to react at all. Was she still angry that he'd left her in a bind with the children? He must make that up to her.

How he wished he'd been there with her when he'd

said the words, to see her reaction, to look into her eyes as he made love to her. He would be there soon. And soon, he prayed, they would be one again.

Saturday afternoon, Courtney was as nervous as a cat, waiting for Mark to come home. Even though she still had doubts about their marriage, she couldn't wait to touch him and hold him again. She straightened her apartment, took a bubble bath, primped for more than an hour, then dressed in green slacks and a matching, curve-hugging sweater.

When her doorbell rang at three-thirty, she literally ran across the room and flung open the door.

Holding a bouquet of roses in his hands, Mark stood there dressed in wrinkled khakis and a rumpled blue shirt, looking exhausted, slightly bleary-eyed, and unshaven. But never had he appeared more beautiful to her—especially when his eyes lit with love and tenderness at the sight of her.

"Mark," she whispered.

"Darling—you look so beautiful."

He was barely inside, the door shut behind him, when he pulled her into his arms and kissed her passionately. The roses fell in a heap on the floor nearby. Courtney moaned in delight, loving the taste of his warm lips, not at all minding the rub of his whiskers. His arms felt so warm and strong about her, and his male scent aroused her desires.

After a moment they broke apart to breathe; then he buried his face in her throat. "I missed you so much."

His mouth felt heavenly against her soft skin. "Me, too."

"Forgive me for leaving you in such a pickle?"

"You're here now."

"Yes. I'm here."

When abruptly he pulled her close and kissed her more intimately, Courtney knew precisely what he had in mind, and she knew she was powerless to resist. He lifted her into his arms and with quick strides crossed over to the couch. He laid her down and gently covered her body with his own. His gaze burned into hers, and the warm weight of him was sheer ecstasy.

His touch was bold as he hiked up her sweater, undid the clasp on her bra, and buried his face between her breasts. With a hoarse cry, Courtney thrust her fingers into his hair. He flicked his tongue teasingly all over her breasts, then suckled at nipples that were already tender from her pregnancy. Tears sprang to Courtney's eyes as desire and love flooded her deeply. She was losing control with Mark again, and there was no way to stop it. She had missed him so much, and she needed him now with a fierceness that was all-consuming, that hurt with its intensity. If he wasn't inside her soon, she felt she would die.

Fingers trembling, she fumbled at his trousers. His response was immediate as he seized her mouth in a devouring kiss. She was amazed at how quickly he tugged off her own slacks and panties. Then he was inside her, deeply, greedily inside her, thick and hot just as she wanted him.

With a groan, he pulled back and gazed down into her eyes. "God, how I missed you."

"Me, too. So much." Courtney could barely gasp out the words. She hauled him closer and kissed him deeply, while lifting her hips to take more of him. . . .

*　　*　　*

Afterward, they cuddled together on the couch, both slightly dazed.

"I hope I didn't hurt you," he said, nuzzling her temple.

Her hand roved down his muscular thigh. "No, I'm fine."

"Are you?"

His hand stroked her lower belly, and she wondered if he were searching for evidence of their child. All at once she found this unbearably sexy. She took his hand and guided it slightly lower. "There, Mark."

"There what?" he teased.

"There's our child," she told him almost shyly. "Run your fingers along there, and you can feel the outline of my uterus rising up."

He stroked her gently, then grinned with pride. "So I can. *Our* child." He leaned over and kissed the spot. "Hello, there, little one."

"You think he hears you?"

Mark glanced up at her face. "He?"

"Or she."

He nodded. "Yes, I think he hears me. You know, I meant what I said on the phone."

Heart pounding, she gazed at him breathlessly. "About what?"

"About our getting away. Why don't you and I drive up to Central City for the night?"

"You mean stay at a hotel together?"

He chuckled. "After what we just shared, a thoroughly shocking suggestion, my love."

"Mark, be serious."

"I am. We need to talk."

"Why do I sense that's not what's *really* on your mind?"

He rolled her beneath him and spoke huskily. "Don't worry, love. There'll be plenty of that, too."

"I'm not wor—" But the rest was lost in his drowning kiss, and her own moan of pleasure as his body claimed hers once more.

Chapter Thirty

Sitting beside Mark in his car, Courtney wondered what on earth she was doing. Throwing caution to the winds, that was for sure. Her husband looked far too appealing, especially with his fresh clothing and clean shave; before they'd left her apartment, he'd showered and changed while she had packed a bag.

What had happened to her caution, her resolve? For weeks she had scolded herself that she must take things slowly with Mark, work out their problems before they made love again. But an hour ago she had rushed into his arms and torn his clothes off. Now she was going off with him for what would certainly be a lovers' tryst. Even though he had argued that they must get away to talk, she had no doubt that they would spend almost all of the next twenty-four hours in bed together.

The setting was certainly both dramatic and romantic, as Mark wound the car through stately rock canyons carved through tall majestic mountains topped with snow and ringed by mists. The mountains wore the lush green coat of full-blown summer. Along the roadside delicate wildflowers blossomed and yucca blooms spiked toward the heavens; horned larks and bluebirds soared about, while in the valleys, near sparkling streams, muledeer munched on green grasses. The setting was awe-inspiring and made Courtney feel as though many of her current problems were very small. . . .

Sitting across from his wife, Mark wondered what Courtney was thinking. Her lovely face held a curious expression—part perplexity, part fascination with the landscape rolling by. Making love with her earlier had been beautiful and humbling. He wanted to feel she was truly his now. But he was realistic enough to know that the physical intimacy had hardly resolved all their problems. He was deeply concerned for her, for their child, for their marriage. They might be together now, but they faced so many stumbling blocks.

"Are you all right, dear?" he asked her. "You know, I hadn't thought of our going high up into the mountains with respect to your pregnancy. Should we be concerned?"

"No. I've lived around these mountains all my life, and my doctor says I'm healthy as a horse."

"You're familiar with Central City, then?"

"Sure. We used to go there for excursions when I was little. By the time I was in college, the casinos were established, so I used to go gambling there with friends."

"Misbehaving, eh?"

"Blowing off some steam."

"I've been to Central City once before," he admitted. "Grandfather took me there when the two of us went trout fishing. We stayed at a charming bed-and-breakfast on the outskirts of town. If it's still in operation, I'm hoping we can stay there tonight."

"You and your romantic cottage getaways."

"You seemed to enjoy Mackinac well enough."

A slow smile pulled at her mouth. "Yes," she admitted. "I did."

"I do like staying at places with character. Traveling as much as I do, I find 'world class' hotels grow bland and predictable after a while."

A few moments later the town of Central City appeared before them, a collection of historic homes and old buildings nestled in a high mountain pass. Mark gestured toward a glitzy complex of buildings off the roadway. "Aside from the addition of the casino, the town hasn't changed much since I was last here. Let's see if I can remember the way to that B & B."

He turned onto a narrow sidestreet flanked by charming Queen Anne–style cottages, then stopped the car before a two-story Victorian house painted a muted lavender with white trim. Pointing toward a sign in the front yard that read, "The Lavender Blossom Bed-and-Breakfast," he announced, "Look, it's still there."

"Indeed it is," murmured Courtney. She stared at the ornate edifice. With wraparound verandas curling about both stories, beautifully carved pillars and porch railings, and gleaming windows hung with Cape Cods, the setting could not have been more charming. A gaslight beckoned in the yard, pointing the way toward fern-lined steps leading to cozy porch rockers and rattan chairs.

"You're pleased?" he asked.

"It looks delightful."

Sporting a proud grin, Mark hopped out his side of the car, hurried around and opened her door. As he escorted her through the gate and into the yard, Courtney could smell the delightful scents of roses, blooming lavender, and freshly mown grass.

Before they even reached the house, the front door opened and a smiling elderly woman appeared. "Are you Mr. Billingham?"

As Courtney glanced, puzzled, at Mark, he replied, "Yes, ma'am. And you must be Libbie Walters."

The slender gray-haired woman in a flower-printed dress and apron moved toward them on the porch. "Indeed. Your room is all ready for you, sir."

"Jolly splendid."

As Mark led Courtney up the steps, she turned to him mutinously. "You already had this planned!"

"Guilty as charged. I wanted to surprise you, so I called the lady from the plane."

"You were being pretty darn presumptuous."

He raised an eyebrow and grinned mischievously. "You mean you're not going to call me hopelessly romantic again?"

Courtney bit her tongue, tempted to do just that.

Their room was gorgeous, airy and large, with a polished wooden floor and several large windows offering a mountain view. A king-size brass bed dominated the space, while an alcove with a comfortable sofa and huge bay window invited leisure sitting and nature viewing. But the bathroom was the best of all. Almost as large as the bedroom, it had a matching wood floor, plush white rugs, both a shower and a huge bathtub with a jacuzzi.

Turning back toward the room, Courtney saw Mark staring at her. "Nice plumbing."

He only chuckled. "Want to go exploring while we still have some light?"

"Sure."

The Great Baby Caper

Grabbing jackets, they left the cottage and strolled hand-in-hand through the charming old town, which in many ways still resembled a mining town of the late nineteenth century. They marveled at the ornate store-fronts, toured the Teller House Museum, and stopped in at the "Face Bar" to see the famous "Face on the Barroom Floor" that had been painted as a practical joke on a traveling actor who had recited the poem there. Afterward they dined on prime rib at a nearby restaurant. They said little during dinner, but the tension in the air was palpable.

Over cheesecake, Mark suddenly snapped his fingers. "You know, I almost forgot." He retrieved a small velvet box from his jacket pocket and handed it to her.

Courtney fingered the box. "Mark, you shouldn't have."

"Nonsense, open it. You deserve something nice after I left you in the lurch that way. Besides, how could I go to London and not bring you back a souvenir?"

She opened the box, only to gasp at the sight of a two-carat, brilliant round diamond, dangling on a gold chain, flanked by equally dazzling solitaire earrings.

"My God, *this* is a souvenir?"

"A small token of my esteem."

"Mark!" she cried. "You're talking a small fortune in diamonds here."

"Seeing the expression on your face makes it all worthwhile."

"Mark, I can't—"

He clasped her hand and pinned her with a look of intense pleading. "Don't, Courtney. Put them on, please."

His words proved as unaccountably sexy as the diamonds themselves. Unable to resist, she placed the pendant around her neck, removed her modest pearl earrings and put on the matching diamonds.

Mark whistled. "Wow!"

Courtney grinned. "I feel like that scandalous Baby Doe Tabor the tour guide told us about today. Didn't she say Baby Doe's husband bought her a diamond necklace purportedly owned by Queen Isabella of Spain?"

"Baby Doe Tabor could not hold a candle to you." He lifted his wineglass and spoke solemnly. "To us, darling."

She clicked her water glass against his wine goblet. "To us."

After they toasted, he leaned close and whispered, "I can't wait to get you alone and see you with nothing on but those diamonds."

His words so rattled her that when she tried to set down her glass, she tipped it over. Mark only laughed wickedly and called for the waiter.

When they arrived back in their room, Courtney was charmed to see that a bottle of champagne in an ice bucket awaited them on the coffee table in the alcove. Mark caught her hand. "Come on, darling, let's go look at the stars."

His husky tone alerted her that the stars would no doubt be given short shrift tonight. "Mark, you're tempting me with champagne. And after I was so good, not having wine at dinner."

"I believe the bottle is a gift from our hostess," he explained. "Tell you what—I'll pour myself a glassful, and you can steal just a sip or two."

"Okay, you've got a deal."

They sat side by side in the cozy alcove, sipping from Mark's glass and gazing out at the beautiful starlit mountain pass. After a moment Mark set down the glass and turned to Courtney. The intense look in his eyes made clear his intentions and only further inflamed her wayward senses. He leaned over, taking her lips in a teasing, fluttering kiss, until, with a low cry, she threw her arms around his neck and kissed him back hungrily. Meanwhile his hands caught the hem of her sweater and began pulling it upward.

"Mark." The word was a moan.

He pulled the sweater up over her head, then ran his fingertips over her bare arm. "My God, your skin is like satin." He kissed her shoulder and touched the solitaire dangling between her breasts. "I told you I wanted to see you with only those diamonds on." He reached for the clasp on her bra. "You're not cold, are you, darling?"

"I-I could be," she managed.

"I won't allow it." He undid her bra and caught her bare breasts in his hands, kneading them gently. "How's that?"

Feeling his wonderful hands on her flesh, Courtney was no longer cold but hot, very hot. "Um—nice."

He pushed her down, and she felt his hot mouth taking her aching nipple. She cried out.

She heard his grunt of satisfaction. "I'm going to undress you now."

"Are you asking me or telling me?"

A low chuckle escaped him. "Do I need to ask?"

Clearly he didn't, for Courtney was way beyond resisting as he removed her bra, then unzipped her slacks, pulling them off, followed by her panties. By now, Courtney was panting, covered with gooseflesh. Already heat pulsated inside her just at the thought of him touching her intimately.

He gazed down at her naked body, the winking diamonds. "My God, you're lovely." His hand slid between her thighs, opening them, his finger stroking the nest of curls between.

Courtney writhed, the aching need pushing harder, deeper, throbbing insistently. "Mark . . . my heaven."

"I want to show you just how much I missed you," he rasped.

"But you've already done that."

"Hastily, yes. But not like this."

He was right. Not like this. Tears burned Courtney's eyes when Mark leaned over and kissed her there. The need inside her grew explosive, became sweetly unbearable.

"Look at the stars, darling," he directed.

She did, gazing at the glorious heavens while Mark's lips worked their potent magic, kissing, caressing. When his tongue began to explore, touching her deeply and boldly, she cried out ecstatically, and his hands grabbed her thighs to hold her still.

"Mark, it's so beautiful."

"Mmm." He lingered a long moment, than at last slid up her body. He entered her deeply, smiling at her sound of raw joy. "Are you looking at the stars?"

"No, at you," she sobbed back. "Always at you."

His mouth ravenously took hers and his strokes quickened. She caught him closer and dug her fingernails into his spine, pleasure inundating her again and again as her body urged him home.

For a long time afterward, he cradled her in his arms and kissed her. Deeply moved and wanting to give him the same ecstasy he'd given her, she leaned over and took him in her mouth. She gloried at the feel of him, hard and pulsing, and flicked her tongue over him. He pleaded but she was relentless, slowly tasting and torturing him. At last he pulled her on top of him, plunged into her, and climaxed quickly inside her. Afterward he wouldn't let her go and they rocked there, adrift in passion, for hours.

Finally, late the next morning, they had their talk. They hiked halfway up a mountain and sat on boulders looking down at the town. The morning was sweet and cool; a hawk circled in the clear skies.

Courtney noted the look of tense preoccupation on Mark's face. There was so much that was good between them, so much emotion and passion. But there were also the problems—partly practical, partly much more personal.

"All right, Mark," she said at last. "We've postponed this long enough. Talk."

He sighed. "I suppose you're right. I guess I've avoided this because . . ."

"It could threaten us?"

His nod was sober. "Yes. I mean, I hope it won't. But yes."

"Go on. Be frank."

He picked up a twig and aimlessly toyed with it. "Courtney, while I was gone, I thought a lot about our relationship. It's not true, as you seem to think, that I'm opposed to your career on principle. Indeed, back when I first met you through those videos, I thought you'd make the perfect executive wife, that we could both have our careers and a good marriage, as well. I don't think I was being very realistic then."

"Go on."

He gazed into her eyes. "Ever since I met you, I've found I've wanted more. You were no longer a distant fantasy, but a real woman I needed in my life. Then once you became pregnant, I realized my original ideal of our relationship could never work. The baby changed everything."

"Yes, it did."

"Now . . . I just don't see how we can make it without some changes. I've neglected my responsibilities in London and don't think I can continue doing so. You're loaded up with work here. With our baby on the way . . . something has to give."

"What do you suggest?"

He regarded her with longing. "If only you'd come back with me to London."

Courtney shook her head. "You mean give up my dreams and ambitions, make all the sacrifices myself."

"But Courtney, you're going to become a mother."

"Thanks for clueing me in, Mark," she replied with some sarcasm. "And you're going to become a father. I intend this to be an equal opportunity marriage."

"Meaning what?"

"Meaning, why don't you give up your businesses, settle here, become an American citizen, and take care of our child while I work?"

"Courtney, that's totally unrealistic."

"And it's *realistic* to ask me to make the same concessions?"

He fell silent.

"I suppose we could try both," she suggested after a moment.

"What do you mean?"

"Well, we could split our lives between here and London."

"And shuttle a small child back and forth?"

She gave a groan. "Okay, it's not a perfect solution. I'm only trying to offer options."

He reached out, took her hand, and braved a smile. "I suppose we'll both get a taste of bi-continental marriage in coming months, since I will have to travel to London often. Will you come with me?"

She bit her lip. "I'll try to, if I can. With all that's going on at corporate, it won't be easy."

He scowled. "Courtney, are you sure—"

"Sure about what?"

"Sure you're being forthright about your feelings? That deep down, you're not still angry at me—and especially at my grandfather?"

Courtney took a long moment to steady herself. "Mark, you still don't get it. The real problem is, I'm the only one being asked to do the giving. I don't see you offering to radically change your life as you seem to expect me to do. And yes, I suppose I am still mad at your grandfather, but that has no bearing on our problems."

"Doesn't it?" he countered. "Then answer me this: If Grandfather's behavior has no bearing on our problems, then why are you still working for him?"

"To further my career."

"And not to nurse a grudge? Not to win against him?"

She hesitated a long moment, then expelled a deep sigh. "Okay, maybe a little. But that's hardly my sole reason for having a career."

He sadly shook his head. "Frankly, Courtney, this is why I've avoided this discussion. I knew nothing would be resolved. I'm going to lose you, aren't I?"

Hearing the pain in his voice, Courtney was filled with regret, with compassion for him, and concern for their marriage. "Mark, I think you're forgetting something.

We haven't been together that long. In many ways, we're still strangers."

"Are we?" His reached out and touched her face. "Well, this stranger loves you."

Feeling equally torn, she whispered back, "So you say."

"You don't believe me."

"Mark, I want to," she said miserably. "But the truth is, no one falls in love as quickly as you claim to have. Infatuation maybe, but not real love. You can't really love a woman until you get to know her, come to respect what *she's* about, and share yourself on the deepest level."

"We've shared."

"To a degree, we have. But you haven't really revealed your deepest thoughts and feelings—about losing your parents, about why you think you fell for me through watching videos. And about why you seem so determined to change and control me now."

"We have a long way to go, don't we?"

Staring at his anguished face, Courtney wished she could somehow magically make things right, but she couldn't, for she was far from sure it was possible.

Chapter Thirty-one

"Mrs. Billingham, you must get over here at once," exclaimed the frantic female manager at the east Denver store. "We have a major problem."

On Monday afternoon, sitting at her desk with the phone at her ear, Courtney sighed. "Can you elaborate, please?"

"You'll have to see this to believe it."

Courtney laughed. "That's what everyone else has said."

"Well, I've got videotape, and *believe me,* you've got to see this to—"

"Right, okay," Courtney interrupted wearily. "I'm on my way."

Hanging up, Courtney hesitated a moment, then dialed Mark's cell-phone number. He answered tensely. "Yes?"

"Are you busy?"

His tone softened. "Hi, darling. I'm on a conference call with three of my staff in London, but it can wait."

"Oh, never mind, then."

"Courtney, tell me what's up."

"Well, there's a problem at the east Denver store, and I'm on my way there now."

"Give me the address, and I'll meet you."

"But your call—"

"It can wait, Courtney."

She gave him directions, feeling grateful that he was willing to drop everything for her.

Twenty minutes later she walked up to the store in the strip mall to find a "closed" sign posted. After she knocked, the young female manager, Nickie Keenig, let her in, greeting her with a nervous smile. "I'm so glad you're here, Mrs. Billingham."

"Thanks, Nickie." Courtney stepped inside, only to gasp at the sight of the store. It was a complete shambles. Racks had been overturned, merchandise pulled down off shelves, packages of toys ripped open and their contents scattered everywhere.

"What happened?" she demanded.

"As I said, you'll have to—"

"Right. See it to believe it."

"The security tape is in my office."

The two women turned at the sound of a British-accented voice. "What in the name of Babel is going on here?"

Courtney smiled at the sight of Mark, looking very dapper in his beige, long-sleeved shirt and brown slacks. She realized she felt stronger now that he had come to join her. "Mark, come on in. This is the store manager, Nickie Keenig. Nickie, this is my husband, Mark."

Nickie extended her hand. "Pleased to meet you."

"Likewise," he said, shaking her hand.

"Nickie and I were about to go view the video of this

newest catastrophe," Courtney went on. "Want to join us?"

"Indeed."

The three hurried to the back room, where Nickie ran the video on a small TV screen. Black-and-white surveillance footage floated by, at first revealing a store operating normally, with a few mothers shopping, some with small children.

"That's shortly after we opened this morning," Nickie explained. "Then this."

Nickie fast-forwarded the tape, then started up again at a point where, amazingly, ten small children of various shapes and sizes ran screaming into the store, followed by two adult women. The youngsters wore matching T-shirts, caps, and shorts, the women casual summer dresses. Courtney noted that the children's T-shirts sported writing on the fronts and backs, but she couldn't actually make out any words. Several of the kids carried foam rubber bats and balls; all created an incredible racket, shouting or howling Indian yells as they stormed the store, sending customers fleeing in their wake.

Courtney watched flabbergasted as the group went to work. Several began swinging bats at one another; four others threw themselves down on the floor and staged temper tantrums, their little arms and legs thrashing wildly, while the rest of the crew began pillaging shelves and dumping over racks. Nickie and several store clerks tried to intervene, racing about and waving their arms, to no avail. Soon more horrified customers fled the store with their own children. Meanwhile, the adults directing the small troupe kept applauding, cheering, and otherwise egging the children on.

"I can't believe I'm seeing this!" Courtney exclaimed.

"Who are those people, and what is written on the children's T-shirts?"

"They're the Brat Brigade," Nickie explained.

"The *what* Brigade?"

"Brat Brigade." Nickie motioned at the screen. "If you'll look there, you'll see me confronting the adults, and one of the women waving papers in my face."

"What papers?"

"She claimed they're a theatrical troupe, and they were paid by corporate to stage a performance at this store."

"You're joking," interjected Mark, who appeared every bit as baffled as Courtney.

"That's what I told the woman, sir. I also threatened to call security." Again Nickie motioned to the screen. "As you can see, that's when both women gathered up the kids and left. One of them even had the audacity to scold me for having my facts wrong, while the other one bragged that they had two more stores to visit this morning, anyway."

"Two more stores?" cried Mark and Courtney in unison.

Before Nickie could respond, her desk phone rang. She grabbed the receiver. "Hello? Oh, hi, Roger. My heavens, you say they're there now? Well, I have Mrs. Billingham here with her husband, and I'll tell them." Lowering the receiver, Nickie said, "It's Roger Cambridge. The troupe is at the south Denver store now. And there's a news crew there filming them, too."

"A news crew?" cried Courtney, aghast. "Tell Roger to detain them all, and we'll be right there."

"You bet."

Courtney and Mark rushed out of the store and into

the parking lot. "My car okay?" he asked Courtney, taking her arm.

"Fine."

"Do you have any idea who might have done this?"

"I haven't a clue."

Mark quickly drove them to their next stop. When the two stepped inside the south Denver store, it was only to find it in a similar state of disarray, with only Roger Cambridge present; the poor man stood helplessly surveying the carnage. Courtney introduced Mark to Roger, then asked him where everyone had gone.

Roger shook his head. "I'm sorry, Courtney. Nickie passed on your order to detain everyone, but I'm afraid I couldn't convince that troupe of hellions, their handlers, or the news people, to stick around."

"That's okay, Roger. I'm sure you tried."

"Do you have security footage?" Mark asked.

Roger nodded. "This way."

He took them to his office and showed them the security video of the troupe creating general chaos, this time with a reporter and cameraman covering the disaster from every angle.

Courtney shook her head. "Any idea who alerted that news crew?"

"I think one of the women said she had," replied Roger.

"But why would they do any of this?" asked Mark.

"Both women claimed they'd been hired by corporate," replied Roger with a skeptical air. "But they left before I could verify anything."

"Any idea where they went?" Courtney asked.

"Well, I heard one of the leaders mention the Pueblo store to the other."

Mark and Courtney looked at each other and simultaneously cried, "Let's go!"

While Mark drove them toward Pueblo, Courtney called the office to alert her entire staff about the new assaults. She also spoke with Janis Jacobs, asking her to run interference with the local news channel, to try to convince them not to run the piece they'd filmed at the south Denver store, even though Courtney realized her chances of success were slim to none.

An hour and a half later, when she and Mark rushed through the doors to the Pueblo store, they at last caught the troupe in the act! Stopping in her tracks, Courtney spotted several children in "Brat Brigade" T-shirts running around howling like banshees, while others were busy looting merchandise and dumping over racks. A three-year-old boy was using a crib mattress as a trampoline, squealing gleefully as he bounced up and down, while a five-year-old girl broke new speed records, careening past Mark and Courtney pushing a baby carriage crammed full of three screeching toddlers.

There were no customers to be seen, and the young assistant manager, Chris Whitman, was chasing several of the terrors or waving his arms. Off to the side Courtney recognized the two women leaders of the troupe whom they had seen in the videos; again, both were playing the role of cheerleader, urging on the rowdy bunch with bravos and applause.

Even as Courtney and Mark stared flabbergasted at the scene, Mark was hit in the head by a foam rubber ball. At once he stuffed two fingers in his mouth and whistled, loud. "Hey, you little hooligans, I've got an expectant mother here!" he shouted in a voice that brooked no nonsense.

All of the children froze in their tracks to stare at

Mark. Courtney shot him a chiding look for blurting out news of her pregnancy.

Chris Whitman rushed toward Courtney. "Mrs. Billingham, wow, I'm so glad you're here! As you can see we've been invaded, and, er . . ." Abruptly he broke into a boyish grin. "Are you expecting?"

"Never mind that," Courtney snapped back. "What's going on here, Chris?"

"Ma'am, I wish I knew," he answered.

Meanwhile the two women, both sporting frowns, marched toward Mark and Courtney. Courtney noted that one was middle-aged, plump, and wore glasses; the other was younger, dark-haired and sharp-featured. The children, still subdued from Mark's scolding, began to gather behind their leaders.

"Is there a problem?" the younger woman asked Courtney.

"Darn right there's a problem," Courtney answered. "I'm Courtney Billingham, CEO of Bootle's Baby Bower. What on earth do you people think you're doing, terrorizing three of our stores this way?"

"Terrorizing?" gasped the woman. "Why, I'll have you know we're a perfectly legitimate theatrical troupe, organized by Ms. Lucille Deaton here, a prominent psychotherapist." She pointed to her middle-aged companion.

The other woman spoke up archly. "I'm Ms. Deaton, and as to your absurd accusations, I happen to believe that children who act out their hostilities in a safe environment are more emotionally healthy overall. That's why May and I organized The Brat Brigade to give our youngsters an opportunity to work out their anger and aggression. We perform at birthday parties and other celebrations." She paused to grin. "As a matter of fact, other children just love watching The Brats perform. It makes them feel empowered."

"Well, good for you," Courtney replied sarcastically. "That still doesn't explain what you are doing here. You have no right whatsoever to ransack our stores, disrupt our trade and scare off our customers this way."

The woman named May gave a gasp. "But we were hired by your corporate special promotions coordinator."

"You were not!" Courtney shot back.

"Well, I never!" Her expression outraged, May dug in her bag and pulled out some folded papers. "I have here written authorization from your corporate offices. We received that along with the legal release we demanded—and a cashier's check for five thousand dollars to cover our services this morning."

"Five thousand dollars?" cried Mark.

Lucille Deaton drew herself up with pride. "You heard May correctly. The Brats may be obnoxious, but they don't come cheap."

"My God," Mark muttered, scratching his head.

"This whole thing is ridiculous!" declared Courtney. "Let me see those papers!"

"Of course." May handed them over.

Courtney quickly perused the documents and voiced her thoughts aloud. "My Lord, these are both printed on our company letterhead, meaning they must have been forged—"

"Forged?" cried Ms. Deaton.

"Yes, forged, by someone with access to our offices. Let me see, the first is from Anna Edsel, Corporate Promotions Coordinator." She glanced at May. "There's no such person working for us. How did she contact you?"

"Ms. Edsel telephoned us," May replied, "making all

the necessary arrangements. Then she messengered over the letters you hold, along with our payment."

Courtney was still staring, stunned, at the first letter, and began reading parts aloud. " 'As agreed via telephone, you are hereby authorized to perform at the three stores designated. . . . Your payment is enclosed, along with the required legal release. . . .' " Quickly she turned to the second document. "You are hereby released from any and all liability that may result as a consequence of your performances . . . Sincerely, Thomas Cheatham, Chief Legal Officer, Bootle's Baby Bower." She glanced up. "He doesn't work for us, either. Didn't the 'Cheatham' tip you off at all?"

"No, not at all," answered May. "May I have the papers back?" She smiled tightly. "Just in case we face legal action from you nice folks."

Courtney hesitated. "May I make a copy first?" As May would have protested, she added, "Please don't worry, we're not going to sue you. We're a baby products company, after all."

"Very well," May conceded reluctantly.

Courtney asked Chris to make copies of the papers, and afterward returned the originals to the women. She was grateful when Mark briskly ushered everyone out the door. He and Courtney were leaving, too, when they all but collided with M. Billingham as he strode inside.

Glancing mystified at the store, he demanded, "Courtney, what in heaven's name is going on here? I called in to headquarters, and Mildred informed me about the latest assault on our enterprises. Three stores hit by these brats on wheels. I've never heard of anything so preposterous! How could you have allowed this to happen?"

Before Courtney could manage to reply, Mark spoke

up sharply. "Hello, Grandfather, it's jolly good to see you again. As for what has transpired here, my wife had nothing whatsoever to do with this, thank you."

Indignant, Courtney turned on her husband. "Look, Mark, I don't need you defending me."

"Aha," interjected M. Billingham with a superior look. "So you *are* responsible for this calamity, Courtney?"

"Of course not!"

The old man frowned fiercely. "Well, I'm beginning to suspect that marriage has softened your brain. You've clearly lost your killer instincts."

"I've lost nothing of the kind."

"Our product line has been tampered with, our stores buried in egg rolls—and now we're ransacked by these spawns of hell. If you were still performing up to snuff, you would have stopped this malarkey long before now. Well, if you can't put an end to this rein of terror, I'll find someone who will."

Courtney was all set to issue a retort when Mark again intervened, his voice cold with anger. "Sir, your attack on Courtney is totally unwarranted. Don't you ever speak to her that way again. You're addressing my wife, and the mother of my child."

M. Billingham's face went utterly blank. "Courtney's pregnant?" Abruptly, he broke into a delighted grin. "Why, what splendid news. And no wonder the little mother has lost charge of things."

Courtney could no longer contain her own outrage. "I've lost charge of nothing. And you, sir, are a male chauvinist pig." She spun about and exited the store.

"Ditto," snapped Mark, rushing after her, leaving a scowling M. Billingham to stare after them.

*　　*　　*

Mark caught up with Courtney in the parking lot and grabbed her arm, but at once she struggled to free herself from his grip. "Mark, let me go."

"Damn it, Courtney, don't be mad at me."

"Don't be mad when you spoke for me again?"

"Grandfather was totally out of line. No one speaks to my wife that way."

She spun about to face him, breathing hard. "Mark, I'm not your possession. I can stand up for myself. Furthermore, you had no right to tell M. Billingham about the baby."

He flung a hand outward. "Who would you have tell him and your family? The stork?"

She shot him a seething look. "That's not the point."

"Isn't it? Besides, he was bound to find out soon anyway, after I let the cat out of the bag back at the store."

"Right. Thanks so much for that, as well."

He grasped her by the shoulders. "How can you allow Grandfather to speak to you that way, and not quit on the spot?"

She lifted her chin. "Maybe because that's just what you want."

"So we're back to blaming me again. And you're keeping your job to spite me?"

"No. I'm keeping it because it's what I want."

"You want to work for a man who has no respect for you?"

Courtney took a deep breath. "Mark, you can't make him respect me. Only I can."

"Right. Then why do you need me?"

Courtney thought of replying, then bit her tongue.

Later when they entered Courtney's apartment, the tension between them remained thick. Glancing at his watch, Mark grabbed the remote from the coffee table and turned on the TV. "It's five o'clock. Want to see if the local news ran the piece?"

"Sure." Going into the kitchen to grab a glass of water, Courtney saw Mark seat himself on the couch. "Mark, I don't mind if you watch the news, but I'm not sure you should be staying here."

He shot to his feet. "Courtney, are you going to put me out like a naughty tomcat every time we have a little tiff?"

She was about to reply when she was distracted by a reporter's voice. Glancing at the grinning anchorman, she heard him say, "Our top story of the day: Who is terrorizing BBB, the Denver-based baby products company?"

Numbly Courtney went to sit beside Mark, and watched the news footage flash by. There was the Brat Brigade attacking their south Denver store, while a grinning young male reporter described their antics. A few times she caught Mark struggling not to laugh. Finally, at her wit's end, she grabbed the remote out of his hand and flipped off the TV.

He glanced at her sympathetically. "Too bad your PR person couldn't talk them out of running the piece."

"Try talking a reporter out of running anything. It's almost as frustrating as trying to reason with you."

"What do you mean by that crack?"

Courtney gazed at him narrowly. "You really don't want me working for BBB, do you, Mark?"

"I just feel it's a bit much, what with your pregnancy and all. And now all of these new frustrations have been added to the brew."

"You find all of this pretty funny, don't you?"

"Funny?"

"Admit you were struggling not to laugh over that news broadcast."

"Courtney, have mercy. The antics of the Brat Brigade are rather amusing."

"Well, I'm not laughing. In fact, I'm wondering . . ."

"What?"

She took a deep breath. "Mark, are you involved in this?"

He paled. "This? You mean the industrial espionage at BBB?"

"It all began when we moved back to Denver together. It stopped while you were gone in London, then started up again on your return."

He made a sound of disbelief. "I can't believe I'm hearing this."

"So you're telling me all of this is just a coincidence?"

"Yes. Damn right, I'm telling you."

"And you don't want me to leave the corporation?"

He sprang to his feet, facing her with eyes flashing. "Yes, I want you to leave. But do you honestly think I would resort to terrorizing my pregnant wife and the mother of my child just to get my way?"

Courtney fell silent, already regretting having accused him. It *was* far-fetched. But so was everything that had happened to her ever since she'd met Mark Billingham.

He continued speaking with an air of hurt. "Courtney, how could you mistrust me so?"

"I'm sorry, Mark, but you have to understand," she replied plaintively. "Men have always felt threatened by me—in my jobs, my relationships. And you seem so determined to speak for me, to take charge of me."

"But does that mean I'd stoop to such underhanded tactics? Haven't I demonstrated that I have more character than that? I should think you'd suspect Grandfather before me."

"Actually, I do suspect your grandfather."

He slowly shook his head. "Don't you trust anyone?"

"Well, maybe all that has happened to me doesn't inspire a lot of trust."

He snapped his fingers. "I knew it! You are still angry."

"Well, maybe I am."

His expression was one of keen disappointment. "Courtney, all along I've tried to have faith in us but now . . . I just don't know."

Courtney stared at him, feeling miserably torn. She knew she had hurt him, and she longed to make things right. But the truth was, she just didn't know, either.

They hardly spoke for the remainder of the evening. Finally Mark got up and walked toward the guest bedroom. "Guess I'll turn in."

Courtney couldn't take any more. She rushed over and grabbed his hand. "Please don't. I mean—don't sleep alone."

She watched his face, saw surprise, followed by joy and then suspicion. "Do you really think this will resolve things?" he asked sternly.

Courtney thrust herself into his arms. "I don't know. I don't care. I'm sorry we fought. Just kiss me, please?"

This time he didn't hesitate, crushing her closer. "Okay, darling. A gentleman never makes a lady wait."

He didn't. They barely made it to the bedroom.

Chapter Thirty-two

"All right—who's responsible for this?" Courtney demanded.

The next morning, she stood in the conference room at work, waving the bogus corporate authorization papers in the blank faces of half a dozen colleagues. After a very tense moment, her legal counsel, Milton Davies, cleared his throat. "Courtney, anyone could have forged those documents."

"Anyone working for us, you mean."

"Not necessarily. Anyone who has ever received a correspondence from us could have cloned our stationery."

Courtney glanced at the documents again. "Yes, you're right. Between scanners and desktop publishing software, it would be simple enough."

Lon Wilson frowned. "Don't you think it's time for us to involve the police? These incidents are becoming serious."

Courtney hesitated, then shook her head. "No, let's try to keep this in house. It's bad enough that the media is involved." She turned to Janis Jacobs. "How are we doing on that front? I noticed a blurb on us in the *Denver Times* this morning—basically a rehash of the television news story yesterday evening."

"Courtney, I was sorry I couldn't stop the local channel from running the piece. As you're aware, I wanted to keep a lid on this because I was afraid we'd be hit by copycats. But actually, the news coverage has been a blessing in disguise. The local papers and several other TV stations have picked up the story, and as a result traffic has increased at all our stores."

"Really?" asked Courtney.

"I spoke with Roger Cambridge right before this meeting, and he's already had two mothers come in today with their children, hoping to get free egg rolls."

As laughter erupted around the table, Courtney could only shake her head. "You mean there's actually an upside to our being targeted?"

"So it seems," replied Janis. "Several other managers have reported shoppers coming in hoping to catch some of the shenanigans. Of course most have made purchases, too."

"Amazing," murmured Courtney.

"In fact, I was thinking we could really turn this around to our advantage," Janis went on. "Enlist the public in finding the culprit."

"How on earth would we do that?" asked Gil Getz.

"Well, we could organize a contest to find the guilty party. We could put entry blanks in the stores, asking customers to guess who is terrorizing BBB. Those who guess the true culprit or culprits would be finalists for a drawing, with the prize being a thousand-dollar shopping spree at BBB. Of course we would need to offer smaller prizes for second and third places."

Lon Wilson whistled. "Hey, I like that idea. That could

be a couple of thou well spent, like a reward for turning in the perp."

"Exactly," said Janis.

"But couldn't this backfire if the public decides this is all just a stunt we staged to increase our business?" posed Milton Davies. "Especially if the terrorist turns out to be someone among us."

That comment spurred a moment of sober silence.

"It's a risk," Janis agreed.

"And what if the perpetrator is never found?" asked Courtney. "It seems unlikely that any customer could guess correctly. They aren't familiar with our operations."

"Yeah, and this terrorist has shown himself to be a pretty crafty individual so far," put in Al Gideon.

Courtney couldn't resist flashing a saccharine smile at Al. "Are you speaking from personal experience there?"

Before he could reply, Gil Getz snapped, "Yeah, Al and me, we engineered this whole scheme together. Everyone knows we're criminals at heart."

Courtney held up a hand. "Very well, gentlemen. I was only trying to add a bit of levity."

"No, Courtney, I think you were trying to accuse me," Al rejoined tensely.

Courtney resisted the urge to comment. "Janis, please continue."

"Well, Courtney, you're right that maybe no one will correctly guess the culprit, and maybe some will speculate that we're involved. But the contest could still significantly increase our store traffic and sales. I think it's worth the gamble. We'd need to put a time limit on it, of course. If no one correctly guesses the perp, or if he's never found, we'll just have a drawing for the winners."

"Sounds like a plan to me," agreed Courtney. "Janis,

could you get back to me when you have this fleshed out a little more?"

"Will do."

Courtney consulted her agenda. "Okay, then, let's move on. I want reports on the investigations all of you are doing. Lon, let's start with you and Milton. What have you heard from the private detectives?"

During the next half hour, Courtney listened to reports from each of her executives and learned the disappointing news that the private detectives had yet to find a successful lead, and that none of her staff had made any real progress in tracking the criminals, either. Though dispirited, she politely thanked everyone and adjourned the meeting.

In the hallway she ran across a frowning M. Billingham. "Well, Courtney, I see that on top of everything else, we got pilloried on the local news last night."

She felt her hackles rising. "Actually, Mr. Bootle, if you'd bothered to attend the meeting this morning, you'd know that the attacks on our stores have actually increased our traffic—and sales."

He raised a white brow. "Really? How very amusing. But this is a conservative company, Courtney. That's not how I want to expand our business."

Courtney gave an incredulous laugh. "This from the man who staged an Old West shootout at last year's convention, and an insane scavenger hunt at this year's?"

His expression softened to one of conciliation. "Courtney, I really didn't want to have another argument with you today."

Stunned by his show of humility, she replied, "Well, you could have fooled me."

"Actually, I've been meaning to offer you and Mark my sincere congratulations on your coming child."

"Thank you," she crisply replied. "Mark will be thrilled to hear it. Is there anything else?"

"Well, yes. Are you sure you're up to continuing with your duties now that you're expecting my great-grandchild—and especially considering all these assaults on our stores?"

"Don't worry, I'm on top of the espionage."

"Are you? Don't forget what I said—"

"Right. Resolve this, or I'm history."

He gave a groan. "Courtney, when I said those things, I had no idea you were—"

"In this delicate condition? Don't worry, I don't expect you to cut me any slack because of my pregnancy, Mr. Bootle."

"Courtney, I'm trying to extend an olive branch here," he went on with frustration. "The truth is, I really do think you and Mark suit each other well, and I've hoped from the outset that this marriage would be a great success. The boy needs it. He's been through a lot."

Courtney felt a stab of guilt. "I know what Mark's been through. And he's a fine person—I've never said otherwise."

"Well, I must say you're being most uncooperative toward me, even hostile."

"*I'm* being hostile?" She rolled her eyes. "You know, for a man who's supposed to be spending his retirement years trotting around the globe, you sure are in the office a lot these days. Every time one of these terrorist incidents occurs, you show up conveniently to give me the third degree. Makes me wonder how deeply you really are involved in this."

For once, instead of denying any connection, M. Billingham flashed her a cagey smile. "Well, you won't *really* know until you nab the culprit, will you, Courtney?"

Before she could challenge him further, he strode away. She watched him, openmouthed. Had her illustrious boss just admitted he was involved in sabotaging his own company?

Feeling at her wit's end, Courtney called Vanessa and invited her to lunch. The two women met in the coffee shop of a nearby hotel. Courtney told her friend about the latest incidents of industrial espionage—how they'd made no progress in tracking the responsible party, and how M. Billingham was blaming her for the incidents, while audaciously hinting that he might even be involved.

"Why, that old snake!" declared Vanessa afterward. "Talk about the guilty party pointing a finger! How on earth does Ham Bootle justify blaming *you* for the crimes of an industrial terrorist—who may even be Ham himself?"

Courtney sighed. "Well, it's all happening on my shift, or so he seems to believe. He says I'm losing control of our operations."

"The arrogant old ass. I could slap him senseless."

"He does have a point. The buck does stop with me."

"Assuming he isn't responsible."

"Agreed."

Vanessa frowned in concentration, tapping her polished fingernails on the tabletop. "I think you should have those P.I.'s you hired follow Ham around and get the goods on him."

Courtney mulled over the suggestion. "It's a thought, but . . . Vanessa, it's still his company. Whatever I do will get back to him."

"What does Mark think of his grandfather's trying to blame you?"

Courtney gave a dry laugh. "Actually, when Mark and I ran across Mr. Bootle at the south Denver store, Mark really lit into him, insisting his grandfather not treat his wife and the mother of his child that way."

Vanessa smirked. "So now Ham knows about the baby?"

"I think half the world knows by now. Mark announced my pregnancy to everyone at the store. The man must lose all sense of discretion when he's angry."

"My dear, you can't hope to keep it secret much longer."

"I know. I'm going to have to tell my family. I can't wait to hear all the whispers and snickering."

"Your family will snicker?"

Courtney ground her jaw. "They'll find it amusing. Courtney, the liberated career woman, becomes a little mother like the rest of her sisters."

"And you don't think heads will turn if the baby simply arrives six months after your wedding?"

"You're right." Courtney patted her stomach. "I'm already more than four months along. Pretty soon I'm going to be out of my regular clothes, and unable to hide it, anyway."

Vanessa stirred her tea. "How are you and Mark getting along?"

Courtney glanced away. "Well, there are still many of the same tensions between us."

"Still separate bedrooms?" Vanessa pressed.

"Vanessa," she scolded.

Vanessa clapped her hands. "Oh, I knew it! You're back together, aren't you?"

Courtney could only shake her head; Vanessa was better at cross examination than a killer attorney. "Well, yes, I guess we are. Mark has a way of growing on me.

And after he returned from London this last time—well, I just missed him so. We still fight, but—"

"Then you make up?"

Courtney grinned. "Yeah. That making up part . . . Wow."

Vanessa laughed in delight. "Why don't you just kiss old Ham good-bye and go live with Mark in merry old England?"

"*Vanessa.*" Courtney's expression revealed her misery. "What about what *I* want? My goals and ambitions? You're the last person who should be urging me to give up my life for Mark, as you did with Floyd."

Vanessa's mouth tightened into a frown. "But the truth of the matter is, I never loved Floyd as much as I suspect you love Mark. You must ask yourself what matters most."

As usual, Vanessa had put her finger on the heart of the matter: what matters most. Was Vanessa right? Did she love Mark? Courtney could think of little else for the remainder of the day.

Chapter Thirty-three

When Courtney arrived home, it was to see Mark sitting in her rocking chair, rocking a six-month-old-baby. Noting her approach, Mark grinned and the infant, in a frilly pink dress and booties, gurgled up at Courtney. With her wispy blond curls, rounded face and huge blue eyes, she was absolutely adorable.

"What is Hannah doing here?" Courtney asked.

Mark stood with the child. "Christy and Steve dropped her off."

"You're kidding! Why?"

Mark grinned. "Why don't you guess."

For a moment, Courtney was dumbstruck. "Oh, no, you don't mean—"

"They've left on a cruise, too. Your mom has their older girl, Mary Ellen, but didn't feel she was up to watching an infant—"

"Because she still has a bum ankle?" Courtney finished.

"Precisely. It's not healing as quickly as the doctor had hoped."

Courtney groaned. "Mark, this is a conspiracy! Why did you agree again?"

"Look at her, love. Wouldn't you agree?"

Courtney glanced down at the baby, who grinned back at her toothlessly. She remembered Vanessa's words and began laughing. Tender, joyous laughter. "You know, you're right. I would have agreed. Give me that little angel."

Mark slipped the baby into Courtney's arms. As Courtney inhaled the baby's sweet scent and touched the soft skin of her little arm, Hannah hugged Courtney and cooed, then planted a juicy kiss on her cheek.

"Ah, yes, Christy said to warn you Hannah is at the kissing stage."

Courtney was making faces at Hannah, who chortled in response. "That's okay. I love kisses."

"Do you?" Mark kissed the baby's cheek, then Courtney.

"Hey, that wasn't an invitation."

"It sounded like one to me."

"As if you need one. So we'll have the little darling—"

"For five days."

"Why am I not surprised?"

For a moment Mark proudly watched the two. "When I see you with her, all I can think of is the two of us and our coming child. When are you doing to tell your family, Courtney?"

Realizing he deserved an answer, she replied, "Well, I'm not sure. Perhaps when we can catch everyone in town together."

"You're not going to wait till you're really showing and just let them guess, are you?"

"No, I wouldn't do that."

He slipped his arms around her. "Look at her, Courtney."

"I know."

"We'll have one just like her soon. Nothing's more important, right?"

Courtney cuddled the baby close. She remembered Vanessa's wise words, so like Mark's now. "You're right. Nothing's more important."

Mark stayed in Denver for five days to help with Hannah, then left for another weeklong trip to London. Courtney was too busy to go with him, but missed him terribly. She also spent her time planning a dinner party for her entire family, so she and Mark could break the news about the baby.

The evening Mark was scheduled to return home, Courtney again took special care with her appearance, bathing and donning a brand-new, blue lace negligee and matching peignoir. As she paced the living room, eager for his arrival, she felt a funny fluttering deep inside her belly. Stopping in her tracks with a gasp of awe, she placed her fingers on her stomach, and felt the tiniest kick. She shouted in joy and felt tears burning her eyes. During her last checkup, her doctor had told her the baby should start moving soon, and she was overwhelmed by this evidence that the child lived inside her.

Then she heard Mark's key at her door.

She hurried across the room and flung it open. Mark was there, rumpled and weary as before, but there. Never had she been so glad to see him.

He took one look at her face and asked, "What's wrong?"

"Nothing!" She pulled him inside the apartment, throwing her arms around him and stretching up to kiss him. "Welcome home, Mark. I just felt our baby move for the first time."

He backed away, eyes reverent. "He moved?"

Taking his hand, she drew it to her belly. "Yes. Feel it."

Mark waited in rapt anticipation, until the fluttering began against his fingers. "My God, you're right."

Courtney smiled radiantly. "He knew his daddy was coming home."

Never had she seen such joy as lit Mark's eyes then. He pulled her close. "Oh, Courtney, Courtney, I think that's the dearest thing you've ever said." He kissed her fervently.

"Welcome home, Daddy."

They didn't reach the bedroom, making beautiful love on the couch again.

Two nights later, Mark and Courtney treated her entire family to dinner at her favorite Italian restaurant. The gang gathered around a long table in the private dining room.

Halfway through the meal, Jason called out, "Hey, Courtney, Mark, what's the occasion?"

Courtney was seated next to Mark at the head of the table. The two exchanged a conspiratorial look, then Courtney called back, "Do Mark and I need a special occasion to invite my family to dinner?"

"Jason's got a point," put in Lyle Sr. "The last time you invited the whole crew out was several years ago, when you announced you'd been hired at BBB."

Courtney laughed. "Okay." She glanced at Mark, and he winked. "Mark and I are expecting."

As cheers went up from all, Brenda Kelly declared, "I was wondering when you'd tell us."

"Mom!" cried Courtney.

"A mother always knows," Brenda replied smugly.

Courtney glanced around the table. "Did the rest of you know, too?"

"Well, we had our suspicions," admitted Carla. "You know, quick weddings and all."

Brittany popped up, ran over and hugged Mark. "I knew you and Aunt Cor'ney would have a baby soon! Didn't I tell you, Aunt Cor'ney?"

"Yes, dear, you sure did." She ruffled the child's hair.

Brittany addressed Mark. "Will you make it a girl, please, Uncle Mark? I already have a brother boy."

Mark chuckled. "We'll try our best, dear."

"When's your due date?" called out Caryn.

Before Courtney could answer, Lyle interjected, "Wait a minute. Aren't you forgetting that congratulations are in order?"

"Congratulations, Mark and Courtney," said Caryn, and quickly the others followed suit with good wishes of their own.

"Thank you all," said a grinning Mark.

"So when's your due date?" Caryn repeated, and everyone laughed.

Courtney took a deep breath, then admitted, "January 9." She glanced about the table and saw her sisters and her mom exchange meaningful looks, though no one snickered.

"Oooh—a New Year's baby," put in Christy ecstatically, clapping her hands.

"Perhaps a Christmas baby," suggested Lyle Jr.

"I can't wait to give you a shower!" exclaimed Brenda. "Buying for babies is so much fun."

"Especially at Bootle's Baby Bower," put in Courtney, and sounds of merriment again poured forth.

Lyle Kelly lifted his glass. "To Mark and Courtney, and a healthy, happy baby."

"Hear! Hear!" shouted the others.

As her family toasted them, Courtney glanced at Mark and melted at the look of pride and love in his eyes. He squeezed her hand and leaned over to whisper at her ear. "That wasn't so terrible, was it, darling?"

She happily shook her head.

"Don't worry," he added huskily. "I'm going to reward you as soon as we get home."

Courtney beamed back at her husband; she could hardly wait.

Chapter Thirty-four

August stretched toward September. Courtney's belly continued to grow, she advanced into maternity clothes, and felt the baby kicking every day. Her doctor pronounced that she was thriving.

She kept busy with her duties at work, and Mark made a couple more trips to London. Although they enjoyed their times together, the tension of all the issues still unresolved between them still simmered beneath the surface.

As far as their love life was concerned, Courtney had pretty much given up on keeping Mark out of her apartment, much less her bedroom. Staying away from him only seemed to make matters worse for them both, and she didn't need that kind of stress in her life right now. As much as she fought it, she grew closer to him with each passing day.

They had some good times together, too, especially when it came to planning for their baby. They began turning her spare room into a nursery, decorating it around the cradle Mark had bought her on Mackinac

Island. Mark painted the room yellow and installed the wallpaper border of nursery animals that Courtney had chosen. Together they selected all the other furnishings and accessories for the room at Bootle's Baby Bower.

Courtney read as much as she could about pregnancy and labor, and after consulting with her doctor, decided she wanted to give natural childbirth with a midwife a try. When she informed Mark, she found he was surprisingly supportive and learned he had already read much on the subject, too.

Together they began interviewing midwives, and also registered for birthing classes at a local hospital. Mark managed to attend most of them, missing only a few while he was out of the country. At the classes they met some other young parents and learned that their anxieties regarding parenthood were quite common.

She and Mark were further reassured on this score on Labor Day weekend. Her sister Caryn left her twin boys, Jake and Jeff, with Courtney and Mark while she and her husband Mike went on a cruise. By the time this third set of young houseguests landed on them, Courtney and Mark were seasoned veterans and had come to accept the enforced baby-sitting with a sense of fun and humor. And Courtney had to admit that the three sessions had given her and Mark training and confidence in their own parenting skills.

During this same period, there were no more incidents of espionage at Bootle's Baby Bower, although Lon Wilson did report to Courtney several failed attempts to penetrate the computer network firewall at corporate headquarters. Lon suspected a single perpetrator was behind the mischief, although their IT people were unable to track down the offender.

Otherwise, their operations were left unscathed.

The Great Baby Caper

Courtney often wondered at this. Why had the mischief cropped up so suddenly, then just as abruptly come to a halt? She did note that this latest lull had occurred soon after Courtney had confronted M. Billingham about possibly being involved. The coincidence bothered her a lot.

Then something really strange happened in mid-September, when BBB hosted its annual dinner party to honor its founder's birthday. Courtney and Mark attended the posh gala held at a downtown private club and were seated on either side of M. Billingham at the head table. Courtney gritted her teeth during all the gushing tributes to the chairman; she made a short speech herself, mostly praising her boss's business prowess. Then Mark stood and led a toast to his grandfather. Courtney noted a lot of pained looks during the speeches, particularly from Gideon and Getz, who kept whispering to each other.

The next day, as was also traditional, M. Billingham dispatched a previously prepared memo to all company employees, thanking them for their support. But this time when the official-looking document landed on Courtney's desk, she read it in stunned silence. She just couldn't believe what it said:

Dear Employees of Bootle's Baby Bower:

This is to thank you for your undying patience and support in dealing with the world's biggest jackass. I am taking this opportunity to inform you that I, M. Billingham Bootle, am a bad-tempered tyrant, a disloyal skunk, and a generally rotten person. I am deserving of neither your respect nor the chairmanship of this company. Instead I should be pilloried, throttled, drawn and quartered, slapped silly, and generally hoisted on my own petard.

I admit before God and this company my myriad and heinous crimes. I am a martinet, a slave driver, a scoundrel, and a heathen. I have rotting teeth and bad personal hygiene. I terrorize my employees and send small children running out of my path. I never tip the paperboy, and have books overdue at the library. I steal candy from babies.

Being worthy of nothing more than a drop into the nearest tar pit, I hereby beg your forgiveness and bid you adieu, so that I may go shoot myself and put myself out of my misery.

Regretfully yours,
M. Billingham Bottle

Courtney finished the missive, then choked up with laughter. A moment later, Deb burst into her office, panic-stricken. "Boss, did you read that memo?"

"Did I ever!"

"I just heard from Mr. Bootle's assistant, Mildred. She's totally freaked out, and informed me Mr. Bootle just summoned all executives to the conference room."

Lips twitching, Courtney stood. "Guess that means me."

When Courtney slipped into the conference room, most of the executives were already present. A red-faced M. Billingham was pacing and waving a copy of the memo.

"I repeat, who did this?" he demanded. "I've already spoken with my assistant, and Mildred swears she put the right memos in everyone's mailboxes last night. I tend to believe her, since she hasn't the imagination for this." Furiously, he crumpled the paper and tossed it, hitting Al Gideon in the head. Al flinched and several others snickered, but no one dared make a comment.

A harried-looking Lon Wilson spoke up. "Sir, I just checked with IT, and evidently someone hacked into our computer system last night using your password."

"My password!" M. Billingham bellowed. "How the hell did anyone get that?"

"We don't know, sir." Lon nervously consulted some notes. "But the letter was revised at 8:30 P.M., while all of us were at dinner."

"Aha!" cried M. Billingham, glancing suspiciously about the table. "A nice little alibi one of you has managed to create."

"Sir, this was most likely done by someone actually here at the office, which rules out anyone present now."

"Not necessarily," M. Billingham shot back. "One of you could have hired it done, or hacked in remotely."

"Well, I suppose," Lon replied. "At any rate, the perp— or hired gun—would also have had to take all of the legitimate copies of your memo out of the mailboxes, then replace them with the fraudulent ones."

M. Billingham turned to Courtney. "Who *was* here last night?"

She frowned. "Really, no one but the cleaning people—although I believe Deb mentioned that an additional, special crew was coming in to shampoo the rugs."

"So someone from this office might have bribed someone from this rug crew?"

"I suppose," Courtney muttered. "But doesn't it stretch credibility to assume a carpet shampooer would know how to access our computers and hack into your personal files?"

"Damn it." M. Billingham waved a hand and began

prowling about again. "This is outrageous! I can't believe someone had the gall to do this to me. A heathen I'm called. Why, I attend church every Sunday in my late wife's memory, I'll have you know. And rotting teeth. My dentist would have apoplexy at the very thought. Not to mention bad personal hygiene." He swung about toward Courtney.

"Definitely not true, sir," she assured him, while struggling not to smile.

Gil Getz chimed in. "It's just a terrible affront, Mr. Bootle—totally unwarranted. Especially calling you a bad-tempered tyrant."

"Indeed." M. Billingham made a growling sound and pounded a fist on the table. "Now all of you get off your overpaid fannies and go find the responsible party!"

"We will, sir, you can rest assured," said Lon Wilson.

"Well, I'm not resting at all till this infiltrator is found, and I'd advise that the rest of you not park your posteriors, either. Otherwise, heads will roll."

"Yes, sir," said Al Gideon.

"And one more thing," M. Billingham ranted. "I want all of you to get something straight. I may be a slave driver. I may have a very short fuse. But this is BBB Ltd., a wholesome enterprise promoting family values." Drawing a seething breath, he finished, "I have never, *ever*, stolen candy from a baby."

He turned about and marched out of the room, slamming the door. There was a moment of silence, then everyone, including Courtney, burst out laughing. Wiping her eyes, Courtney glanced about the table, then sobered somewhat as she remembered Gideon and Getz snickering together at the dinner party. She must ask Lon to keep a special eye on those two.

* * *

Courtney was aware that Mark had another trip to London planned. A few days before he was scheduled to leave, he surprised her over breakfast by simply handing her a ticket. "Please come with me this time."

Courtney hesitated. Mark had asked her to accompany him several times before, and she'd said no. But things weren't as hectic at work right now. True, they hadn't yet found the person who had roasted M. Billingham with the fake memo, but no further mischief had occurred since.

Then she saw the love and hope on Mark's face, and totally melted. She reached out and squeezed his hand. "Okay."

His eyes lit up. "Really?"

She nodded. "My doctor says that if I'm to do any traveling, it's best done during my second trimester, and that will be over soon."

He reached out to pat her burgeoning belly. "Quite true, my love."

"And I would like to see your London."

"I'd like to make it *our* London."

Feeling a bit put on the spot, she went on, "I'd also like to meet your sisters and their families while we're there, if that's possible."

"Absolutely. I've already mentioned to Beth and Merry that I hoped you might come with me next time. They told me just to say the word, and we'll all get together for dinner." Mark leaned over the table to kiss her. "Darling, you've no idea how happy you've made me."

Courtney was tempted to reply, *Don't assume this means I'll live there with you.* But Mark seemed so delighted, she didn't have the heart to burst his bubble.

Chapter Thirty-five

A few days later they left Denver on an afternoon flight, connecting to a Transatlantic carrier in New York. They arrived at Heathrow early the next morning, just as a misty dawn was creeping over the landscape. Exhausted by so many hours in flight, Courtney slept in the cab as they sped to Mark's flat, and her arrival there also passed in a blur.

Hours later she awakened in a soft bed to a blinding stream of sunshine and the smell of warm tea. She realized her clothing had been removed, and she now wore one of Mark's oversize T-Shirts emblazoned with "St. Katherine Racket Club." That and nothing more . . . not even her panties.

She looked up to see him hovering over her, smiling and extending a steaming cup. He smelled delicious and appeared clean-shaven as well as smartly dressed in fresh slacks and a sports shirt.

"Hello," she murmured.

He leaned over and kissed her brow. "Good afternoon, sleepyhead."

"Afternoon? What time is it?"

"Three P.M."

"Wow. I slept that long?"

"Just as well you slept off your jet lag." He extended the cup to her. "I figured the smell of hot tea might awaken you."

She sat up, took the cup, and slowly sipped the strong, sweet tea. "Ummm, thanks, this is good." She gestured about. "So this is your flat."

"Be it ever so humble."

Courtney glanced around at the large, airy loft with its high ceilings crisscrossed with industrial pipe, polished plank floors, handsome brick walls, contemporary furnishings and huge, sunny windows. Off to one side, a handsome open kitchen gleamed with chopping board islands and stainless-steel appliances. Beyond, an open door revealed a large modern bathroom; Courtney vaguely recalled stumbling into it shortly after their arrival.

"Very nice," she pronounced. "Did you say this building used to house a plumbing supply warehouse—I mean, before the area became trendy?"

"So you remember what I said on our arrival? You seemed just about dead to the world when I carried you in this morning."

"I do vaguely remember the loft, the bathroom . . ." She plucked at her T-shirt. "But not you undressing me."

"I do." He leaned over, kissed her, and spoke in a sexy voice. "A more distinct pleasure I've never known."

"You stinker." Setting down her cup on the end table, she rose, and saw Mark draw his gaze over her long, bare legs. "So you like the sight of a fat woman."

He drew her closer, wrapped his arms around her and gently stroked her rounded belly. "A beautiful woman,

353

plump with my child. I'm so glad you came here with me, darling."

"Me, too." Impulsively kissing his jaw, she strolled over to the window and looked out at an array of yachts gleaming in the Thames. "What a grand view."

"A big reason I bought this loft."

"It's large, but obviously made for a bachelor."

He curled an arm around her waist. "It could be partitioned off. A bedroom, a nursery. And the flat next door is up for sale. I could buy it, we could expand. . . ." Wickedly he leaned over and kissed her tummy. "Much as you've already done so beautifully, my love."

As one of Mark's hands boldly stroked her bare thigh, Courtney moaned. "So you have it all planned out? You spirit me away here, hoping I'll agree to stay?"

He straightened, regarding her solemnly. "Not at all. Nothing has been that well organized since the day I met you. I'm just offering suggestions."

She smiled, realizing she had been a bit hard on him. "Okay, so you are."

He grinned. "Are you up to going out for a bit? That is, before we go over to Beth's place for dinner tonight?"

"Sure. I'm so glad I'll get to meet everyone."

"The girls and their families are excited, too." He glanced at his watch. "If we hurry, we can get in a bit of sightseeing before we're due there at seven."

She nodded happily. "I can't wait to explore London. I haven't been here since my senior trip a good ten years ago."

"Well before the London Eye and the Millennium Dome," he noted. He picked up her suitcase from the foot of the bed and lifted it onto the mattress. "So get dressed, woman."

"What are you going to do?"

The Great Baby Caper

He plopped himself down in a nearby leather chair. "I'm going to watch you."

And the rascal did just that.

They went out in Mark's car, stopping first for high tea at a charming restaurant near the Victoria embankment. By the time they'd visited a few of Mark's favorite shops in Soho and a gallery or two off Picadilly, it was time to get ready for dinner with his sisters.

Mark's younger sister, Beth, and her family lived in an elegant old town house in Belgravia. When Courtney and Mark arrived, both Beth, a statuesque brunette who greatly resembled Mark, and her younger sister Merry, a pretty woman with light brown hair, greeted Courtney with warm hugs and congratulations. In the formal parlor, Courtney was introduced to the rest of their families: Beth's husband, Peter Penright and their children, five-year-old Peter Jr. and three-year-old William; Merry's husband, Paul Withers, and their two children, three-year-old Madison and two-year-old Dillon.

Although all were polite and friendly toward her, at once Courtney noticed the difference between Mark's kin and her own rambunctious clan. Everyone here was more subdued, particularly the children; all four were neatly groomed and impeccably mannered. Even the youngest, Dillon, was shy and retiring, and Courtney could not coax a smile out of him. Before dinner was served, all four were whisked upstairs by a uniformed nanny.

In the formal dining room, a maid served up a delicious dinner that included clam chowder, vegetables vinaigrette, and salmon with shrimp sauce. Conversation at the table was divided between the sexes. Merry and Beth asked Courtney countless polite questions about her background, her family and the expected baby, while offering all sorts of motherly advice.

The three men, better acquainted, hashed out familiar issues: Paul, an estate agent, complained because the council tax was being raised in the posh district where he sold many of his properties; Peter, a solicitor specializing in international law, argued his opposition to the European Monetary Union. By dessert, the men had shifted to an animated discussion of the latest test cricket match between England and Australia.

That was when Beth waved a hand and protested. "Gentlemen, please! Not cricket again. Merry and I are going to whisk Courtney off to the parlor before she becomes so disgusted that she tosses the lot of you in the Thames."

The men chuckled, and Peter said contritely, "Are we boring you, Courtney? If so, I apologize."

"Please, don't," she replied. "Actually this sports talk is making me feel quite at home. You see, every time my family gathers in Denver, my dad and brothers-in-law are busy discussing the Denver Broncos. Here, evidently, it's cricket."

As the men chuckled, Merry spoke up. "Well, Beth and I are stealing Courtney away, anyway. We must have an opportunity to grill her in private."

"Don't you two girls get carried away, now," said Paul.

"Yes, dear, let me know if you need help," added Mark.

"Oh, I'll be fine," Courtney assured him.

The women took their tea and adjourned to the parlor. Courtney sat on the settee with Beth, while Merry occupied a wing chair flanking them. Solemnly Beth picked up a handsome leather photo album off the coffee table and extended it toward Courtney. "Actually, I had an ulterior motive in bringing you in here. I thought you might want to see this. It belongs to Mark."

Courtney took the album. "Really, it's Mark's?"

Beth nodded. "There's a story behind that. After Mum and Dad lost their lives, I went through all their old photos and had the best ones reproduced, so I could make an album for each of the three children. This one is Mark's."

"How thoughtful of you." Courtney frowned. "But why doesn't he have it?"

Beth touched Courtney's hand and smiled compassionately. "He told me to keep it for him until he had a family of his own. I don't mean to pry into yours and his affairs, Courtney, but Mark has mentioned to Merry and me that you two haven't decided as yet where you're going to live. Selfishly of course, we would like you to choose the U.K. But regardless of that, Mark does have a family now, doesn't he? So I want the two of you to have the album."

Courtney was touched. "Beth, that's so sweet of you. But I still wonder why Mark had you keep it all this time."

"I think Mark took our folks' deaths really hard, even harder than Beth and me," put in Merry.

"Oh, yes," agreed Beth. "Being the oldest, Mark took the responsibilities so much to heart. Even with Grandfather Bootle around to oversee things, Mark was constantly fretting over me and Merry. Were we at the right schools, were we happy? On top of that, he had his own education to think of, and Dad's businesses. He turned from a carefree lad to a solemn man overnight. He's lived in a shell for so many years—a true introvert."

"Really?" asked Courtney. "He's always seemed so friendly and outgoing to me, with such a sense of fun."

"But that was mostly after you came into his life," explained Merry. "Beth and I have remarked so many times since then that we can't believe the change in Mark. Almost like a dead man springing back to life."

"I . . ." Again Courtney felt choked up with emotion. "I had no idea."

"He loves you so, Courtney," Beth added, feelingly. "He can't stop talking about you and the baby. We're so thrilled to have you in the family."

"I—I'm truly honored to be a member." Blinking at a tear, Courtney managed to smile brightly at both women. Then she flipped open the album and began perusing its pages. Otherwise, she would have burst out crying.

Courtney took the album with them when they left. Mark noticed the volume tucked beneath her arm, but made no comment as he drove them back to his loft. Instead he asked, "What did you think of my family?"

"Oh, they're wonderful. Your sisters seemed reserved at first, but I soon discovered they're very warm in their way."

"Good. I'm glad they passed muster."

"Mark, this wasn't a contest."

"They certainly all loved you."

"Then I'm glad *I* passed muster."

Inside Mark's loft, Courtney laid the photo album down on the bed, then went off to the bathroom to get undressed. When she emerged, Mark, wearing only his trousers, stood staring at the album on the bed. He'd turned off the lights except for the nightstand lamps, but she could see the strain in his face.

"Mark, I want you to show me the album," she said.

He glanced up at her. "Why did you bring it back with us?"

"Beth gave it to me, to take home with us." She smiled. "Because you have a family now."

For a moment he stood silent, a muscle working in his jaw. At last he said, "Courtney, I haven't claimed that album before because—well, I haven't been able to face . . ."

"All the memories of family life, the pictures of your parents?" she asked gently.

He nodded.

She went over and hugged him. "I've noticed how tense you become when we discuss them. Mark, you mustn't be afraid to feel things."

He stroked her cheek with his fingertips. "Mustn't I, Courtney?"

She took his hand. "Come on. Show me."

They sat down on the bed together, and reluctantly Mark opened the album. After turning a page or two, he laughed. "Hey, there's my baby picture."

Courtney stared at the adorable, blue-eyed baby with chubby cheeks and curly dark hair. "Yes, I know."

"You know?"

"Well, I had a peek at the album with Merry and Beth," she admitted. When he would have protested, she added, "But I still want *you* to show it to me."

He gave a groan, but continued turning the pages. "Ah, there I am at three, on my trike outside our house in Mayfair." He hesitated a moment. "That's my mom in the background talking to our neighbor." He flipped to another page. "There I am riding my bike at Hampstead Heath, and here I am out on the lake in the sailboat with my dad." He paused again.

She squeezed his hand. "He looks just like you, Mark. It makes me so sad to realize I'll never get to know him— or your mom."

He nodded, his voice thick as he continued. "Here are Beth and me, showering Merry with confetti at her birthday party. There's Mother and Dad at their fifteenth wedding anniversary . . ." His voice faded, and he closed the album. "Courtney, this is hard."

Gently she took his hand, raised it to her mouth and kissed it. "Why? Because you retreated into yourself when your parents died? That's what Beth and Merry told me."

His troubled gaze met hers. "I suppose that's true."

"What changed, Mark?"

Abruptly he smiled. "You, darling."

"Tell me more about that, Mark. About why seeing me in those videos brought you halfway across the world to meet me."

He sighed and glanced away uneasily. "Courtney, I think it will sound very strange."

"No, it won't. I want to know."

He gazed back at her, and this time she could see the love in his eyes. "When I first saw you, darling, there was so much life and vitality in you, so much heart. I couldn't stop looking at you. I watched those videos endlessly, until I'd memorized your every word, your every look, your smile. You might say I became obsessed. I told myself, that's the woman I want to share my life with." He drew a shuddering breath. "I know it sounds weird now, almost like I became a stalker or something."

"No, it doesn't. I think it's very sweet. That you were so locked up in yourself, and I touched something that brought you out."

He regarded her soberly. "Courtney, I still don't think you get it. I knew before I ever met you that I wanted to marry you. I think I even knew I loved you. Mind you, I never intended to force you as Grandfather attempted.

The Great Baby Caper

But I knew you were the one." He drew a shuddering breath. "Now you know. Admit that if I'd told you all this before, it would have scared you away."

She looked at him with her heart in her eyes. "Perhaps so, back then. But I'm not scaring away now, Mark. You've worked your way into my heart. And don't you know that the more I learn about you—"

"Yes?"

She almost blurted, *the more I love you.* Instead she caught him to her fiercely and whispered, "You don't have to be afraid anymore, Mark. I understand you now and believe your feelings. You're not going to lose me like you lost your parents. You can look at those pictures, and if they make you sad, I'll hold you. We're in this together now, with our child, and I'm not letting you go. You're mine now."

"Oh, Courtney." Voice breaking, he pushed the album aside, pulled her close and kissed her. Then he drew back at the sound of her sob. "Darling, what's wrong?"

"I just feel like such a chump," she admitted. "Here I've been worried about trusting you, giving you such a hard time, and not allowing myself to see how much you love me."

"It's all right, darling," he reassured her, pulling her closer. "Besides, I haven't been guiltless in all of this, either. I think I have tried to control you. I did want to pull you away from your job, bring you here and have you to myself. I felt so threatened by it all, so afraid I'd lose you."

"And I felt threatened because you seemed so much like my family, my former boyfriends, not respecting my career or me as a person."

"I do respect you, Courtney," he acknowledged quietly. "Part of what drew me to you in the first place was

Eugenia Riley

your confidence and ability. But I think I may have some blind spots about family life. Mine wasn't the best, so I've tried to compensate. When my parents died, I coped by throwing myself into my responsibilities, so my sisters could have the best. When you came along, I think I clung to the same value system, seeing myself as the one who should take care of you, and the baby as more your responsibility." He kissed her brow. "But no more. We'll find a better way to share things."

"I know we will. But I've been very stubborn, too, and I'm ready to start giving more. Now that I know where you're really coming from." She kissed his neck.

"I'm glad, darling." Smoothly he pulled off her nightgown, then feasted his eyes on her. "Lovely. So lovely." He leaned over to press his lips against her belly. "I think I'm going to die if I can't kiss you now. Is it still okay to make love?"

"Very much okay."

He kissed her, passionately, and after a moment pulled her astride him. His hands boldly roved her spine, and he buried his face in her neck. "Unzip me, will you, love? Touch me."

Without hesitation, she did as he bid, caressing his hardness. He leaned over, nipping her breast with his teeth, while his fingers moved between her thighs. Courtney gasped in mindless arousal.

"Take me inside you now," he urged hoarsely.

Courtney sank onto him, for once not minding his taking charge of her at all. Pleasure flooded her to the core. She moaned.

"Ahhh," he murmured. "That's so good, darling. But don't let me hurt you. Mind the baby."

His words were so sweet that Courtney lost control, tears stinging her eyes. She pushed him back on the bed and stared down into his eyes. "You would never hurt me. I know that now."

Her mouth took his. Her body claimed his heat. First he had taken charge of her. Now she was possessing him. . . .

The rest of their London stay passed in a blur of enjoyable activity. While Mark conducted his business during the day, Courtney went sightseeing, taking a boat ride down the Thames, touring Westminster Abbey and the British Museum. A couple of times she joined Beth and Merry for lunch and shopping; she was quickly coming to love both women as sisters.

Mark joined her whenever he could leave work early. One afternoon he took her to visit the flagship Billingham's store near Burlington Arcade—and created quite a stir when he arrived unannounced, then decided to buy himself and his bride matching bathrobes, wryly requesting an "employee discount." They spent another afternoon shopping together in the street market on Portebello Road; Courtney bought souvenirs and gifts for everyone in her family, and Mark bought an entire handmade linen layette for their baby.

Their last evening in London, they went up for a ride in the London Eye, the gigantic, 450-foot ferris wheel built to honor London's millennium. Standing with Mark inside one of the large glass capsules, Courtney was awed by the spectacular view of London—the Thames directly below, Big Ben and Parliament just beyond them. She could even see past London proper to the trees and hills ringing the horizon.

"Happy, darling?" Mark asked.

"This is amazing."

"I know. There was great skepticism here about the

London Eye when it was first proposed, but it's become a smashing success, an eighth wonder of the world. Unlike the Millennium Dome . . ." He pointed down the Thames. "Which has been more of a White Elephant as far as the general public is concerned."

Staring out at the lights of the Tate Modern Museum, she murmured, "Well, this can't be beat. You know, I've had the time of my life, Mark."

He smiled. "As I have, darling. And we're not done yet. After this, I'm taking you over to Simpson's in the Strand for a grand dinner. It's quite an historical old restaurant."

"Sounds great."

"So what do you think of London?"

"I love it. There isn't quite the hustle and bustle of the States. It's much safer, and very interesting."

"Perhaps a good place to raise a family?"

"Perhaps."

He stroked her cheek. "Thank you for recognizing that."

She smiled wistfully. "I just know that we're together now, and we'll work it out, though we may not have all the answers yet." She squeezed his hand. "Anyway, this trip has been so wonderful, and it's our last night in London. I don't want anything to spoil it."

"Of course not." He kissed the tip of her nose. "Tonight it will be just the two of us."

"Yes, just the two us."

She smiled bravely at him, and he at her. But Courtney knew how uncertain they both felt inside. They'd made such progress here. However, the problem wasn't just the two of them, but how they and their child would fit into this world. That was the real issue, and it was still a stumbling block to their future happiness together.

Chapter Thirty-six

"So, Courtney, are you and Mark having a boy or a girl?" Caryn asked.

Sitting on the couch in her mom's living room, Courtney stared blankly at her sister for a moment. It was now mid-November, and her mom and sisters were hosting a baby shower for her. Gaily wrapped presents were stacked on the coffee table in front of her, and on the floor nearby. Over a dozen women were in attendance, including some of Courtney's friends from the office and from high school, and of course, Vanessa.

"Caryn, really," scolded Brenda Kelly. "Courtney may want the sex of her child to be kept a secret."

"Oh, everyone knows these days," replied Caryn, waving off her mother.

"Well, certainly you and Mike knew, since you were expecting twin boys," put in Carla. "But some couples like to maintain an air of mystery."

As several women laughed, Courtney addressed her oldest sister. "Actually, Carla, you're right. The doctor wanted to tell Mark and me, but we decided we wanted it to be a surprise."

"Oh, how romantic," put in Deb. "You won't know what the little darling is till it pops out."

More laughter erupted. Feeling the baby kick her, Courtney pulled a face. "From the size of this kid, I have a feeling I'm going to pop before he or she pops out."

"Don't worry, hon," reassured Christy. "It's certainly no worse than the proverbial putting a camel through the eye of a needle."

"That's just what I'm afraid of," Courtney said dryly.

"And where are you planning to have the baby?" asked Melissa, an old high school friend of Courtney's.

"Well, I've pretty much decided on the birthing wing at the hospital," said Courtney. "I've already found a midwife I like, and I think a water birth would be nice."

"You mean all natural—no drugs?" asked Christy.

"It is better for the baby."

"Wow—you're really brave," said Caryn. "I never could have had my two without being medicated."

"Come on, girls," chided Vanessa from across the room. "Don't frighten Courtney. If she's made her decision, we should support her."

"You're right," agreed Caryn. "Good for you, Courtney."

"Tell me that on the day I deliver, when I'm screaming for narcotics," Courtney added,

Amid more merriment, Brenda clapped her hands. "So which present will you open first, dear?"

Courtney smiled at Vanessa, who sat across from her in a wing chair. "I think Vanessa's. She's always so creative."

"Why, thank you, dear," said Vanessa. "I do hope you like my little contribution."

The Great Baby Caper

Brenda handed Courtney Vanessa's gift bag, and oohs and aahs were heard as Courtney pulled out the present—an exquisite baby quilt with a bunny appliqued at its center, and pink-and-blue gingham piping on its edges. "Oh, Vanessa! Did you make this?"

"It's nothing," replied Vanessa modestly.

"Nothing!" declared Deb, looking on. "Why that design is so lovely, we should sell it at BBB."

Courtney turned to Deb. "You know, you're right. We need a new design for the Bootle Baby Quilt. What do you think, Vanessa?"

Vanessa smiled lovingly at Courtney. "I think I want to reserve that design just for your child, Courtney."

"Oh, how sweet!" put in Christy. "Come on, Courtney, open another one."

Courtney folded the quilt and smiled at Vanessa, feeling grateful to have so many friends and so much support. Things were going well between her and Mark, too. She was falling for him more each day, and she couldn't wait until they could hold their precious baby in their arms.

That evening Mark helped Courtney put all the baby gifts away in the nursery. She was folding Vanessa's quilt and placing in it the crib when she realized Mark hadn't moved or spoken for several moments. She turned to see him staring at her solemnly. "Is something wrong?"

"No, I'm just watching the mother of my child as she pads about."

Courtney rolled her eyes and rubbed her lower back. "Padding about is getting harder all the time."

"You must be tired, darling. Go on to bed. I'll finish up here."

Eugenia Riley

"You're sweet."

He brushed a strand of hair from her eyes. "I'm worried about you. Dash it all, I have to be in London again next week."

Courtney forced a cheerful expression. "Mark, I'll be fine."

"I wish you could start your maternity leave now."

"You know we agreed that I wouldn't until the Christmas holidays. That way I can take eight full weeks and nurse the baby."

"I just think it's too much for you."

"It really isn't, Mark. Now that the incidents of industrial espionage have pretty much stopped, things are much smoother. We still haven't nabbed the culprit, but we're no longer in a panic mode. I'm already working a more limited schedule. Besides, I need the distraction of work. Otherwise, I'll just worry."

"Worry? About what?"

"You know—the baby. Will he or she be okay—"

"He'll be perfect."

"Will the delivery go well—"

"I'll be there to ensure that it does."

She laughed. "As if you have any control. I guess that's what's scary." She patted her belly. "We don't have control. It's all in Mother Nature's hands now."

He kissed her brow. "I'll see to it that the old girl toes the mark."

"Let's hope you'll be successful."

"I will." Gently he patted her rear. "Now go on to bed before I carry you."

"Come in and rub my back?"

"Of course. I'll be along soon."

Mark kissed his wife, watching her amble out of the room, her movements slow and awkward due to her advanced pregnancy. Despite his reassurances to the contrary, he was terribly worried about her these days. Would she and the baby come through the delivery all right? Would the child be normal and healthy? Would Courtney feel terrible pain on its birth?

Though he had supported her choice of natural childbirth with a midwife and agreed with her that it was better for the baby, the entire prospect was daunting to him. How he wished he could go through the delivery for her.

Despite all his anxieties, he felt such pride that she was his, that they were together now, that she carried his child and was willing to endure such pain for its benefit. They'd drawn so close, especially after all they had shared during their London trip. But they still had a ways to go, and some important decisions to make regarding their lives together. Perhaps the coming of their child might put matters in better perspective for them both.

Chapter Thirty-seven

In the next month the baby growing inside Courtney became even larger. Each checkup revealed that mother and baby were thriving.

Although Courtney's due date wasn't until January 9, in early December she began to feel occasional, mild pains in her belly. When she checked with her midwife, she was told that these were perfectly normal "Braxton-Hicks" contractions that weren't actual labor.

Courtney packed her suitcase for the hospital, and she and Mark did their Christmas shopping early. Already a proud daddy, Mark bought several toys and plush animals for the baby, even though the child was not expected by Christmas.

As of late November he'd also quit making trips to London, telling Courtney he would not leave the country again until after the child was born. Knowing she could count on him to be there for the baby's birth left Courtney both relieved and grateful.

On Christmas Eve, Mark and Courtney drank wassail and decorated the tree. Since she was thoroughly exhausted, they went to bed early. But within minutes of dozing off, Courtney was awakened by one of those odd twinges; she sat up in bed, grimacing.

Mark sat up beside her. "You okay?"

She rubbed her belly. "Just another false labor pain."

He raised an eyebrow. "You're sure it's false, darling?"

"From what my sisters have told me, this is nothing like the real thing."

He smiled and touched her belly. "Wow, your tummy is hard. Has he been active?"

"She's been doing somersaults."

Mark leaned over and kissed her. "Want some warm milk to help you get to sleep?"

She grimaced. "Yuck. I've never really been a warm milk fan. I'll leave that for our baby."

He chuckled.

"How 'bout some of that caffeine-free orange tea you make me? We could sip it and watch a movie for a while."

"Sure, I'll have it brewed up in a jiff."

Moments later they were both sipping the warm tea in bed and watching *It's a Wonderful Life* when the phone rang. Thinking it might be her mom calling to remind them about Christmas dinner tomorrow, Courtney grabbed the receiver. "Hello?"

"Hello, Mrs. Billingham, this is Lon Wilson."

Bemused, she replied, "Oh, hi, Lon. Strange hearing from you. I should think things would be really quiet down at corporate headquarters tonight, with everything shut down."

"Well, not exactly."

"What do you mean?"

"I think we've found the mole."

Courtney sat bolt upright. "You've what?"

"We've found the culprit responsible for the espionage. And I'd suggest you come see this for yourself. I've already called Mr. Bootle."

Courtney glanced out the window at snowflakes falling. "Do you really think that's nec—"

"Yes, ma'am, if you want to be here when we confront the responsible party."

"Okay, then, we'll be right down." She hung up and turned to Mark, who was eyeing her quizzically. "Lon thinks he's found the infiltrator, and wants us to come down to headquarters."

Mark gave a dry laugh. "You're joking. Such high drama. Couldn't he have told you on the phone?"

"He didn't want to."

"But to drag you downtown this late at night . . . Courtney, it's snowing outside."

"A light snow, and besides, it's not even ten yet. I can't sleep after that call, anyway."

"Are you sure you're up to this?"

"Absolutely."

"But, darling, you've been having labor pains—"

"*False* labor pains. For almost a month now. Come on. Let's go."

"Very well," he acquiesced wearily.

They bundled up and left in Mark's car. Half an hour later, as the couple entered the security office at corporate headquarters, Courtney spotted a scowling M. Billingham standing next to Lon, a few feet away from a bank of small tv monitors that were flashing footage of various corridors and offices.

M. Billingham's expression was grave. "Courtney, Mark, I hope you're both well."

"We are, Grandfather," Mark answered.

Courtney turned directly to her security chief. "Lon, what do you have for us?"

He motioned toward a far screen. "The culprit in the act, Mrs. Billingham."

Courtney was starting toward the screen when M. Billingham touched her arm. "I hope this won't be too much of a shock for you, my dear."

"What does that crack mean?" she asked.

He shrugged. "On the other hand, perhaps it won't be a shock at all."

Courtney flashed him a perturbed look and moved toward the screen. What had M. Billingham meant? Was the old coot still convinced she was somehow responsible for the espionage? She studied the screen, only to gasp as she spotted a familiar figure huddled at the computer terminal in M. Billingham's office; the culprit wore the uniform and hat of a cleaning crew person.

"Oh, my God!" She turned back to Lon. "Are you sure you've caught the right party?"

Lon nodded grimly. "A week ago, I received an alert from IT that our financial files had been penetrated. We've been watching the perp come in and out ever since—sometimes disguised as a building maintenance person, today posing as an upholstery cleaning person. I'm only allowing the shenanigans to continue in order to gather evidence before we notify the police."

"You've known about this for a week, and you didn't tell me?" Courtney demanded.

"There was no point in proceeding before we had a solid case."

Courtney groaned.

"Shall we go confront the perpetrator?" M. Billingham asked.

Courtney turned to him sharply. "I think Mark and I should."

Ignoring her tone, M. Billingham strode to the door and opened it. "We'll all go. Courtney, dear, after you."

Courtney marched out the door and down the hallway toward M. Billingham's office. She flung open the door and confronted the figure at the desk. "So, it was you! How could you? And here I thought we were friends."

The figure at the computer terminal flinched. Then Vanessa Fox stood and calmly removed her cap, staring impassively at her accusers. "Hello, Ham," she murmured.

"Van," he replied sternly.

She flashed an apologetic look at Courtney. "Hello, Courtney, Mark."

Courtney started toward her friend, almost tripping over an upholstery cleaning machine on the floor. She spoke in an intense whisper. "Vanessa, please, don't you realize you're in big trouble here?"

Vanessa drew herself up proudly. "I've gathered as much. I believe 'caught red-handed' is the phrase. But no matter. It was all well worth it just to make Ham Bootle squirm."

"Make me squirm?" M. Billingham repeated.

"Yes, make you squirm," Vanessa replied spitefully. "Ever since I saw you at Mark and Courtney's wedding, I knew I had to take action and give you your just desserts at last. I almost made it, too, altering records so it would seem as if you had embezzled company funds. Of course I also intended to see that those funds would be recovered—once you were in prison. What sweet revenge that would have been!"

Stunned, M. Billingham stepped forward. "But why

would you want to wreak vengeance on me, Van? I've been more than generous with you."

"Ah, yes, very generous, driving my husband until he died of a heart attack," Vanessa retorted bitterly.

M. Billingham paled. "But I warned Floyd to slow down, especially after his first attack—"

"Sure you did, but you also kept piling on the work. Then after he died you forced me out of the company. You had known for years that I wanted to join Bootle's Baby Bower as a designer. I had ideas for an entire new product line. But oh, no, that was too much of an assault on your ego, having a woman spearhead your product line. So once my husband was gone, you forced me out. It was only when Courtney came along and you saw her as a potential future wife for your grandson that you revised your sexist policies. At least I can be thankful she got the opportunities I never had."

M. Billingham drew a trembling hand through his white hair. "Van, I never knew you felt that way."

"Indeed. A true Bootle you are. Self-absorbed and oblivious to the feelings of others."

Crestfallen, Courtney stepped forward. "Vanessa, I can't believe I'm hearing this. So you were responsible for everything—the egg roll fiasco, the grumpy-face stickers, our website being attacked, the Brat Brigade?"

Vanessa nodded. "Yes, I was responsible. It took a bit of planning and skullduggery—hacking into e-mails, hiring various crews, bribing people—but I was more than equal to the task. As you've so often reminded me, I am a genius with computers, so I also knew how to cover my tracks."

Courtney blinked at sudden tears. "But how could you do this to *me*? Here I thought you were my friend, someone who wanted women to get their just due in the business world. Yet you undermined me this way. Were you jealous of my accomplishments?"

With a cry of anguish, Vanessa touched Courtney's arm. "Oh, no, darling, never. Whatever else you may think of me, please know that I never intended to do any of this to *you*. My pride over your achievements knows no bounds." She shot a hostile glance at M. Billingham. "You must understand that *everything* I did, I did to hurt Ham, to make *him* suffer. Remember that day last summer when we met for lunch?"

"Yes."

"Well, that's when you told me what a hard time Ham was giving you over this. When I realized he was blaming you, that I was hurting you instead of him, I was devastated. Immediately I ceased my activities at the stores and website and turned to your computer system instead. I was the one who rewrote Ham's annual memo to his employees, revising it for accuracy—"

"Accuracy?" bellowed M. Billingham.

"And I knew you wouldn't get blamed for that, since you were at the dinner the night that particular foul deed was done. Since then I've been hacking into your computer system, trying to get some dirt on Ham. My theory was that anyone who was such a self-centered jackass was probably a criminal, too."

"A criminal! How dare you!" exclaimed M. Billingham.

Ignoring him, Vanessa forged on. "I was looking for any clue to illegal activity on Ham's part—offshore accounts, dummy corporations, evidence of money being funneled. But I found nothing. That's when I decided to 'create' proof of Ham's embezzling funds from the company. And I would have succeeded, too, except for the efforts of Mr. Wilson here. I almost had Ham where

I wanted him—in an orange jumpsuit at county jail."

As Vanessa spoke, M. Billingham had grown ashen. "My God, Van, do you hate me that much?"

Vanessa gazed at him sadly. "Actually, while you may not believe this, I never hated you, Ham. At one time I genuinely liked and respected you. Then, after what happened with Floyd, after you forced me out, I felt deeply hurt, and betrayed. I wanted you to pay." She turned to Courtney, offering a contrite smile. "Courtney, darling, I'm so sorry to disappoint you, or to cause you any distress so close to the birth of your child. And that's pretty much my story." She gazed frostily at M. Billingham. "I presume you'll call the authorities now and cart me off to the calaboose?"

For once, M. Billingham appeared at a loss. "I'm not sure."

"We really should, Mr. Bootle," urged Lon.

"May I say something, Mr. Bootle?" asked Courtney.

He waved a hand. "Why not?"

Courtney leveled a fierce look on him. "You deserve this."

"I what?"

"I agree, Grandfather," put in Mark. "You can't just treat people as shabbily as you have, for years and years, and expect them not to retaliate."

"Now my own family betrays me," grumbled M. Billingham. "Things have reached a pretty pass, indeed."

Lon cleared his throat. "Sir, that still doesn't solve our current dilemma." He jerked his head toward Vanessa. "What should I do about her?"

M. Billingham scowled from Lon to Vanessa. He was opening his mouth to speak when suddenly Courtney uttered a low cry.

Mark grabbed her arm. "Darling, what is it?"

Courtney was still gasping, feeling as if a huge fist had just grabbed her insides and given them a very hard twist. "I think I just felt a *real* labor pain."

He went wild-eyed. "Oh, Good Lord. But the baby isn't due for another two weeks."

"Well, from everything I'm feeling, she hasn't looked at the calendar lately."

"You're going to have my great-grandchild *now*?" cried M. Billingham. Distraughtly he turned to Lon. "Don't just stand there, man, do something."

He gulped. "What should I do, sir? Call 911?"

"Yes. Call 911."

"No!" protested Mark. "We'll just go straightaway to the hospital."

M. Billingham nodded nervously. "Splendid idea. We'll do just that."

Listening to the men and realizing she could put their confusion to her advantage, Courtney grabbed Vanessa's arm. "Will you come with me to the hospital? I really can't make it without you."

Vanessa's expression melted. "You mean you've forgiven me, darling?"

"Of course I have. Will you come?"

"Certainly I will, that is . . ." She glanced pointedly at M. Billingham.

He at once took her cue. "Of course. We'll all go to the hospital." He gazed wryly at Vanessa's costume. "Perhaps they'll have a couch or two for old Van here to scrub."

"Why, you snake!" she declared.

"Now if that isn't the pot calling the kettle black." M. Billingham wheeled about to Lon, snapping his fingers. "Run along downstairs and inform my driver we're on our way with a lady in labor."

"Yes, sir." Lon dashed out of the office.

Abruptly M. Billingham brightened, grinning at Mark. "A Christmas baby. Won't that be jolly, grandson?"

"Yes, sir." He took Courtney's arm. "You all right, darling?"

"Yes. Can we just go, please?"

A secret smile curved Courtney's mouth as the group headed out of the office and toward the elevator. Normally she would have objected to M. Billingham's coming along to the hospital. But he had spared Vanessa, at least for the moment, and she wasn't about to look a gift horse in the mouth.

Besides, she had a much more pressing matter on her mind: She and Mark were about to have their baby!

Chapter Thirty-eight

The ride to the hospital passed in a blur for Courtney. She felt a small bump or two as they sped along and was aware of a light snowfall outside the limousine windows. She and Mark sat huddled together in the passenger compartment across from Vanessa and M. Billingham, who looked on in tense silence; Courtney took a moment to marvel at how panic had forced the two to set aside their usual enmity.

By now her pains were hard, coming three minutes apart, and as she cried out, the worried look on Mark's face alarmed her even more. Nonetheless, his arms were steady about her, his voice calm as he murmured, "Easy, darling. Remember your breathing exercises. Slow, deep breaths."

"I'm in too damn much pain to breathe deeply."

"Then try panting and blowing like our birthing teacher discussed."

Courtney tried the technique, and found that it did help somewhat. "I'm so worried about the baby. She's early."

"He'll be fine." He hesitated. "Do you want me to call your parents, darling?"

She shook her head. "Not yet. The whole gang will come rushing down, and I don't think I can take a mob scene right now."

When they arrived at the hospital entrance nearest the birthing wing, M. Billingham sprang to life. Leaning toward the driver, he barked, "Don't just sit there, Hinkham. Go fetch a stretcher!"

"Yes, sir."

Even as the chauffeur was opening his door, Mark yelled, "Really, Hinkham, a wheelchair will do."

Nodding, the chauffeur shot out of the car, returning momentarily with an orderly pushing a wheelchair with a blanket folded across it. As Hinkham opened the passenger compartment door, Courtney felt a blast of cold air and shivered violently.

The orderly peered inside, grimacing as he spotted the look of pain on Courtney's face. "You the lady in labor?"

"No, *I* am!" declared Vanessa across from her. "Will you kindly quit gawking, young man, and help my friend get inside before she freezes to death?"

"Yes, ma'am."

With assistance from both Mark and the orderly, Courtney was helped into the wheelchair and quickly wheeled inside. At once M. Billingham grabbed the arm of a man rushing by. "Sir, my grandson's wife needs your immediate assistance. She's having a baby."

"Sorry, sir, but I'm the hospital chaplain."

M. Billingham waved him off. "Then start praying, for heaven's sake!"

In the meantime Mark had pushed Courtney up to the registration desk and spoke in a rush to the woman sitting there. "Hello, my wife is in active labor, and she's already pre-registered for a birthing suite. Mrs. Mark Billingham is the name."

"Just a moment, sir." The woman consulted a computer screen. "Courtney Billingham?"

"Precisely."

She picked up a receiver. "Someone will be right out from the birthing wing to take her down."

"Thank you."

Mark was turning away from the woman when his grandfather charged up, followed by Vanessa. "Can't anyone help us?"

"Someone will be right down to get Courtney."

"Well, they're certainly taking their sweet time about it. I've half a mind . . ." He paused as Courtney let out a low cry.

Vanessa turned on M. Billingham. "Now look what you've done—she's in agony."

He was aghast. "I may be a real snake, Vanessa, but I'm hardly responsible for *that!*"

As the two continued to bicker, Mark touched Courtney's shoulder. "Darling, are you all right?"

"No, I'm splitting in two!" she wailed.

"Pant and blow, darling."

"I can't!"

"Sure you can. I'll show you."

To Courtney's amazement, Mark began panting and blowing, quickly turning red in the face, and she was so amused and amazed by this, she almost forgot her pain. She uttered a laugh that ended in a new moan.

An attractive, middle-aged blond woman in a pink uniform hurried up. "Courtney Billingham?"

"Yes!" the four cried in unison.

"I'm Edith Milberry, your midwife. I'm going to take you to your birthing suite."

"Thank God," uttered M. Billingham, mopping his brow.

They proceeded down several corridors, then stopped outside a private room in the birthing wing. The midwife paused and spoke to Courtney. "Do you want all of these people to go in with you?"

Courtney gazed at Mark, at her friend Vanessa, and finally at M. Billingham. Even though she had thought her heart was hardened toward the latter, the look of anxiety on his face made her relent. She addressed the nurse. "I want Mark and Vanessa with me." Her gaze shifted to M. Billingham. "*He* may visit, if he stops barking at everyone."

M. Billingham grinned. "Courtney, I assure you my barking days are over. You just concentrate on delivering my great-grandson, and I promise you I'm a changed man. You can have anything you want."

This opportunity was too good for Courtney to resist. "Really?"

He nodded.

Courtney glanced lovingly at Vanessa. "Then don't put my friend in jail."

Vanessa squeezed Courtney's hand, and tears thickened her voice. "Darling, please, you don't have to—"

But before Vanessa could finish, M. Billingham smoothly interrupted, "Done. Is there anything you need, Courtney?"

Vanessa glanced at M. Billingham, her jaw dropping open.

"Well, I'd like to have my suitcase," Courtney told him.

"I'll have the chauffeur go fetch it. Just give me your apartment key."

Mark handed his grandfather the apartment key

Courtney had given him. "Tell Hinkham that Courtney's bag is sitting just inside the doorway."

"Will do."

He strode off, and the midwife wheeled Courtney into her room, which was large, with low lighting. Off to the side stood a hospital bed including various monitors, and opposite it was a large sunken tub.

The midwife helped Courtney get undressed and into her hospital gown. Once she was in bed, the nurse checked her progress, then hooked Courtney up to a fetal monitor. "You're already more than halfway dilated and the baby's heartbeat is strong," she pronounced. "But since the baby is early, we'll see what the doctor says. He may want to transfer you upstairs to maternity."

A few moments later, Courtney's doctor came in, examined her, then said, "Unless you want an epidural, I see no reason to transfer you. This baby may be a bit early, but he's a good size, and his heartbeat is very strong. In fact, I wonder if we got your date of conception wrong."

"No, we got it right," Courtney and Mark said in unison, and everyone laughed.

Half an hour after the doctor left, M. Billingham came in with Courtney's suitcase. Setting it down next to the bed, he clasped her hand and gazed at her with genuine concern. "How are you doing, my dear?"

"Just swell," she managed, then cried out as she was hit by the most powerful pain yet.

The midwife stepped forward and spoke to M. Billingham. "Sir, you may want to leave. I'm going to start the water in the bath now. Mrs. Billingham's labor is progressing really fast, and she may already be entering transition."

"My, my, that sounds grave," he said. "Good luck, my dear."

"Thanks," Courtney panted.

M. Billingham leaned over and kissed Courtney's brow. He was heading for the door when Vanessa spoke up. "Hold up, Ham. I'm coming, too."

"You're leaving?" Courtney asked Vanessa.

Vanessa turned to Courtney, kissing her cheek. "Darling, this part should be just for you and Mark. I'd only spoil it." She paused, winking gravely. "Besides, someone must keep old Ham from terrorizing the staff."

"I heard that!" declared M. Billingham.

"Thanks, Vanessa," said Courtney, giving her a hug.

"Thank *you*, darling. And good luck. You'll do great."

After she left, Courtney all but doubled up with the next contraction. Mark worriedly patted her back. "Darling, are you sure you don't want medication?"

Courtney violently shook her head, panting, "Better—for her—if I don't."

The midwife, who had been filling the bathtub, hurried back over to Courtney. "You okay, Mrs. Billingham?"

"I—think this baby wants *out*," she managed.

"I agree." She turned to Mark. "Sir, are you planning to join your wife in the birthing pool?"

"Indeed."

"Then you need to change now."

"Righto. I've swim trunks in Courtney's suitcase."

He grabbed the suitcase and dashed off for the bathroom.

The midwife squeezed Courtney's hand. "Are you having another pain?"

She nodded.

"As soon as it subsides, I'll examine you again. But I

385

think it's time to get you in the warm water."

"Sounds great."

The midwife examined Courtney and confirmed that she was fully dilated. She actually giggled at the sight of Mark returning from the bathroom in his swim trunks. "All you need is goggles and some flippers," she teased.

"Funny, love." He helped Courtney change into the exercise bra she'd brought along to wear while in the pool, then he and the midwife helped Courtney out of bed and across the room. Mark stepped into the pool first, settling Courtney in front of him and wrapping his arms around her.

"I'm here, darling," he whispered. "We'll get through this together."

Courtney sighed at the feel of the warm water surrounding her. But Mark's arms were an even greater comfort. "I'm so glad you're here."

Soulfully he whispered, "I love you so much."

Courtney was very touched, on the verge of telling Mark she loved him, too, when the next pain all but tore her apart.

"I can see his head," the midwife declared.

"Oh, and I can feel it," Courtney said, groaning.

"Time to push, honey," the midwife said.

For long moments, Courtney pushed with all her might while Mark comforted and held her. Just as she could feel the baby's head breaking through, the midwife cautioned, "Wait—stop." She examined Courtney, then said "Okay, there's no cord around his neck. You can pushed again."

Courtney gave a mighty cry and pushed, then seconds later she saw the midwife holding her baby aloft—a tiny gray creature locked in the fetal position, with a cap of dark hair.

"Congratulations, you have a boy," the woman announced.

Tears blurred Courtney's eyes as she stared at her son, so beautiful and perfectly formed, but also gray and barely moving. "He's not breathing."

"Don't worry, hon, he will be in a minute." The midwife quickly clamped off the chord and let Mark cut it, then took the infant away to a nearby cart. Courtney watched anxiously as the nurse suctioned out the baby's mouth, then she heard her son's first, strong cry. She thought her heart would break with joy at the sound of it.

Seconds later, when the midwife slipped the baby back in Courtney's arms, he was whimpering softly and struggling to open his eyes.

"Oh, look, Mark—he looks just like you!" Courtney cried. "Look how pink he's turning. And—oh, my God—he's opening his eyes and staring at us!"

"He's beautiful—just like you, darling," Mark murmured back, his voice breaking. "Thank you for my son. The best Christmas gift you could ever give me."

Overwhelmed by feelings of joy, she twisted about to gaze up at him. "Merry Christmas, Mark. I love you."

She saw tears in his eyes then. "I love you, too, darling. You and this child are my world."

The three cuddled together, their world united by love.

Epilogue

A week later Courtney was at home, in bed, nursing her tiny son. Mark Billingham III looked exactly like his handsome dad, with Mark's dark hair and eyes that Courtney was certain would be blue. He'd weighed in at six pounds six ounces, and seemed intent on doubling his weight during his first week of life. Even now he was gulping down breast milk like a champ, his tiny fist clenched about Courtney's index finger.

Everyone in Courtney's family had come by to visit the baby and bring him presents, and already they all adored him. Courtney loved her child more than she could bear. She had never expected to be so fascinated by her son. In just a short week he'd become her world—he and Mark, too, of course.

In that brief time all her priorities had shifted. Maternity leave would no longer be enough for her—she wanted time with her baby, lots of time. She didn't want to leave the corporation in a lurch; but her heart was no longer there. It was here, with Mark and her son.

As if he'd heard her thoughts, the door creaked open

and Mark stepped inside, grinning at the sight of his wife and baby. "How are you two doing?" he whispered.

"Great."

"Vanessa and my grandfather are here—along with scads of gifts for the little one."

"Here? You mean they came together?"

"Astonishing though it seems. They want to say hello to you, and see the little guy. Should I ask them to return later?"

She stared down at the baby and smiled. "No. But he's already asleep."

Stepping closer, Mark extended his arms. "So he is. You just rest, and I'll go show him off, then put him down for his nap. I know you must be tired with all of your family stopping by so much. Are you up to seeing Grandfather and Vanessa?"

"Yes, I'd like to. I've actually been worried about Vanessa ever since we caught her in the act at corporate headquarters."

He took the baby, looking down at him with a father's pride. "For shame, darling. I forbid you to worry. You just sit there and take it easy. I'll bring them in shortly."

Courtney fastened her nursing bra and buttoned her bed jacket. Soon, Mark ushered Vanessa and his grandfather into the room. Vanessa wore a red wool dress and M. Billingham a sharp black suit. Both appeared inordinately happy.

"Courtney, dear!" he exclaimed, rushing over to kiss her. "We've just seen the little one, and a more handsome baby was never born."

"Thanks," she replied.

"He's beautiful, darling," declared Vanessa.

"The spitting image of my grandson," M. Billingham added.

"Don't forget that Courtney was in on the production of this perfect little angel, too," Mark chided.

"Oh, of course, never," M. Billingham assured him.

Vanessa stepped over to the bed and hugged Courtney. "How are you feeling, darling?"

"I'm fine." Quizzically, she studied the high color in her friend's cheeks, the sparkle in her eyes. "And you're looking positively radiant."

"Indeed," seconded Mark. He raised an eyebrow at his grandfather. "I take it you and the lovely Mrs. Fox have mended your fences?"

M. Billingham laughed. "Better than that." He winked at Vanessa. "Do you want to tell them, Van, or should I?"

Her lips twitched. "Be my guest, Ham."

"Vanessa and I plan to marry," M. Billingham announced.

"What?" cried Mark and Courtney in unison.

"Explain that, sir," added Mark.

Appearing pleased as punch, M. Billingham stepped over to take Vanessa's hand and spoke with uncharacteristic humility. "The truth is, I think I've loved Vanessa since the very day I met her. Ah, she was always a thorn in my side, but her beauty, intelligence, and spirit fired my blood. Unfortunately when we met, she was married. I considered Floyd my friend, so of course I was aghast at my own feelings, which also seemed disloyal to my late wife's memory." He gave a sigh. "After Floyd died, I felt terrible guilt for his death and couldn't bear having Van around then, either." He gazed at her fondly. "Too much temptation."

"But you never even considered being honest about your feelings," Vanessa scolded.

"True—but were you honest about yours?"

"To tell you the truth, Ham, I didn't even realize I had feelings for you until you admitted yours." She grinned at Courtney. "Do you know what this old tyrant said when he proposed?"

"Now, Van, you know I was only kidding," he blustered.

Ignoring him, Vanessa told Courtney, "He said, 'My dear, it's either incarceration for you, or wedlock with me for the rest of your life.' "

Courtney gave an outraged cry. "Why, you old rascal! After you promised me you wouldn't press charges against my friend!"

"I already told you ladies it was a bluff," grumbled M. Billingham. He gazed at Vanessa, and for once his emotions were evident for all to see. "I just couldn't risk her giving me the wrong answer. I was taking quite a chance."

Vanessa took his hand and regarded him warmly. "I'm glad you took the risk, Ham." She turned to Courtney. "Funny how close anger and hurt can be to love."

Mark and Courtney exchanged a knowing glance. "Well, congratulations," he said with a grin.

"Yes, congratulations," added Courtney.

"Are you two off to some exotic locale for a honeymoon?" Mark inquired.

The old man chuckled. "Actually, we'd like to have a small, private wedding here, as soon as Courtney and the baby are up to attending it. Then we'll be off for a three-week cruise of the Mediterranean. Afterward . . . well, Vanessa will be joining our company as senior product designer."

"Oh, Vanessa, that's wonderful!" cried Courtney.

"You see, it's not true that I never appreciated Vanessa's talents," M. Billingham explained. "I just couldn't take the torture of having her around."

Vanessa winked. "And now I get to torment you for the rest of our lives, eh?"

M. Billingham chuckled. "I'll anticipate the suffering with great relish. And one more thing," he added, to Courtney. "I don't think we should take the company public, after all."

"We shouldn't? But the deal promises to be so lucrative—"

"I don't care about that anymore," he admitted heavily. "I don't want to answer to stockholders, nor to make Bootle's Baby Bower a household name. I think smaller, more intimate, more family oriented, is better."

"I see," murmured Courtney. "In that case I think you need a new CEO."

"What?" cried M. Billingham.

"I resign," Courtney happily declared. "And I want Vanessa to have my job."

"Me?" cried Vanessa.

"You're absolutely capable of it. You and M. Billingham can run the company together. Especially if you don't have to tackle all those SEC filings."

"Courtney, are you sure about this?" asked Mark.

She nodded. "I've been thinking about this ever since the baby was born. The only thing that held me back was our plans to go public. I didn't think it would be fair to bail out at such a critical time." She smiled at Vanessa and M. Billingham. "But now I know the company will be in excellent hands."

Vanessa appeared both shocked and flattered. "Why, thank you, dear, that's quite a vote of confidence—I mean, if you are *really* sure."

Courtney nodded solemnly. "Don't worry, Vanessa, I

won't spend my life being bitter like . . . well, like you. Sorry if I sound blunt there, but—"

"No, darling, you're absolutely right," Vanessa cut in firmly. "Life is much too short for anger and bitterness. If only Ham and I had learned our lesson long ago." Brightening, she turned to him. "Well, what do you think, Ham?"

He raised and kissed her hand. "My dear, I think you'll make a world-class CEO, and the two of us will be an excellent team. Now let's leave these two alone and go plan our wedding."

The two hugged and kissed Courtney, then left. Silence descended, and she realized Mark was staring at her in awe.

"What is it?"

He came over to the bed, sat down, and took her hand. "Why would you want to quit your job now, love?"

Choked with emotion, she whispered, "Because I want to live with you in London."

His eyes lit with wild hope, then his expression sobered again. "But—are you sure? I'm perfectly willing to liquidate my holdings and live here with you. I'll even become an American citizen if you want me to."

She shook her head. "No, Mark, that won't be necessary."

"But what changed your mind?"

"You—and our baby." She threw herself into his arms. "Oh, Mark, it used to be I had such a chip on my shoulder, with so much to prove. By damn, I'd show my family that a woman was meant to be so much more than just a little housewife. When your grandfather pulled that stunt on me, it only made matters worse. You were right. I was caught up on my pride."

"But Courtney, I didn't make things easy for you, either," he admitted humbly. "As I admitted in London, I did try to control you—because I was just so afraid of losing you."

"As you lost your parents," she added wisely. "You know, I think we both had some issues relating to our lives as children. Remember how left out we both felt?"

He nodded. "Me with the socialite mother, you the fourth of five children."

"I think I always felt like an outsider, so different from my sisters and mom, my ambitions out of step with their domestic values. I came to see home and family as synonymous with losing my identity. That was so silly of me. Now I've found my real self with you."

"Oh, Courtney." He pulled her close and buried his face in her hair.

She clutched him tightly. "When our baby was born, I realized nothing mattered more than him, and the three of us. I want him never to feel left out, or not supported in whatever he wants in life. And I have nothing left to prove—except how much I love you and him."

"Done. I'm convinced." Passionately he kissed her.

"Can you forgive me?"

"For what?"

"For not coming to my senses sooner?"

"Darling, there's nothing to forgive. But have you really thought all this through? Moving to London is a big step. Can you leave your family, your job behind?"

"We can fly back and forth to see everyone. As for my job, later on I'm sure I'll want to resume my career. If so, I'll manage one of your companies, or start up one of my own. But in the meantime, I just want to be with you and our child. And I want our son to be brought up in England."

"Courtney, if you ever change your mind . . ."

"I won't. Now come here, handsome."

She pulled Mark close and kissed him, again and again and again, until she had him thoroughly convinced.

Dear Reader:

Imagine my delight recently when I watched my eighteer month-old grandson pause outside to have a conversation with small, fluorescent pink flag left by a utility company: "Flag! H flag! Hug?" The idea of having an animated conversation with a inanimate object is just one of the wonders of the very young, an spending time with my first grandchild has reacquainted me wit that magical time. I hope I've managed to capture that sense c wonder in *The Great Baby Caper*—as well as the feelings of jo and adventure that falling in love, and becoming a parent, ca bring.

If you liked *The Great Baby Caper*, I'm sure you'll also enjo my previous contemporary romance from Love Spell. *Lovers an Other Lunatics* is a zany and adventurous story set in Galvesto Texas. And for more delightful baby stories, please try *New Year Babies*, an anthology that includes my funny and touchin Victorian time-travel novella, "The Confused Stork."

I have several other titles still available from Dorcheste Publishing under the Love Spell and Leisure Books imprints *Embers of Time* (Love Spell), an emotional and mystical time-trav el romance that commences in post-World War II Charleston, S.C *Bushwhacked Bride* (Love Spell), a fun, sexy time-travel romanc set in the Old West; and *Strangers in the Night* (Leisure Books), poignant collection of love stories set in the 1940s, featuring m novella "Night and Day." And I'm sure you'll be pleased to kno that my first time-travel romance, the classic *A Tryst in Time*, now back in print from Love Spell!

I hope you'll order these titles from Dorchester Publishing or our local bookseller. And please watch for my future releases om Leisure Books and Love Spell.

Thanks, as always, for all your support and encouragement. I elcome your feedback on all my projects. You can reach me via mail at eugenia@eugeniariley.com, visit by website at ww.eugeniariley.com, or you can write to me at the address list- below (SASE appreciated for a reply, free bookmark and wsletter available).

Eugenia Riley
P.O. Box 840526
Houston, TX 77284-0526

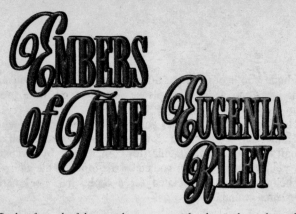

Embers of Time — Eugenia Riley

In the aftermath of the second great war, two lonely people are destined to meet in the splendor of Charleston, South Carolina. He is a handsome RAF pilot; she is a beautiful young army nurse. Each has known the horror of war and both have experienced devastating loss, the death of a beloved child in a recent, tragic fire.

But are the children really lost? Even as Adrian and Vickie forge a deep bond, both are haunted by poignant glimpses of the children's ghosts in the Charleston streets, visions that soon lead the couple back to search for the children in an earlier time. There, they discover a city as grand and mysterious as time itself, and a miracle that will heal their wounded hearts.

___52408-2 $5.99 US/$6.99 CAN

Dorchester Publishing Co., Inc.
P.O. Box 6640
Wayne, PA 19087-8640

Please add $2.50 for shipping and handling for the first book and $.75 for each book thereafter. NY, and PA residents, please add appropriate sales tax. No cash, stamps, or C.O.D.s. All orders shipped within 6 weeks via postal service book rate.
Canadian orders require $2.00 extra postage and must be paid in U.S. dollars through a U.S. banking facility.

Name _____
Address _____
City_____ State_____ Zip _____
I have enclosed $_____ in payment for the checked book(s).
Payment <u>must</u> accompany all orders. ☐ Please send a free catalog.
  CHECK OUT OUR WEBSITE! www.dorchesterpub.com

Lovers and Other Lunatics

Eugenia Riley

Get Ready for . . . The Time of Your Life!

Teresa Phelps has heard of being crazy in love. But Charles Everett seems just plain mad. Her handsome kidnapper unnerves her with his charm and flabbergasts her with his accusations. He acts under the misguided belief that she holds the key to finding buried treasure. But all Tess feels she can unearth is one oddball after another.

While Charles' actions resemble those of a lunatic, his body arouses thoughts of a lover. And while Charles helps to fend off her dastardly and dangerous pursuers, Tess wonders if he has her best interests at heart—or is she just a pawn in his quest for riches? As the madcap misadventures ensue, Tess strives to dig up the truth. Who is the enigmatic Englishman? What is he after? And most important, in the hunt for hidden riches is the ultimate prize true love?

___52371-X $5.99 US/$6.99 CAN

Dorchester Publishing Co., Inc.
P.O. Box 6640
Wayne, PA 19087-8640

Please add $1.75 for shipping and handling for the first book and $.50 for each book thereafter. NY, NYC, and PA residents, please add appropriate sales tax. No cash, stamps, or C.O.D.s. All orders shipped within 6 weeks via postal service book rate. Canadian orders require $2.00 extra postage and must be paid in U.S. dollars through a U.S. banking facility.

Name_____
Address_____
City_____State_____Zip_____
I have enclosed $ _____ in payment for the checked book(s).
Payment <u>must</u> accompany all orders. ❑ Please send a free catalog.

ATTENTION
BOOK LOVERS!

Can't get enough of your favorite **ROMANCE**?

Call **1-800-481-9191** to:

✳ order books,

✳ receive a **FREE** catalog,

✳ join our book clubs to **SAVE 20%**!

Open Mon.-Fri. 10 AM-9 PM EST

Visit **www.dorchesterpub.com**
for special offers and inside
information on the authors you love.

We accept Visa, MasterCard or Discover®.
LEISURE BOOKS ♥ LOVE SPELL